Amitav Gho

Amitav Ghosh was born in Ca
Bangladesh, Sri Lanka and In
universities of Delhi and Oxford, ...
of institutions and written for many magazines.
The first novel in his *Ibis* trilogy, *Sea of Poppies*, was
shortlisted for the Man Booker Prize.

Praise for *Gun Island*

'A rich and rewarding novel that reaffirms the transformative
power of topographical and human connection, and registers
the rhythms of the quiet and the unquiet life' *The Spectator*

'A book of reckless and persuasive scope, a huge,
rambunctious reckoning with our environmental
declension' *Sunday Times*

'A compelling book – a sinuous and often gripping piece
of storytelling, satisfyingly shaped and beautifully written'
Prospect

'With sweeping exuberant style and extraordinary linguistic
facility Ghosh takes us into a world where desperate refugees
trickle through borders like water from melting ice . . .
This important novel is an account of our current world,
the one few writers have had the courage to face'
Annie Proulx

'An extraordinary reading experience from one of our greatest
living storytellers. Ghosh masterfully collocates disparate
worlds to create a story of family, self, history, and destiny'
Neel Mukherjee

Gun Island

Amitav Ghosh

JOHN MURRAY

First published in Great Britain in 2019 by John Murray (Publishers)
An Hachette UK company

This paperback edition published in 2020

1

A CIP catalogue record for this title is
available from the British Library

Paperback ISBN 9781473686687
Ebook ISBN 9781473686663

Typeset in Adobe Caslon Pro by Palimpsest Book Production Ltd,
Falkirk, Stirlingshire

Printed and bound in Great Britain by Clays Ltd, Elcograf S.p.A.

John Murray policy is to use papers that are natural, renewable and recyclable
products and made from wood grown in sustainable forests. The logging and
manufacturing processes are expected to conform to the environmental
regulations of the country of origin.

John Murray (Publishers)
Carmelite House
50 Victoria Embankment
London EC4Y 0DZ

www.johnmurraypress.co.uk

For
Anna Nadotti
and
Irene Bignardi

Part I

The Gun Merchant

Calcutta

The strangest thing about this strange journey was that it was launched by a word – and not an unusually resonant one either but a banal, commonplace coinage that is in wide circulation, from Cairo to Calcutta. That word is *bundook*, which means 'gun' in many languages, including my own mother tongue, Bengali (or Bangla). Nor is the word a stranger to English: by way of British colonial usages it found its way into the *Oxford English Dictionary*, where it is glossed as 'rifle'.

But there was no rifle or gun in sight the day the journey began; nor indeed was the word intended to refer to a weapon. And that, precisely, was why it caught my attention: because the gun in question was a part of a name – 'Bonduki Sadagar', which could be translated as 'the Gun Merchant'.

The Gun Merchant entered my life not in Brooklyn, where I live and work, but in the city where I was born and raised – Calcutta (or Kolkata, as it is now formally known). That year, as on many others, I was in Kolkata through much of the winter, ostensibly for business. My work, as a dealer in rare books and Asian antiquities, requires me to do a good deal of on-site scouting and since I happen to possess a small apartment in Kolkata (carved out of the house that my sisters and I inherited from our parents) the city has become a second base of operations for me.

But it wasn't just work that brought me back every year: Kolkata was also sometimes a refuge, not only from the bitter cold of a Brooklyn winter, but from the solitude of a personal life that had become increasingly desolate over time, even as my professional fortunes prospered. And the desolation was never greater than it was that year, when a very promising relationship came to a shockingly abrupt end: a woman I had been seeing for a long time had cut me off without explanation, blocking me on every channel that we had ever used to communicate. It was my first brush with 'ghosting', an experience that is as humiliating as it is painful.

Suddenly, with my sixties looming in the not-too-distant future, I found myself more alone than ever. So, I went to Calcutta earlier than usual that year, timing my arrival to coincide with the annual migration that occurs when the weather turns cold in northern climes and great flocks of 'foreign-settled' Calcuttans, like myself, take wing and fly back to overwinter in the city. I knew that I could count on catching up with a multitude of friends and relatives; that the weeks would slip by in a whirl of lunches, dinner parties and wedding receptions. And the thought that I might, in the midst of this, meet a woman with whom I might be able to share my life was not, I suppose, entirely absent from my mind (for this has indeed happened to many men of my vintage).

But of course nothing like that came to pass even though I lost no opportunity to circulate and was introduced to a good number of divorcees, widows and other single women of an appropriate age. There were even a couple of occasions when I felt the glow of faint embers of hope . . . but only to discover, as I had many times before, that there are few expressions in the English language that are less attractive to women than 'Rare Book Dealer'.

So the months slipped by in a cascade of disappointments and the day of my return to Brooklyn was almost at hand when I went to the last of my social engagements of the season: the wedding reception of a cousin's daughter.

I had just entered the venue – a stuffy colonial-era club – when I was accosted by a distant relative, Kanai Dutt.

I had not seen Kanai in many years, which was not entirely a matter of regret for me: he had always been a glib, vain, precocious know-it-all who relied on his quick tongue and good looks to charm women and get ahead in the world. He lived mainly in New Delhi and had thrived in the hothouse atmosphere of that city, establishing himself as a darling of the media: it was by no means uncommon to turn on the television and find him yelling his head off on a talkshow. He knew everyone, as they say, and was often written about in magazines, newspapers and even books.

The thing that most irritated me about Kanai was that he always found a way of tripping me up. This occasion was no exception; he began by throwing me a curveball in the shape of my childhood nickname, Dinu (which I had long since abandoned in favour of the more American-sounding 'Deen').

'Tell me, Dinu,' he said, after a cursory handshake, 'is it true that you've set yourself up as an expert on Bengali folklore?'

The almost audible sneer rattled me. 'Well,' I spluttered, 'I did some research on that kind of thing a long time ago. But I gave it up when I left academia and became a book dealer.'

'But you did get a PhD, didn't you?' he said, with barely concealed derision. 'So you *are* technically an expert.'

'I would hardly call myself that . . .'

He cut me short without apology. 'So tell me then, Mr Expert,' he said. 'Have you ever heard of a figure called Bonduki Sadagar?'

He had clearly been intending to surprise me and he succeeded: the name 'Bonduki Sadagar' ('Gun Merchant') was so new to me that I was tempted to think that Kanai had made it up.

'What do you mean by "figure"?' I said. 'You mean some kind of folk hero?'

'Yes – like Dokkhin Rai, or Chand Sadagar . . .'

He went on to name a few other well-known characters from Bengali folklore: Satya Pir, Lakhindar and the like. Such figures are not quite gods and nor are they merely saintly mortals: like the shifting mudflats of the Bengal delta, they arise at the conjuncture of many currents. Sometimes shrines are built to preserve their memory; and almost always their names are associated with a legend. And since Bengal is a maritime land seafaring is often a prominent feature of such tales.

The most famous of these stories is the legend of a merchant called Chand – 'Chand Sadagar' – who is said to have fled overseas in order to escape the persecution of Manasa Devi, the goddess who rules over snakes and all other poisonous creatures.

There was a time in my childhood when the merchant Chand and his nemesis, Manasa Devi, were as much a part of my dream-world as Batman and Superman would become after I had learnt English and started to read comic books. Back then there was no television in India and the only way to entertain children was to tell them stories. And if the storytellers happened to be Bengali, sooner or later they were sure to circle back to the tale of the Merchant, and the goddess who wanted him as her devotee.

The story's appeal is, I suppose, not unlike that of the Odyssey, with a resourceful human protagonist being pitted against vastly more powerful forces, earthly and divine. But the legend of the merchant Chand differs from the Greek epic in that it does not end with the hero being restored to his family and patrimony: the Merchant's son, Lakhindar, is killed by a cobra on the night of his wedding and it is the boy's virtuous bride, Behula, who reclaims his soul from the underworld and brings the struggle between the Merchant and Manasa Devi to a fragile resolution.

I don't remember when I first heard the story, or who told it to me, but constant repetition ensured that it sank so deep into my consciousness that I wasn't even aware that it was there. But some stories, like certain life forms, possess a special streak of vitality that allow them to outlive others of their kind – and since the story of the Merchant and Manasa Devi is very old it must, I suppose, possess enough of this quality to ensure that it can survive extended periods of dormancy. In any event, when I was a twenty-something student, newly arrived in America

6

and casting about for a subject for a research paper, the story of the Merchant thawed in the permafrost of my memory and once again claimed my full attention.

As I began to read the Bangla verse epics that narrate the Merchant's story (there are many) I discovered that the legend's place in the culture of eastern India was strangely similar to the pattern of its life in my own mind. The origins of the story can be traced back to the very infancy of Bengal's memory: it was probably born amidst the original, autochthonous people of the region and was perhaps sired by real historical figures and events (to this day, scattered across Assam, West Bengal and Bangladesh, there are archaeological sites that are linked, in popular memory, to the Merchant and his family). And in public memory too the legend seems to go through cycles of life, sometimes lying dormant for centuries only to be suddenly rejuvenated by a fresh wave of retellings, in some of which the familiar characters appear under new names, with subtly changed plot lines.

A few of these epics are regarded as classics of Bengali literature and it was one such that became the subject of my research thesis: a six-hundred-page poem in early Bangla. This text was conventionally agreed to have been composed in the fourteenth century – but of course nothing is more grating to an aspiring scholar than a conventional opinion, so in my thesis I argued, citing internal evidence (such as a mention of potatoes), that the poem did not find its final form until much later. It was probably completed by other hands, I claimed, in the seventeenth century, well after the Portuguese had introduced New World plants to Asia.

From there I went on to argue that the life cycles of the story – its periodic revivals after long intervals of dormancy – were related to times of upheaval and disruption, such as the seventeenth century was in those parts of India where Europeans established their first colonies.

It was this last part of the thesis, I think, that most impressed my examiners (not to speak of the journal that subsequently published the article in which I summed up my arguments). What amazes me in retrospect is not the youthful hubris that allowed me to make these arguments but rather the obtuseness that prevented me from recognizing that the conclusions I had reached in relation to the legend might apply also to the history of its existence in my own memory. I never asked myself whether the legend might have surfaced in my mind because I was myself then living through the most turbulent years of my life: it was a period in which I was still trying to recover from the double shock of the death of a woman I had been in love with, and my subsequent move, by grace of a providential scholarship, from the strife-torn Calcutta of my youth to a bucolic university town in the American Midwest. When at last that time passed it left me determined never to undergo that kind of turmoil again. I spared no effort to live a quiet, understated, uneventful life – and so well did I succeed that on that day, at the wedding reception in Kolkata when the Sadagar entered my life anew, in the guise of the Gun Merchant, it never occurred to me that the carefully planned placidity of my life might once again be at an end.

'Are you sure you have the right name?' I said to Kanai, dismissively. 'Maybe you misheard it or something?'

But Kanai stood his ground, insisting that he had used the phrase 'Gun Merchant' advisedly. 'I'm sure you know,' he said, in his maddeningly superior way, 'that the figure of a Merchant crops up under many different names in our folklore. Sometimes the stories are linked to certain places – and my feeling is that the legend of Bonduki Sadagar is one of those, a local tale.'

'Why?'

'Because his legend is tied,' said Kanai, 'to a shrine – a *dhaam* – in the Sundarbans.'

'The Sundarbans!' The idea that there might be a shrine hidden inside a tiger-infested mangrove forest was so far-fetched that I burst into laughter. 'Why would anyone build a dhaam in a swamp?'

'Maybe,' said Kanai coolly, 'because every merchant who's ever sailed out of Bengal has had to pass through the Sundarbans – there's no other way to reach the sea. The Sundarbans are the frontier where commerce and the wilderness look each other directly in the eye; that's exactly where the war between profit and Nature is fought. What could be a better place to build a shrine to Manasa Devi than a forest teeming with snakes?'

'But has anyone ever seen this shrine?' I asked.

'I haven't been there myself,' said Kanai. 'But my aunt Nilima has.'

'Your aunt? You mean Nilima Bose?'

'Yes, exactly,' said Kanai. 'It was she who told me about Bonduki Sadagar and the dhaam. She heard that you were in Kolkata and she asked me to tell you that she would be glad if you could go and see her. She's in her late eighties now and bedridden, but her mind is as sharp as ever. She wants to talk to you about the shrine: she thinks you'll find it interesting.'

I hesitated. 'I don't know that I'll have the time,' I said. 'I'm heading back to New York very soon.'

He shrugged. 'It's up to you.' Pulling out a pen he scribbled a name and a number on a card and handed it to me.

I peered at the card, expecting to see his aunt's name. But that was not what he had written.

'Piya Roy?' I said. 'Who's that?'

'She's a friend,' he said. 'A Bengali American, teaches somewhere in Oregon. She comes here for the winter, like you, and usually stays with my aunt. She's here now and she'll make arrangements if you decide to visit. Give her a call: I think you'll find it worth your while – Piya's an interesting woman.'

Kanai's aunt's name added heft to what had so far seemed a tall tale. A story that came from Nilima Bose could not be scoffed at: wooed by politicians, revered by do-gooders, embraced by donors and celebrated by the press, she was a figure whose credibility was beyond question.

Born into a wealthy Calcutta legal dynasty, Nilima had defied her family by marrying an impoverished schoolteacher. This was way back in the early 1950s; after the marriage Nilima had moved with her husband to Lusibari, a small town on the edge of the Sundarbans. A few years later she had founded a women's group that had since grown into the Badabon Trust, one of India's most reputed charitable organizations. The trust now ran an extended network of free hospitals, schools, clinics and workshops.

In recent years I had kept track of Nilima's doings mainly through a chat group for members of the extended family: my personal acquaintance with her dated back to my adolescence, when I had crossed paths with her at a few family gatherings. The last of these had occurred so long ago that I was surprised – and more than a little flattered – to learn that Nilima remembered me. Under the circumstances, I told myself, it would be rude if I didn't at least call the number that Kanai had given me.

I dialled the number next morning and was answered by an unmistakably American voice. Piya had evidently been expecting my call for her opening words were: 'Hello – is that Mr Datta?'

'Yes – but please call me Deen, it's short for Dinanath.'

'And I'm Piya, which is short for Piyali,' she said, sounding both brisk and friendly. 'Kanai said you might call. Nilima-di's been asking about you. Do you think you might be able to come see her?'

There was something about her voice – a forthrightness combined with a certain element of gravity – that arrested me. I remembered what Kanai had said – 'Piya's an interesting woman' – and was suddenly very curious about her. The excuses I had prepared slipped from my mind and I said: 'I'd very much like to come. But it would have to be soon because I'm leaving for the US in a couple of days.'

'Hold on then,' she said. 'Let me have a word with Nilima-di.'

It took her a few minutes to come back on line. 'Could you come this morning?'

I had made many plans for that morning but suddenly they didn't seem to matter. 'Yes,' I said. 'I can be there in an hour, if that's okay.'

The address that Piya gave me was of Nilima's ancestral home in Ballygunge Place, one of Kolkata's poshest neighbourhoods. Although I had not visited the house in many years I remembered it well, from childhood visits with my parents.

I discovered now, on stepping out of the Ola cab that had brought me to Ballygunge Place, that the old house was long gone; like many other grand Calcutta mansions it had been torn down and replaced with a modern apartment block that was large enough to accommodate everyone who had a claim to the ancestral property.

The new building was unusually stylish and the lift that took me up to Nilima's floor was decorated with elegant 'designer' touches, as were the front doors of every apartment that I passed on the way. Nilima's door was the only exception in that it had no embellishments except a sign that said NILIMA BOSE, BADABON TRUST.

I rang the bell and the door was opened by a slim, small woman with close-cropped hair that was just beginning to turn grey at the edges. Her clothes – jeans and a T-shirt – accentuated the boyishness of her build; everything about her was spare and streamlined except her eyes, which were large and seemed even more so because the whites stood out sharply against her dark, silky complexion. Her face was devoid of make-up and she wore no ornamentation of any kind. But on one of her nostrils there was a pinprick that suggested that she had once sported a nose stud.

'Hello, Deen,' she said as we shook hands. 'I'm Piya. Come on in – Nilima-di's waiting for you.'

Stepping inside I discovered that the apartment was divided into two sections: the outer part, which served as an office for the trust, was filled with the glow of computer screens. A dozen earnest-looking young men and women were hard at work there; they spared us scarcely a glance as we walked through to the rear where lay Nilima's living quarters.

Opening a door Piya ushered me into a tidy, sunlit room. Nilima was lying on a comfortable-looking bed, propped up by a few pillows and half covered by a bed-sheet. Always tiny, she seemed to have shrunk in size since I had last seen her. But her face, round and dimpled, with steel-rimmed eyeglasses, was just as I remembered, down to the sparkle in her eye.

Piya found me a chair and pushed it close to the bed. 'I'll leave you two alone now,' she said, giving Nilima's hand an affectionate squeeze. 'Don't tire yourself out, Nilima-di.'

'I won't, dear,' Nilima said, in English. 'I promise.'

A fond smile appeared on her face as she watched Piya leave the room. 'Such a sweet girl,' she said, switching to Bangla. 'And strong too. I don't know what I would do without Piya.'

Nilima's Bangla, I noticed, had acquired the earthy tones of a rural dialect, presumably that of the Sundarbans. Her English, by contrast, still retained the rounded syllables of her patrician upbringing.

'It's Piya who keeps the trust going nowadays,' Nilima continued. 'It was a lucky day for us when she came to the Sundarbans.'

'Does she spend a lot of time out there?' I said.

'Oh yes, when she's in India she's mostly in the Sundarbans.'

Nilima explained that it was Piya's research, in marine biology, that had first brought her to the Sundarbans. Nilima had given her a place to stay and supported her work, and over the following years Piya's involvement with the trust had deepened steadily.

'She spends every vacation with us,' said Nilima. 'Summer and winter, she comes whenever she can.'

'Oh, really?' I said, trying not to sound unduly inquisitive. 'Doesn't she have a family, then?'

Shooting me a shrewd glance, Nilima said: 'She's not married, if that's what you mean –' at which I dropped my eyes and tried to look disinterested.

'But Piya does have a family of sorts,' Nilima continued. 'She's adopted the wife and son of a Sundarbans villager who died while assisting with her research. Piya's done everything possible to help the wife, Moyna, in bringing up the boy.' She checked herself: 'Or at least she's tried . . .'

Then she sighed and shook her head, as if to recall why she had asked me to come. 'I mustn't ramble on,' she said. 'I know you're pressed for time.'

Truth to tell I was so eager to know more about Piya that I wouldn't at all have minded if she had rambled on in this vein. But since I couldn't very well say so, I reached into my jacket pocket and pulled out the small voice recorder that I usually take with me when I'm scouting for antiquities.

'Are you planning to record this?' said Nilima in surprise.

'It's just a habit,' I said. 'I'm a compulsive note-taker and record-keeper. Please forget about the gadget – it's not important.'

Nilima knew the exact date on which she had first heard of the Gun Merchant. She had entered it that very day in an account book that bore the label 'Cyclone Relief Accounts, 1970'. The book had recently been retrieved for her from the archives of the Badabon Trust. Flipping it open, she showed me the entry: at the top of a page, in Bangla script, were the words 'Bonduki Sadagarer dhaam' – 'the Gun Merchant's shrine'. Below was the date 'November 20, 1970'.

Eight days earlier – on November 12, 1970, to be precise – a Category 4 cyclone had torn through the Bengal delta, hitting both the Indian province of West Bengal and the state that was then called East Pakistan (a year later it would become a new nation, Bangladesh). Storms had no names in this region back then but the 1970 cyclone would later come to be known as the Bhola cyclone.

In terms of casualties the Bhola cyclone was the greatest natural disaster of the twentieth century; its toll is conservatively estimated at three hundred thousand lives lost but the actual number may have been as high as half a million. Most of those casualties were in East Pakistan where political tensions had long been simmering. West Pakistan's laggardly response to the disaster played a critical part in triggering the war of independence that resulted in the creation of Bangladesh.

In West Bengal it was the Sundarbans that absorbed the impact of the cyclone. Lusibari, the island where Nilima and her husband lived, suffered a great deal of damage: a large chunk of the island was ripped away by the storm surge, houses and all.

The damage to Lusibari was, however, a pale shadow of what was visited on the islands and settlements to its south. But Nilima did not learn of this till several days later. She was told about it by a young fisherman of her acquaintance, Horen Naskar: he had been out at sea, fishing, and had witnessed the devastation with his own eyes.

Horen's account prompted Nilima to assemble a team of volunteers to collect and distribute emergency supplies. With Horen at the helm of a hired boat, Nilima and her team had ferried supplies to some of the villages near the coast.

On each outing they saw horrific sights: hamlets obliterated by the storm surge; islands where every tree had been stripped of its leaves; corpses floating in the water, half eaten by animals; villages that had lost most of their inhabitants. The situation was aggravated by a steady flow of refugees from East Pakistan. For several months people had been coming across the border, into India, in order to escape the political turmoil on the other side; now the flow turned into a flood, bringing many more hungry mouths into a region that was already desperately short of food.

One morning, Horen steered the boat to a part of the Sundarbans where the mighty Raimangal River ran along the border, with different countries on its two shores. Nilima usually avoided this stretch of river: it was notoriously frequented by smugglers and its currents were so powerful that boats were often inadvertently swept across the border.

Not without some difficulty Horen managed to keep the boat close to the Indian side, and in a while they came to a sandbank where a village had once stood: nothing was left of the settlement but a few bent poles; every last dwelling had been swept away by the wave that followed the cyclone.

Spotting a few people on the riverbank, Nilima asked Horen to pull in. From the look of the place, she assumed that many of the hamlet's inhabitants had been killed or wounded – but on enquiring, she received an unexpected answer. She learnt that no one from that hamlet had suffered any bodily harm; they had even managed to salvage their belongings and stocks of food.

To what did the village owe its good fortune?

The answer startled Nilima: her informants told her that the miracle was due to Manasa Devi, the goddess of snakes, who, they said, was the protector of a nearby shrine.

Shortly before the storm's arrival, as the skies were turning dark, the shrine's bell had begun to ring. The villagers had rushed there, taking whatever food and belongings they could carry. Not only had the shrine's walls and roof kept them safe from the storm, it had continued to shelter them afterwards, even providing them with clean, fresh water from its well – a rare amenity in the Sundarbans.

Nilima had asked to see the shrine and was led to it by the villagers. It was a good distance from the sandbank, situated on a slight elevation, in the middle of a sandy clearing that was surrounded by dense stands of mangrove.

Of the structure itself Nilima retained only a vague memory – there were hundreds of people milling around and their belongings were stacked everywhere. All she could recall was a set of high walls and a curved roof with the profile of an upturned boat: its shape had reminded her of the famous temples of Bishnupur.

Nilima had asked whether there was a custodian or caretaker that she could speak to. In a while, a middle-aged Muslim man, with a greying beard and white skull cap, had emerged from the interior. Nilima learnt that he was a *majhi*, a boatman, and that he was originally from the other side of the Raimangal River. As a boy he had occasionally worked for the people who then tended the shrine: they were a family of Hindu *gayans* (or ballad singers) who had kept alive the epic poem (or *panchali*) that narrated the legend of the shrine, passing it down orally through many generations. But over the years the family had dwindled to one last remaining member, and it was he who had asked him, the boatman, to take care of the shrine after his passing. That was a long time ago, a decade before the partitioning of the Indian subcontinent in 1947; the boatman had been looking after the dhaam ever since; it had become his home and he now lived there with his wife and son.

Nilima had asked if it was strange for him, as a Muslim, to be looking after a shrine that was associated with a Hindu goddess. The boatman had answered that the dhaam was revered by all, irrespective of religion: Hindus believed that it was Manasa Devi who guarded the shrine, while Muslims believed that it was a place of jinns, protected by a Muslim *pir*, or saint, by the name of Ilyas.

But who had built the shrine, and when?

The boatman had been reluctant to answer. He did not know the legend well, he said, and could only remember a few snatches of the poem.

Wasn't there a written version of the poem? Nilima asked. No, said the boatman; it was the Gun Merchant's express desire that the poem never be written down but only passed on from mouth to mouth. Unfortunately the boatman had never memorized the poem and remembered only a few verses.

At Nilima's insistence the boatman had recited a couple of lines and the words had lodged themselves in Nilima's memory, perhaps because they sounded like nonsense verse (a genre of which she was very fond).

Kolkataey tokhon na chhilo lok na makan
Banglar patani tokhon nagar-e-jahan

Calcutta had neither people nor houses then
Bengal's great port was a city-of-the-world.

Nilima cast me a glance and laughed, a little awkwardly, as though she were embarrassed to bring such a piece of silliness to my notice.

'It doesn't make any sense, does it?' she said.

'Not immediately,' I said. 'But go on.'

Nilima had continued to question the boatman and he had responded by becoming increasingly reticent, pleading ignorance on the one hand, yet insisting on the other that it was impossible for most people to make sense of the legend. But Nilima had persisted and had succeeded in getting him to divulge the general outline of the story. It proved to be quite similar to the legend of the merchant Chand.

Like Chand, the Gun Merchant was said to have been a rich trader who had angered Manasa Devi by refusing to become her devotee. Plagued by snakes and pursued by droughts, famines, storms, and other calamities, he had fled overseas to escape the goddess's wrath, finally taking refuge in a land where there were no serpents, a place called 'Gun Island' – Bonduk-dwip.

Here Nilima stopped to ask me whether I had ever heard of a place of that name.

I shook my head: 'No, never,' I said. 'It must be one of those fairy-tale countries that crop up in folk tales.'

Nilima nodded. There were some other such places in the story, she said, but she couldn't recall their names.

But not even on Gun Island had the Merchant been able to conceal himself from Manasa Devi. One day she had appeared to him out of the pages of a book and had warned him that she had eyes everywhere. That night he had tried to hide himself in an iron-walled room, but even there she had hunted him down: a tiny, poisonous creature had crept through a crack and bitten him. Having barely survived the bite, the Merchant had escaped from Gun Island, on a ship, but while at sea he was once again captured by pirates. They threw him into a dungeon and were taking him to be sold, at a place called 'The Island of Chains' (Shikol-dwip) when Manasa Devi appeared before him once again. She promised that if he became her devotee and built a shrine for her in Bengal, she would set him free and make him rich.

Now at last the Merchant gave in and swore that he would build a temple for the goddess if only she would help him find his way back to his native land. So she set him free and wrought a miracle: the ship was besieged by all manner of creatures, of the sea and sky, and while the pirates were fighting them off, the captives managed to take over the ship and seize their captors' riches. The Merchant's share of the spoils allowed him to turn homewards and on the way he was able to make many profitable trades. On his return to Bengal he brought with him a fortune so vast, and a tale so amazing, that it earned him the title Bonduki Sadagar – the Gun Merchant. This was how the shrine had got its name.

'And that was all there was to it,' said Nilima with a shrug. 'I told the boatman that it really made no sense at all. He didn't seem at all surprised. He said: "I told you, didn't I? The legend is filled with secrets and if you don't know their meaning it's impossible to understand." And then he added: "But some day, when the time is right, someone will under-stand it and who knows? For them it may open up a world that we cannot see."'

Nilima gave me a self-deprecating smile. 'I don't know what it was but there was something about the story that got into my head: it haunted me and I wanted to know more about it. But there was always so much else to do that it dropped out of my mind – until just the other day, when I was reading something

18

about the great cyclone of 1970. Then suddenly it all came back to me.'

'But you only visited the temple that one time?' I asked.

'Yes,' she said. 'It was the only time I actually went there. I did see it again once, from a distance, but I didn't have time to stop. That was about ten years ago. I believe the dhaam's still there, but who knows how much longer it'll remain? The islands of the Sundarbans are constantly being swallowed up by the sea; they're disappearing before our eyes. That's why I feel that some record should be made of it; for all I know that temple might be an important historical monument.'

Trying to be helpful I said: 'Have you tried to contact the Archaeological Survey of India?'

'I wrote to them once but they showed no interest at all.'

Then she glanced at me and her face broke into a dimpled smile. 'So then I thought of you.'

Taken aback, I said: 'Me? Why me?'

'Well you have a passion for antiquities, don't you?'

'Yes, but not of this kind,' I said. 'I mainly deal with old books and manuscripts. I often visit libraries, museums, old palaces and so on – but I've never done anything remotely like this.'

'Still, wouldn't you at least like to see the place?'

The only reason I didn't say no straight away was that it would have seemed rude. At that moment a visit seemed impossible to me – because I was due to leave for New York at the end of the week; because I already had a packed schedule of appointments for the days ahead; and (most of all) because I didn't much care for swamps and mangroves.

I tried to get out of it by mumbling an excuse: 'I don't know that I'll have the time; I have to catch a flight home . . .'

But Nilima was not a woman to give up easily.

'It wouldn't take long,' she persisted. 'You could go there and be back in a day. I'd be glad to arrange it.'

I was trying to think of a polite way to decline when who should walk in but Piya.

Nilima lost no time in roping her in: 'Tell him, Piya – a visit to the shrine won't take long. He's afraid of missing his flight to America.'

Piya turned to me and asked when I was scheduled to fly. I told her and she reassured me: 'Don't worry – you'll be back in good time for your flight.'

'Are you sure?'

'As sure as it's possible to be.' She added apologetically: 'I'd have liked to accompany you myself. Unfortunately I can't because I'm on my way to a conference in Bhubaneswar and won't be back till next week. But if you do decide to go I'll see to it that you're well looked after.'

Her smile made me reconsider the matter. 'I'll think it over,' I said.

Gathering my things together I said goodbye to Nilima. Then Piya led me to an adjoining room, where she introduced me to a matronly, heavy-browed woman in a nurse's uniform – a blue and white sari.

'This is Moyna Mondal,' said Piya, 'Nilima's favourite nurse.' She threw an arm around the nurse's shoulder and gave her a hug. 'Moyna and I are like family; we've become sisters over the years. If you decide to go she'll arrange everything. You don't need to worry about anything: it'll be quick and easy.'

Piya's tone was so encouraging that I was tempted to say yes. But something held me back.

'I just need to check a few things,' I said. 'Will it be okay if I get back to you tomorrow morning?'

'Sure. Take your time.'

Cinta

My mind was in a muddle when I left Nilima's flat. The reasonable, practical, cautious parts of me were dead set against going. I have always been a nervous traveller and the thought of missing my flight filled me with dread. Nor could I imagine that I would find anything of special interest, from a professional point of view: if ever there had been anything of value at the shrine it was sure to be long gone.

But then there was Piya: there was something about her that reminded me of Durga, my first, long-ago love. It wasn't so much her appearance as something about her manner, her gaze; I sensed in her a single-mindedness, an idealism that was reminiscent of Durga.

I knew that if it had been possible for Piya to accompany me I would have been glad to go. This frightened me, and added to my confusion. Some months before, my therapist, back in Brooklyn, had told me that I was in a peculiarly vulnerable state and was likely to delude myself about relationships that had not the slightest chance of working out. She had warned me especially about situations in which I found myself fixating on women who were unattainable or ill-matched for someone in my circumstances: 'Don't set yourself up to fail, yet again.'

Those words echoed in my ears all the way back to my apartment.

By dinner-time I had more or less made up my mind that I would not go. But that evening I was invited to dinner by one of my sisters and when I went up to her apartment I found her, and her whole multi-generational household, sitting rapt around a television set. And what should they be watching but a (bizarrely modernized) version of the legend of Manasa Devi and the Merchant? I was told that this was now the most popular show on regional television: evidently the legend of the Merchant was undergoing one of its periodic revivals, not just in my own mind, but in the culture at large.

The thought disquieted me.

Later, back in my own apartment, I was tidying away my things when my eyes fell on my voice recorder. I reached for it, thinking that I would erase my interview with Nilima, but by accident I pushed the wrong button and the interview began to play from the start. I listened idly until the recording reached the bit where Nilima had recited the following lines:

> Calcutta had neither people nor houses then
> Bengal's great port was a city-of-the-world.

Here something caught my interest. I hit the pause button and replayed that bit several times over.

The lines seemed nonsensical at first, but as I listened to them it struck me that their metre and rhythm were consistent with a particular genre of Bengali folk poetry, one that has been known to yield some valuable historical insights. It struck me as interesting also that the boatman had recited the couplet in answer to Nilima's question about when the shrine was built. Was he perhaps trying to suggest a date or a period?

Needless to add, poems of this kind are often intentionally cryptic. Yet, in this instance, the first line was not particularly mystifying: what it probably implied was that the Merchant's shrine was built at a time when there was no Calcutta – that is to say, before the city's founding, in 1690.

But what of the second, more enigmatic line?

The words 'Bengal's great port' were clearly intended to refer to Calcutta's predecessor as the most important urban centre in

Bengal. And there could be no doubt about the identity of that city: it was Dhaka (now the capital of Bangladesh).

But the phrase 'city-of-the-world', on the other hand, made no sense in this context: I had never heard of the Persian or Urdu phrase, *nagar-e-jahan*, being used in relation to Dhaka. How had it found its way into this couplet?

It struck me presently that this line, like the first, might also be a cryptic reference to a date.

As it happens my own family's origins lie in the part of the Bengal delta that is now Bangladesh: my parents and grandparents had crossed over to India when the subcontinent was partitioned. But before that they had spent a lot of time in Dhaka – and now, as I tried to recall the Dhaka stories of my older relatives, something flashed through my mind. Flipping open my laptop I started a search.

An answer appeared within seconds.

What I learnt was this: Dhaka had served as the capital of Bengal when it was a province of the Mughal Empire. The fourth Mughal monarch was the emperor Jahangir ('World-Conqueror') and during his reign, and for some years afterwards, Dhaka had been renamed Jahangir-nagar in his honour.

Could it be that *nagar-e-jahan* was a play on words, a cryptic reference to Dhaka in the seventeenth century?

If this were the case, it would follow that the shrine had been built at some time between 1605, when the emperor Jahangir was enthroned, and 1690, when Calcutta was founded by the British.

Once this idea had entered my head other details began to fall into place. For example the evident Persian influence in the couplet: the seventeenth century was a period in which Bangla had absorbed many words and phrases from Persian, Arabic and for that matter, Portuguese and Dutch as well.

A date range of 1605 to 1690 was supported by another detail in Nilima's story: the fact that the shrine had reminded her of the temples of Bishnupur. For it was precisely in this period that the Bishnupur style of architecture (which married Islamic and Hindu elements to marvellous effect) had flowered across Bengal.

Equally intriguing was the recurrent theme of the gun (or *bundook* – a word that had entered Bangla through Persian and Arabic). The Mughals were of course famously a 'gunpowder empire'. Like their contemporaries, the Turkish Ottomans and the Persian Safavids, their power had rested largely on firearms. Could it be that the Gun Merchant's shrine was some sort of folksy commemoration of this process?

It was an interesting possibility but not, I decided, worth the trouble and risk of a trip to the Sundarbans.

With that settled, my mind turned to my other existence, in Brooklyn. It was not entirely an accident then that it occurred to me to wonder whether my American cellphone had run out of charge. While in India I always used a local SIM card and a different device, so my Brooklyn phone had lain unused on a corner of my desk for the last several weeks.

Switching it on now I saw that the phone was indeed almost out of charge. After rummaging around for a bit I found the charger and plugged it in. Then, flipping through my apps I discovered that absolutely no one, or at least no sentient being (rather than bots) had attempted to call or text me in all the time I had been away.

I was reflecting on this, with that passing sense of injury that such a discovery is bound to bring, when suddenly, like a dying ember coming to life, the phone's screen began to glow. An instant later the device let forth a trill, so piercing that the stray cat that had been yowling outside my window took to its heels.

I was so startled that for a couple of rings I sat frozen, staring at the screen. My astonishment was further compounded when I noticed that the call was from an Italian number and that the caller was an old friend, or rather mentor, Professoressa Giacinta Schiavon. I recalled also that Cinta (as she was known to her friends) had been unwell the year before. I had not heard from her since and had been wondering whether her health had taken a turn for the worse.

But Cinta's voice, always resonant, sounded as brisk and cheerful as ever: '*Caro! Come stai?*'

'I'm very well, Cinta,' I said in surprise. 'And you? How's your health?'

'Oh I am fine; *tutto a posto.*'

'Good. And where are you?'

'In Venice,' she said. 'At the airport.'

'Where are you going?'

'To Heidelberg, for a conference.' Then she added: 'I am doing the keynote, you know.'

The explanation was unnecessary: it went without saying that Cinta would be the star of any conference that was lucky enough to have her. She was a giant in her field, which was the history of Venice; in her youth she had studied with such greats as Fernand Braudel and S. D. Goitein and was fluent in all the major languages of the Mediterranean. Few indeed were the scholars who could match her, either in erudition or name recognition – so it was touching, as well as a little amusing, to see that fame had not dulled the small, and rather absurd, streak of vanity that was among her most endearing traits.

'And you?' she said. '*Dove sei?*'

'In Calcutta,' I said. 'In my bedroom. Do you remember it?'

'*Certo, caro!*' Her voice softened. 'How could I forget? And do you still have that – how do you call it? "The Dutchwoman"?'

'"Dutch wife".'

I remembered how she had smiled when I told her that this was the English name for the 'lap-pillows' or bolsters that Bengalis love to have in their beds. 'I had to get rid of that one – the moths got to it. I'm all alone now.'

'But you are well?'

There was a note of concern in her voice that puzzled me. 'Yes, I'm fine. Why do you ask?'

'I don't know, *caro* – I just had a dream.'

'At the airport?' I said incredulously.

'*Beh!* But it's not so strange ... I am in a nice lounge, in a big chair – my flight is delayed because of some flood somewhere. And while I sit here waiting some nice young *camerieri* are bringing me glasses of prosecco. You understand?'

'Yes.'

I could imagine all too well the drama of Cinta's entry, with every eye in the lounge turning towards this tall, wide-shouldered woman with flashing black eyes and a mass of white hair curling down to her neckline, in a style made famous by the film-stars of her youth. No one who knew Cinta could doubt that every *cameriere* in the place was clustering around her, racing to fetch glasses of prosecco as she settled into a chair.

'I was sitting here, *caro*,' she continued, 'and I fell into a doze and an image appeared before my eyes – I don't know whether it was a dream or a memory. That happens you know, as you grow older – you can't tell the dreams from the memories.'

'What exactly did you see in your dream?'

'I saw you standing in front of a tent – a big one, like a circus tent. There were many people inside, watching something, a *spettacolo* – I don't know what exactly. Do you know what this could be?'

I scratched my head. 'Yes, I think I recall something – maybe it happened when you came to Calcutta for the first time. How long ago was that?'

'Twenty years? Twenty-five?'

'Anyway it was a very long time ago,' I said. 'We went to the Indian Museum, on Chowringhee, and afterwards you wanted to go for a walk in the Maidan. Do you remember it? It's a big stretch of green in the centre of the city. You caught sight of a huge tent where there was a *jatra* going on – a kind of folk opera performance. You wanted to see what was happening so we stopped at the entrance and you looked inside.'

'*Ah, sì!* I remember.'

It struck me as very strange that she should recall such a trivial and fleeting moment while sitting in an airport in Venice. 'We were there for just a few minutes,' I said. 'I wonder why you would remember that, of all things, after all these years?'

'*È vero*,' she said, sounding more than a little puzzled herself. 'I don't know why it seemed important. Anyway, I hope I didn't wake you?'

'No. Not at all. I'm really happy to hear your voice.'

'Yes, yours too,' she said hurriedly. I could tell that she was baffled by what had happened and was now eager to get off the phone. 'Ciao, *caro*, ciao! We'll speak again soon. *Tanti baci!*'

Unsettled by the sheer randomness of the call I lay down on my bed and tried to think back to that decades-old day when Cinta and I had gone walking in the Maidan. But try as I might I could remember nothing of interest, nothing that might cause that moment to linger in her memory.

Then I had an idea. Being the avid note-taker and journal-keeper that I am, it struck me that it was not unlikely that I had made an entry that day. If so it would not be hard to find for the journal was close at hand, stacked in the rusty steel trunk that served as a repository for my papers, jottings, diaries and so on.

Reaching under the bed I pulled the trunk out, amidst a cloud of dust. The hinges squeaked and tiny weevils scattered over the floor as I pushed back the top. Underneath a powdery layer of dust, the contents of the trunk were as I had left them, neatly sorted and labelled.

And there it was! A slim pocket diary with a russet cover. The page for the day of Cinta's arrival in Calcutta included the flight details (I had received her at the airport). The entry for the next day read as follows: 'Tour of Old Calcutta with Cinta and then Indian museum. Thought she might like to see the bright lights of Park St but she wasn't interested. Wanted to walk in the Maidan. There was a jatra going on, with a big billboard that caught Cinta's interest; a female figure with snakes wrapped around her body – Manasa Devi.'

Then it began to come back to me.

I had met Cinta the year before, in the United States. I was then in my early thirties and Cinta was some ten years older. I had recently found a job at the library of the Midwestern university from which I had graduated with a PhD (I had of course applied for all sorts of academic positions, but with no success; it seemed that there was no great demand in America for specialists in early modern Bengali folklore).

Already then Cinta was a figure of note on many counts. Both glamorous and brilliant she was already a well-regarded historian and had published an authoritative study of the Inquisition in Venice. But it wasn't because of her book that her name was as well known as it was: she owed her fame (or notoriety) to a personal tragedy that she had endured in the full light of public attention.

In her mid twenties Cinta had had an affair with the editor of a prominent Italian newspaper, a much older man. He had left his wife for her and they had had a daughter together. Their relationship was by all accounts a very happy one and Cinta had continued writing her first book while raising her daughter, Lucia.

Cinta's book was published when her daughter was twelve, and soon afterwards she was invited to a conference in Salzburg. She and her husband had decided to turn the trip into a family vacation and Cinta had gone on ahead, by plane. Her husband, who had a penchant for fast cars, had followed a few days later, with their daughter. But on the way, while crossing the Dolomites, the brakes of his Maserati had failed, sending him and Lucia plummeting down a steep mountainside.

The circumstances of the accident, and the fact that it involved a famous journalist, would probably have been enough to attract a great deal of attention in Italy. But it was the ensuing mystery, and the suspicion of wrongdoing, that put the story on the front pages of newspapers around the world.

Earlier that year Cinta's husband had published a series of exposés on the Mafia. After his death rumours began to circulate that he might have been the target of a planned assassination. The matter eventually reached the Italian parliament and a judge was appointed to conduct an investigation. Inevitably Cinta found herself at the centre of a maelstrom of unwanted publicity and was finally driven to escape the paparazzi by taking a sabbatical in America.

I, and many of my colleagues in the library, had followed this story as it unfolded in the tabloids and gossip magazines. But where exactly Cinta had taken refuge was not widely known so it came as a great surprise to us when we learnt that she was somewhere nearby, in the Midwest, and had written to the director of our library asking for permission to use our Rare Books Room (which happened to possess an important collection of historical documents, bequeathed by an Italian scholar who had emigrated just before the war).

Permission was readily granted and on the day that Cinta first showed up at the library I don't think there was a single member of the staff who didn't find some reason to drop by the Rare Books Room to catch a glimpse of her as she sat enthroned behind a massive bookstand. And quite a sight she was too, with her elegant yet sombre clothes, and her indefinable air of melancholy.

In that library the Rare Books and Special Collections Room was regarded in much the same light as mortuaries are in hospitals (the fact that gloves had to be worn in both gave rise to any number of laboured witticisms). Sepulchrally quiet, the room was usually empty except for the occasional scruffy graduate student. So far as the staff was concerned there was no assignment less desirable than that of the person who had to fetch and carry for the users of the room – and since I was new to the library the position of Catalog Assistant for Rare Books and Special Collections naturally came to me.

So it happened that during Cinta's two weeks in the library I was the gofer who had to fetch the materials she called up, which I did with a will, if only for the pleasure of hearing her say, in her rich, smoky voice, '*Grazie mille.*' She had an extraordinary ease of manner and within a day or two she had invented her own name for me, 'Dino' ('Dean in Italian'), but beyond a few occasional words we said hardly anything to each other within the walls of that room. I owed my acquaintance with her, rather, to the fact that I was a smoker then, as was she.

It was bitterly cold that spring and we smokers had to huddle together in a faux grotto near the library's main entrance. On one occasion we happened to find ourselves alone there and in an effort to make small talk I asked if she was finding it difficult to deal with the harsh Midwestern weather.

'Oh no!' she said emphatically, blowing out a cloud of smoke. 'You know I am half Midwestern myself: my mother is from Lexington.'

'Lexington, Kentucky?' I said.

She answered with a nod and a smile. 'Yes. Alice – my mother – is from Lexington.'

Cinta explained that Alice was from a Kentucky brewing family, one whose name I knew well, as it happened, because their bourbon was one of my favourites. As a young woman Alice had yearned to travel in Europe, especially Italy. The outbreak of the Second World War had forced her to defer her dream for a while but she had gone there soon after the war and had fallen in love with Venice.

This was a time when just to be American was to be a celebrity in Italy; everyone was eager to try out their English. One day, while going down the Grand Canal in a vaporetto, the *conducente* – a very good-looking young man – had recognized Alice as an American and had said: 'Can I ask you for some help please? With English? I am trying to learn . . .'

'*Sì,*' she had answered, '*certo!*' At which he had pulled a book out of his leather shoulder bag and asked her to explain a sentence that he had underlined. An avid reader, Alice was delighted to see that the book was Henry James's Venetian novella *The Aspern Papers*. After that she had begun to wait for that particular vaporetto and that particular *conducente*. Within a few months they were married.

'She has always been a great romantic, my mother,' said Cinta. 'You would have to be, wouldn't you, to give your daughter a name like Giacinta?'

'And your father?'

She laughed. 'Oh, he is a Venetian, born and bred. He likes to buy and sell things and is very good at it. They have been very happy together.'

'Do they live in Venice?'

'Yes, always, so I too was born and raised there. I'm a Venetian, one of the last.' She smiled and blew out a puff of smoke: '*Basta*, enough about me. What about you? What brought *you* here, to this part of the Midwest?'

'A scholarship,' I said. 'For a PhD.'

'Ah, so you are a scholar then? You came here only to study?'

I don't know what got into me then for I rarely talked about the circumstances of my departure from Calcutta. But Cinta had been so forthcoming herself that almost without knowing it I blurted out the words: 'No, that wasn't all.'

'There was something else then?'

I nodded.

She turned her black eyes on me and it was as if she were looking right into my soul.

'A woman?'

'Yes.'

'Were you setting out in search of her? Or running away?'

'Neither,' I said. 'She died, very suddenly and I had to leave.' I took a deep breath. 'It's a long story.'

Her eyes narrowed but she did not press me. 'Where did you grow up then?'

'Calcutta,' I said. 'In India.'

'*Calcoota?*' she said, in her inimitable way. 'That is where the Indian National Library is, *giusto?*'

I learnt then that at the end of her sabbatical Cinta intended to return to Italy by way of Asia and was planning to spend a week at the Indian National Library. Why? Because her current research project was on the role of Venice in the medieval spice trade.

It came as news to me that Venice had ever played a part in the spice trade. But Cinta assured me that this was indeed the case: 'Spices were a big part of the Venetian economy; for centuries the city had a Europe-wide monopoly on the spice trade.' She threw her head back and blew out a coil of smoke. 'The profits were so great that everyone became envious. That is why the Portuguese and the Spanish set off on those voyages of discovery – they wanted to break the Venetian monopoly on spices.'

I don't know whether it was because of what she said, or how she said it, but in any case I was captivated: it seemed wonderfully original to me that someone should want to travel to India to study the history of Venice. And Cinta being who she was I assumed that she would be travelling in great style and that the arrangements for her visit had already been made. Little did I expect that she would ask me – a mere Catalog Assistant! – to suggest a place where she might stay. But so she did, and after giving the matter some thought I said: 'I suppose you might want to try the Grand Hotel.'

'Is it very grand?'

'It is certainly the grandest hotel in Calcutta,' I said (which was true at that time).

She shook her head: 'Then it's not for me. I would like a quiet place, modest but clean – the kind of place where serious scholars stay.'

She blew out a smoke ring and waved it away. 'You see,' she said softly, dropping her gaze. 'I want to be incognito, if you know what I mean. I want to be quiet and to work – and also to see the city. You understand? I don't want many people – especially the papers – to know that I am there.'

This was the closest she came, during those two weeks, to mentioning her bereavement and the firestorm of publicity that had followed it.

'Yes of course I understand,' I said. 'I know just the place for you – a clean, quiet guest-house, not far from my own flat. I will be there myself this winter and if you like, I would be glad to show you around the city.'

She gave me one of her heart-stopping smiles. 'Yes – I would like that . . . *Grazie!*'

It was on Cinta's second day in Calcutta that we went walking in the Maidan. This being the largest open space in the city it often happened in those days that circuses and troupes of performers would pitch their tents there. That day, as I remember, one such tent seemed especially popular: people were streaming towards it from every direction.

At the entrance to the tent was a large (and to my eyes, hideous) billboard depicting a female figure entwined by serpents. It was inevitable perhaps that the image would catch Cinta's eye: when she asked me about it I explained that there was a performance going on in the tent, and that it was based on a popular legend about the goddess of snakes.

I said this flatly and without enthusiasm, hoping that she would let the matter drop. But my explanation only whetted her curiosity.

'*Posso?*' she said, gesturing at the tent. 'Can I take a look?'

My heart sank. I had no taste for jatra performances, which often go on for hours with absurdly costumed figures screeching in falsetto voices. The worst part, as far as I was concerned, was that these performances tended to reduce classic texts to simple-minded parodies.

But to explain all this to Cinta would have taken a long time so I allowed myself to be led towards the tent, although not without indulging in a little bit of sarcasm. 'I suppose,' I said, 'that this is the India you had expected to see, isn't it?'

She turned to me with a puzzled expression. 'Why do you say that?'

'It's exotic, isn't it?' I said. 'Especially if you think of India as a land of snake-charmers, as many foreigners do.'

She raised an eyebrow. 'And all these people inside?' she said, pointing to the crowded tent. 'Are they foreigners? Do you think this is exotic for them too?'

I shrugged. 'They are just simple people, with time to kill.'

She smiled. 'Well, I feel like I have a little time to kill as well – so I hope you won't mind if I go inside for a bit?'

'Not at all,' I said. 'And I hope *you* won't mind if I leave you here and go for a little walk? I could come back in, shall we say fifteen minutes?'

'Yes. Perfect.'

So I left her there and came back a short while later to find her already at the entrance.

'Did you enjoy the show?'

She nodded vigorously. 'Yes, very much. I couldn't understand a word of it of course, but I enjoyed watching the audience. I have never seen an audience so completely spellbound. It was as if they were *stregato* – bewitched.'

'I'm sure they were,' I said. 'People of that sort will believe anything, won't they?'

She glanced at me in surprise. 'You really don't like this story do you? It is perhaps too vulgar and common for you?'

This was near enough to the bone to nettle me. 'I think you've misunderstood me,' I protested. 'I grew up with this story. In fact it was the subject of my research thesis – I've even published an article on one of the epic poems on which this performance is based.'

It occurred to me suddenly that it would be a coup for me, career-wise, if the great Giacinta Schiavon were to read (and, better still, comment on my article).

'I could show you the article, if you like,' I said. 'It's not too long, just ten pages or so.'

'Why of course,' she said. 'Please do. I will read it with pleasure.'

I seized upon this invitation with an eagerness that is a little embarrassing to look back upon now (in my defence it could be said that I felt I had slipped in Cinta's regard, having come across as a priggish and overly westernized snob and was therefore keen to exonerate myself). The very next morning I went by the guest-house of the Ramakrishna Mission, where she was staying, and dropped off a copy of my article – 'A Note on the Dating of a Bengali Folk Epic'.

We had arranged to have dinner that evening, at a restaurant that was a twenty-minute walk from the guest-house. Cinta was waiting for me when I went to pick her up and within a few minutes, just as we reached the quiet sidewalks of Southern Avenue, she said: 'I read your article. Just now, before you came.'

'Oh? What did you think?'

'*Bravo!* Very interesting. I'm sure you're right about the potatoes!'

The hint of mockery in her voice warned me that she had more to say. I waited.

'I find it interesting how you write about this poem. You are like an archaeologist examining a pottery shard. Your language is so clinical, so precise!'

'Thank you,' I said. 'Your words are high praise, so far as I am concerned.'

She cast a puzzled, sideways glance at me as we passed under a streetlight.

'Is that all it is for you then, this poem? A lifeless fragment that is of interest only because it can be carbon-dated?'

'I suppose it is,' I said. 'I'm not a literary critic after all.'

'*Però* . . . those people at that performance yesterday, they were not critics either. And how they listened! Just to look at them you could tell that for them the story is not dead.'

'How do you mean?'

'You should have seen how rapt they were!' she said. 'And so many of them too! You would never see a crowd like that in Europe today, for such a performance. If someone staged, say, *Orlando Furioso* they might get an audience of learned critics and professors but that would be all. You would never get people like that – simple people, young and old, men and women. Only for *calcio* – football – do you see such a crowd. But even that is not the same for you would not see so many women at a football match. No, for those people yesterday that poem is alive! It is about the here and now! It is more real than real life.'

'Well, what can you expect?' I retorted. 'Those people are, as you say, simple and uneducated. Wasn't it Marx who said that peasants are like sacks of potatoes? Is it surprising that their lives are filled with gods and goddesses and demons?'

She glanced at me again. 'You really do not care for ordinary people, do you?'

The imputation of elitism made me bridle. 'Why you're quite wrong!' I said. 'I consider myself a person of the left. As a student I was a Maoist fellow-traveller. I've always stood in solidarity with peasants and workers.'

'Oh yes, *certo!*' she said, suppressing a giggle. 'I knew many Maoists and fellow-travellers in Italy. They had every regard for the bellies and bodies of poor people – but not, I think, for what is in their heads.'

'Not if it goes against reason,' I said. 'I pride myself on being a rational, secular, scientifically minded person. I am sorry if this does not conform to stereotypes of Indians – but I am not religious and don't believe in the supernatural. I will not, on any account, go along with a whole lot of superstitious mumbo-jumbo.'

She was quiet for a couple of paces. 'If that is true,' she said softly, 'why do you use all these religious words?'

'What religious words?'

'Like "superstitious" and "supernatural"?' she said, sketching apostrophes in the air with her index fingers. 'Don't you know that it was the Catholic Inquisition that put these words into currency? It was the Inquisitor's job to stamp out "superstition" and replace it with true religion. It was the Inquisitor also who decided what was "natural" and what was "supernatural". So to say that you don't believe in the "supernatural" is a contradiction in terms – because it means that you also don't believe in the "natural". Neither can exist without the other.'

'Oh come on,' I said impatiently. 'That's just semantics.'

'Yes, you're right. But the whole world is made up of semantics and yours are those of the seventeenth century. Even though you think you are so modern.'

This stung me in a particularly sensitive spot and I struck back harshly.

'I suppose in your eyes no Indian can be modern or rational? We're all supposed to believe in goddesses and witches and demons?'

'*Madonna!*' She stopped suddenly and flung up her hands in a gesture of disbelief. 'Why? Do you think that people elsewhere don't believe in such things? You are so wrong! I can tell you that to this day there are many people in France and Italy for whom witches and spirit-possession are just simple facts of life.'

'Impossible!'

The word sprung spontaneously from my lips; I could not square what she was saying with my conception of Europe, which I had always regarded as the wellspring of scientific rationality.

'I don't believe you.'

'But it is true!' she insisted. 'Have you never heard of tarantism, for example?'

'No. What is that?'

'The word comes from *tarantola* – a kind of venomous spider that lives in southern Italy. Its bite can have strange effects on

37

people. In some parts of southern Italy people believe that spirits can enter you through the bite of a tarantula. The victims have to be exorcized by music, and especially dance – that is where the *tarantella* comes from.'

'But Cinta,' I said, 'the tarantella is just a musical form, isn't it? A very old one, as I recall, going back to the seventeenth century? Surely things like that died out a long time ago?'

'Actually no!' said Cinta. 'Tarantism still exists. Someone I knew published a brilliant study of it not long ago – Ernesto de Martino. Have you heard of him?'

'No,' I said. 'The name doesn't ring a bell.'

'I'm not surprised. De Martino is very little known outside Italy even though he was, in my opinion, one of the most important intellectuals of the twentieth century. He was a historian, a folklorist and an ethnographer – and also a communist and disciple of Gramsci. But what he is famous for are his studies of tarantism, which he conducted in the 1960s when such practices were thought to have died off long before. That is what makes his work so interesting: he showed that in some parts of Italy – the very birthplace of Renaissance rationalism! – tarantism was thriving. And unlike all the others who have studied such practices he approached it with an open mind. He did not assume that these poor peasant women – and they *were* mainly women – were deluded. He did not rule out the possibility that they experienced something that falls outside our usual range of explanations.'

'You mean,' I said, in disbelief, 'that he believed that spirits and demons are real? That they can communicate with people through spider bites?'

'No, no!' said Cinta. 'His argument was that we cannot start with the label of the "supernatural", as rationalists invariably do. They assume that unexplained forms of causation cannot *in principle* exist. Yet, as de Martino shows, there are many well-documented instances of things that cannot be explained by so-called "natural" causes.'

'Like what?'

'Hmm . . .' She paused to think. 'For example, foreknowledge – what they call pre-cognition nowadays. Knowing that something will occur before it does.'

'As with soothsayers and oracles?' I scoffed. 'You're not telling me you seriously believe in that kind of thing?'

'Really?' she said. 'But then how do you explain what happened with the Aztecs?'

'I'm sorry? You've lost me.'

'But have you not heard about the Aztec predictions? Long before the Spanish arrived the Aztecs knew that invaders would be coming across the seas. They knew that they would be carrying "sticks of fire", and they even knew about the shapes of their helmets. And it was because they knew these things that they were helpless when the invasion actually came about. People think that knowing the future can help you prepare for what is to come – but often it only makes you powerless.'

At this point I almost burst out laughing. But fortunately we had now reached our destination, a Chinese restaurant on Lansdowne Road. Opening the restaurant's big red moon-door I said, on what I hoped was a light note: 'If there's one thing I have confident foreknowledge of it's that the food in this restaurant will be more Indian than Chinese.'

I was, I must admit, a little shaken by this argument, not because Cinta had said anything particularly strange – many people say strange things after all – but because she had tried to defend what she had said. It seemed unseemly, inappropriate, even rude. It's one thing, after all, to tell a child a fairy tale at bedtime; it's quite another to tell the same story to an adult, in all seriousness.

But still, I liked Cinta, and did not want to lose her friendship, so I decided that I would let the subject drop. And evidently Cinta too had come to a similar decision, so the dinner went by pleasantly enough. But our disagreement was neither settled nor forgotten and the strain that it had created lingered in the air as we walked back to the guest-house. It was on an awkward note that I said goodnight but I gave her my phone number anyway and asked her to call if she needed anything.

However, I didn't think that Cinta would want to see me soon and was not surprised when the next couple of days passed without any word from her. I knew that she was in town for the rest of the week so I decided that I would let another day or two go by before seeking her out, perhaps at the National Library.

But instead it was Cinta who sought me out. One evening, just as I was finishing dinner, my phone (the old-fashioned kind, with a dial and finger holes) began to ring. To my surprise it was Cinta: 'Ciao, *caro!*'

Her voice sounded strained. 'How are you, Cinta?' I said. 'Is everything all right?'

'Not really,' she said. 'I have had some news. I have to go back to Italy immediately. I am flying out tomorrow.'

I didn't want to pry but nor did I want to seem unconcerned. 'It's nothing serious I hope?'

She hesitated and then added, reluctantly: 'Perhaps you know about my husband and daughter . . . what happened?'

'Yes, of course.'

I could sense that she was struggling with herself, that she wanted to talk, but not over the phone.

'Look, Cinta,' I said, 'would you like me to come over?'

'Yes, please.'

'I'll be there in ten minutes.'

She was waiting for me at the entrance to the guest-house. 'Can we go somewhere?' she said. 'For a walk maybe?'

The weather was not pleasant that evening. As often happens in Calcutta in January, the streets were shrouded in a heavy, noxious-smelling fog.

'A walk may not be a good idea today,' I said. 'Maybe we could go back to my apartment instead? It's not far.'

'*Va bene.* Let's go.'

The usually busy streets were silent and almost deserted. Neither of us said anything until we had reached the house.

My apartment isn't large but the living room is comfortable enough. Cinta seated herself on the divan and I poured us both a shot of brandy from a bottle that I had bought at Duty Free.

She took a sip and sat staring into the glass. Then, without any prompting from me, she began to talk about the phone call she had received, earlier in the day, from the Italian ambassador in New Delhi. He was relaying a request – a summons, in all but name – from the judge who had been appointed to enquire into the accident that had killed her husband and daughter.

A new piece of evidence, a police report, had turned up and he wanted to question Cinta about it.

'Do you have any idea,' I asked, 'of what's going on?'

She nodded. 'Yes, I do.' After a moment's pause she added: 'It is about something that happened that day in Salzburg, just before the accident, when I was in a hotel, waiting for my daughter and husband to join me. They were coming by car from Milan. Giacomo loved to drive you see . . .'

That night, in her hotel in Salzburg, Cinta had woken up in the small hours with a nagging sense of unease. This wasn't exactly new; she had been on edge ever since her husband, Giacomo, started receiving threats from unknown sources. But that morning the sense of foreboding was unusually strong, so much so that she threw up a couple of times.

She waited until dawn and then put a call through to Giacomo, in Milan, and begged him to call off the trip.

He was incredulous: 'Why?'

She didn't know what to say except 'it's just a feeling, a *presagio* – after all, you've been getting these threats'.

Giacomo had brushed her words impatiently aside. A confident, headstrong man, he was accustomed to dealing with threats: he told her not to worry, he was not going to let himself be intimidated by low-life *malavitosi*. Their daughter Lucia had been looking forward to this holiday, he said, and would be bitterly disappointed if it were cancelled.

And then he sprang a surprise. He told her that his paper had just given him a satellite phone and that she would be able to call him at any time during the drive from Milan to Salzburg: he read out the number and made her take it down.

This mention of advanced technology had made Cinta doubt her intuitions; she had stopped pressing him, partly because she knew he wouldn't listen anyway, and partly because she didn't want to sound like a credulous fool. Besides, Giacomo's confidence and certainty had reassured her, dispelling some of her anxiety. By the end of the call Cinta was almost back to her usual self. She told Giacomo and Lucia that she missed them and couldn't wait for them to get to Salzburg.

But later that morning, at the conference, her apprehensions returned and she was unable to keep her mind on the proceedings. She went to a payphone and called the number Giacomo had given her. He answered after a couple of rings. He was laughing: '*Ecco!* See the satellite phone works! Here we are on the autostrada and I am speaking to you!'

'Where are you?'

'Somewhere between Bressanone and Innsbruck. We'll be in Salzburg in a couple of hours.'

He handed the phone to Lucia.

'Mamma!' cried Lucia. 'It's so beautiful here. I wish you were with us.'

'I wish so too, *tesoro!*'

They chatted on for a little bit and then Cinta said goodbye. But somehow, even though everything seemed all right, she wasn't reassured. Instead of going back to the conference she made her way to the hotel and went up to the suite that she had taken. She was sitting in a chair, staring blankly at a window, when she heard Lucia's voice saying: '*Mamma! Mamma! Ti voglio bene . . .* I love you!'

The words were so clear that she whipped around, thinking that Giacomo and Lucia had arrived early and somehow let themselves into the room. Not seeing anyone there she wondered whether Lucia was playing a practical joke. She went through the whole suite, looking inside closets and under the beds. When it became clear that there was no one else in the suite, she picked up the phone, dialled an outside line and keyed in the number of Giacomo's satellite phone.

All she got was the sound of static so she tried again, struggling to hold her fingers steady. Again there was no answer so she called the hotel's telephone operator, thinking that she might have made a mistake with the country codes, or some other detail. She gave the number to the operator and sat down to wait, staring at the phone. There followed a delay of several minutes during which she grew increasingly frantic. When the wait became unbearable she called the reception desk and demanded that the clerk talk to the phone operator. She thought she would hear back in a minute or two and when that didn't happen she left the suite and ran down the stairs to the reception desk.

The receptionist and the telephone operator were huddled together in an office. Cinta went straight in and demanded to know what was going on. They told her that they had tried the number of the satellite phone several times and there had been no response.

The receptionist asked her when she had last heard from her husband and where he was at the time. 'Between Bressanone and Innsbruck,' she told him. After noting down her answers he begged her to calm herself and go back to her suite: he would find out who was responsible for patrolling that stretch of the highway and contact them.

Cinta went slowly back to her suite and shortly afterwards the phone began to ring. She snatched it up: at the other end was some kind of *poliziotto*, an Italian patrolman. She gave him the number of Giacomo's car and told him that she was worried that something had gone wrong because he wasn't answering his satellite phone. The patrolman told her not to worry, some stretches of the road were outside satellite coverage – but he would put out an alert anyway, just in case.

Cinta's phone rang an hour later. It was the patrolman; he had called back to tell her that a helicopter had spotted Giacomo's car, at the bottom of a steep gorge; there were no survivors.

'So you see,' said Cinta, 'I knew that somewhere there was a record of my call and the time when it was made. I knew that if anyone ever examined the reports carefully they would see that I had called the police more than an hour before the accident was reported. They would wonder how I could have known that something had gone wrong before the police did. I think that is what has happened.'

'And what will you tell them?'

'It's simple: I will say that I just happened to call Giacomo's satellite phone and grew worried when there was no answer.'

'And the rest? Your daughter's voice?'

She cast me a scornful glance. 'Of course I will say nothing about that. You know very well that it cannot be said. They would think me a *pazza* . . .'

All through this Cinta had held herself upright, with a steely calm. But now her shoulders began to shake and she covered her face with both hands.

It was painful to listen to her dry, gasping sobs. After a while I went to the divan and put an arm around her. She leaned into my shoulder and began to weep, with a silent desolation such as I had never heard before. Such raw pain would have been hard to behold in anyone but was especially so in her because she was usually so contained. Without her saying so I knew that she had never before spoken of her experience in that Salzburg hotel.

I am not sure how long we sat there like that but I remember saying after a while that she was in no state to go back to the guest-house: I would make up the bed in my bedroom for her, and I'd sleep in the living room, on the divan.

She nodded and when my bedroom was ready she went off there while I stretched myself out on the divan.

I slept fitfully and woke at dawn to find Cinta on the other side of the living room, standing at a window, smoking, and watching the stirrings of the street below.

When she saw that I was awake she came to sit beside me. Putting an arm around my shoulder she gave me a peck on the cheek.

'*Grazie, grazie!*'

'It's nothing, Cinta – you don't need to thank me.'

'But I do! You listened to me so sympathetically. Even though you are such a big rationalist! I am grateful to you for that.'

'It's really not necessary.'

She smiled, holding me at arm's length. 'And now you know so much about me. But I know almost nothing about you.'

'There's nothing much to tell,' I said. 'Don't you know what they say? Indian men have no inner lives. The only thing they really care about is their digestion.'

'Can that be true?' She seemed to ponder this in all seriousness. 'No, I think not, Dino. I seem to remember you telling me something quite interesting – about why you left for America . . .'

'Oh that. You really want to know?'

She nodded. 'Yes, tell me.'

I got up to put a kettle on the stove.

'I told you, didn't I, that I was a Maoist fellow-traveller back in my student days? Those groups were very strong here back then. All the brightest and most idealistic students were drawn to them.'

She nodded. 'Yes, it was the same in Italy when I was a student.'

'Were you . . . ?'

She shook her head. 'No. Those ideas always seemed too simple to me. But maybe you felt differently?'

'I don't know that ideas had much to do with it.'

'A woman then?'

'Yes. She was named after Durga, the warrior goddess, and that was what she was for me. I was a bookish young fellow with my head in the clouds; I dreamed of travelling and seeing the places I had read about. And then Durga burst into my life – she was a legend already, known for her reckless courage. She would take incredible risks, carrying messages to armed insurgents in the countryside. I was in awe of her – she made me feel worthless and selfish and petit bourgeois.'

'So you fell in love with her?'

'Yes.'

'And she? Did she love you?'

'I think so: I was as much of a mystery to her, I suppose, as she was to me. We had an affair anyway, which was a risky thing for her because I wasn't one of her Maoist comrades, just a kind of hanger-on. They were like a cult, her party and her comrades – everyone who wasn't "inside" was an object of suspicion. And this must have been especially so in my case because they knew that I had an uncle who was high up in the police. Perhaps they thought that I was trying to get secrets out of Durga or something, I don't know. Anyway, one day Durga went out of town without telling me anything about where she was going. This was not unusual of course, except that this time she didn't come back. A few days later I found out that she'd been shot by the police in an "encounter".'

'Who told you?'

'My policeman uncle: he said that she was betrayed by her own comrades.'

'Why?'

'Probably because of her relationship with me. Or possibly because her comrades wanted to stir up trouble for my uncle. In any case someone had planted my name and address on her.'

'*Incredibile!*'

'Yes. My uncle said he would hush it up but I had to leave

46

the city at once. So I was packed off to stay with relatives in New Delhi. That was when I started applying to American universities – and I got lucky, I suppose . . .'

Cinta rose to her feet and came to stand beside me. 'It wasn't your fault you know. You mustn't blame yourself.'

It had been a long time since I had thought of those events, and now I could feel my composure beginning to dissolve. I didn't want to run the risk of breaking down, not just then, so I glanced at my watch.

'Cinta, we really must go. I don't want you to miss your flight to New Delhi.'

In the taxi, on the way to the airport, Cinta asked whether I was happy in the Midwest, working at that library. I told her I didn't much care for my job but couldn't see any way out.

'Well, we must do something,' she said. 'We must find you something more suitable.'

Sure enough, six months later, when I was back in the Midwest, I received a letter from a New York company that dealt in rare books and antiquities: they were looking to recruit someone for their Asian division and had written to me because I had been very highly recommended by Professoressa Giacinta Schiavon, who was a close friend of one of their directors.

The offer was tempting but I hesitated: moving to New York was a daunting, even frightening prospect. Everyone I knew said that I would be overwhelmed by the city.

I was still dithering when Cinta called, out of the blue, and told me not to surrender to my apprehensions. It's always a mistake, she said, to do the easy thing, just out of habit.

The call tipped the balance: I took the job and it proved to be exactly what I needed. I did well enough that within fifteen years I was able to set up on my own, in Brooklyn.

Those years happened to coincide with Cinta's rise to scholarly stardom. She began to travel more and more and when she passed through New York we often met, usually for a leisurely meal. Sometimes our paths would cross also at conferences, meetings and auctions. So, in one way or another, even though we lived on different continents, we saw each other several times a year. She often sent clients my way, many of whom were Italian, so over the years I even acquired a working knowledge of the language.

What Cinta saw in me was, I must admit, something of a mystery to me, and it made me all the more grateful for her friendship: I could never forget that if not for her I might well have remained forever entombed in that sepulchral library in the Midwest. Such was the part she had played in my life that I could not take a call from her lightly, even when it appeared, as on that day in Kolkata, to have been made unmindfully. It was almost as though she had wanted to tell me, once again, not to do the easy thing, just out of habit.

Looking at my watch I saw that it was not too late to call Piya. I dialled her number and she answered after a couple of rings.

'Hello, Piya,' I said. 'Look, I've decided to go to that temple after all.'

'Good!'

'Could it still be arranged for tomorrow? Or did I call too late?'

'Tomorrow's fine. Moyna is taking one of the trust's minibuses early in the morning – she'll accompany you to Basonti, which is the major river port for the Sundarbans. You'll be met there by a man called Horen Naskar; he'll take you to the shrine in a boat and get you back to Basonti before nightfall. We'll arrange a taxi to bring you to Kolkata from there. With a bit of luck you'll be home by dinner-time.'

'Sounds good.'

'Could you be at the Gol Park roundabout at 5 a.m.? The bus will pick you up from there.'

'Sure. No problem.'

'One more thing,' said Piya. 'It'll be windy and a bit chilly on the boat at that time of the morning, so be prepared. And you might want to bring along a change of clothes.'

'Why?'

She laughed. 'Let's just say there's a lot of mud in the Sundarbans. And a lot of water too.'

'I get it. And what about you? When do you leave for Bhubaneswar?'

'Tomorrow morning. I don't suppose you'll be here when I get back?'

'No, but maybe,' I said hopefully, 'we'll run into each other again next year?'

'Yeah, sure. Goodbye till then. Take care.'

'And you too. Take care.'

Tipu

The next day I went to the Gol Park roundabout a little before five, wrapped up in a light sweater and windbreaker. Slung over my shoulder was a canvas backpack: I had taken Piya's warning to heart and had brought along not one but two changes of clothes, as well as a camera, voice recorder and e-reader.

The sky was dark and the roundabout was shrouded in the usual foul-smelling winter smog, with the streetlights glowing eerily in the gloom. A few minutes after five I heard a faint echo of angry voices in the distance. The voices grew steadily louder and then the dull glow of a pair of headlights appeared within the mist. Shortly afterwards a yellow minivan, emblazoned with the logo of the Badabon Trust, came to a halt in front of me: pouring out of its door and windows were the sounds of a heated altercation.

The quarrel quietened as I climbed in. Moyna was seated at the front of the bus and had kept a place for me, beside her.

The silence lasted only until I was seated. As soon as the bus began to move, the altercation flared up again.

Looking over my shoulder I saw that I was the only adult male in the bus; the other passengers were all women and children. The front rows were filled with employees of the trust, all dressed in prim, starched, cotton saris, like Moyna. The women at the rear were a motley lot, clothed in bright, tinselly synthetics; some were accompanied by children and a few were breast-feeding their babies, under cover of their saris.

As the quarrel raged on Moyna began to whisper into my ear, explaining that the women at the back were 'sex workers' (she used the English phrase) and had been rounded up by the police from various red-light districts in Kolkata and elsewhere. They were all originally from the Sundarbans, she said, so the police had called on the trust to help rehabilitate them, through its workshops and employment generation schemes.

But the trust could not offer much by way of money and this was what the dispute was about. The women at the back were protesting that they would not be able to support themselves on the wages they had been promised; the trust's staffers were angrily refuting this claim.

Unfortunately, Moyna told me, this was a losing battle. The trust's experience showed that many, if not most, of the rescued women would soon go back to the lives they had been living before.

'How can you be so sure?' I asked.

Moyna gave a weary sigh.

'We've been dealing with these problems for many years,' she said. 'Ever since Aila.'

This was how I made the acquaintance of Cyclone Aila, which hit the Sundarbans in 2009.

The way this disaster had unfolded, Moyna told me, was quite different from the cyclones of the past. Starting in the late 1990s warning systems for storms had been put in place across the region so there was plenty of time to prepare. Mass evacuations had been planned in advance and millions of people were moved to safety, in India and in Bangladesh. As a result the casualty count was surprisingly low, at least in relation to the cyclone of 1970.

Yet Aila's long-term consequences were even more devastating than those of earlier cyclones. Hundreds of miles of embankment had been swept away and the sea had invaded places where it had never entered before; vast tracts of once fertile land had been swamped by salt water, rendering them uncultivable for a generation, if not forever.

The evacuations too had produced effects that no one could have foretold. Having once been uprooted from their villages many evacuees had decided not to return, knowing that their lives, always hard, would be even more precarious now. Communities had been destroyed and families dispersed; the young had drifted to cities, swelling already-swollen slums; among the elderly many had given up trying to eke out a living and had taken to begging on the streets.

The Sundarbans had always attracted traffickers, because of its poverty, but never in such numbers as after Aila; they had descended in swarms, spiriting women off to distant brothels and transporting able-bodied men to work sites in faraway cities or even abroad. Many of those who left were never heard from again.

Sometimes, said Moyna, it seemed as though both land and water were turning against those who lived in the Sundarbans. When people tried to dig wells, an arsenic-laced brew gushed out of the soil; when they tried to shore up embankments the tides rose higher and pulled them down again. Even fishermen could barely get by; where once their boats would come back loaded with catch, now they counted themselves lucky if they netted a handful of fry.

What were young people to do?

Making a life in the Sundarbans had become so hard that the exodus of the young was accelerating every year: boys and girls were borrowing and stealing to pay agents to find them work elsewhere. Some were slipping over the border into Bangladesh, to join labour gangs headed for the Gulf. And if that failed they would pay traffickers to smuggle them to Malaysia or Indonesia, on boats.

The only way to avoid this fate was for the young to get an education. But how could boys and girls who had been brought up in mangrove country, studying by candlelight and sharing old textbooks, compete with city folk with their tuition centres and easy access to the Internet?

Moyna's voice had become unsteady now and she was dabbing her eyes with the hem of her sari.

It wasn't long before another torrent of words came pouring out of her.

When her son was born, she said, she had had many dreams for him – that he would be the first in the family to finish college, that he would study medicine or engineering. But nothing had ever turned out well for him; he had been dogged by misfortune since he was little, starting with the death of his father, who had been killed while working for Piya.

Of course, said Moyna, everyone had been very kind – Nilima, the trust, her neighbours, and Piya most of all. They had never had to ask Piya for anything: the burden of the accident weighed so heavily on her that she had given them more than they would ever have thought to expect. She had bought a small house in Lusibari for Moyna and her son, and had opened bank accounts for them, one for their everyday needs, and one for the boy's education. She had spent countless hours tutoring the boy in English; when she was away in America she would give him lessons over the phone and the Net. She had gifted him laptops, tablets, the latest phones, games consoles, music systems – and when the boy complained that he was often unable to use his gadgets because of power cuts, Piya had paid to have their house solarized.

'Can you imagine,' said Moyna, 'what it was like for him to have all this, in the Sundarbans, where no one has seen such things . . . ?'

I understood that the list of gifts that Moyna had recited was a metaphor for the peculiar predicament that Piya's generosity had created for her and her son, enclosing them both in a bubble of affluence within the increasingly impoverished terrain that they actually inhabited.

All of this was well meant of course, said Moyna, but the upshot was that her son had found it increasingly hard to fit in. While still quite young the boy had begun to say that he wanted to go to the United States. When he reached thirteen, and was old enough for high school, Piya had taken him with her to the small university town in Oregon where she lived and worked. But the experiment had ended badly, as it was bound to: Piya lived alone, in a small apartment, eating food out of boxes and travelling frequently for work; it was not as if she had a family, or knew anything about bringing up children. Being often left to fend for himself the boy had fallen in with the wrong crowd and had even had a couple of brushes with the police. After a couple of years Piya had brought him back to India, fearing that he might end up in the American juvenile detention system.

Moyna had been astonished by how much her son had changed in the interim. His clothes, his manner, his hair – nothing was the same. Even his name was different: he had told her that his real name, Tutul, was difficult for Americans so he had changed it to Tipu. He had insisted that everyone get used to his new name and wouldn't answer to any other.

For Tipu to go to school in Lusibari was clearly impossible so Piya had admitted him into an expensive boarding school in Kolkata. But that too had turned out badly. The attitudes that Tipu had brought back from America had not sat well with his fellow students and teachers. Things had become worse still when his schoolmates discovered that he was a Dalit, from the Sundarbans. One day a classmate had said to him that only servants and whores came from the Sundarbans. Tipu had lost his temper and given the fellow the beating he deserved. But the other boy was from an influential family and they had ensured that Tipu was expelled.

After returning to the Sundarbans, Tipu had flatly refused to go on with his schooling, and neither Moyna nor Piya nor anyone else had been able to change his mind. If they tried to press him, he would say: 'I can learn more on the Net than any of those teachers can teach me.'

And it was true that he was very good with computers; and since he spoke English like an American, he had plenty of resources to fall back on. At that time he was only in his mid teens yet people would come from all around to ask for his help. Soon he began to earn money and would sometimes disappear for a few days – where he went and where exactly his money came from Moyna didn't know; if she asked he would say that he was doing some work for a call centre. He was of an age to go to college now, and had long since outgrown whatever sway she had ever had over him – he did what he liked and went where he pleased. He was like a stranger to her now.

Moyna dabbed her eyes again and fell silent, staring out of the window at the rice-fields and fish ponds that were flashing past us.

I did not imagine that it would fall to my lot to meet Tipu. But at Basonti, as we were walking along an embankment, Moyna suddenly cried out: 'Why there he is! Tipu!'

'Where?'

She pointed ahead, to a small, slight youth who was slouching towards us, with his hands thrust deep into the pockets of his slack-waisted jeans.

'I didn't think he would be here,' said Moyna. 'Nilima-di must have told him you were coming. She's the only one he listens to.'

Moyna's description of her son had led me to expect an abject, morose young fellow. But it was evident at a glance that Tipu was a creature of an altogether different kind; he had the probing eyes and darting movements of a hungry barracuda. He even glinted, barracuda-like, because of a silver ear stud and glittering highlights in his hair, which was spiky on top and flat at the sides. As for his clothes – a Nets T-shirt and baggy jeans that kept slipping down to expose his bright red boxers – they would not have looked out of place in Brooklyn.

We soon learnt that it was indeed Nilima who had asked Tipu to meet us at Basonti. 'She asked me to go along and get the GPS co-ordinates of this shrine,' said Tipu. 'She wants me to record the location.'

He had been speaking Bangla all this while, in an unenthusiastic murmur, but his voice rose as he turned to me and stuck out his hand.

'Hey there,' he said in English, sticking out his hand. 'How you doin'?'

Shaking his hand, I said: 'Hi. I'm . . .'

'I know who you are, Pops,' said Tipu, grinning. 'I know all about you.'

I was dumbfounded. 'How?'

'Looked you up on the Net.'

I don't know what annoyed me more: the insolence of his tone or that he had decided to call me Pops, as though I were a character from a comic book. But being unable to think of a suitable rejoinder I decided that it would be best to ignore his sallies.

'Where's the boat?' I said.

'Over there.' He pointed to the riverfront which was packed with vessels of all kinds.

'Which one is ours?'

'That one.'

I had imagined that I'd be carried to the shrine in a sleek, powerful motor launch that would skim swiftly over the water, propelled by a churning white wake. But the boat that awaited me was an ungainly tub, rigged out to appeal to day trippers from Kolkata, with hideous images of tigers and crocodiles painted on its sides. Neither the garish colours nor the banner that hung from the deck rails (SUNNY SUNDARBANS TOURS, PROP. HOREN NASKAR) could disguise the fact that this was just an old-fashioned, rather diminutive version of the kind of steamer that is known in Bangla as a *bhotbhoti*.

Moyna now began to show signs of lingering: she would, I think, have liked to join us on the trip, if only to spend a little time with her son. But Tipu would have none of it: dismissing his mother with a peremptory wave, he ushered me along the embankment to a waiting gangplank. 'Come on Pops,' he said briskly. 'We can't be shooting the breeze now. Skipper's getting antsy – wants to catch the falling tide. You'd better get your ass on board.'

The gangplank was a little too narrow for my comfort but I managed to make it safely across. As I was stepping on to the steamer's deck I heard a raucous laugh behind me.

'Good going Pops!' said Tipu as he scrambled nimbly across the plank. 'You made it! Looked like you were going to take a tumble there for a bit.'

Pulling in the gangplank, he darted away to cast off the steamer's moorings. Down in the bowels of the vessel an engine began to throb and a plume of thick black smoke appeared above us. A moment later we were under way, wallowing along to the rhythm of the engine's steady *bhot-bhot-bhot*.

Suddenly Tipu materialized beside me again. 'So are you staying over tonight Pops?'

'No,' I said. 'I have to get back to the city.'

'Too bad. I could have arranged for you to have a good time.' He winked and cupped his hands over his chest as though he were fondling a woman's breasts. 'You know what I mean?' he said, pumping his hips and elbows. 'I could'a found you some action; there's lots of it around here if you know where to look.'

I stared at him speechlessly, unable to summon any words.

'Or maybe you'd like some of this?' he said, pulling out a joint. 'I'll let you have the first one free, seeing that you're an old dude and all.'

I could tell that he was trying to get a rise out of me. Without another word I turned around and headed towards the wheelhouse.

Horen Naskar looked to be in his sixties: squat and stocky he had broad shoulders and a belly that strained against his white shirt and belted lungi. The upper part of his face was shielded by enormous steel-rimmed eyeshades; the part below had the weathered look of an old tyre, with deep wrinkles etched into the sun-scorched skin.

Seating myself beside him, on the helmsman's bench, I pulled out a notebook: 'So, about this shrine we're going to: do you remember the time you went there with Nilima-di?'

'Of course,' said Horen. 'It was in 1970, soon after the great storm. That was a terrible one, that storm, even worse than Aila . . .'

Storms, I soon discovered, were Horen's measure of time. In the same way that the Chinese speak of the era of the Qianlong or Jiajing emperors, or Americans of the Kennedy or Reagan administrations, Horen spoke of the Bhola cyclone, and of Aila, as events that bookended extended spans of time.

Aila, in particular, had affected his life in very important ways. He had been in the fishing business before, with several vessels to his name. But the 2009 storm had capsized two of his trawlers and a couple of other boats as well. Afterwards he had decided to get out of fishing altogether: profits had been declining for years and it had become increasingly clear that things would only get worse. He had decided instead to use his insurance payments to go into the tourism industry – and he had made the switch at a good time, just as the Sundarbans was beginning to become popular with tourists.

The great cyclone of 1970, Horen remembered for a different reason – because he had come close to losing his life. He had been out at sea, with his uncle, when the storm struck. Their boat was swept ashore, but on the wrong side of the border. The boat had not survived the landing but they had managed to climb on to a tree. After two days they had spotted some fishermen from their own village, in India; they were in a boat that was miraculously intact, and they had offered to take Horen and the others back with them. On the way home they had witnessed scenes they could never have imagined: they had had to fight off stranded mobs; they had been forced to evade thieves and river bandits, who had descended like vultures, to take advantage of the chaos.

These events were less than a week in the past on the day when Horen steered Nilima's boat to the Gun Merchant's shrine. As a result his recollections of the legend were quite different from hers: the calamities that figure in it loomed much larger in his memory than they did in hers. He remembered vividly, for example, the disaster that had forced the Gun Merchant to flee his homeland: a drought so terrible that the streams, rivers and ponds had dried up and the stench of rotting fish and dead livestock had hung heavy in the air. Half the people had died of starvation; parents had sold their children and people had been reduced to eating carcasses and cadavers.

As I listened to Horen's telling of the legend, I was struck by another difference between his version and Nilima's. Her account of the story had presented the Merchant in the light of a victim. As Horen told it, on the other hand, the Gun Merchant's misfortunes were due to his own arrogance, and his conviction that he was rich enough, and clever enough, to avoid paying deference to the forces represented by the goddess of snakes.

In Horen's telling, the reason the Gun Merchant had fled downriver, with his fortune and his family, was that he had believed that he could escape the powers of the goddess. But a giant wave (to be exact, a *baan*, or tidal bore – a common phenomenon on Bengal's rivers) had struck his boats and he had lost most of his riches. His family was spared however, and they had found refuge in a small riverside village. Here, with what little remained of his wealth, the Gun Merchant had lodged his family in a large and solid house, thinking that it would keep them safe. Then he had gone off to a city to acquire goods to trade – but on his return, he learnt that in his absence there had been a flood and the house had been invaded by swarms of snakes and scorpions. They had killed his wife and seven children.

But even then the Gun Merchant had persisted in his attempts to give Manasa Devi the slip: taking passage on a ship he had set sail for a distant land. But halfway there the ship had been attacked by sea bandits who had enslaved him and taken him to their stronghold. There the Gun Merchant had had the good fortune to be purchased by a kindly ship's captain (the word that Horen used was *nakhuda*, a term that was in wide use in the old Indian Ocean trade: it had the dual meaning of 'ship owner' and 'ship's captain').

Here Horen paused to scratch his head.

'The *nakhuda* had a Muslim name,' he said. 'It began with "Il" . . . that's all I remember.'

'Was it perhaps "Ilyas"?' I prompted him.

Horen gave the wheel a thump: 'Yes!' he said. 'That's it – his name was Nakhuda Ilyas! It was with him that the Merchant travelled to one land after another until he came at last to Gun Island.'

'Do you remember what those other lands were called?' I asked.

Horen scratched his head again.

'I seem to recall,' he said, 'that there was a land of sugar, where everything was sweet; and also a country made of cloth, and an island of chains.'

He shrugged apologetically.

'*Maaf korben*,' he said. 'I'm sorry – it was a long story, and much of it made no sense to me.'

'And what became of the Muslim boatman who told you the story? He had a family, didn't he?'

'They stayed on in the dhaam until the old man died. All that's left of the family now is a boy, his grandson. His mother died recently I believe.'

'Do you know the boy?'

Horen nodded. 'A little; I see him around on the water sometimes. His name's Rafi; he's young, only seventeen or eighteen.'

'What does he do?'

'He's a fisherman, mainly. He scrapes by as best he can.'

'Do you think it might be possible for me to meet this Rafi

fellow?' I said. 'I'm sure he knows a thing or two about the shrine.'

Horen pursed his lips. 'It would have been easy to arrange a meeting if you were staying longer,' he said. 'But you're here only for the day, aren't you?'

'Yes.'

'Too bad!'

My disappointment must have been evident for Horen added: 'For all you know, you might run into Rafi today, at the shrine. I believe he often goes by there when he's out fishing.'

The steamer now made a sharp turn, leaving behind a wide river and entering a creek; it was so narrow that we seemed to be passing through a tunnel inside the forest. The falling tide had lowered the steamer and raised the mangroves above us, so that the channel was now overlooked on both sides by impenetrable battlements of mud and tangled foliage. There was scarcely a creature to be seen but every element of the landscape – forest, water, earth – seemed to be seething with life.

All of Horen's attention was now fixed upon the winding, treacherous watercourse ahead and his words, which had been flowing freely for a while, now began to run dry. Not wanting to distract him I stepped out of the wheelhouse and went down to the steamer's main deck.

I was standing in a gangway, gazing at the mangroves, when Tipu appeared beside me. The joint that he had showed me earlier was now stuck behind his ear; in his right hand he was holding a pair of binoculars.

'Wanna take a peek Pops?' he said, offering me the glasses. 'I won't charge ya nothin', being that you're not really a tourist.'

I ignored him, which only made him laugh.

'You still mad at me Pops?' he said, thrusting the binoculars into my hands. 'Look, I was only yanking your chain.'

To refuse the offer would have seemed petulant, so I accepted with what little grace I could muster. I raised the glasses to my eyes and was trying to bring the lens into focus when the steamer rounded a bend; all of a sudden the end of the creek came into view, revealing an expanse of water that stretched almost to the horizon.

'That over there is the Raimangal River,' said Tipu. 'Bangladesh is on the far bank.'

'I can see it, but it's just a blur.'

'You ever been there Pops?'

I heard the whir of a lighter and caught the acrid smell of marijuana smoke.

'I've been to Dhaka a couple of times,' I said. 'My family was from East Bengal, you know. They came over during Partition.'

Without missing a beat, Tipu said: 'Yeah, sure I know. Your family was from Madaripur district, right?'

I lowered the glasses and stared at him. 'How do you know that?'

'I saw something you'd posted,' he said, narrowing his eyes against the smoke of his reefer. 'On your family chat group.'

'What?' I cried indignantly. 'But that's a private group, strictly by invitation only. How did you get access to it?'

'Oh, I have my ways,' he said, grinning, baring his barracuda-like teeth.

I glowered at him speechlessly, not knowing what to say.

He began to laugh.

'It's no big deal Pops. I handle some of Nilima's social media accounts. She's on your family chat group, right?'

'Yes.'

'Yeah – anyways, that's how I read about your grandparents being from Madaripur. I know that 'hood well.'

This came as yet another surprise. 'You've been to Bangladesh? To Madaripur?'

My incredulity – and, no doubt, naiveté – drew another peal of laughter from him. 'Sure! I've been there a coupla times. All you gotta do is cross this river – it's easy if you know how. Wanna go?'

'No!' I said. 'Not illegally anyway.'

He shrugged, with his reefer hanging off his lip. 'So I guess you believe in passports and visas and shit like that?'

'*Believe?*' I retorted. 'Passports aren't a matter of belief.'

'So why'd you sound so shocked then?'

'Well . . .'

I realized then that he was right: I did indeed believe in passports, visas, permits, green cards and the like. For me these weren't just pieces of paper or plastic; they possessed a certain kind of sacredness that attached also to the institutions that issued them. I thought of all the hours I had spent at passport and visa counters and the stark terror that an immigration officer's frown could still send through me. I can't deny that I felt a twinge of envy, not unmixed with resentment, for his blithe disregard for all of that.

'But you've got a passport, haven't you?' I said. 'Didn't you spend some time in the US?'

'Sure I did,' he said. 'And yeah, I did have a passport back then. But it expired and I haven't renewed it. Who needs to spend all that time in government offices? There are easier ways of getting a passport, and if you've got the money you can choose whichever kind you want – Bangladeshi, Indian, Malaysian, Sri Lankan, you name it, they've all got a price. But if it's just a matter of going over for a couple of days you don't need any of that – all you have to do is cross the river and you're in Bangladesh.'

'But why do you need to go to Bangladesh anyway? I thought you worked for a call centre or something.'

'A call centre?' He recoiled, as though from a mortal insult. 'What made you think I worked for a call centre?'

'That's what your mother said.'

'Yeah, well, what does *she* know?' he said with a dismissive snort. 'Call centres are strictly for losers – I'd never work for one of those.'

I saw that he was nettled and couldn't resist prodding him a

bit. 'So who *do* you work for then? Some drug kingpin somewhere, so you can smoke free weed?'

He shrugged this off with a derisory laugh. 'Drugs? Jeez Pops,
that's no industry to be in – declining margins, shrinking profits,
bad risk profile. No, that wouldn't work for me at all. I like
growth industries, like the one I'm in.'

'And what would that be?'

'The people-moving industry Pops,' he said, grinning. 'It's
already one of the world's biggest and still growing fast. Turnover
last year was in the billions. But I don't suppose you know
anything about that, do you?'

'You're right. I have no idea what you're talking about.'

'Let me put it this way,' said Tipu. 'My clients are people who
need help finding a better life.'

At last I began to understand what he was getting at. 'You
mean migrants?'

'Sure. People like you. Or like you musta been when you were
my age.'

'But I went abroad legally,' I said. 'What you're talking about
sounds like human trafficking.'

He laughed again. 'Whoa there Pops – you sure like those
big words! What I'm doing is I'm offering an essential service.
In these parts, there's a whole bunch of dirt-poor, illiterate people
scratching out a living by fishing or farming or going into the
jungle to collect bamboo and honey. Or at least that's what they
used to do. But now the fish catch is down, the land's turning
salty, and you can't go into the jungle without bribing the forest
guards. On top of that every other year you get hit by a storm
that blows everything to pieces. So what are people supposed
to do? What would anyone do? If you're young you can't just sit
on your butt till you starve to death. Even the animals are moving
– just ask Piya. If you've got any sense you'll move and to do
that you need someone who can help you find a way out.'

'You mean someone like you?' I said incredulously. 'A kid
sitting in some small town in the Sundarbans?'

'Kids are good at some things Pops! And one of them is called the Internet. You know what that is, right?'

'What does the Internet have to do with it?'

'Everything Pops, everything.' His voice was now insultingly patient, as though he were speaking to someone of limited intelligence. 'The Internet is the migrants' magic carpet; it's their conveyor belt. It doesn't matter whether they're travelling by plane or bus or boat: it's the Internet that moves the wetware – it's that simple Pops.'

'But wait a minute,' I retorted. 'Didn't you just say that many of these people are dirt poor and illiterate? How do they go on the Net?'

'Pops! It's not the twentieth century any more. You don't need a mainframe to get on the Net – a phone is enough, and everyone's got one now. And it doesn't matter if you're illiterate: you can call up anything you like just by talking to your phone – your virtual assistant will do the rest. You'd be amazed how good people get at it, and how quickly. That's how the journey starts, not by buying a ticket or getting a passport. It starts with a phone and voice recognition technology.'

'You mean they call someone?' I said.

'No. It goes much deeper than that. Where d'you think they learn that they need a better life? Shit, where do you think they even get an idea of what a better life *is*? From their phones of course. That's where they see pictures of other countries; that's where they view ads where everything looks fabulous; they see stuff on social media, posted by neighbours who've already made the journey – and after that what d'you think they gonna do? Go back to planting rice? You ever tried planting rice Pops? You're bent over double all day long, in the hot sun, with snakes and insects swarming around you. Do you think anyone would want to go back to that after they've seen pictures of their friends sitting in a cafe in Berlin sipping caramel lattes? And the same phone that shows them those images can also put them in touch with connection men.'

66

'What's a connection man?'

'They're called *dalals* in Bangla. They're the ones who make all the necessary connections for migrants, linking them from one phone to another to another. From there on the phone becomes their life, their journey. All the payments they need to make, at every stage of the journey, are made by phone; it's their phones that tell them which route is open and which isn't; it's their phones that help them find shelter; it's their phones that keep them in touch with their friends and relatives wherever they are. And once they get where they're going it's their phones that help them get their stories straight.'

'Stories? What does that mean?'

'Oh, that's the best part of my job Pops – making up stories for my clients! That's what I'm known for, my stories.'

'I don't understand.'

'See, it's like this . . .'

At this point Tipu wasn't just talking; he was dancing, like a rapper, to the rhythm of his own voice, flicking his arms from side to side and stabbing the air with his reefer.

'Suppose a guy's applying for asylum in Sweden – he'll need a story to back him up, and it can't be just any old story. It's gotta be a story like they want to hear over there. Suppose the guy was starving because his land was flooded; or suppose his whole village was sick from the arsenic in their ground water; or suppose he was being beat up by his landlord because he couldn't pay off his debts – none of that shit matters to the Swedes. Politics, religion and sex is what they're looking for – you've gotta have a story of persecution if you want them to listen to you. So that's what I help my clients with; I give them those kinds of stories.'

I couldn't judge whether he was telling the truth, or just trying to make an impression, but either way I was both appalled and fascinated. 'Tell me more about these stories; give me an example.'

'Like if they're from Bangladesh, I tell them to say they're Hindus or Buddhists and are being oppressed by Muslims. And if they're from India I tell them to go at it the other way around – that works pretty good too. And then there's sexual orientation of course, and gender identity – they love those kinds of stories over there. But that's where the art comes into it Pops – you've got to judge who can carry off what. You gotta know your clients and what kind of story fits each of them. So you could say that what I'm providing is a point-to-point service.'

'But how do your clients hear about you?' I said. 'Do you advertise or something?'

'Nope. It's all word of mouth, going out on social media. A guy might see something that a previous client has posted and then decide that he wants to take the same route. Or else maybe he and his friends will just get curious. They'll come and talk, and if they want to go ahead, and can raise the money, I connect them to dalals.'

He stretched out a hand and twisted his body, in what seemed to be a dance move. Pointing to the far shore, he said, 'And most of those dalals are over there, in Bangladesh – and quite a few of them are in Madaripur, which is why I need to go over from time to time.'

'You mean those services aren't available in India?'

'Sure they are. But the systems are better in Bangladesh – they've been doing it longer, so they're just better at it. I guess it goes back to families like yours Pops – once they got moving they never stopped. And don't tell me your grandparents had passports and visas when they crossed this river. They didn't, right?'

'That's true,' I said. 'But things were different back then. I'm sure the border is patrolled now. Aren't you afraid of getting caught? This area must be swarming with border guards?'

'So what?' he said, drawing on his reefer. 'You think it's easy to seal a border that runs through a forest like this one, half land and half water? Anyone who knows their way around these parts can get around the patrols. And if, by chance, you get unlucky and end up in the hands of the Man – hey, he knows the score too. It's just a matter of money – and in this industry there's more than enough to go around.'

Suddenly he turned to me, eyes glinting. 'Hey listen Pops,' he said, flicking the reefer's stub into the water. 'You're not going to talk about this with my mom or Piya, are you?'

'Not if you don't want me to.'

'I don't. I don't want you to mention any of this to anybody at all, okay?'

'All right. I won't.'

'You better not Pops.' There was a hint of menace in his voice despite his jokey grin. 'Or else bad stuff might happen.'

'What stuff?'

He grinned again, baring his teeth. 'Like I might get into your computer – and who knows where that could lead?'

The Shrine

The water level was now so low that the riverbank ahead of us snaked away into the distance like a towering wall of mud, topped by an impenetrable tangle of leathery leaves and spidery roots.

To my unaccustomed eyes the matt browns and greens of the landscape looked almost featureless, unreadable. Yet I could tell, from the way that Horen's eyes kept flickering from detail to detail, that to those who knew what to look for, the forest teemed with signs that could, in fact, be deciphered and read, like some antediluvian script.

Yet in a while even Horen began to look perplexed.

'As I remember, the dhaam should be somewhere there,' he said, pointing ahead. 'But this stretch of river has changed a lot since I was last here.'

In the end it was Tipu who spotted the site, with the help of his binoculars.

'*Oijé!*' he shouted, pointing directly ahead. 'There it is!'

Pushing up his sunshades Horen squinted at a distant smudge on the riverbank.

'The boy's right,' he grunted. 'It isn't where I had thought.'

'How can that be? It can't have moved, surely?'

'It's the river that's moved,' came the answer. 'When I last saw the place it was still a good way inland. Now it's at the water's edge.'

As the steamer drew closer to the site it became clear that to get to the temple we would have to walk across a couple of hundred yards of mud, much of it pierced by spear-like mangrove spores. When I went down to the lower deck I saw that Tipu was already making preparations for the crossing, taking off his shirt and sneakers and rolling his jeans up above his knees. I noticed also that he had lit another stubby little joint and was drawing on it as he changed.

He saw me looking and gave me a wink. 'How about it Pops?' he said, holding out the joint. 'Like a toke? You'll feel better for it.'

I shook my head brusquely and turned away.

But Tipu wasn't done with me.

'And how the hell're *you* gonna manage Pops?' he said, grinning slyly at my trousers and windbreaker. 'If you go into the mud dressed like that, you'll come out like this . . .' He mimicked a zombie. 'I'd lose some of those threads if I was you.'

He was right of course. In the end I had to strip down to my underwear and wrap one of Horen's spare lungis around my waist, like a loincloth. As for my wallet, phone and other equipment, Horen took them from me and placed them inside a locker.

'None of this will be any use to you if you fall in the mud,' he said. 'We can fetch your stuff later if you need it.'

As he was stepping up to the gangplank, Horen offered me a few pointers on dealing with the mud: 'Use your big toe like a claw and dig it in – see, like this . . .'

Then, with his lungi girded around his crotch, he went nimbly down the gangplank and stepped into the soft, shining silt. For a few moments, as he was sinking in, he stayed completely still; only when the sludge was up to his thighs did he pull one foot out, stork-like, and step forward.

'Be patient!' he shouted to me over his shoulder. 'Move very slowly.'

It was all in vain.

I had not imagined that slimy, slithering things would brush against my legs and feet as they were sinking into the almost liquid slurry. I panicked and tried to move ahead without pulling my foot out all the way. Next thing I knew I was lying face down in the velvety, melting mire, with Tipu's laughter ringing in my ears.

Nor was that my only fall: I tipped over with every second step, even with Tipu and Horen holding my arms. Mud seeped into my mouth, my ears, my eyes: it was as if my body were being reclaimed by the primeval ooze.

It seemed to me then that my eyeglasses were my last connection with civilization and I held them in place with a panicked, maniacal ferocity even though they were plastered with slop, as indeed were my eyes. So completely was I blinded that even when the depth of the mush dwindled to a few inches I still had to be held up and guided by Tipu and Horen. At a certain point I understood that I was climbing up a slope and then stepping over a door frame on to a paved surface.

Tugging at my elbow Horen brought me to a standstill: 'Stay there! Don't move!'

I did as I was told, shivering in the January chill, vaguely aware of a clanging, metallic sound somewhere nearby. Suddenly a bucketful of water descended on my head like a shower of ice; it was so cold that I was instantly numbed, unable to move or make a sound. A moment later something – a fingertip – dug into my ear and scraped out a plug of sludge.

'See Pops,' said Tipu giggling. 'You'd have had a better trip if you'd taken a toke.'

When Horen fitted my glasses – freshly washed and dried – over my eyes, it was as though I had woken from a nightmare. I saw that I was standing next to a well that had a half-filled aluminum bucket perched on the rim. We were in a paved courtyard, facing what looked like a dwelling with a collapsed roof. One part of it was curtained off with a length of blue tarpaulin and looked as though it were still in use. In front of it lay a couple of pots and a cooking fire with fresh embers.

From the look of the place, said Horen, it seemed that Rafi had come by earlier in the day. He had hung up a couple of fishing nets outside the compound, and collected a pile of bamboo. He was probably somewhere nearby and would be back soon.

'Where do you think he might have gone?'

Horen scratched his head.

'There are a couple of spots downriver,' he said, 'where fishermen go at this time of year. Tipu and I could go look for him in the bhotbhoti, if you like.'

I seized eagerly upon the suggestion.

'Yes, you should both go,' I said.

'And what about you?' said Horen.

'I'll stay here. I need some time to look around.'

Horen nodded: 'All right. We'll be back soon.'

Only after they had left did I get to look around properly – and then suddenly it was as though everything I had gone through to get there – the mud, the humiliation, the chilly baptism – had all been worth it.

I discovered now that I was standing at the centre of a rectangular courtyard with my back to the temple, which was at the other end of the walled enclosure: it wasn't till I had turned around that the facade came into view.

The building wasn't large – no bigger than the familiar thatched huts of the Bengal countryside – and time had not been kind to it. Yet the structure was so unexpected – and so lovely – that the sight fair took my breath away.

The roof had the convex outline of an upturned boat, and it was this, I guessed, that had reminded Nilima of the temples of Bishnupur. Nor was that surprising, for everything about the structure – its burnt sienna colour, the shape of the roof, and the panels on its facade – spoke of Bengal's most celebrated style of architecture, which had originated in the kingdom of Bishnupur in the seventeenth century.

This is a style which is perfectly attuned to the place in which it was born, in the sense that it echoes the shapes and forms of the Bengal countryside. It also makes ingenious use of the region's most easily available materials. Rather than aspiring to the grandeur of stone (of which Bengal has very little) it relies instead on brick, made with the delta's ample supplies of mud and silt. The rich colour of these thin, hard bricks is, to my eyes, one of the glories of the Bishnupuri style.

However, a shrine built of brick cannot be carved in the manner of the great stone temples of south and central India (or for that matter Cambodia and Java) – so the temples of Bishnupur discharge the function of storytelling (essential to all such structures) by means of terracotta friezes and bas reliefs. These are set into the walls like plaques or tablets.

The shrine in front of me was, of course, only a minor example of the Bishnupur style – but I was delighted to note that its facade was decorated with a good number of friezes. It struck me that if the building were indeed associated with the legend of the Gun Merchant, surely some of those panels would bear depictions of guns (or, rather, muskets).

All thought of my recent discomfitures, and my still damp clothing, now vanished from my mind: I was aware only of a tingling frisson of curiosity as I tucked up my lungi and approached the facade.

My main concern was that the panels would be too weathered to be legible – and this fear proved to be well founded, for the contours of the reliefs had indeed been greatly eroded by the passage of time. But soon, to my utter delight, I discovered that the outlines of the original reliefs (or so I presumed them to be) had been preserved nonetheless, and that too in a most curious fashion. Someone had traced over the outlines on the panels with great care, using shards of red pottery! I suspected immediately that these marks had been made with fragments of clay cups, like those in which chai used to be served at tea stalls everywhere in India – and on glancing down I spotted several bits of broken pottery lying scattered along the foot of the facade.

The tracings had the look of simple, crudely drawn hiero-glyphs. Although some of the lines had begun to fade, they were mostly still legible. As with hieroglyphs, some symbols and motifs recurred again and again, in different combinations. The most prominent of these were a couple of turbaned figures, each paired with a distinctive symbol. One of these symbols was easy to decipher: it was an image of the palm of a hand, sheltered by a cobra's hood. Guessing that this sign stood for the goddess of snakes, Manasa Devi, I assumed that the figure with which it was paired represented the Gun Merchant. If this were correct, it would seem to follow that the second figure stood for the sailor, 'Captain Ilyas'. I was fairly sure that this was indeed the case, but I could make no sense of the symbol that was paired with the sailor.

I had never seen this symbol before and could not imagine what it meant.

Some of the friezes were easy to interpret. There were several panels, for example, in which the Merchant and the Captain were shown to be seated in a boat: these were clearly intended to represent episodes from their travels. In one panel they were depicted with a number of shell-like objects: I took these to be conches, picked up at one of their ports of call. Another panel depicted a book, in the form of an illuminated palm-leaf manuscript. The penultimate panel, in which the Merchant seemed to be tied up, was also easy to interpret: this was presumably a depiction of the episode in which the Merchant was being taken to the Island of Chains to be sold as a slave.

But many of the figures and symbols were impossible to understand. For example, a panel with an image of a mound, sheltered by two palms; and another that seemed to be filled with fluttering flags and pennants. But the strangest symbol of all was a recurrent image of two concentric circles.

What could this possibly mean? And as if this were not baffling enough, in one of the panels the circles were overlaid with criss-crossing lines.

Equally puzzling was the absence of the things I had most expected to see – guns and muskets. There was only one sugges-tion of a weapon, in a panel that included a helmeted figure, armed with an elongated object, something that could have been a musket or a spear. I guessed that the image was a representa-tion of a European pirate (or *harmad* as they were known in Bangla). The figure was certainly armed, but I could not be sure that his weapon was a gun.

I stared hard at each panel, trying to imprint them on my mind. Never had I so greatly regretted the absence of my phone: if only I had had it with me I would have been able to preserve these images forever. But let aside a phone, I had not even a sheet of paper, or a pencil, to make sketches . . .

I decided that as soon as the steamer returned, I would ask Horen to fetch my phone and camera.

So caught up was I in thinking about the shrine's exterior that it was almost as an afterthought that I wandered through the arched gateway that led to its interior.

It was very dark inside and seemed even more so because of the contrast with the bright, mid-morning sunlight outside. But as soon as I had stepped past the gateway I knew, from the echoing of my bare feet, that I was in a cavernous, domed hallway, of a kind that is characteristic of this style of architecture: the interiors of Bishnupuri temples are often open, in the manner of congregational spaces, possibly because of Islamic or Christian influence. But exactly how tall or wide this space was I could not tell, for I was aware only of a slippery mossiness beneath my feet and a chilly, slightly fetid, dampness around me.

As I was looking around I became aware of a low, growling sound, somewhere behind me. I spun around thinking that a dog had followed me inside. But no! Framed in the arched gateway was the face of a shaggy-haired boy who was staring at me in what seemed to be utter disbelief.

Who could this be but the much awaited Rafi? I was so delighted to see him that I hurried eagerly towards the entrance, crying out loudly: '*Ei to!* Here you are! I've been waiting for you.'

He began to back away fearfully as I approached and this did not entirely surprise me; I was, after all, a stranger, possibly an intruder. But still, his response was so excessive as to be almost amusing; he seemed to be seized by utter, eye-popping terror, as though I were some kind of monster.

'I'm just a visitor,' I said, in a soothing tone. 'I've come from Kolkata . . .'

But this did not stop the boy's retreat; he continued to back away from me until his withdrawal was halted by the rim of the well. There at last he came to a standstill. Dropping his eyes he began to breathe heavily, as if in relief at a narrow escape.

He looked to be in his late teens, with a lightly feathered upper lip and long, supple limbs. His face was narrow, with large, long-lashed eyes and a full deep-brown mouth that was down-turned at both ends. His feet were bare, thickly coated with mud, and he was dressed in a frayed shirt and a faded cotton lungi that was doubled up above his knees. With his mop of unkempt hair and glistening, watchful eyes, he was at once feral and delicately graceful, like some wild, wary creature that could at any moment take flight.

'I seem to have caught you by surprise,' I said. 'You're Rafi, aren't you?'

He nodded and straightened himself. 'And who are you?' he said; I noticed that his Bangla accent was marked with the rustic lilt of the Sundarbans. 'What are you doing here, all by yourself?'

'I'm Dinanath Datta,' I said, in what I hoped was a soothing tone. 'I just came to look at the temple. It was Horen Naskar who brought me . . .'

'Is that so?' said Rafi. 'But where is he? I didn't see his boat.'

'He went to look for you,' I said, 'he thought you might be somewhere nearby. I asked him to find you.'

His wary eyes widened. '*Keno? Ki chai?*' he said. 'Why? What do you want with me?'

'I just want to ask a few questions about the shrine.'

'I don't know that I can tell you anything,' he said brusquely. 'I never had much to do with the dhaam.'

'But then who was it who traced the outlines on the walls?'

'That was my mother's doing,' he said. 'She died last year.'

'I'm sorry to hear that,' I said. 'Did she talk about the dhaam much?'

'Only a little bit,' he said, shuffling his feet.

I couldn't tell whether he was telling the truth or being evasive.

'But I'm sure your mother and grandfather told you stories about the place,' I said, trying to encourage him. 'Surely you remember something?'

'Just a little,' he said reluctantly.

'All right then,' I said. 'Let's go look at the pictures together. Tell me what you remember.'

Perhaps Rafi's memory was more tenacious than he imagined; or perhaps stories heard in early childhood are not easy to forget. In any event, once we started examining the panels he was able to identify many of the images and confirm several details.

It turned out that I had guessed correctly about the figure of the Gun Merchant and the symbol that he was paired with. I had been right, too, in identifying the other turbaned figure as the Merchant's mentor and companion, Captain Ilyas – but as for the symbol that was paired with him, Rafi had no more of an idea of what it represented than I did.

But he did confirm my identification of the helmeted figure: this was indeed a pirate, none other than the leader of the *harmads* who had captured the Gun Merchant as he was fleeing overseas in order to escape Manasa Devi's wrath.

But my interpretations had also been wrong in several instances, most notably in my reading of the panel with the shells. These objects were not conches but cowrie shells – and in pointing this out Rafi clarified a vital link in the legend.

The story went that after his capture by the pirates the Gun Merchant had been taken to a port and put up for sale, as a slave. That was when Captain Ilyas had entered his life: recognizing the Merchant to be an intelligent and well-travelled man, the Captain had bought him from the *harmads* and set him free. In return the Merchant had guided the Captain to an island that abounded in cowrie shells; that was where the two of them had amassed their fortunes.

Rafi's mention of cowries set me thinking. I remembered reading somewhere that for many centuries cowrie shells had served as a currency throughout the Indian Ocean region and beyond. I remembered also that most of these shells came from a single island, the name of which I could not immediately recall – and nor was there time, for Rafi had moved on to another panel.

After collecting a trove of cowries, said Rafi, the Gun Merchant and Captain Ilyas had taken their shells to another land – and here he pointed to the panel that depicted a mound, sheltered by two palm trees. This, he said, was the 'Land of Palm Sugar Candy' (*Taal-misrir-desh*) and no sooner had they arrived there than they were set upon by poison-spitting monsters so they had been forced to flee to yet another land – and he pointed now to the panel that was covered with flags and banners. This was a place called the 'Land of Kerchieves' (*Rumaali-desh*) – but here too the Gun Merchant and the Captain had been dogged by misfortune. Manasa Devi had sent scorching winds against them and the land had become so dry that one day a burning wind had set their house afire, incinerating everything around them. The blame had fallen on the unfortunate travellers, and their neighbours had risen up against them and driven them away. It was now that Captain Ilyas had decided that they would go to the one place where they were sure to be safe from Manasa Devi, a place where there were no snakes – and this refuge was none other than Gun Island (Bonduk-dwip). It was this island, said Rafi, that was symbolized by the image of the two concentric circles: for not only was Bonduk-dwip an island, it was an island within an island – hence the circle enclosed by another circle.

And what of the image in which the circles were overlaid with criss-crossing lines?

Rafi scratched his head. 'My grandfather told me about it once,' he said. 'But I don't remember any more.'

It was clear from his tone that he had had enough of my questions. Turning his back on the shrine he made a gesture of dismissal.

'Of course it's all nonsense,' he said, tossing his hair as though it were a mane. 'There is no Land of Palm Sugar Candy or a Gun Island. It's just a fairy tale. No one can rule over snakes.'

This was said with great vehemence, yet there was an undertone in his voice that led me to wonder whether his scepticism about the legend had something to do with some long-ago crisis of disappointment, maybe of the kind that besets children when they learn that there is no Santa Claus and no Toy Factory at the North Pole.

'You're right,' I said, humouring him. 'And it's obvious, isn't it, that this dhaam has nothing to do with Manasa Devi?'

His long-lashed eyes glinted, as if in puzzlement. 'Why?' he said. 'Why do you say that?'

'Because,' I said, 'if Manasa Devi had anything to do with this place, surely there would be a snake around here, wouldn't there? A cobra?'

I glanced at him again and saw, to my surprise, that his face had gone rigid. He was staring fixedly at me now, with a hand over his mouth.

'What's the matter?' I said. '*Ki hoyechhe?*'

Slowly his hand fell away from his mouth.

'But there is,' he whispered.

'There is what?'

'There *is* a cobra – inside the dhaam. It has been there many years.'

It was my turn to stare now, in disbelief.

'Impossible,' I said. 'I went inside the dhaam – I didn't see anything.'

'It was right behind you,' he said. 'When you came out of the dhaam I could see it behind you. Its hood was raised and its head was above your shoulder. I've never seen it like that before; it never comes out when I'm here and I leave it alone too – it keeps other snakes and animals away. I never go in there – you must have disturbed it when you went in.'

'No,' I said, shaking my head. 'No – it's not possible . . .'

At that moment I was absolutely certain that he was joking or deluded. It was simply unimaginable that I had stepped into a cobra's lair; such things just don't happen to people like myself – reclusive antiquarians who spend most of their waking hours staring at screens and old books.

At this point we were at one of the dhaam's far corners, where the facade joined the compound's surrounding wall: from that angle almost nothing was visible of the building's interior, except the arched entrance and the darkness inside.

My incredulity at what I had just heard was such that my feet began to move of their own accord. Before I knew it they had brought me face to face with the entrance so that I could confirm, with my own eyes, that everything was as I had thought.

And then suddenly there it was, appearing out of the darkness like a whiplash, rearing up as if it had been waiting for me, the intruder, to show himself again.

Staring at it now, at a distance of only a few feet, I realized that it was no ordinary cobra but a king cobra – a hamadryad – of a size such that its upraised head was level with mine.

Its tongue flickered as I looked into its shining black eyes, and I became aware of a growling sound (I would learn later that this species does not hiss but emits this other sound instead).

I stood frozen, as if welded to the ground – yet, although it was well within reach of me, I am convinced, to this day, that the cobra would not have harmed anybody if not for what came next.

Unbeknownst to me Tipu had arrived at the compound's gate moments earlier and had observed the scene as it was unfolding. Imagining that I was about to be attacked, he had snatched up a fishing net and crept stealthily into the courtyard.

It was only when the net was cast at the cobra that I became aware of Tipu's presence – and it was then too that the creature struck, with astonishing speed and power. Even as the net was descending over its hood, it flung itself at Tipu and succeeded in striking him, with one fang, just above the left elbow.

And then, just as suddenly as it had appeared, the cobra was gone, and the net was lying empty on the ground. Tipu was on his knees, hunched over his elbow, staring at the wound on his arm. Then he slowly crumpled to the ground and looked straight into my eyes.

'What . . . what do I do now, Pops?' he said in a whisper.

I was in shock and could do nothing but stare, helplessly.

'Why'd you bring us here, Pops?'

I glanced at Horen but he was a still as a statue, with an expression of horror stamped on his face.

'What's happening, Pops?' said Tipu, clutching his arm. The pupils of his eyes had begun to float upwards, so that only the bottom halves were visible.

Then I heard the sound of footsteps and looked up to see Rafi racing towards us. To my relief he seemed to know exactly what to do. Hitching up his lungi he knelt on the ground and raised Tipu's quickly swelling arm to his mouth. Then, clamping his lips around the spot where the snake's fang had punctured the skin, he began to suck on the wound, with an intensity of effort that deepened the colour of his face.

When his mouth was full he raised his head and turned aside, to spit. But before he could empty his mouth a gagging sound burst from his throat and his hands flew to his chest.

'Did you swallow some?' said Horen.

He nodded, grimacing.

'Don't worry,' said Horen. 'It won't do you any harm so long as it stays in your belly and doesn't get into your blood.'

Rafi was hawking and spitting furiously. After a minute he drew a hand across his mouth and looked up at Horen. 'If a cobra puts something in you,' said Rafi, 'you can never be rid of it. That's what my grandfather used to say.'

Turning back to Tipu, Rafi fastened his hands on his arm and began to squeeze.

'I need some rope.'

Horen tore off a length of cord from the net that Tipu had thrown and handed it to Rafi, who wound it around Tipu's arm, using a bit of wood to tighten the tourniquet.

In the meantime, Horen had fashioned a makeshift hammock from the fishing net. 'We can use this to carry Tipu to the steamer,' he said. 'With any luck we can get him to the hospital in Lusibari in a couple of hours.'

When Rafi had finished with the tourniquet he rolled Tipu into the net. Then he and Horen picked up the two ends and started on the way back. I followed close behind.

As we were approaching the mud bank, Horen barked at me over his shoulder. 'Be careful – you'd better not fall into the mud now. We don't have any time to waste.'

Visions

Tipu kept his eyes closed and made scarcely a sound until he had been placed on a mattress in the shaded interior of the steamer's main cabin. Even when the engine started up and the steamer began to move, with a loud throbbing, he lay deathly still. For a while he seemed to lose consciousness. But then his eyes flew suddenly open and he turned his head to look at his arm, now hugely distended and discoloured. His eyes widened as they passed over the tourniquet and came to rest on the wound, which was like a crater sitting atop a mound of swollen flesh.

'*Eta ki?*' he said in a plaintive, almost childlike voice. 'What's this? There seems to be something inside of me. It's taking hold of me. What is it?'

'Don't look at your arm,' said Rafi. 'Try not to think about it.'

Swinging his long, lean frame on to the mattress Rafi crossed his legs and took Tipu's head gently but firmly into his lap. Then he ran a hand over Tipu's beaded forehead. 'Don't be afraid. The snake that bit you is no ordinary snake – my grandfather used to say that it had been sent to protect us.'

Tipu's eyes were glassy and he seemed not to have understood what Rafi had said. 'Who are you?' he said. 'I feel I know you.'

'That's true,' said Rafi. '*Amader kono porichay nei.* We've never met till today but I also feel that I know you.'

'Why? How?'

'It doesn't matter,' said Rafi. 'You should try to be calm now. That's what's important.'

'Be calm?' said Tipu. 'How can I be calm when there's a burning ember inside my body?'

I fetched a bottle of water and Rafi held it carefully to Tipu's lips. He drank thirstily, his Adam's apple bobbing up and down as the water poured into his mouth in a steady stream. Then he pushed the bottle aside and said, 'But it's still there, inside me, the fire.'

'Drink some more water,' said Rafi.

Tipu's head fell back into Rafi's lap, with the eyes wide open. Then his expression began to change: the pupils of his eyes slowly floated upwards so that only the whites were visible. His mouth dropped open and ribbons of drool trickled out of the corners. All at once his body began to twitch and shake, making spasmodic little motions, like those of a dreaming animal. And all the while his head remained motionless, flung backwards in that strange position, with empty white eyes and a slack, open mouth.

After an eternity the twitching gradually stopped and the pupils returned to the centre of Tipu's eyes — yet it was not as though he were coming awake. He seemed to be returning rather to the state of consciousness that he had been in before he drifted away: a condition that was not really one of awakeness because he did not seem to be aware of his surroundings.

'Where am I? Where am I?' he said, as his eyes came slowly into focus.

'You're in Horen Naskar's steamer,' I said. 'And we're with you, right here.'

Tipu's right hand shot out, as if to push me away. 'No! No! I'm in the water and they're coming for me.'

'*Ke?* Who?' said Rafi, running a hand gently over Tipu's sweat-drenched forehead. 'Who's coming for you?'

'I can't see them, I can only see their shadows and they're coming closer and closer. But they can't reach me.'

'Why?'

'Because of them.'

'Who?'

'The snakes.'

'What snakes?'

'Don't you see them? They're everywhere.' His right hand rose and the index finger began to point. 'See – here, there, there. They're everywhere. Can't you see?' He seemed genuinely surprised that whatever he was seeing was invisible to us.

I was deeply unsettled now and my voice rose. '*Na!*' I cried. 'No! There's nothing and no one here but us . . .'

This earned me an angry retort from Rafi. 'How do you know,' he snapped, 'that there's no one here but us? *Chup korun!* Be quiet! Let him say what he has to say. And if you can't take it, go away.'

The protective snarl in his voice startled me; Rafi was like a wild creature, standing guard over its young.

In the meantime, words were still flowing from Tipu's mouth. '. . . they're all over my body, they're wrapped around my hands, they're under my feet . . . but I'm not afraid of them; they're trying to help me . . . or else they would have got me already . . .'

'Who?' said Rafi. 'Who would have got you?'

'They. The shadows.'

'And who are they?'

'I can't see them . . . they're just moving voids . . . and they want to pull you in, with them . . .'

His voice trailed away and his head fell back with the eyes open; once again his pupils began to drift away. Then the muscular twitching started up once more and I realized that he had returned to the other state that he had been in before.

All the while Rafi's hand continued to stroke Tipu's head and face. They could not have been more unlike each other, Tipu with his ear stud and highlights, and Rafi with his shaggy hair and feral wariness, yet an odd bond seemed to have arisen between them; it was as if the venom that had passed from Tipu's body into Rafi's mouth had created an almost carnal connection.

Soon Tipu's convulsions became too much for me to watch. I stepped out and went up to the wheelhouse.

Horen glanced at me as I stood in the doorway. 'I heard Tipu's voice,' he said. 'He seems to be raving – *baje bokchhé*, talking rubbish.'

The earthy plainness of the Bengali phrase did much to re-assure me. Yes, of course, I said to myself, that's all it is – a delirium – which often sets in after a shock.

'That's right,' I said to Horen. 'He's talking a lot of rubbish.'

'It's not necessarily a bad thing,' said Horen. 'If he's yammering at least we know that he's fighting for his life.'

'But how much longer till we get to the hospital?'

Horen glanced at his cellphone which was propped up in front of him.

'Another hour and a half at least.'

He gestured to me to come into the wheelhouse. 'Could you take the wheel for a bit? We've just came into cellphone range and I want to call Moyna. She'll get everything ready at the hospital.'

I put my hands gingerly on the wheel while Horen stepped outside and dialled a number. We were on a wide, untrafficked stretch of water and there was nothing much for me to do. It was bracing to be up there, in the bright sunlight, with the river stretching away ahead. I didn't hesitate when Horen asked if he could go down to check on Tipu.

'Yes, go,' I said. 'I'll be fine for a few more minutes.'

Horen was gone a little longer than I expected, maybe five or ten minutes. He looked oddly shaken when he stepped back into the wheelhouse.

'Did something happen down there?' I said, as I handed the wheel back.

'Tipu was carrying on again,' said Horen gruffly. 'He kept asking Rafi what his name was, and Rafi kept saying it, again and again. But every time he said it Tipu would shake his head: "No, no, that's not it." Seeing them going on like that I said to

Rafi: "Don't bother to answer, he's just talking nonsense, he's not in his right mind." But then suddenly Rafi spoke up, saying that Tipu was right – "Rafi" was just a pet name, he said. His real name, given to him by his grandfather, was Ilyas – like the character in the story. And only when he heard this name did Tipu stop saying no. He fell quiet for a bit and said: "Yes, that's right: I recognize him now."'

Horen glanced at me with a raised eyebrow. 'According to Rafi only his grandfather had ever used that name.'

He pulled a face. 'Strange, isn't it? How could Tipu have known about the name? He's never met Rafi before.'

'There's nothing strange about it,' I said brusquely. 'Tipu must have overheard us when we were talking about that story this morning. He must have heard us mention the name "Ilyas" so it would have been on his mind. And it's hardly surprising that Rafi's grandfather gave him that name, is it, considering that he was the custodian of that shrine?'

'Yes, of course, that must be it,' said Horen, sounding rather relieved. He glanced at his cellphone.

'We're making good time – not much longer now. You'd better go down and keep an eye on the boy.'

I was about to step into the cabin when Tipu's voice brought me to a halt.

'They're very close now, very close; I can feel the cold of the shadows. I'm so cold – hold me, hold me.'

Rafi placed the palms of his hand on Tipu's chest. 'I'm here. I'm holding you. You're safe.'

The words seemed to have a reassuring effect on Tipu. He gave a long sigh. 'They're turning back. *Phire jachhé*. They can't get past . . .'

'Past what?'

Tipu did not answer the question directly. Instead his hand floated through the air, inches above his body, as though he were caressing something that was wrapped protectively around him. For a moment he seemed calmer but then suddenly he began to scream: 'No! No! They're going after something else. I can't see what.'

A long moan leaked slowly out of his open, drooling mouth and his body went rigid and arced upwards, like a bow, almost breaking out of Rafi's grip. He moaned again and said something that I couldn't catch.

'What's he saying?' I asked Rafi. 'Can you make out?'

'It's a name, a woman's name – "Rani".'

Now suddenly Tipu's body went slack; his head flopped downwards and the pupils slowly returned to his eyes. He seemed spent, exhausted, yet he continued to mumble something under his breath.

Uncoiling his legs Rafi stretched himself out beside Tipu and enveloped him in his arms, almost as though to prevent him from being snatched away.

Suddenly Tipu's convulsions stopped and his body went limp.

'Is he still breathing?' I said in alarm.

'Yes,' said Rafi. 'He's just passed out – and maybe that's for the best.'

'Did you hear what he was saying, just before he passed out?'

Rafi nodded. 'He was saying that we should phone someone – a woman by the name of Piya. Do you know who that is?'

'Yes. Why did he want us to phone her?'

'He said we should warn her.'

'About what?'

'About Rani.'

'But who is Rani?'

'I don't know,' said Rafi impatiently. 'But you should call Piya anyway.'

It struck me that Piya would certainly want to know about Tipu's condition.

'All right,' I said. 'I'll call her right now.'

I went to the steamer's prow, dialled Piya's number and raised the phone to my ear, but only to be answered by a couple of beeps. Glancing at the screen I discovered that the signal icon had gone blank; evidently we were once again out of range.

I was staring at the device in frustration, hoping that the bars would bounce back, when Rafi appeared beside me. Jerking his head in the direction of the main cabin, he said: 'Tipu seems to have exhausted himself. He's sleeping.'

With my eyes still fixed on my phone, I said: 'Good.'

Rafi watched me for a minute and then shook his head. 'It's no use,' he said, in his rustic accent, 'you'll have to wait a bit.'

The uninvited words of advice irritated me. 'Wait for what?'

'What you're looking for,' said Rafi, sounding very sure of himself.

I frowned at him, looking him up and down. With his shaggy hair, frayed shirt and mud-caked feet, he looked like a creature of the wild: it seemed unlikely to me that someone like him, a backwoods fisherman, could have any idea of how cellphones worked.

'How would you know what I'm looking for?' I said sharply.

Rafi stared at me, his long-lashed eyes opaque. Then he reached for the waist of his faded lungi and took out a small plastic-wrapped package. When the wrappings came off, I saw, to my astonishment, that what he had in his hands was a cellphone, not unlike mine. He turned it on, and after a minute or two thrust the device at me, tapping the top of the screen.

'See,' he said, 'no reception. You won't see any bars until we reach the next river over there –' he raised a hand to point ahead – 'and even there you'll only get two bars. For three bars or more you'll have to wait till we get there.' His hand rose to point to a spot that was still more distant.

Then he craned his head to steal a glance at my phone. 'But your phone is an old model,' he said. 'So you may have to wait longer.'

I could not begrudge him the smirk that now appeared on his face. He was evidently well aware that the tables were turned – it was my ignorance that had now been laid bare.

It shamed me to think that I had assumed that Rafi would be unacquainted with cellphones simply because he was a Sundarbans fisherman. I knew of course, at some level, that the assumptions that Indians like myself had grown up with – that rural people were 'backward', especially where it concerned modern gadgets – no longer held, if indeed they ever had; I had seen for myself that young Indians, no matter whether rich or poor, educated or not, had an ability to deal with phones and computers that far surpassed my own. Nor was I so out of touch as be unaware that in India, as in many other poor countries, there were great numbers of people whose digital skills were completely disproportionate to their material circumstances and formal education. And yet, knowing all this, I had still embarrassed myself by assuming that someone like Rafi would not know about the workings of a gadget as ubiquitous as the cellphone.

Rafi was watching me with a half-smile: his lustrous eyes and the downturned corners of his mouth gave his face an extraordinary expressiveness, leaving no room for doubt that he knew exactly what was going through my mind.

'Tourists are often surprised,' he said, 'to see that we have cellphones here too. Though why it surprises them I don't know, for we need phones even more than city people do. For us it can be a matter of life and death.'

'In what way?'

'Because of the weather alerts. You could get caught in a storm if you don't follow the alerts. And the GPS can be a big help too, at least where there's reception. But back there –' he pointed downriver, in the direction we had come from – 'you still have to remember the way, just as my grandfather did. He never needed a GPS – it was all in his head.'

'Did you learn a lot from him?'

'Some things. But there was much that he didn't want to teach me.'

'Like what?'

He shrugged. 'Things about animals, and fish, and the water – he'd tell me that I didn't need to learn what he knew because the rivers and the forest and the animals are no longer as they were. He used to say that things were changing so much, and so fast, that I wouldn't be able to get by here – he told me that one day I would have no choice but to leave.'

'And go where?'

He shrugged. 'I don't know. Wherever people go. Bombay, Delhi – I don't know.'

'So you're thinking of leaving?'

'Maybe. I couldn't leave while my mother was alive. But now . . .'

Without finishing the sentence he turned on his heel and headed back to the main cabin.

Glancing at my phone again I saw that the signal bars had bounced back. I dialled Piya's number and was answered by a taped message that told me, in Hindi, that the user was on another call. I called back a few minutes later and got the same message again. It went on like this for a frustratingly long time and I was getting close to giving up when at last I heard Piya's phone ring.

She picked up after several rings, sounding flustered and impatient.

'Is that you, Deen?'

'Yes.'

'I'm sorry, I can't talk now. I'll have to call you back later.'

'It's urgent. I'm calling about Tipu.'

'Oh? What about him?'

'He was on the boat with me today – apparently Nilima had asked him to go to the shrine?'

'Yes, yes, go on.'

'I'm afraid there's been a mishap.'

'What do you mean by mishap?'

'Tipu was bitten. By a snake. He's delirious but we're on our way to the hospital now.'

She paused to take a breath. 'Did anyone get a look at the snake? Do you have any idea of the species?'

'Yes,' I said. 'It was a very large cobra. I'm almost certain it was a king cobra.'

She gasped. 'Oh, hell! A king cobra's bite can kill an elephant.'

I began to stutter. 'But surely . . . surely . . . the hospital will be able to . . . ?'

'No! They won't have the right antivenin. It's rare and very expensive—' Suddenly she broke off. 'Wait!'

Her voice faded away but I was able to hear some ambient noise at her end. I got the impression that she had run into a crowded room and was talking to someone in an urgent whisper. A few minutes later she was back on the phone, with good news: she had spoken to a herpetologist friend who was at the same conference. He was about to go into the jungle, for a field trip, so he had brought along supplies of antivenins, including one for a king cobra. He had agreed to donate some to Piya.

'But how will you get it to us?' I asked. 'We need to have it as soon as possible, right?'

'I'll bring it myself,' she said. 'I'm flying back to Kolkata in a couple of hours. I should be able to get to the Lusibari hospital before midnight.'

'But what about your conference? Didn't you just arrive in Bhubaneswar today?'

'Yes, but there's been an emergency and I've had to change all my plans. In fact I was on the phone with the travel agent just before you called. He managed to get me on a flight that leaves very soon.'

I could tell that she was getting impatient. I was just about to ring off when Rafi suddenly appeared beside me. He whispered in my ear: 'Have you told her about Rani?'

Turning to one side, I said: 'Piya, listen, there's something else I need to tell you.'

'Go on – but quickly please.'

'You remember I said that Tipu was in a delirium?'

'Yes, go on, quickly please.'

'While he was in this delirium he said we should call and warn you.'

'About what?'

'About someone called Rani.'

I heard a sharp intake of breath. When she spoke again there was a quiver in her voice. 'How long ago did he say this?'

'About forty-five minutes, I'd say.'

'That's impossible!' she shot back. 'Are you sure about the time?'

'No, not exactly. But it was around forty-five minutes ago. Why?'

'Because that's when my alert went off.'

'What alert?'

'About Rani.'

'And who's Rani?'

'Rani is . . .'

She changed her mind. 'It would take too long to explain – I'll tell you when I see you.'

'All right.'

'But wait,' she said. 'I don't suppose I'll see you, will I?'

'Why not?'

'You're going back to the city, aren't you? Haven't you got a plane to catch?'

'Oh that!' I had completely forgotten about my flight. 'We'll see about that later. I can't leave Tipu in this condition – after all, the reason this happened to him was that he was trying to protect me.'

Rani

On arriving at the hospital in Lusibari, Tipu, now more or less comatose, was immediately rolled off to the intensive care unit on a stretcher.

A good half-hour passed before we were at last able to speak to a doctor. He confirmed that Piya was right: the hospital didn't stock the right kind of antivenin because it was expensive and difficult to obtain. But there was still reason for hope: fortunately Tipu had received only a small dose of venom having been struck by only one of the snake's fangs (Piya would explain to me later that a strike of this kind was uncharacteristic of the king cobra, *Ophiophagus hannah*, which rarely attacked humans but was reputed to be very persistent when it did).

Now everything depended on the antivenin, said the doctor, and how soon it was administered. In the meantime, there was nothing for us to do but wait.

As the hours crept by the wait became harder and harder. At a certain point, when a nurse came to tell us that Tipu's breathing was become increasingly uneven, I had the impression that we were being prepared for bad news.

But Piya arrived earlier than expected, almost an hour before midnight. She was clearly under great strain: there was a haunted look in her eyes and her face was so weighted with anxiety that she looked skeletally thin. Yet she was neither breathless nor flustered, and her manner, as she handed over the container that she was carrying, was completely composed. She remained calm even when Moyna fell upon her and burst into tears.

An hour or so later a doctor appeared and announced, to our great relief, that the serum had begun to take effect and that Tipu's condition was improving. There was no need for us to remain at the hospital, he said; we would be well advised to get some sleep.

It was too late for me to go back to the city now and since there were no hotels in Lusibari, Piya arranged for me to stay the night in the Badabon Trust's guest-house. This proved to be the second floor of Nilima's Lusibari residence. It was a pleasant place with clean, comfortable rooms and all the facilities that one could wish for, including high-speed Internet. I was not surprised to learn that Piya made her home in the guest-house when she was in the Sundarbans, and that it was she who had refurbished the place and put in the Wi-Fi.

In the kitchen there were two large refrigerators. Like almost everything in the building they ran on solar power. One of the refrigerators was especially stocked for Piya, who, I soon discovered, subsisted on a very idiosyncratic diet, consisting mainly of energy bars and peanut butter and jelly sandwiches. Neither of us had eaten in a long time so when she offered to make me a sandwich I accepted with alacrity.

It was over this unexpectedly toothsome meal that I heard the story behind the name that Tipu had mentioned in his delirium: Rani. This, said Piya, was the name of an individual river dolphin, of the species that she had been studying for most of her professional life: the Irrawaddy dolphin, known to science as *Orcaella brevirostris*. Rani happened to be a member of a pod of *Orcaella* that had been especially important to Piya's research. She had kept careful records for each individual in the pod and knew all of them intimately, especially the females, whom she had tracked through every breeding season. She had also mapped the pod's movements over many years, following their diurnal, seasonal and annual migrations.

Piya's language was carefully neutral – no doubt because she was loath to anthropomorphize the animals that she studied – yet it was clear that her relationship with Rani was strong enough, and durable enough, to qualify as what humans might regard as an old friendship. Their connection stretched back for more than a generation because Piya had also known Rani's mother: she was the first dolphin in that pod that Piya had learnt to identify as an individual, because she was the only one with a newborn calf. But that calf hadn't survived; it was killed in a collision with a motorboat when it was just a few weeks old. Its death had shocked and grieved Piya so she was delighted to discover, on her return the following year, that the mother dolphin had calved again.

Tipu, who was then a little boy, had been with Piya at the time of the discovery – back then he would often insist on accompanying her when she went into the forest – and it was Tipu who had shortened the calf's official name, RN1, to Rani. A year later Rani had gone missing one day. Piya had launched a frantic search, scouring the pod's favoured routes, and sure enough, at one of their feeding grounds she had found Rani entangled in a length of nylon netting.

Piya wasted no time in cutting Rani loose and after that the dolphin had begun to make eye contact with her, in a manner quite different from other members of the pod – a manner that suggested something more than mere recognition (the word 'gratitude' suggested itself all the more strongly because Piya was so careful to avoid using it).

That was many years ago and Rani was now the oldest living member of the pod and a true matriarch, having raised a dozen calves. More than any other member of the pod it was she who had helped Piya track the family's migrations.

During the early years of Piya's research these patterns of movement had been regular and predictable. But then the tracks had begun to vary, becoming increasingly erratic; this was due, Piya believed, to changes in the composition of the waters of the Sundarbans. As sea levels rose, and the flow of fresh water diminished, salt water had begun to intrude deeper upstream, making certain stretches too saline for the dolphins. They had started to avoid some of the waterways they had frequented before; they had also, slowly, begun to venture further and further upriver, into populated, heavily fished areas. Inevitably some had been ensnared by fishermen's nets and some had been hit by motorboats and steamers. Over the last few years the pod had lost so many members that its numbers were now down to Rani and just two others.

To Piya it had begun to seem increasingly likely that the pod would not survive as a group, so she had done something that she generally avoided doing: she had fitted Rani with a GPS-enabled tracker that provided real-time information on her whereabouts and general condition. This device was programmed to send alerts to her cellphone in certain situations.

'And that's what happened yesterday,' said Piya. 'I got an alert while I was at the conference.'

'What kind of alert?'

Piya grimaced. 'Let's just say – it was the worst possible kind of alert; one that would be sent only if the dolphin was no longer in the water.'

I suddenly recalled television images of beached whales.

'You mean Rani may have been stranded or beached?'

'I don't know. But it was that kind of alert.'

'And am I right to think that the alert was sent out at around the time that Tipu began to talk about Rani?'

'That depends,' said Piya, with a shrug, 'on whether you got the time right.'

'But even if my estimate was off by half an hour or more,' I said, 'it would still be very odd, wouldn't it? After all, Tipu was in a delirium – how could he possibly have known where Rani was?'

'Let's not jump our guns,' said Piya. 'We don't actually know that anything has happened to Rani. That's still TBD. These devices have been known to malfunction. I'm not going to come to any conclusions until I've checked out the situation on the ground.'

'And how are you going to do that?'

Piya got up and began to clear away our plates. 'I have the GPS co-ordinates of the place where the tracker ended up. The location is an island called Garjontola. I'll be going there as soon as I can, maybe even tomorrow if Tipu is okay.'

As she was reaching for my empty plate she stopped to cast a glance at me. 'Would you like to come?'

'Would you have room for me?' I said, trying not to sound too eager.

'I think so. I'm hoping to hire one of Horen's faster boats. It can carry ten passengers and I'm taking only a couple of my local assistants. There should be plenty of room. You're welcome to come along, if you like.'

'Thank you,' I said. 'Yes, I'd like to come along.'

'Good, let's hope it works out.'

Later that night I regretted the impulse that had made me accept Piya's invitation. When I woke up next morning I was half hoping that the trip would be called off. But while we were eating breakfast Moyna arrived: she said that Tipu's condition had improved markedly and that he would probably be discharged from the hospital the next day.

That left us free for the day, so Piya went ahead with her plans. A little after 10 a.m. we set off for Garjontola accompanied by a couple of local fishermen whom she had trained to help with her research.

To my relief, the boat was a big improvement on that of the day before; although not quite a speedboat, it was certainly much faster than that ungainly steamer.

'Do you see how many shades of colour there are in the water?' said Piya, squinting at me from under the bill of the baseball cap she had placed on her close-cropped hair.

Narrowing my eyes against the spray, I focused my gaze on

the river below. Slowly, as I followed Piya's finger, what had seemed at first to be an unvarying mud-brown colour revealed itself to be a composite of many different hues. Nor was there any uniformity to the pattern of the river's flow: once my eyes had grown accustomed to scrutinizing the water I was able to spot pools, whirlpools, braids, striations and many sorts of ripples.

These were signs, said Piya, of the innumerable streams that were contained within the course of this one river. Each of these streams differed from the others in small ways, and each was freighted with its own mixture of micro-nutrients. In effect, each was a small ecological niche, held in suspension by the flow, like a balloon carried along by a wind. The result was an astonishing proliferation of life, in myriad forms.

'Each of these rivers,' said Piya, 'is like a moving forest, populated by an incredible variety of life forms.'

'That's a beautiful image,' I said. 'A forest that's been moving for millions of years.'

'But the fact that a river flows,' said Piya, 'means that it carries traces of everything that happens upriver. And that's the part that really worries me.'

'Why?'

She scratched her cheek doubtfully, as though she were wondering what level of explanation I might be able to follow.

'Have you heard of oceanic dead zones? No? Well they're these vast stretches of water that have a very low oxygen content – too low for fish to survive. Those zones have been growing at a phenomenal pace, mostly because of residues from chemical fertilizers. When they're washed into the sea they set off a chain reaction that leads to all the oxygen being sucked out of the water. Only a few, highly specialized organisms can survive in those conditions – everything else dies, which is why those patches of water are known as "dead zones". And those zones have now spread over tens of thousands of square miles of ocean – some of them are as large as middle-sized countries.'

'Really?'

'Yes. And they're not just out in mid-ocean any more,' said Piya. 'They've started appearing in rivers too, especially where they meet the sea, as in the estuaries of the Mississippi and Pearl Rivers. Which figures, of course, because it's through rivers that agricultural effluents reach the oceans.'

'I see what you're saying,' I said. 'You're suggesting the same thing may be happening here?'

'Something like that,' said Piya, 'except that I don't think it's just agricultural effluents in this case. I have a feeling that something else is to blame.'

'And what's that?'

She pointed upriver. 'I have a feeling that the culprit here is a refinery that started up a couple of years ago – it's not far from here as the crow flies. We'd been fighting it for years – I mean the trust and an alliance of environmental groups – but we were up against some very powerful people, a giant conglomerate that's got politicians in its pocket on both sides of the border. They organized a campaign against us, called us "foreign agents", tried to cut off our funding, had protesters arrested, attacked our demonstrations, not just with the police but also with paid goons – every kind of dirty trick you can think of and then some. And the online stuff! You wouldn't believe what comes at me through social media: death threats, hate mail, constant trolling.'

'Doesn't it scare you?'

'It does, to be honest. But the trust is so well known in the Sundarbans that I feel safe when I'm here. And anyway, someone has to do the work – we can't just let them get away with poisoning the Sundarbans.'

'What exactly have they been doing?'

'I can't say for sure because they've been pretty careful to hide whatever it is that they're up to. That's because we did manage to get the courts to impose a pretty tough regulatory regime on the refinery. As a result they've had to put systems in place to make sure that their discharges of effluents are kept to so-called "safe levels". But I'm beginning to suspect that they've been dumping effluents into the rivers when they think they can get away with it. We've been seeing things we'd never seen in these waters before – massive fish kills, for example.'

'What's a fish kill?'

'It's when you find thousands of dead fish floating on the surface or washed up ashore. It's happening all round the world with more and more chemicals flowing into rivers. But here I'm pretty sure that it's the refinery that's responsible.'

'Has this stuff affected your dolphins?'

'I believe it has,' said Piya. 'My guess is that this is why Rani and her pod have abandoned their old hunting grounds. I'm certain that it's been a huge source of stress for them – I mean, wouldn't you be stressed, if you had to abandon all the places that you know and were forced to start all over again?'

She sighed, gazing into the distance. 'And it must be hardest on Rani, knowing that the young ones depend on her. There she is, perfectly adapted to her environment, perfectly at home in it – and then things begin to change, so that all those years of learning become useless, the places you know best can't sustain you any more and you've got to find new hunting grounds. Rani must have felt that everything she knew, everything she was familiar with – the water, the currents, the earth itself – was rising up against her.'

The words had an oddly familiar ring. 'It's funny you should say that. Moyna said something similar when she was talking about the people who're leaving the Sundarbans.'

Piya nodded. 'You'll hear those words often here. We're in a new world now. No one knows where they belong any more, neither humans nor animals.'

A half-hour later Piya tapped my shoulder and pointed ahead. 'There it is – Garjontola.'

To me the island seemed no different from any other stretch of the mangrove forest – a featureless green smudge squatting upon a ledge of mud. But soon enough it became clear that something unusual had happened there: a tall column of birds could be seen circling above the island, in widening spirals.

Piya studied the island carefully with a pair of binoculars.

After a while I asked, 'What do you see?'

She turned to me and handed me the glasses: 'Here, take a look.'

I couldn't see much – it wasn't easy to focus the glasses in that fast-moving boat – but I did manage to catch a glimpse of some oblong patches of grey, outlined against the mud.

'Are those your dolphins?' I said.

'I won't know till I take a closer look.'

The boat came to a stop about a hundred yards from the shore. Moments later we were hit by a putrid odour; it was so strong that I had to hold a hand over my nose.

Piya gave me a wry smile. 'I think you'd better stay back – it's going to stink like hell out there.'

I didn't argue; I remained on the boat while Piya and her assistants went over in a rubber dinghy.

They came back after an hour with a reek of putrefaction wafting around them. Under her cap and sunglasses, Piya's face was unreadable; without so much as a glance in my direction she busied herself in putting away her equipment and the samples she had collected. When the boat turned around to head back she went to the prow and sat huddled over her camera, going over the pictures she had taken. It was clear that she was in no mood to talk.

We were more than halfway back when she came to sit beside me, at the rear of the boat.

'It was them all right,' she said grimly. 'Rani and her pod. They seem to have beached themselves, all at the same time. I've never seen anything like it.'

'Were they trying to get away from something, do you think?'

'It sure looks like that. I don't think the corpses were washed ashore. They wouldn't be lying next to each other, with their heads pointing in the same direction, if they'd died in the water.'

'Could a predator have attacked them?'

'I didn't see any signs of injury,' she said. 'Of course, the remains have been torn up by birds and crabs so it's hard to tell. But I don't think a predator could have done this: a shark or a croc wouldn't have been able to sneak up on them without their knowing. *Orcaella* are used to dealing with sharks and crocs: they detect them with their sonar. Anyway, a croc wouldn't have attacked all three at once.'

'Do you think it could have something to do with those dead zones that you were talking about?'

She shook her head. 'No. I don't think a dead zone could spook them into beaching themselves.'

'What do you think it was then?'

She thought this over, frowning. 'It's not uncommon, you know, for whales and dolphins to beach themselves – in fact it's been happening more and more frequently. There's a theory that man-made sounds – from submarines and sonar equipment and stuff like that – could be behind the beachings. As you know, marine mammals use echo location to navigate so if something messed with that they could become disoriented and run them-selves aground. But nothing like that could have happened here – there's no vessel anywhere nearby with that sort of capability.'

'So what could it be then?'

She made a despairing gesture. 'I don't know – I don't think we'll ever know. Clearly something spooked the hell out of them. But I have no idea what it was. There are just so many aspects of marine mammal behaviour that we don't understand, especially when it comes to beachings.'

Putting her arms around her legs Piya fell into a reverie, her chin on her knees. When she spoke again her voice was softer: 'Some of the old stories about beachings are so weird that they sound almost like witchcraft.'

'What do you mean?'

'Like there are these stories, you know,' she said, 'about islands in the southern Pacific where shamans claimed to be able to summon dolphins. They'd do some mumbo-jumbo on the beach and sure enough dolphins would arrive. It was probably just coincidence, but they took the credit for it anyways.'

'Or maybe they had visions,' I said, 'like Tipu did yesterday?'

I regretted the words almost as soon as I had said them. Casting me a sharp, scornful glance she said: 'You think Tipu had a vision?'

'Well,' I said, defensively, 'he did want to send you a warning, didn't he? At around the time your alert went off?'

'But you're not sure about the time, are you?' she shot back, in a tone of annoyance. 'And Tipu was probably just remembering something from the past. There's nothing else to it.'

'Still,' I persisted. 'Even if it's just a coincidence, don't you think it's interesting?'

'No, not particularly,' she said dismissively. She thought this over for a minute and then added: 'I guess that's the difference between you and me. I'm just a field biologist, trying to figure out my data. And you're a . . . hell, I don't even know what you do.'

'I'm an antiquarian book dealer.'

She gave a dry laugh. 'Yeah. It's like we're from different planets.'

After this exchange Piya's manner became markedly less friendly; I had the sense that my reference to visions had annoyed her and that she wanted to be rid of me.

Just before we arrived in Lusibari I looked at my watch and realized that there was still time for me to make my flight if I hurried straight back to Kolkata. With Piya in this mood there was no reason for me linger; I asked if she could arrange for me to return to the city and she answered with a nod.

Pulling out her phone she made a couple of calls. 'It's done,' she said. 'You can leave when you want.'

As soon as the boat had docked we went back to the guest-house where I put my things together. Then Piya walked me down to Lusibari's jetty, where a boat was waiting to take me to Basonti.

'Listen,' I said. 'I'm sorry I didn't get to say goodbye to Tipu.'

'That's all right,' she said offhandedly. It was clear now that she was relieved to see me go. 'He'll understand.'

'But I'd like to know what he says.'

'About what?'

'About Rani, and how he knew that she was in danger.'

'Oh that,' she said disinterestedly. 'I wouldn't hold my breath if I were you. Tipu's probably forgotten all about it. People never remember what they say when they're delirious.'

We were at the jetty now, and as I was shaking her hand I said: 'Do you ever come through New York?'

She looked startled. 'Why?'

'That's where I live. And I thought perhaps if you came through . . .'

She had begun to shake her head before I could finish the sentence. 'Look, I'm sorry,' she said in a tone that was clearly intended to dampen any expectations that I might have. 'I live between Oregon and here – these are the only places I spend time in, and I don't think that's ever going to change. As for New York, I can't remember when I was last there – maybe ten years ago? And I can't say I care for it, frankly.'

I nodded and tried not to look unduly snubbed. 'Well maybe you could drop me an email about Tipu?'

'Sure,' she said. 'Can you text me your address?'

'I'll do that,' I said. 'Take care.'

'Take care.'

On the way back to the city I felt as though I were slowly waking from an extended hallucination. I could no longer remember why I had embarked on this absurd expedition and cursed myself for having gone. Once again my therapist had been proved right; I had allowed my hopes of romance to get the better of my judgement.

I don't think I have ever been as glad to see an airport as I was when I reached Dum Dum later that night: it was as if a gateway of escape had appeared magically in front of me. Even the processes of checking in and going through immigration and security didn't seem as tedious as they usually did: they were like rituals that signalled a return to sanity.

I was in the departure lounge when my phone pinged to alert me to an email. It was from Piya.

'Tipu says hi. He's fine – he's sitting up in bed, chatting with Rafi. He says he doesn't remember a thing after he got bitten – just as I thought. Said to say goodbye to you. By the way does he really call you Pops?' This was followed by a string of incomprehensible emojis.

Fortunately my automatic Away responder was still on: I decided that there was no need to reply. At that moment I didn't want to spend one more second thinking about this strange episode; all I wanted was to put it out of my mind.

I stepped on to the plane with a great sigh of gratitude: it was as if I had entered an impregnably metallic, mechanical, man-made womb, where everything served to protect me from that world of mud and its slithering, creeping inhabitants.

Dawn was breaking when the plane took off and its flightpath took it, briefly, over the Sundarbans. From my seat, by a window, I had a clear aerial view of the silted, tidal landscape below, densely matted with vegetation and veined with rivers. The sight made me shudder: that I had ventured voluntarily into that wild tangle of mud and mangrove seemed incomprehensible now.

What had I been thinking of? Had I gone mad?

Brooklyn

Experience had taught me that to travel between Calcutta and Brooklyn was to switch between two states of mind, each of which came with its own cache of memory. For me this alternation had happened so reliably in the past that it was not unduly optimistic, I think, to assume that my memories of that visit to the Gun Merchant's shrine would recede once I had settled into my Brooklyn apartment.

But this expectation was soon belied. For several weeks after my return I found it hard to focus on my work. While sitting at my desk I was frequently ambushed by snatches of recollection from that day; worse still, my nights were often interrupted by dreams from which I would awake drenched in sweat, with a burning sensation stewing in my guts ('Heartburn,' said my doctor).

It was as if some living thing had entered my body, something ancient that had long lain dormant in the mud. I could only think of it in analogy to germs or viruses or bacteria, yet I knew it was none of those things: it was memory itself, except that it was not my own; it was much older than me, some submerged aspect of time that had been brought suddenly to life when I entered that shrine – something fearsome, venomous and over-whelmingly powerful, something that would not allow me to be rid of it.

I spent hours sitting at my desk but was unable to get anything done. I urgently needed to finish my first catalogue of the year but hours would go by without a single word being written. To fill the silence I would play music, sometimes classical Indian ragas, sometimes qawwalis by Sufi musicians. They would lull me into a stupor and hours would slip by without my being aware of it. My portable Bluetooth speaker became my constant companion, accompanying me from room to room as I wandered listlessly around my apartment.

After two wasted months I went to my doctor and got a prescription for anti-anxiety pills. But even these didn't help. If anything they made me feel even less my own self, my own master; they seemed only to strengthen the hold of whatever it was that had gained ascendancy over me.

I was sitting at my desk one day, staring blankly at my computer, when a pop-up window appeared on the screen. Inside the window were the words: 'Does the word BHUTA mean "ghost"? Or does it mean something else?'

Unnerved by this strange manifestation I went to the bathroom and washed my face. When I came back the window was still on the screen, blinking. But now I noticed a line in small print; it said 'Bonduki@bonduki.com wants to start a chat session with you.'

I sat down and typed: 'Is that you, Tipu?'

The answer appeared after a couple of seconds. 'Sure it's me. Now answer the question.'

'Why are you asking me this?' I wrote. 'Why don't you look it up on the Net?'

'I did. And now I'm asking u. What exactly does BHUTA mean?'

I scratched my head for a bit and then fetched a dictionary.

'Look, I'm no expert on this,' I wrote. 'All I can tell you is that the Bangla word "bhoot" or "bhuta" comes from a basic but very complicated Sanskrit root, "bhu", meaning "to be", or "to manifest". So in that sense "bhuta" simply means "a being" or "an existing presence".'

There was a long pause.

'So are u and I bhutas then?'

'I suppose you could say so.'

'And what about animals? Snakes? Dolphins?'

'In the sense that they exist and are beings, yes, animals are bhutas too.'

'Then why do people mean "ghost" when they say "bhoot"?'

'Because "bhuta" also refers to the past, in the sense of "a past state of being". Like when we say "bhuta-kala" or "times past".'

Another long pause.

'But if the same word means both "exist<u>ing</u>" and "exist<u>ed</u>" wouldnt it mean that the past wasnt past? That the past was present in the present?'

'In a sense yes.'

'But thats impossible isnt it? How can the past be present in the present?'

'In the same way that you might say in English "the present is haunted by the past". I suppose that's how the word "bhuta" has come to mean "ghost".'

This time his response was instantaneous. 'So are u saying that ghosts exist?'

'NO!'

I yelped. My fingers had hit the keyboard so hard that I had split a fingernail. But I typed on, without stopping. 'I'm not saying that AT ALL. I'm just telling you what the word means.'

Several minutes went by before Tipu's response appeared: 'OK, got it.' This was followed by a thumbs-up emoji, and then the window closed.

I slammed shut my laptop and stared at it, shivering, half expecting it to open of itself. It was as though the most sterile object in my safe, man-made world had suddenly become a portal through which the primeval mud could draw me back into its depths.

Time became almost meaningless to me now. The days flowed by and I scarcely noticed.

Then one day another pop-up window appeared on my screen.

'What is a SHAMAN?'

I recoiled, frowning. 'Tipu, why do you keep asking me these things?' I wrote. 'Why don't you look them up yourself, on the Net?'

'I did. I found a site that said shamans can communicate with animals. And even with trees, and mountains, and ice and stuff.'

'That's your answer then.'

'So do you think its true? That these guys can communicate with animals? And trees and mountains?'

Pushing my chair back, I forced myself to consider this seriously.

I must have sat there for a long time because presently another balloon appeared within the pop-up screen. 'Hey Pops! u still there?'

Startled out of my trance, I wrote: 'I was just thinking about your question. I suppose the answer depends on what you mean by "communication". For example, if a dog barks at me then I know that it's trying to communicate <u>something</u>. Maybe that it's angry, that it doesn't want me to come any closer. Whatever it is, it's certainly some sort of communication, isn't it?'

'I guess. But u know what I mean. Can they like communicate more complicated stuff?'

I thought about this for a bit. 'Look, if someone like me, who knows pretty much nothing about animals, can figure out what a dog is trying to communicate when it barks, then I imagine that people who actually work with animals, like farmers, or dog walkers, or horse trainers, can understand some pretty complicated stuff.'

A minute went by and I found, to my puzzlement, that I was sitting on the edge of my seat as I waited for his response.

'Horen says my dad cud understand animals. And not just animals.'

'What else then?'

'He says that he cud see and feel things that others cudnt.'

'Like what?'

'Oh you know.' His rate of typing was suddenly very slow.

'Like we were talking about that time? What did u call them? Beings?'

'I don't know that I would take Horen's word for any of this,' I wrote. 'What does your mother say?'

Tipu didn't answer my question. When he began to type again the words that appeared before me were: 'Rafi's grandad was a bauley. Do u know what that means?'

I had a quick look at the dictionary. 'A bauley is a man who leads people into the jungle, right? In the Sundarbans?'

'Ya. They get to do that coz they have this special thing with some animals. Rafi sez his grandad was like that. Wud that make him a shaman?'

A feeling of being very far out of my depth took hold of me now.

'You know who you should ask about this stuff?' I wrote. 'Piya. She works with animals.'

A pause. 'You think Piya communicates with animals?'

'She hinted that she recognized gratitude in one of her dolphins. That's communication of a sort, isn't it? Though of course she could never say so.'

'Why culdnt she say so?'

'Because scientists aren't allowed to say things like that.'

A string of laughter emoticons scrolled past me, and then: 'Catch ya later.'

The next day it struck me that I now had a legitimate reason to send Piya an email.

'Hi, Piya,' I wrote. 'How are you? Are you in the US? I've been wondering about how Tipu's getting on. Could we talk some time? Yours. Deen.'

She wrote back a few hours later. 'Hi, Deen. I'm in Oregon. Call me any time. Here's my number.'

I waited a while, so as not to seem too eager.

'Hi, Piya.'

'Hi there, Deen.'

I'd prepared myself for a brisk brush-off but she didn't seem to be in a hurry. We chatted casually for a while before turning to the subject of Tipu: 'So how's he doing?'

'To be honest,' she said, 'Tipu's not doing too good. It's weird – he seemed to have recovered completely, but then he had a relapse. Started getting these blackouts and migraines. We tried to get him to see a doctor but he wouldn't. The only thing that seemed to help him was hanging out with Rafi.'

'Oh, so they've become good friends, have they?'

'I guess.'

'That's interesting,' I said. 'They're so different. I suppose they bonded over that awful incident. Anyway, I'm glad they've become friends.'

The line went quiet for a moment.

When Piya spoke again, it was in a quiet, confiding tone. 'You know, Deen, I think they may be more than just friends.'

'Oh?'

'Yes. I've wondered about Tipu's sexuality in the past. He's not said anything to me but I think it's possible that Tipu may have something special going on with Rafi. They certainly spend a lot of time together.'

'He mentioned Rafi in one of his messages to me.'

'What?' She sounded very surprised. 'Has Tipu been in touch with you then?'

'Yes he has. He's been sending me these weird questions. "What's a ghost?" "What's a shaman?"'

She burst out laughing. 'That's Tipu. He always finds a way to pull your chain.'

'You think that's what he's doing?'

'Sure sounds like it. Anyway, I wouldn't worry about it if I were you.'

'I'm glad to hear it,' I said. 'And what about you? Are you heading back to the Sundarbans any time soon?'

'Not for a few months.' She sighed. 'I'm dreading it actually. The news from there isn't good. More shoals of dead fish drifting up. And my assistants even found a big crab die-off – a huge swarm of them lying dead on a mud bank. That's seriously bad news because crabs are a keystone species in the Sundarbans.'

'Do you think the refinery is to blame?'

'That's what I suspect, yeah, but there's no proof yet. And in the meantime, all the other stuff – the harassment, the hate mail – all of it just keeps getting worse.'

'So it must be a relief to be back in Oregon then?'

'It is,' she said. 'Not that things are much better here, though. In fact I'm not even at home. I'm up in the mountains with my college room-mate, Lisa. She's been going through a bad time . . . it's a long story.'

'Tell me.'

'Okay. So Lisa's an entomologist and teaches in a community college up here, in the mountains. Some years ago she started a research project on bark beetles – they're these insects that eat up trees from the inside so that when there's a dry spell the dead wood is like kindling, just waiting to go up in flames. Bark beetles have been extending their range, as the mountains warm up, and Lisa found that they've invaded the forests around the town where she lives. She went to the town council to warn them that they had to do something. But no one paid any attention, not the mayor, nor anyone else, least of all the people who were in harm's way. To them she's just a pushy outsider who doesn't know anything about the mountains and is trying to make a name for herself. Well this year there was a long drought and a couple of weeks ago a huge wildfire broke out, just as Lisa had warned. The state had to declare an emergency and send in helicopters and stuff. Two people died and dozens of houses were burnt down.'

Piya paused to take a breath.

'You would think that afterwards people would have thanked Lisa for her warnings and treated her as a hero or something. But no: what they did was that they blamed *her*! A rumour went around that she had started the fire herself because she wanted more funding for her research. Soon it was all over the social media. She was even questioned by a cop. Then she began to get threats – even death threats. Someone fired a bullet into her porch; a tree in her yard was set on fire. Luckily it didn't do much harm but now she's terrified, so I'm spending a few days with her, just to cheer her up.'

Piya paused again.

'Can you believe it? It's like we're back in the Dark Ages – women being attacked as witches!'

For several months Tipu disappeared from my screen. I began to think that he had at last tired of his pranks – this should have pleased me but instead I felt just a little disappointed.

And then one morning the interface for the online telephony program that I was then using popped up on my screen, accompanied by a shrill ringing.

'You have a call from Bonduki@bonduki.com.'

I hit Answer and Tipu's face appeared in front of me, grinning, pixie-like, but without the ear stud and the blond highlights.

'Hey, man! Turn on your camera.'

'Why?'

'I want to see where you are.'

'I'm in my study.'

'Yeah, so lemme see it.'

Grudgingly I turned on the camera. 'There's not much to see here.'

But Tipu wasn't listening to me. 'Wow! You got a shitload of books out there.'

'Yes, well that's what I do. I sell old books.'

He snickered. 'You mean people still read those things?'

'Fewer and fewer.'

Now Tipu made a whistling sound: '*Eeeew.*' This was intended, I soon realized, to express concern. 'And what's the deal with you, man?'

'What do you mean?'

'Dude, you don't look too good . . .'

'I'm fine,' I said pre-emptively.

'You've got these dark circles under your eyes. And that heavy stubble – that ain't doing much for you, man, I can tell ya that.'

I ran a hand over my chin. 'I just forgot to shave.'

'Yeah, like for a month. What's the matter widdya man? You look like ya got something inside a'ya.'

'Of course I've got something inside of me,' I retorted. 'We all do. Don't you know that bacteria are a big part of your body weight?'

He gave a screech of laughter. 'Yeah, that's it! You've been taken over by bacteria. Isn't there a word for it? What do they call it? Poss— something.'

'You mean "possession"?'

'Yeah, that's it.'

'Don't be silly,' I snapped. 'Possession is when someone is taken over by a demon.'

'"De" what?'

'Demon.'

'What's that?'

'It's nothing. Just a metaphor for greed. An imaginary thing.'

'Y'think greed's imaginary?' He chuckled. 'Hey Pops, I got news for you: greed's real, it's big. You got greed, I got greed, we all got greed. You want to sell more books. I want more phones, more headphones, more everything. Fuck man, it's not parasites we got inside of us, it's greed! If that's what a demon is then there's no way it's imaginary. Shit no! We're all demons.'

I decided to play along.

'You may be right, Tipu, but you know what? That's really bad news, because according to Hindu mythology, when demons take over is when the world ends. There's something called *pralaya* that happens – everything dissolves, even time. But it could happen in other ways too. The Zoroastrians say rivers of molten metal will flow over the earth. The Christians say death, disease, famine and war will bring the Apocalypse. The Incas thought it would start with earthquakes; Muslims say the oceans will burst forth and the dead will turn in their graves . . .'

'Hey! Pops!'

Glancing at the screen I was surprised to see an expression of genuine fear on his face.

'Stop! You're scaring me.'

'Well, you started it,' I said. 'Where are you anyway?'

'I'm in . . .'

I noticed now that there was a white sheet hanging behind him. I couldn't tell whether he was indoors or outdoors.

His grin broke out again. 'I'm in Bangalore.'

'Bangalore? What're you doing there?'

'Working for a call centre.'

'Really? I thought you hated call centres.'

'Yeah, but sometimes you gotta take what you can get. And these call centres sure love my American accent.'

'That makes sense.'

'Anyway,' he continued, 'that's not why I called.'

'Why did you call then?'

'Just wanted to ask you something.'

'Yes?'

'You've got a friend in Venice, right?'

I caught my breath.

'How do you know?' And then it dawned on me. 'Tipu, have you hacked my computer? Or my phone?'

He gave a squeal of laughter.

'Maybe I just hacked your head, Pops! If I'd hacked your computer I wouldn't need to ask.' He grinned. 'So tell me – it's true, right? You have this friend in Venice?'

'Yes, it's true.'

'Have ya heard from her recently?'

'No, but I'm going to see her next month, in Los Angeles.'

'Good. Don't let anything scare you off.'

This mystified me. 'What could scare me off? I'm looking forward to seeing her.'

'Yeah, well, shit happens. Like that day when I got bitten.'

'That was in the Sundarbans, Tipu. I'm going to LA. There aren't any snakes there.'

'Yeah? You sure?'

'Of course there aren't. Don't be silly. I'm not going to get bitten in LA.'

'That's too bad though – a snake bite might be just what you need.'

'Tipu, what the hell are you talking about?'

'Never mind. Anyway, when you see your friend, be sure to listen to her carefully.'

'Why? What're you getting at?'

'Just that she's a good person. You need to listen to her carefully Pops.'

'How do you know whether she's a good person or not?'

'She's been good to you, right? And some day you're going to have to return the favour.'

'What favour? I don't understand. How did you even know about my friend?'

He laughed. 'Maybe someone whispered something in my ear. Maybe I've got a secret pal who knows your friend very, very well and wants to be sure that you don't chicken out of your meeting in LA.'

'Of course I'm not going to chicken out of seeing her. That's why I'm going to LA.'

'Yeah, but something might happen that'll get you all freaked out.'

'Like what?'

He giggled. 'Maybe you'll see a snake or somethin' on the way.'

'Tipu,' I said patiently, 'I'm going to LA in a plane, business class if you must know.'

'Great – I'm happy for ya, Pops! But hey, you never know – shit happens. Anyways, don't get freaked out and skip meeting your friend.'

'I have no intention of skipping anything.'

'Good. You need to do this. And you know what? You need to go through with this for your own sake too.'

'Why?'

He winked. 'Don't you want to get rid of that bacteria or whatever that's got into your head?'

'Tipu, I can't make any sense of this.'

Raising a hand he flicked his fingers across the screen. 'Gotta go. Take care.'

Then my screen went blank.

Wildfires

The prospect of seeing Cinta was the one thing that had sustained me through this strange twilit time. It was she who had arranged for me to come to Los Angeles: a museum was hosting a conference, to celebrate its acquisition of a very valuable seventeenth-century edition of *The Merchant of Venice*, and Cinta was to deliver the concluding address. A number of rare book dealers had been invited and she had prevailed on the hosts to include me in the list.

It happened, moreover, that the museum in question was a famously wealthy institution so we were to be hosted in great style, and were being flown out business class. This became yet another reason to look forward to the trip – and such was my state of mind at that time, that for several weeks I thought of little else.

Long before it came time to catch my flight I made sure to reserve a window seat for myself. On the day of journey, when I boarded the aircraft, I was aware, for the first time in many months, of a pleasurable sense of anticipation. My seat, with its console of buttons and its elaborate entertainment system, was all that I could have asked for; I settled in contentedly, intending to make the most of the next seven hours. But just as I was about to try out the noise-cancelling headset, I caught the sound of an excited conversation across the aisle: an elegantly dressed blonde woman and a sun-tanned man in a business suit were loudly exchanging words like 'fire' and 'evacuation'.

I thought, at first, that they were talking about a film (they looked like Hollywood people). But then, as others joined in, it became clear that they were concerned about some sort of emergency that was currently unfolding in Los Angeles.

I had not kept up with the news that week. Now, looking at my smartphone, I learnt that massive wildfires had been raging around Los Angeles for several days. Thousands of acres of land had been incinerated and tens of thousands of people had been moved to safety.

Startled by the news I rose inadvertently to my feet. My intention was to ask the stewardess whether our flight was likely to be delayed – but no sooner had I stirred than two uniformed members of the crew came barrelling down the aisle to tell me, very brusquely, that I couldn't get up, the FASTEN SEAT BELT sign was on, and the plane was about to start taxiing.

'I'm sorry,' I said. 'I was wondering whether there's any danger—'

Before I could say 'of a delay', I was cut off.

'Sir! You need to lower your voice . . . And you need to fasten your seat belt.'

'But I just saw this . . .' I held up my phone to show her a news item about the wildfires. In the process my forefinger inadvertently touched an icon on the screen and suddenly an eerie, keening sound burst out of the overhead luggage bin, filling the whole cabin and turning every head in my direction.

Being well aware of the complications of flying in these times, I knew exactly how unwise it was for someone of my appearance to draw attention to himself. I always exerted myself to avoid doing so – but now here I was, the cynosure of all eyes.

Such was my state of mind that I did not immediately recognize the sound that was pouring out of the luggage bin as one of my favourite pieces of music, a passage from Nusrat Fateh Ali Khan's 'Allah Hoo'. Although I loved this recording dearly, no sound could have been more unwelcome to my ears at that moment, especially when I saw its effect on the people around me.

An eternity went by before I realized that I had accidentally turned on a music sharing app that was linked to my portable Bluetooth speaker (which I had snatched up at the last minute and stuffed into my hand luggage). Instead of tapping my phone, to turn off the app, I panicked and leapt up to reach for the luggage bin – and the stewardess in turn leapt to intercept me. There followed a short scuffle. It ended with me collapsing on my seat while the stewardess stood in the aisle, hands on hips, glowering at me.

'Sir, if you don't calm down immediately you will be removed from this aircraft.'

'I'm sorry . . . I'm sorry . . . I'm sorry . . .'

In the meantime, 'Allah Hoo' was still blasting from my Bluetooth speaker. Only now did it occur to me to turn the app off, and even this took a while because my hands were shaking uncontrollably.

As my gaze rose, trembling, from my phone, it encountered ranks of faces staring at me with expressions that ranged from bewilderment to terror.

I shrank into my seat, mumbling abjectly: 'I'm sorry, I'm sorry, I'm sorry . . .'

I managed to get through the next few hours without incident and it was not until the plane began its descent that I remembered the wildfires. It was the captain's pre-landing announcement that reminded me of them: our flightpath had changed, he said, because the wildfires had shifted direction; passengers on the left side of the plane might even be able to see some smoke as we were coming in to land.

It was my good luck (or so I thought at the time) to be seated on the left side of the plane. Leaning forward, I scanned the horizon with my nose against the window.

It wasn't long before dark smudges appeared in the distance. They quickly grew into dense masses of smoke. Then leaping waves of flame came into view too, lining the horizon with flickering tints of yellow and orange.

Even more striking was the landscape that lay beneath our flightpath – a charred, smouldering stretch of forested hillside that had already been laid waste by the fires. The plane was now flying low enough that I could see a great mass of blackened tree trunks rising out of a vast field of ash. I noticed also that many birds were circling over the ashes of the burnt-out forest – this astonished me because the destruction was so complete that it was difficult to think that any living thing would be drawn to this incinerated landscape.

I would learn later that the remains of a wildfire are by no means a wasteland. For certain species of birds – hawks, eagles and other raptors – they present rare opportunities for hunting: the loss of tree cover makes it easy to spot those rodents and reptiles that have survived the fire by burrowing underground. For birds of prey the conditions are so favourable that some species of raptor have even been known to actually start, or spread, wildfires by carrying burning twigs afield in their beaks.

But of course I did not know this at the time, so I watched the circling birds in fascinated amazement. Even from that distance, some could be seen diving steeply down to forage among the ashes.

Presently I caught a glimpse of two birds arrowing downwards together, on convergent paths: they had both evidently targeted the same prey and it seemed inevitable that they would collide. They were no larger than specks and I lost sight of them as they dropped down, towards the blackened earth. But a minute or two later I spotted them again, one in pursuit of the other. They shot up together, twisting, manoeuvring, rising higher and higher and moving all the while, in the direction of the plane.

As the birds grew larger I saw that one of them was holding something in its talons; this was the prize that its rival was trying to prise away. So absorbed were the birds in their pursuit that they were rising ever higher, at great speed. And since the plane was descending steeply it wasn't long before the birds were actually above us. Then at last the bird in the lead seemed to tire of the chase. Flipping itself over it tossed away its prey – a twisting, writhing, sinuous animal.

As I watched the creature flying through the air a sound burst from my throat – I would later hear it described as a 'scream'.

I was not aware then of what I had done, and when I heard raised voices and cries of alarm I did not imagine that they had anything to do with me.

But suddenly a steward and stewardess converged on my seat, along with a big, burly man in a dark suit – I knew at a glance that he was a security agent in plain clothes.

'That's enough, sir!'

The agent reached over, unbuckled my seat belt and pulled me to my feet. 'You need to come with me, sir.'

Within a couple of minutes I was sitting beside the agent, with a plastic tie around my wrists. I sat there stunned, with my eyes closed, listening. All around me voices were whispering about the suspiciousness of my behaviour and how I had been disruptive from the start.

Squads of policemen and blue-suited agents were waiting for me when I was finally allowed to leave the plane. They led me to a blindingly bright, neon-lit room, where they unfastened my hands and demanded that I hand over my cellphone and laptop, along with my passwords. Too rattled to resist, I complied, and was left to wait alone at a steel desk.

There was nothing for me to do but stare at my watch, and the more I stared the more convinced I became that this trip had been a terrible idea from the start, that there was something ill-fated about it and that I should go back to New York on the next available flight.

By the time the door opened again more than an hour had passed, and I had decided that if I was not detained after my interrogation I would go straight to the ticketing desk and get on a flight to New York, no matter what the cost.

But to my surprise there was no interrogation. I was handed

my cellphone and laptop by two blue-suited agents, one of whom held the door open and told me I was free to go.

'Is that all?' I was almost disappointed.

'Yes, sir. That's all. You're free to leave.'

As I was getting my things together one of the agents said: 'What made you do that?'

'Do what?'

'The crew said that you kept screaming "Snake! Snake!" You should know that you can't do that on a plane.'

I moistened my lips, trying to think of something to say.

'I'm sorry, sir,' I said. 'I don't know what got into me.'

I was almost out of the room when the other agent said: 'Do you always get a lot of calls from Turkey?'

My mouth fell open. 'Sir,' I said guardedly, 'I very rarely get calls. And I don't think I've ever got a call from Turkey in my life.'

The agent raised an eyebrow. 'Really? That's weird.'

'Why?'

'Because your phone kept ringing this last hour. The caller's number had the country code for Turkey.'

I gaped at him, dumbfounded. 'Oh? I have no idea . . .'

Wandering out to the arrivals halls, I stopped to check my phone. I saw that I had ten missed calls, all from a number that was preceded by the code + 90. Hesitantly I touched the return call button and raised the phone to my ears: it rang a few times but there was no answer.

When I put the phone away I realized that I had wandered out of the airport and was standing near a taxi line. To go back into the airport to arrange a return flight was more than I could bring myself to do; I was exhausted. Instead I got into a taxi and gave the driver the name of my hotel.

By the time I reached the hotel it was almost midnight. My room was on the fifteenth floor and it was even more luxurious than I had expected.

I was now completely exhausted and eager to get into bed.

But as I was slipping between the soft, white sheets I noticed a strange orange glow around the edges of the curtains. Rousing myself, I went to the window and pulled back the curtains. They opened on a landscape that seemed to be ablaze with fire and smoke. It took me a while to realize that the fires were actually many miles away; in the darkness of the night they seemed to fill the horizon, from end to end.

The sight was mesmerizing. When at last I fell asleep I saw the fires again in my dreams, with a glowing snake hurtling towards me, through the flames.

Los Angeles

Next morning there was much confusion in the lobby, largely because the hotel had rearranged its dining rooms so that its guests would not have to gaze at waves of flame as they breakfasted.

I had been hoping to have breakfast with Cinta but she was nowhere to be seen. After a long and fruitless search I was told that her flight had been delayed because of the fires. She had arrived very late at night and would not be joining us until later in the day.

Swallowing my disappointment I fell in behind the others as they filed out to board the buses that were to take us to the conference.

The museum that was hosting the conference was celebrated for its architecture and landscaping. The buses and cars that brought visitors to its gates were allowed no further than the car park at the entrance; from there on transportation across the grounds was provided by the museum's own fleet of sleek, electric vehicles.

I had visited the museum several times before and in my experience the system had always worked with clockwork precision: visitors had no sooner set foot in the parking area than they were whisked away in liveried shuttle buses.

But this was not the case when we arrived for the opening event of the conference: there were no shuttle buses anywhere in sight and, odder still, the car park, which usually filled up as soon as the museum opened its gates, was almost empty.

There was only a single security guard at the entrance and all she could tell us was that the museum was drastically short-handed that morning; many of her colleagues had not been able to get to work because of road closures caused by the still-raging wildfires.

This disclosure set off a buzz of consternation among us: What about the conference? Was it to be called off?

The guard put through a call to her boss and a couple of minutes later a voice spoke to us through a speakerphone. It was the museum's director. Everything would go ahead as planned, he said. There was nothing to worry about; he had been assured by the city authorities that the wildfires posed no direct threat to the museum. We just needed to be a little patient because of the shortage of staff – everything would be taken care of very soon.

And sure enough, within a few minutes a convoy of shuttle buses pulled into the car park.

The museum's principal buildings were located on the spine of a steep ridge. The site commanded panoramic views stretching from the hills in the east to the sea on the western horizon.

But that morning nobody looked either at the hills or the sea; every eye was drawn in the same direction, towards the north-east, where a dark cloud had reared up above the horizon, taking the shape of an immense wave, complete with a frothing white top. From where we stood it looked as though a gigantic tsunami were advancing upon the distant outskirts of the city.

The sight was so riveting that ushers had to be sent to herd us into the auditorium for the opening event.

On stepping into the auditorium I recognized several acquaintances. They were bibliophiles, librarians, experts on book-making and of course rare book dealers like myself. It was a largely grey-haired crowd, sprinkled with more than its fair share of blue blazers, bow ties and strings of pearls.

The opening speaker, however, was conspicuously not of our

ilk: he was a trendy young historian who had gained a reputation as a peddler of Big Ideas. The subject that he had elected to speak on (as we discovered on entering the auditorium) was 'Climate and Apocalypse in the Seventeenth Century'.

This grandiose title kindled a certain scepticism in the audience, and that mood was in no part allayed by the speaker's hipsterish appearance: a hirsute youth, he was dressed in pencil-thin trousers and a waistcoat that seemed to be made from straw. Nor did it help that he chose to begin on a bombastic note.

The seventeenth century, declared the historian, was a period of such severe climatic disruption that it was sometimes described as the 'Little Ice Age'. During this time temperatures across the globe had dropped sharply, maybe because of fluctuations in solar activity, or a spate of volcanic eruptions – or possibly even because of the reforestation of vast tracts of land following on the genocide of Amerindian peoples after the European conquests of the Americas.

In any event many parts of the world had been struck by famines, droughts and epidemics in the seventeenth century. At the same time a succession of comets had appeared in the heavens, and the earth had been shaken by a tremendous outbreak of seismic activity; earthquakes had torn down cities and volcanoes had ejected untold quantities of dust and debris into the atmosphere. Millions had died: in some parts of the world the population had declined by a third. In these decades more wars had raged than at any time before: many parts of Europe had been convulsed by conflict; England had experienced the greatest internal upheaval in its history – civil war – and central Europe had been devastated by the Thirty Years War; in Turkey a fearsome drought had led to a devastating fire in Istanbul, shaking the Ottoman Empire to its foundations; elsewhere, as in China, long-established dynasties had been overthrown amidst torrents of blood; in India the Mughal Empire had been beset by famine and rebellion. A great wave of suicides had swept the world; in China multitudes of Ming loyalists had killed themselves; in

Russia an Orthodox sect called the Old Believers had declared the tsar to be the Antichrist and tens of thousands of its members had taken their own lives. And everywhere there was talk of apocalypse: the comets that were streaking through the heavens were thought to be portents of the destruction of the universe; even the creatures of the earth were believed to be conveying warnings of catastrophe. In many parts of the earth clouds of locusts had darkened the sky and vast swarms of rodents had stripped the land bare; in Italy there was a sudden crescendo in visions inspired by the bites of tarantulas – and in England dreams of beasts, from the Book of David, had caused a sect called the Fifth Monarchists to rise up against the government, only to be brutally slaughtered.

But the great paradox of this era, the speaker continued, was that these upheavals had been accompanied also by an extraordinary intellectual and creative ferment: this was the beginning of the Age of Enlightenment, the century of Hobbes, Leibniz, Newton, Spinoza and Descartes, and the world had been enriched by many masterpieces of literature, art and architecture, including . . .

Here he named a number of seventeenth-century masterpieces – and among them there was one that served to jolt my memory: the Taj Mahal. That name took my mind back to India, and it occurred to me that the temples of Bishnupur were built at about the same time as the Taj. This in turn reminded me of the Gun Merchant's shrine . . . and I suddenly recalled the droughts, famines, storms and plagues that played so large a part in the legend.

Was it possible that the legend was born of the tribulations of the Little Ice Age?

For a while I was lost in my own thoughts and when my attention returned to my surroundings I saw that the talk was over. The speaker was now being aggressively questioned by a curmudgeonly antiquarian.

'. . . what you've given us, sir, is merely a list of coincidences

... anybody with a couple of hours to spare could produce a similar catalogue of floods, quakes and wars for other centuries ... you are juxtaposing things that have no connection ... anyway what does Jacobean drama have to do with the weather? ... And people everywhere have always imagined themselves to be heading towards apocalypse ... that's because every generation likes to think that it's special and everything will come to an end when they're gone ... these seventeenth-century zealots were no different from millions of others, before and after them!'

This rebuttal played well with the audience, meeting with a chorus of approbatory murmurs and whispers.

But the stirrings in the auditorium had little effect on the speaker, who would not yield an inch.

'And what if the millenarians were right? Couldn't it be said that it was in the seventeenth century that we started down the path that has brought us to where we are now? After all, it was then that Londoners began to use coal on a large scale, for heating, which was how our dependence on fossil fuels started. Would your Jacobean playwrights have written as they did if they hadn't had coal fires to warm them? Did they know that an angry beast, which had long lain dormant within the earth, was coming to life? Did Hobbes or Leibniz or any of the other thinkers of the Enlightenment have any understanding of this?'

He paused to cast a dramatic glance around the room.

'It would seem that the intellectual titans of the Enlightenment had no inkling of what was getting under way. Yet, strangely, all around the earth, ordinary people appear to have sensed the stirring of something momentous. They seemed to have understood that a process had been launched that could lead ultimately to catastrophe: what they didn't allow for was that the story might take a few hundred years to play out. It has fallen to us, centuries later, to bear witness to the last turn of the wheel. And what we are seeing already –' he paused to point a finger in the direction of the distant wildfires – 'should be enough to remind us that the climatic perturbations of the Little Ice Age were trivial compared to what is in store for us now. What our ancestors experienced is but a pale foreshadowing of what the future holds!'

This answer exasperated the book dealer who turned to the audience and announced, with a roll of his eyes: 'I feel like I'm back in 1999, arguing with some kid who thinks the world is going to end at the stroke of midnight . . .'

A gale of laughter blew through the auditorium. And just as it was receding another, far more strident noise, burst upon us: the wailing of a fire alarm.

I was rising to my feet when the sound died and a voice came over the speaker system: 'I'm sorry about that . . .'

It was the director of the museum; he had stepped up to the podium and was speaking into a microphone.

'We've just been told that we need to evacuate this building, as a precaution. It's something to do with the wind – the wildfires are moving faster than expected. But there's absolutely no need to worry – we only want to keep everyone safe. Our security team will help you find the exits . . .'

We filed out quietly, blinking in the bright California sunlight.

The tsunami of smoke in the distance was still in the same place – or so it seemed to me, although some of the others thought that it had moved a little closer. It was difficult to be sure.

After a few minutes the director's voice was heard again.

He told us that his staff had been hard at work and had found an alternative venue for the conference: none other than the hotel where we were staying! A hall, and a suite of meeting rooms, had been made available to us, so apart from a few minor adjustments everything would go ahead as planned!

He ended with a cry that roused a chorus of cheers: 'We've got to show Mother Nature that we're not quitters!'

This announcement did much to restore our spirits: there were many who felt that the new arrangements were an improvement on the original plan; with the hotel as the conference's venue, it would be easy to slip away to our rooms – or the pool, or the bar, for that matter.

All in all nobody was unduly put out by the changes. And I, for one, welcomed the disruption, because it was then that I caught sight of a great mop of white hair: Cinta was leaning on a balustrade staring at the distant wildfires.

On the way back to the hotel, sitting beside Cinta on the bus, I said: 'What did you think of that keynote? Do you think he was right, about the seventeenth century and today?'

'Oh yes, Dino,' said Cinta. '*Assolutamente*, I feel it all the time now, every day when I read the papers. It's as though the Little Ice Age is rising from its grave and reaching out to us.'

'And to me too – through you.'

Cinta glanced at me with knitted eyebrows. 'What do you mean?'

'Do you remember how you called me, almost accidentally, a couple of years ago? I was in Calcutta and you were in Venice, at the airport, waiting for a flight. You said you had had a dream.'

'Yes, I remember. Go on.'

'That day I had gone to see an elderly relative of mine – a remarkable woman who has spent most of her life living and working in the Sundarbans.'

It occurred to me then that Cinta might not know what I was referring to. 'Have you heard of the Sundarbans? The mangrove forest of Bengal?'

'*Sì, caro!*' Cinta smiled and patted my hand. 'In Italy everyone knows about the Sundarbans. It is because of a famous children's book that was set there. It was my daughter Lucia's favourite book; she used to dream of that forest.'

'The Sundarbans?'

'Yes,' said Cinta, 'but go on with what you were saying.'

'So what happened was that my relative told me about a small temple in the jungle and asked me to visit it; she felt that someone needed to make a record of the structure before it was swallowed up by the mud. Her story was interesting but I wasn't keen to go because I had to leave for New York in a couple of days and was very busy. Actually I had more or less decided not to go when you called, and then, for some reason, I changed my mind and went after all.'

'And what did you find?'

'The temple was there, just as she had said – it was quite distinctive in style, and I'm pretty sure that it was built in the seventeenth century. The temple was also associated with the goddess of snakes, Manasa Devi, about whom there are many legends, some of which are linked to the figure of a merchant. You may remember that I once gave you a piece I'd written about one of those legends.'

'*Sì, mi ricordo.* Go on.'

'The strange thing about this little temple is that the legend that's associated with it was never written down or published – it was only meant to be passed down from mouth to mouth. Apparently there was some kind of prohibition on putting the legend in writing.'

'That's not so unusual,' said Cinta. 'There are many secret legends and stories.'

'But if the story is meant to be a secret then why build a shrine to it? Doesn't it defeat the purpose?'

'Not necessarily,' said Cinta. 'There could be many reasons why whoever built the shrine wouldn't want the story to be written down.'

'Like what?'

Cinta smiled cryptically. 'Maybe they believed the story wasn't over – that it would reach out into the future?'

'I don't get that, Cinta,' I said. 'I don't see how a legend could reach out into the future. After all, it's just a story . . .'

She stopped me with a rap on the knuckles.

'You must never use that phrase, Dino,' she said slowly and deliberately. 'In the seventeenth century no one would ever have said of something that it was "just a story" as we moderns do.

At that time people recognized that stories could tap into dimensions that were beyond the ordinary, beyond the human even. They knew that only through stories was it possible to enter the most inward mysteries of our existence where nothing that is really important can be proven to exist – like love, or loyalty, or even the faculty that makes us turn around when we feel the gaze of a stranger or an animal. Only through stories can invisible or inarticulate or silent beings speak to us; it is they who allow the past to reach out to us.'

'Aren't you exaggerating a bit, Cinta?'

'No, *caro*, no. You mustn't underestimate the power of stories. There is something in them that is elemental and inexplicable. Haven't you heard it said that what makes us human, what separates us from animals, is the faculty of storytelling?'

I nodded. 'Yes, I have.'

'But what if the truth were even stranger? What if it were the other way around? What if the faculty of storytelling were not specifically human but rather the last remnant of our animal selves? A vestige left over from a time before language, when we communicated as other living beings do? Why else is it that only in stories do animals speak? Not to speak of demons, and gods, and indeed God himself? It is only through stories that the universe can speak to us, and if we don't learn to listen you may be sure that we will be punished for it.'

I shifted uneasily in my seat, recalling those months in Brooklyn when I had been haunted by the feeling that something that had long lain dormant in the mud of the Sundarbans had entered me. Then an image flashed past my eyes, of that snake tumbling down through the skies, and as if by instinct I threw up my hands to shield my face.

'What's the matter, *caro*?' said Cinta. 'What just happened?'

'Oh, nothing, Cinta, nothing.'

I couldn't bring myself to tell her about what had happened on the plane the day before. What could I say anyway? That I was having nightmares about snakes? That I had been arrested for disruptive behaviour on a plane? What could she possibly think except that I was losing my mind?

'It's just that I haven't been too well of late.'

'Yes I can see that.' She looked at me closely and then leaned back in her seat.

'I think you have been working too hard, *caro*,' she said. 'Come, let us take a break from this conference. My cousin's daughter Gisella is here from Rome – did I ever tell you about her? Gisa, as we call her, is a very interesting girl. She makes documentary films for television and has won some major prizes. She lives in Trastevere, in Rome, with her girlfriend, and they have adopted two orphaned refugees – a six-year-old girl from Syria and a boy of seven from Eritrea. Now they are all here, in California: Imma, Gisa's partner, does something big with computers, and her company has asked her to spend this year in LA. They have taken a house near Venice Beach.'

Cinta gave a laugh. 'Venice Beach! Isn't that wonderful? Do you know that I have never been there – a Venetian who hasn't seen Venice Beach! But today –' she paused to tap my hand with a forefinger, for emphasis – 'Gisa has asked me to come for an *aperitivo*: and you must come with me of course! We will skip the conference dinner – they are always very boring. Venice Beach will be more *divertente*, no?'

She patted my hand. 'You will like Gisa, *caro*. I am very fond of her: she was about the same age as my Lucia and they were very close. It is always nice for me to see her.'

At the end of the day's sessions I called an Uber to take us to the address that Gisa had sent to Cinta. The driver dropped us off at a charming house in a canal-crossed neighbourhood adjacent to Venice Beach: Gisa's partner was still at work when we arrived so it was Gisa who greeted us at the door.

She was in her mid thirties, slim, willowy, and dressed in dark trousers and a baggy black sweater. She had a silver ring in her left nostril and her short, platinum-blonde hair had streaks that matched her pink eyeglasses. She spoke very fast, often outrunning her own thoughts, slipping unselfconsciously between Italian and English, and gesturing all the while with her slim, eloquent fingers.

That day it was clear from the start that Gisa was on edge. And with good reason too: barely had she opened the door before her adopted children burst out of the house, followed by an excitable young Labrador who almost knocked Cinta over. The children were a lively, high-spirited pair and Gisa had to chase them around the yard for several minutes before she finally succeeded in herding them back inside. The dog, Leola, was the most recalcitrant and had to be literally pushed in: 'Leola! *Calmati!*'

By the end of it Gisa was panting and full of apologies: they weren't always like this, it was just that she had kept the children home from school because of concerns about the air quality. There was too much smoke in the air, for one, but she also did not want to be separated from them at a time when wildfires were raging just a few miles away. She had been caught in a similar situation the year before, she told us, during a vacation in Sicily. They had been sitting on a sun-drenched beach when the police had suddenly appeared to tell them that a wildfire had broken out nearby and was moving rapidly in their direction. In the ensuing melee she had been separated from her daughter for several agonizing minutes. It was not an experience that she wanted to repeat.

All of this poured out of her while we were still outside.

'I think the smoke is better now,' Gisa said, anxiously scanning the sky. '*Non è vero?* Soon we can walk down to the beach. But first come in and have an aperitivo.'

'Or why don't we go to the beach first?' said Cinta. 'It will be sunset soon and it may get too dark later.'

Gisa nodded in agreement and we set off after a few minutes, with the children running ahead with the dog. The sun was setting by the time we got to the beach and it looked empty and rather forlorn, with only a few runners and joggers dotting the broad, seemingly endless runway of sand. Gisa thought that it was the smoke that had kept people away – yet the air was fresher here than elsewhere, with a nice crisp breeze blowing in from the sea. Nor was that distant tsunami of smoke visible from the beach; the dark wave that I had seen the day before was obscured by a haze.

Leola, the retriever, was eager to go into the water, so the children ran ahead, throwing a stick into the waves for her to fetch. The dog clearly loved the game. She watched the stick as though her life depended on it; her eyes stayed riveted on it even as she was plunging into the waves in pursuit – in a dozen throws she did not once fail to bring back the stick.

Then all of a sudden, as she was on her way back to shore with the stick in her mouth, she came to an abrupt halt in about a foot of water. Dropping the stick, she gave a couple of excited barks while snapping at whatever it was that had attracted her attention.

The children cupped their hands around their mouths and shouted to the dog to come back. But Leola paid them no heed and kept dipping her snout in the water. Then she raised her head again and we saw that there was something hanging from her mouth, something that seemed to be alive and writhing.

Gisa was already running as the dog stepped towards the shore. Leola had barely reached the sand when she collapsed and dropped the thing that was in her mouth.

Gisa's adopted son was the first to approach the dog and he began to scream: '*Serpente! Serpente!*' Gisa was only a step behind him; grabbing his shirt she pulled him back.

When Cinta and I caught up, a few seconds later, Gisa was cradling the dog's head in her lap. Her children were crouching around her, crying uncontrollably. A couple of feet away lay a two-foot snake; its colour was darkly metallic with a bright yellow underbelly. It was dead, its head crushed to a pulp.

A couple of red-suited lifeguards appeared beside us now and they took the situation in at a glance.

'Did the dog get bit? By that snake?'

'Yes,' said Cinta. 'It must have bitten her as she was chewing up its head.'

'Too bad,' said the guard. 'What you've got over there is a yellow-bellied sea snake; its venom's lethal.'

'A sea snake?' I said. 'Are they common around here?'

'Didn't used to be,' said the guard. 'But we've had a bunch of yellow-bellies washing up here in the last few months. Wish I knew where the hell they're coming from.'

The guards carried the dog to the boardwalk while Gisa called her partner and Cinta tried to comfort the children. There was an agonizing wait as the dog lay moaning and twitching on the boardwalk. Fortunately the campus where Imma, Gisa's partner, worked was nearby and she was able to run over in a few minutes. She lost no time in taking charge of the situation, quickly summoning an Uber to take them to the vet.

Cinta and I waved them off and then stood on the sidewalk for a few minutes, trying to catch our breath. I was thinking of calling an Uber when I spotted a taxi approaching and flagged it down.

'Come, Cinta, let's go back to the hotel.'

The wildfires had caused so much disruption that we were soon trapped in bumper-to-bumper traffic: the driver warned us that it might take us two hours or more to reach the hotel.

An hour later, as we sat idling on an expressway, Cinta's phone rang; it was Gisa. They had a long talk, in low voices.

Cinta was in tears when she got off the phone.

'*Non posso crederci*,' she said, brushing a hand across her eyes. 'I don't believe it. The dog is dead, of a snake bite! Here in LA.'

'And how are the children?'

'They're all right. I imagine they've seen worse.'

'And Gisa?'

'She's shaken.'

I nodded. 'That's only to be expected. It must have been very upsetting, to see her pet die like that.'

'It wasn't just that.'

'Then?'

'Something strange happened while the dog was dying.'

'Go on.'

Cinta bit her lip. 'I told you, didn't I, that Gisa was very close to my daughter, Lucia?'

'Yes, you mentioned that.'

'Gisa said she felt Lucia was there today, with her, just a little while ago . . .'

Cinta began to dab her eyes, and we were silent for a while, staring at the inferno-like landscape ahead of us where towering columns of flame were advancing upon orderly, neatly designed neighbourhoods.

Then Cinta said in a whisper: 'You know, I feel it too, some-times.'

'What?'

'Lucia's presence. I feel that she is there, beside me. It is very comforting.'

'And do you ever hear her voice? Like you did that time in Salzburg?'

Cinta nodded. 'I did – just one other time.'

'When? Where?'

'A few years after Giacomo and Lucia died. The investigation into the accident was dragging on, with no end in sight. Everyone knew that nothing would come of it – it was all just smoke and mirrors, or as we say *specchietti per le allodole*, "mirrors for larks". The politicians and policemen were either afraid for their lives, or they were in the Mafia's pocket. As time went on my faith in things began to erode until I no longer believed in anything – and I missed Giacomo and Lucia so much that the pain became unbearable and I no longer wanted to live. I almost stopped eating and one day, in that weakened state, it happened that I got wet in the rain and fell ill with pneumonia. To me it was like a deliverance and I embraced my sickness hoping that I would be carried quickly away. But while I was in the hospital – I can still see the room, with its neon lights and a table filled with bouquets – one day I heard Lucia's voice quite clearly. I couldn't see her but I had a sense that she was standing by a window, beside the curtain. She said: "Mamma, mamma – what is this you're doing to yourself? This is not your time, you must fight to stay alive. You must not give in like this: something will happen to renew your faith in the world – you must believe me. Until then you must live and wait – for my sake if not yours. Because if you die now, neither you nor I will ever find peace."'

Cinta's voice faded away and she gave me a halting smile.

'It was a dream, perhaps, or maybe a hallucination. But anyway here I am, still waiting.'

It occurred to me, later that evening, that I knew only one person who might be able to shed some light on the incident at Venice Beach: Piya.

On an impulse I went to my laptop and wrote her an email describing what had happened and asking if she knew of any similar occurrences.

The message sounded a little brusque when I read it over so I added a couple of lines, asking about Tipu.

I didn't know where Piya was and didn't expect to hear back soon, if at all, since she was probably in some distant time zone. But my message reached her in Oregon and she wrote back within fifteen minutes.

Weird coincidence, she said, she had come upon a newspaper article about yellow-bellied sea snakes just the day before (she included the link, which was about an incident in Ventura Beach, California). These snakes generally lived in warmer waters, to the south, but sightings in southern California had become increasingly common: their distribution was changing with the warming of the oceans and they were migrating northwards. This was bad news for southern California because yellow-bellies were indeed extremely venomous – but fortunately fatalities were vanishingly rare. My friend's dog had been very unlucky.

'As for Tipu, thanks for asking about him. He's still in Bangalore and seems to be doing well. He's been very good about staying in touch with Moyna – she says he often calls and sends pictures of himself.'

The message continued: 'And I don't know if you heard about what happened to that temple you visited? There was a bad storm a couple of months ago and it was swept away. I'd been meaning to go see it but I guess it wasn't meant to happen. There's nothing left of it now.'

The message ended with a sunburst of emojis and 'Take care, and let's hope you don't run into any more snakes!'

Gun Island

Cinta's talk was the closing event of the conference and there wasn't an empty seat in the hall when it began.

It wasn't just her books, and her position as Professoressa Emerita at the Università di Padova, that made Cinta such a draw: over the years she had also become an exceptionally compelling speaker. Her rich, rasping voice, her operatic accent and her manner, at once theatrical and impulsive, were the perfect complements of her erudition, and she knew exactly how to use them to the best advantage. Standing on a podium, with her fine features framed by a halo of brilliantly white hair, Cinta often made an unforgettable impression – and so she did that day as she spoke to us about the historical background of Shakespeare's Venice.

A real-life counterpart of Shylock, Cinta told us, would have lived in Venice's Jewish enclave, which dated back to the year 1541, when the Venetian Republic had enacted a law allowing Jews to settle in the city on condition that they wore distinctive clothing, did not consort freely with Christians and lived on an island of their own, in the interior.

Here a large map of Venice appeared on a drop-down screen and Cinta turned to it with a laser pointer: 'You see,' she said, 'this is the *sestiere* – the district – of Cannaregio, in the north-east of Venice. And here –' now the glowing red dot of the pointer moved a little – 'is the island in question. Since Venice is itself an island – or rather an archipelago of islands – the old ghetto is an island within an island, as you can see.'

The phrase 'island within an island' startled me. Where had I heard it before?

A couple of minutes went by before I recalled the curious symbol I had seen on the walls of the Gun Merchant's shrine, of two concentric circles.

'*Dwiper bhetorey dwip*,' Rafi had said, 'an island within an island . . .'

I leaned forward, listening intently as Cinta continued. The island that was allotted to the Jews, she said, had previously been a foundry where armaments, including bullets, were cast. The word for foundry in the old Venetian dialect was *getto* and this had become the name of the city's Jewish settlement. Not only would this settlement become a great centre of Jewish learning, it would also lead to the coining of certain words, of which *ghetto* was only one.

Now, resting an elbow on the podium, Cinta leaned forward: 'Remember that the merchants who lived in the ghetto of Venice traded with the Levant, Egypt and North Africa; many were fluent in Arabic. *Secondo me*, it was through them that my city came to occupy a curious place in the *vocabolario* of classical Arabic: in that language Venice is linked to three apparently unrelated things – hazelnuts, bullets and guns! I say "apparently" because of course the shape of hazelnuts is similar to that of bullets which are, in turn, indispensable for guns! In any event, all three are known in Arabic by a word that derives from the Byzantine name for Venice, which was "Banadiq" – the ancestor of the German and Swedish "Venedig". In Arabic "Banadiq" became "al-Bunduqeyya", which still remains the proper name for Venice in that language. But *bunduqeyya* is also the word for guns, hazelnuts and bullets – and the latter, I like to think, were cast precisely in the foundry of the old *getto*!'

Here she paused for a moment, and then, like a magician who is about to pull a rabbit out of a hat, she made a dramatic gesture.

'And through Arabic the name of Venice has travelled far afield, to Persia and parts of India, where to this day guns are known as *bundook* – which is, of course, none other than "Venice" or "Venetian"!'

It sometimes happens that the circuitry of the brain establishes a connection that creates a jolt like that of an electric shock. That was what happened to me at this point in Cinta's talk. Was it possible that I had completely misunderstood the name 'Bonduki Sadagar'? Could it be that its meaning was not 'The Gun Merchant', as I had thought, but rather, 'The Merchant who went to Venice'?

I must have gasped audibly for many heads turned to look at me. Flushed with embarrassment, I rose to my feet and stumbled out of the hall.

My abrupt exit did not escape Cinta's attention. Later, at the closing party, she took me aside.

'Dino! I saw you walk out of my talk,' she said, putting a hand on my sleeve. 'What happened, *caro*? Are you not well?'

'It's not that,' I mumbled awkwardly. 'It's just that you touched on something that startled me.'

'What? *Dimmi!*'

I cast a glance around the crowded, noisy room. 'Can we go outside? I can hardly hear myself in here.'

'*Certo*, let's go to the garden.'

Helping ourselves to glasses of wine, we went outside, to the hotel's garden, and found ourselves a secluded bench.

'So tell me then,' said Cinta. 'What is it?'

I gulped down some wine and took a deep breath. 'You know that shrine I was telling you about? In the Sundarbans?'

'*Sì*. Go on.'

'There's a legend associated with it – but as I told you, it was never written down and all that survives of it are a few fragments. What I knew of it led me to assume that it was just a kind of wonder tale about fantastic places and people – something that had no connection with reality. But some of the things I've heard at this conference – first from the opening speaker, and then from you today – have made me wonder whether there might not be more to the story than I had thought.'

'Why exactly?'

'Well for one thing the central figure in the legend is called Bonduki Sadagar – which I had interpreted to mean "Gun Merchant". I guess that's how I'll always think of him – but after listening to your talk I realized that it could also mean something quite different. Maybe it means "The Merchant who visited Venice".'

Cinta's eyes widened and she stared at me for a moment.

'What else do you know about this legend?'

'Not much, I'm afraid.'

'Tell me what you know, everything.'

She listened to me intently as I sketched the outlines of the story. Even before I had finished she began to nod: 'You are right, I think. Your Gun Merchant's name probably *is* a reference to Venice, not to guns.'

She frowned and tapped her chin with her forefinger. 'But still, I am not sure what you have in mind. Are you suggesting that the story is an apocryphal record of a real journey to Venice?'

'That thought did cross my mind,' I said, 'but there are too many arguments against it, all those fantastical place names for instance. What can you make of the Land of Palm Sugar Candy and the Land of Kerchieves? Don't they sound like items from a book of marvels?'

Cinta closed her eyes. '*Forse, forse* . . . but tell me: what are the actual names of these places, in Bangla? Do you remember?'

'Yes I do,' I said. 'The name that I translated as the "Land of Palm Sugar Candy" was *Taal-misrir-desh*. *Desh* is "country" in Bengali, and *taal* is a kind of palm tree that produces a sugary syrup which is used to make all kinds of sweets including a crystallized candy. I translated the phrase as "palm sugar candy" because the Bengali word for "sugar candy" is *misri*.'

'*O caro mio!*' Cinta gave a deep, rumbling laugh. 'This is indeed a marvel, but not of the kind you imagined.'

'What do you mean?'

'Do you not know that "Misr" is but the Arabic word for Egypt? *Misri* or *masri* just means "Egyptian" – perhaps crystallized sugar is known as *misri* because the process had come to Bengal by way of Egypt?'

I gazed at her, dumbfounded.

'*Non è possibile?*' she continued. 'Maybe your Sugar Candy Land is just a reference to Egypt?'

'Why . . . yes,' I stuttered. 'I suppose it's possible – the Gun Merchant and Nakhuda Ilyas would certainly have had to go through Egypt in order to reach the Mediterranean . . .'

The solving of the first puzzle had whetted Cinta's appetite. She cut me off impatiently: 'And the other country they passed through?' she said. 'What was that called?'

'The Land of Kerchieves? In the legend it was called *Rumaali-desh*. In Bengali *rumaal* is a handkerchief . . .'

A triumphant cry burst from Cinta's lips: 'Hah! But nothing could be more clear! Of course! That too is a place.'

'What place?'

'Have you not heard of Rumelia? Or of the fort of Rumeli-Hisari?'

I shook my head. 'No? Where is it?'

'In Turkey.'

I gasped. 'Turkey? Really?'

'Yes, *caro*, Turkey. Why do you look so . . . so *sbigottito*? You're shivering.'

I took a deep breath. 'Oh, it's nothing. Go on. Where is this fort?'

'On the outskirts of Istanbul, where the Turks built their first stronghold in Europe. *Rumeli* comes from "Rum", "Rome" – which is how Constantinople, the Byzantine "Rome", was known in Arabic and Persian. The *Rumaali* of your story is probably just a corruption of some version of "Rum" – does it not make sense that the Gun Merchant and Captain Ilyas would have gone from Egypt to Turkey? And wait a minute . . .'

She stopped to rub the tip of her nose: '*È vero* – did you say they were expelled from that land because of a fire?'

I answered with a nod, and she cried out. 'See! Now you even have a date!'

'How?'

'There was a great fire in Istanbul in 1660 – do you not remember what our opening speaker said the other day? A terrible drought had turned Istanbul into a tinderbox and in July 1660 a huge fire broke out in the city, killing forty thousand people and destroying hundreds of thousands of houses. Two-thirds of the city was immolated, and the Jewish neighbourhoods were particularly badly hit. It was a great *catastrofe* because afterwards fanatics placed the blame on the Jews. Many were expelled and a good number came to settle in Venice.'

Cinta took a sip of her wine: '*Che peccato* . . . such a pity that we don't know anything more about this Captain Ilyas. It would be interesting to have a few clues about who he was and where he was from.'

'Wait a minute!' I said, suddenly recalling a detail. 'There is one little clue. On the walls of the shrine, the figure of Captain Ilyas was often paired with a little symbol – a sign I didn't recognize.'

'*Davvero?* Draw it for me.'

I pulled a pen and a paper napkin out of my jacket pocket and closed my eyes, trying to visualize the symbol.

'It looked something like this,' I said.

I handed her the napkin and shone a light on it, with my cellphone.

Putting on her glasses, she peered at the napkin for a moment. 'Why,' she said, 'I think . . . *no, sono sicura!* – yes, I am sure – it's an aleph, the first letter of the Hebrew alphabet! It is all clear now – the Captain was a Jew! The name 'Ilyas' was common among Eastern Jews at that time – and in Hebrew the name begins with an aleph!'

Cinta clapped her hands in childlike delight. 'Sì! Now – all of it begins to make sense! Did you not say that the Gun Merchant was sold to Captain Ilyas by Portuguese pirates?'

'Yes – that was the story.'

'Ah!' She ran a fingertip ruminatively around the top of her wineglass. 'Now, if a seventeenth-century Portuguese pirate had picked up a few captives in the Bay of Bengal, where would he go to sell them? The answer is obvious: Goa, which was the capital of the Portuguese Empire in Asia as well as a hub of the Indian Ocean slave trade.'

She laughed again. 'So you see, Dino, maybe this is not just a wonder tale. The outlines of the story are historically quite plausible. The protagonist is a merchant, whose homeland, in eastern India, is struck by drought and floods brought on by the climatic disturbances of the Little Ice Age; he loses everything including his family, and decides to go overseas to recoup his fortune. On the way his ship is attacked and he is captured by Portuguese pirates who take him to Goa and put him up for sale, as a slave. He is bought by a well-travelled trader and sailor, Ilyas, who recognizes his qualities and sets him free. Ilyas is by origin a Portuguese Jew; his family had come to Goa to escape the Inquisition in Portugal. But now the Inquisition has come to Goa too, so he has decided to leave again and the Gun Merchant decides to accompany him. They set off in Ilyas's ship and go first to the Maldive Islands where they acquire a cargo of cowrie shells. *Poi* they go to Egypt, only to find that it is also convulsed by the "general crisis" of the seventeenth century. The government is split between two warring factions, the economy is under strain, it is not a good time for merchants. So Ilyas and his protégé set off for Istanbul, the capital of the Ottoman Empire, which has long been a safe haven for Jews like Ilyas. But there too, trouble is brewing. The land is in the grip of a fearsome drought; strange messianic figures have emerged. Suspicion stalks the streets of Istanbul, and when a great fire breaks out the finger of blame lands upon the Jewish community. So Ilyas decides that he and his protégé are not safe and must leave again, this time for Venice.'

She made a sweeping gesture, like a conjuror picking something out of the air. '*Ecco!* You have your legend!'

But I was still unconvinced.

'I don't see why Nakhuda Ilyas would have taken the Merchant with him to Italy. Wouldn't a dark-skinned Bengali man have stood out in Venice?'

Cinta's eyes sparkled, brightly enough to pierce the gathering darkness. '*Ah tesoro, non ti ricordi?* Remember Othello? Your Merchant would not have been the first, or last, dark-skinned man in Venice. It was then the most cosmopolitan place in the world. Visitors from other parts of Europe always commented on how many foreigners there were in Venice – including people from the Levant, North Africa, Mali. That was why Shakespeare set those two plays in Venice – it was the only plausible setting for characters like Shylock and Othello.'

Even as I was conceding this, another objection occurred to me: 'But what about the cowrie shells?' I said. 'What use would they be in Venice?'

'They would fetch money, of course! Cowries were for centuries an important article of trade in Venice. They served as a currency in the Malian Empire and at that time Venice was the most important trans-shipment port for that part of Africa. In the seventeenth century the demand for cowries began to rise because they were used for the Atlantic slave trade. It was a time when large quantities of cowries were flowing through the markets of Venice – our heroes could have found no better place to dispose of their shells.'

Her explanation left me scratching my head. 'I still don't understand, Cinta. Why would a roving sea captain like Nakhuda Ilyas want to settle in a ghetto?'

'*Caro,*' she said gently, 'perhaps you have misunderstood the term – the *getto* of Venice was not like the ghettoes of Eastern Europe. Even though Jews were segregated in Venice, they were safer and freer there than anywhere else in Christendom. The place is not as you might think – have you not seen it?'

'No, I don't remember having seen the Ghetto.'

'Well, then you must come back to Venice – to Banadiq. That is obvious I think. You visited me there once didn't you?'

'Yes, a long time ago. I stayed in your apartment.'

'Then you must come back again. Whatever this is, you must follow it through. Don't think of it as something unfortunate that has befallen you. Think of it as an ordeal at the end of which there may be a reward, maybe even just something that will bring you peace of mind. And you are not alone in this. I will be with you too – all the way.'

I knew, from the intensity of her voice, that she was trying to reassure me. But her words had the opposite effect: I felt exhausted and completely out of my depth.

'But what *can* I do to see it through, Cinta? I have no idea.'

'Well you won't know until you come back to Venice.' She reached for my hand and gave it a squeeze. 'Promise me that you will come? You will stay in my apartment of course – it is very close to the *getto*. This time we will make sure that you see it.'

It was impossible to say no. 'I promise,' I said. 'I'll come to Bundook as soon as I can get my business affairs in order.'

My promise to Cinta was not idly made; at that time I certainly meant what I said. But once I was back in New York, ensconced in my apartment, the idea of going to Venice began to seem increasingly implausible. What would be the point of it? What could I possibly hope to find there? I had bills to pay and work to do. I hadn't made a major sale in a long time and had no money coming in. I had already been forced to dip into my 'rainy day' account and could not afford to deplete it further. Venice was sure to be hugely expensive; going there was beyond the means of someone who made his living by hawking wares that nobody seemed to want any more.

As the days passed I began to worry more and more about my finances. Soon I was thinking of little else: I would obsessively check the accounts in which my savings were invested; I would spend hours on the phone, rebalancing my funds and making minute adjustments to my portfolio. And every time I made a change messages would appear on my screen suggesting some new fund or some new strategy for saving still more.

These messages in turn would generate others, some of which exhorted me to consider how long my savings would last if I lived for another twenty, thirty or forty years. Terrifying actuarial figures would scroll down the screen suggesting, very discreetly, that I was heading towards destitution and homelessness.

Some years before I had paid a nostalgic visit to the Midwestern town where I had once studied and worked. Memories of that trip now came back to haunt me. I had been away from the town a long time and was unprepared for the changes that had befallen it: the whole region had been devastated by factory closings and was now a part of the Rust Belt. The damage had been compounded by a recent banking crisis. I drove past the house where I had once lived (paying a rent beyond my means simply because the neighbourhood had reminded me of the

Archie comics I had read, as a child, in Calcutta) and I found the street, with its winding, leafy, picture-perfect curves, festooned with FOR SALE signs: I was told that a wave of evictions, enforced by a bank of near murderous rapacity, had left many of my former neighbours homeless and that some of them had even been reduced to sleeping under sheets of cardboard on the corner of Jefferson and Main, where they subsisted by begging quarters off drunken Chinese and Arab students as they stumbled out of the High Plains Bar and Grill.

Now, staring at my dwindling savings, I began to wonder whether this was the fate that awaited me.

Searching for answers, I immersed myself in the statistics and probabilities that were constantly thrust upon me by anonymous robo-messages: how long would I live? How many years would my savings last if I had to be committed to a nursing home?

What if I lived to ninety-five; did I have enough insurance?

I keyed in the question and stared in alarm at the numbers that appeared before me: the odds were good enough that I felt compelled to reach for my credit card. But no sooner had I paid for the extra insurance than another window popped up, displaying the odds of my living to one hundred and three – and I saw, to my dismay, that they were no smaller than those of a passer-by being hit by an icicle falling off my windowsill. And since that was a possibility against which I was already insured, I could think of no good reason not to reach for my credit card again.

But even that brought me no peace of mind: it was as if I were tumbling down a rabbit hole of mathematical uncertainty. I fell into a kind of paralysis, a state of drawn-out, perpetual panic.

In my occasional moments of lucidity it would occur to me that the only thing that could lift me out of this funk – or depression, or whatever it was called – was to talk to Cinta. But months and months went by and there was neither a call nor a message from her – and the embarrassment and guilt of having reneged on my promise to visit her in Venice weighed so heavily on me that nor could I bring myself to call her.

Sometimes when my phone rang I would glance at the screen, hoping to see the code for Italy. But it was always either a bill collector or a recorded message from some huckstering politician, or a robo-call in Chinese.

But then one day my cellphone rang, and there it was, the code for Italy: + 39. I snatched up the device thinking I would hear Cinta's voice at the other end.

But no: to my great surprise it was Gisa, Cinta's niece.

After we had exchanged a few pleasantries Gisa told me that she was working on a new documentary, commissioned by a consortium of television channels. It was about the recent wave of crossings into Italy, across the mountains and from the far sides of the Mediterranean and the Adriatic.

'You have been following, yes, how thousands of *rifugiati* are coming across the sea, in boats, from Libya and Egypt? Some have been rescued but many have died.'

The truth was that I had paid scarce attention to the news of late and was only dimly aware of this phenomenon. 'I don't know much about it I'm afraid.'

'Over here, in Italy – no, in Europe – everyone is talking about the *rifugiati* and *immigrati*. Our new right-wing government came to power because they promised to be tough on migration. This has now become the biggest political issue across Europe, so everyone wants to know about it. Why are the migrants coming, in such dangerous circumstances? What are they fleeing? What are their hopes? That is why a documentary is necessary.'

'I can see that it's an important project,' I said. 'But I'm not sure that I can be of any help.'

'Oh yes you can,' said Gisa. 'You see – I need a translator and Cinta suggested you. It was she who gave me your number; she thought you might be able to do it.'

'Me?' I said in surprise. 'But I don't think I have the necessary languages. Aren't the refugees mainly from the Middle East and Africa?'

'Most of them are, yes,' said Gisa. 'But there are also many from Pakistan and Bangladesh. *In realtà* last month Bangladeshis were the second largest group coming into Italy.'

'Really? I had no idea.'

'And you speak Bangla, *vero*?'

'Yes, certainly.'

'Yes, Cinta told me. This is why I called you. I have already done many interviews around the country but now I am going to Venice and I was thinking that you could join me there.'

Her train of thought baffled me. 'I don't follow. Are you telling me that you need a Bengali translator in Venice, of all places?'

'Yes. In Venice there are many, many Bengalis. *Tantissimi!*'

I was dumbstruck. 'Is that true? There are many Bengalis in Venice?'

'Yes, it is true. Bengalis have been settling in the Veneto for a long time. Earlier they came to work in the shipyards of Mestre and Marghera. But now many more have come and in Venice they do everything – they make the pizzas for the tourists, they clean the hotels, they even play the accordion at street corners.'

'Amazing. I had no idea.'

'So will you come? Of course we will buy your ticket and pay for your services. There is also a per diem for hotels, meals and so on. But Cinta said you could stay in her apartment so you will not need to spend that money. Altogether it will come to maybe as much as . . .' She named a sum that sounded positively princely to me. 'And maybe you could come early and have a little time to yourself in Venice, so that you can look around and get over jet lag?'

I was so moved that my eyes filled with tears.

'How could I possibly say no to that? And I hope Cinta will be there too?'

'*Purtroppo, no!* Unfortunately she is teaching for the next few weeks. But Padova isn't far and I'm sure she will join us at some point.'

'Wonderful! Thank you for calling, Gisa. This is the best phone call I've had in years.'

She laughed. '*A presto!*'

The ticket arrived next morning, by email, and I boarded a plane a few days later. I had reserved a window seat for myself, as usual, even though the flight was a red-eye.

The sun was up when the plane began its descent and when I turned to look out of the window I found myself gazing down at a sight that reminded me of the patch of Bengal countryside that I had glimpsed on my last flight out of Calcutta, a little more than two years before: an estuarine landscape of lagoons, marshes and winding rivers.

From that height it was possible to mistake the Venetian lagoon for the Sundarbans.

Part II

Venice

The Ghetto

That there is a strange kinship between Venice and Varanasi has often been noted: both cities are like portals in time; they seem to draw you into lost ways of life. And in both cities, as nowhere else in the world, you become aware of mortality. Everywhere you look there is evidence of the enchantment of decay, of a kind of beauty that can only be revealed by long, slow fading.

The kinship of the two cities is nowhere more apparent than in Venice's *getto*: the walls that surround it, the narrow entrances that lead to it, and the slender, crooked houses – all of this reminded me of a part of Varanasi that I particularly love: the area around the Bindu Madhav temple, near Panchganga Ghat. There too you find seclusion and serenity in the midst of noisy multitudes; there too you have a sense of being amidst a community that follows age-old customs, unobserved by the world.

But there is one important difference: the Ghetto of Venice really is an island within an island, surrounded by water on all sides. An arched wooden bridge leads to a tunnel-like entrance, and this in turn opens into a large piazza, enclosed by tall houses and a wall. This square is relatively uncrowded; small groups of tourists sweep through from time to time, like leaves in a gale, but otherwise the place gives the impression of being home to many full-time residents. Washing can be seen, fluttering on lines that stretch between windows, and children of all ages are much in evidence, careening around on bicycles and skateboards.

Sitting on a bench, in a corner, I made an effort to imagine the square as it might have looked, three and a half centuries earlier, trying to envision it as it would have appeared to a traveller from Bengal. I tried to think of the Gun Merchant treading on those cobblestones, surrounded by people in red and yellow headgear – the colours enjoined on the inhabitants of the Ghetto by Venetian law, to mark them out as non-Christians. Warmed by the sun I began to daydream and suddenly the Gun Merchant seemed to appear before my eyes, tall, broad-shouldered, with a yellow turban, walking unhurriedly past on some errand. He glanced at me as he went by and his eyes were clear and untroubled. I could see why he would feel safe here, beyond the reach of Manasa Devi and the creatures and forces that she commanded. This, if any, was a place that would seem to be secure from non-human intrusion: apart from a few ornamental trees and plants there was almost nothing in sight that was not made by human hands. Here surely the Gun Merchant would have known himself to be beyond his tormentor's grasp – yet, here too Manasa Devi had managed to reach him.

How?

What sort of wild creature could intrude upon a place like this?

As I was asking myself these questions a strange thing happened; I seemed to slip through an opening, or a membrane, so that I wasn't looking at the Merchant's predicament from his own point of view but rather from the perspective of his pursuer, the goddess herself. And then the pursuit no longer seemed to be a story of an almost incomprehensible vindictiveness but something more fraught, and even tender, a search driven by fear and desperation.

I remembered my readings of the Merchant legends of Bengal and how inapt the word 'goddess' had seemed to me in relation to the depiction of Manasa Devi in these epics. 'Goddess' conjures up an image of an all-powerful deity whose every command is obeyed by her subjects. But the Manasa

Devi of the legend was by no means a 'goddess' in this sense; snakes were not so much her subjects as her constituents; to get them to do her bidding she had to plead, cajole, persuade. She was in effect a negotiator, a translator – or better still a *portavoce* – as the Italians say, 'a voice-carrier' between two species that had no language in common and no shared means of communication. Without her mediation there could be no relationship between animal and human except hatred and aggression.

But an intermediary must, after all, command the trust of both the sides for which she is mediating. How can a translator do her job if one side chooses to ignore her? And why would her constituents obey her if they knew that those she was addressing on their behalf – the Merchant and his fellow humans – had refused to acknowledge her voice? Hence the urgency of her search for the Merchant: for if he, and others like him, were to disavow her authority then all those unseen boundaries would vanish, and humans – driven, as was the Merchant, by the quest for profit – would recognize no restraint in relation to other living things. This was why the Merchant had to be found; this was why his attempts at concealment had to be thwarted at all costs . . .

My daydream was interrupted by a ball that rolled up to the bench and bumped into my shoes. Picking it up I tossed it to the little girl who was running behind it – and then it was as if a spell had been broken. I couldn't understand why I was sitting there, conjuring up imaginary scenarios based on nothing but some garbled fragments of a fable and a few random incidents and coincidences. It was nothing less than absurd for me to be indulging in this childlike fantasy; here I was, in one of the world's most beguiling cities, and I was wasting time on a daydream instead of sitting in a piazza, drinking a spritz, and reading James's *Aspern Papers*.

A burden seemed to slip from my shoulders now: I rose to my feet and stretched my limbs, as though I were waking from a long night's sleep. It was a moment that I wanted to remember so I took out my phone and snapped a few pictures. When my phone suggested that I post the pictures on a photo-sharing site, tagged with the date and location, I hit the send button without hesitation.

Then a wonderful aroma of garlic and olive oil came wafting through the air, stirring my appetite. I saw that lunchtime was approaching and decided to find something to eat.

There are two parts to the Ghetto of Venice: one is called the New Ghetto (Getto Nuovo) and the other is the Old Ghetto (Getto Vecchio). As with everything in the city, the relationship between the two is very complicated: predictably, the New Ghetto is actually the older of the two.

A narrow lane, with tall houses on either side, leads from the New Ghetto to the Old. That day one of the houses in the lane was under repair: a grid of scaffolding was attached to the facade and the sound of hammers was echoing through the lane.

The scaffolding occupied half the width of the lane, leaving just about enough space for one person to squeeze past it at a time. I had almost made my way through when a shout of warning burst on me, from above: '*Shabdhaan!* Careful!'

The word triggered an instinctive response and I froze. A moment later a slab of masonry came crashing down in front of me. Had I not stopped in my tracks the chunk of plaster would almost certainly have hit me on the head. I stood there shaking, knowing full well that I would probably be dead if I had taken another step.

I was gazing speechlessly at the shattered masonry, frozen in horror, when it struck me that the warning that had saved my life had been shouted in Bangla.

But how was that possible, here in the Ghetto of Venice?

I turned my gaze towards the scaffolding, and found myself looking into the dark face of a worker in a hard hat: he was perched on a crossbeam some two storeys above me.

'Was it you who dropped this?' I shouted in Bangla.

He nodded; his eyes were panic-stricken and he looked utterly aghast.

'What would have happened,' I asked, 'if I hadn't understood your warning?'

'*Maaf korben* – forgive me, sir,' he said in a faltering voice.

He was young, just a boy, with a mop of shaggy black hair spilling out of his red hat.

'You could have killed me!' I said.

'It was a mistake, sir – I've just started this job . . .'

By this time several other workers had clambered down from the scaffolding. Gathering around me they began to talk at once, in Bangladeshi-accented Bangla, murmuring apologies, trying to mollify me, and scolding the fellow who had dropped the masonry.

'Sir, you won't report him to the *questura*, will you?' one of them beseeched me.

A silence fell as they waited for my answer. In their eyes I could see an anxiety that bespoke an existence of extreme precariousness: I understood that an untoward word to the authorities could lead to the unravelling of their lives.

'No,' I said. 'I won't complain, but . . .'

They looked hugely relieved and one of them took hold of my arm.

'Why sir, you're still shaking – you should sit down somewhere and have a cup of tea or coffee.'

The miscreant was now pushed to the front. Tall and thin, he stood in front of me with his shoulders hunched, quailing.

'Go on,' said one of the older workers, elbowing him in the ribs. 'Take the gentleman to Lubna-khala's place. She'll give him some coffee and set things right.'

The youth raised his eyes now and we looked each other full in the face for the first time. His eyes widened and then he flinched and glanced away – and that was when I noticed the downturned corners of his mouth and his long-lashed eyes.

I was about to say his name when he silenced me with a beseeching glance.

It was only after we were out of earshot of the others that I uttered his name. 'Rafi?'

He was wearing the most banal of urban clothes – a T-shirt, jeans, windbreaker and sneakers – yet something still remained of his feral quality.

'Is it really you?'

He gave me a sheepish smile. 'Yes, it's me,' he said. 'But I'm glad you didn't say anything back there.'

'Why?'

'Because I would have had to explain that I had met you back in India. And then there would be many more things to explain as well.'

'Why?'

'Because you see,' he said, after an awkward pause, 'the others don't know that I grew up in India. Everyone here thinks I'm Bangladeshi. It's best to leave it like that.'

We were crossing an arched wooden bridge now and suddenly my knees began to wobble, as if in delayed shock. I recalled the sound of that slab of masonry crashing down upon the paving stones, right in front of me. It was as if a warning, or a message, had been delivered to me – but from whom?

Suddenly I remembered my exchange with Tipu about that mysterious Sanskrit root *bhu*, which means simultaneously 'being' and 'becoming' and much else as well. It seemed to me then that only a word derived from this root could account for our presence in the Ghetto: Rafi and I were both *bhutas* in the sense of being at once conjunctions and disjunctions in the continuum of time, space and being.

My breath became laboured and I came to a stop, leaning heavily against the side of the wooden bridge.

'Are you all right?' said Rafi.

'Just give me a minute,' I said. 'I need to catch my breath.

This is all too much for me . . . that accident . . . seeing you here . . . it's so strange.'

He raised an eyebrow. 'Why do you say that? Why is it so strange to see me here?'

'Don't you find it strange?'

'That I'm here? No. I've been here for some months already. Why is that strange?'

His indifference shook me, making me wonder whether I was making too much of this encounter. My eyes wandered down, to the canal below, and to the fortress-like walls of the Ghetto, and I suddenly remembered a phrase that Rafi had himself used to describe one of the recurrent motifs in the Gun Merchant's shrine – two concentric circles.

'Do you remember, Rafi, that day when we met, how you talked about an "island within an island"? What if I told you that this is exactly where that island was, and that the Bonduki Sadagar had actually been here himself?'

Rafi answered with a nonchalant shrug. 'That's just a story,' he said. 'And anyway what does it matter to me? I'm here to work and I don't want to lose my job.'

I could see that he was getting impatient but I wasn't quite ready to move on yet.

'And what about Tipu? What's his news?' I said.

Rafi's eyes flared for an instant and then his face hardened.

'Why are you asking me about Tipu?' he said testily. 'What makes you think that I would know where he is?'

The look in his eye warned me off from pressing him on this subject.

'And how about you, Rafi? What brought you here? How did you come to Venice?'

He shrugged and started to walk away, at a brisk pace. 'There's no time for all that now. It's a long story.'

Stepping off the bridge we entered a maze of narrow lanes. I had no idea where I was but Rafi seemed to be very sure of the way. I had trouble keeping up with him as he turned from one alley into another.

'Where are we going?' I said as I panted after him.

'They told me to take you to Lubna-khala. So we're going to her office.'

'And who is Lubna-khala?'

Rafi looked back, over his shoulder. 'She's a Bangladeshi lady; she's been here twenty years. She speaks Italian and everything.'

'Why do you call her *khala*? Is she your aunt?'

'No. We just call her that – because she helps us with things. She tells us about our rights under the law and things like that, so whenever there's a problem we go to her.'

He came to a stop at what seemed to be a small travel agency: taped to the window was a sign in Bangla, announcing cheap flights to Dhaka. Opening the door, Rafi let me into a cluttered little room, furnished with a desk, a monitor and a couple of chairs.

The woman who was seated at the desk rose to her feet when she saw us: she was dressed in a dark tunic and a long skirt; her head was covered by a flowered scarf. She was maybe in her early forties, with a hazel complexion, a rounded, dimpled face and large brown eyes.

Her gaze sharpened now as she looked from Rafi's face to mine and back again. '*Ki hoyechhé?*' she said in Bangla. 'What's going on?'

It was only now, I think, that Rafi properly understood that he, no less than I, had had a near miraculous escape; that if the block of plaster had hit me he would have been in a lot of trouble. His voice became unsteady and he choked several times as he described the accident.

Lubna heard him out and then gave him a stern berating: 'Get back to work now – and no more mistakes! You won't get off so lightly the next time. *Buzla?* Understand?'

Rafi nodded and let himself out, head lowered.

I would have left too had Lubna not asked me to sit for a

few minutes. I took the chair she had pointed to and she seated herself across the desk, facing me.

'I feel terrible about this incident,' she said in her lilting Bangla.

For some reason her voice evoked a sense of warmth and familiarity like I had never before experienced in an encounter with a stranger: under its spell the sense of foreboding that had gripped me just a short while ago started to recede. When Lubna began to apologize for what had happened it was I who rushed to reassure her.

'It wasn't your fault, not at all.'

'I know,' she said, 'but I feel responsible for these boys. They've no one else to turn to, you see. Some of them have only just arrived.'

'From Bangladesh?'

'Yes.'

'And is that where you're from?' I asked.

She nodded: 'And you?'

'I was born in India,' I said. 'But my family was originally from Bangladesh. They were among the Hindus who left at Partition.'

'And which part of Bangladesh were they from?'

'My mother's family was from Dhaka. My father's people were from Madaripur district.'

'Madaripur!' She gave a cry of delight. 'But that's where I'm from!'

That was when I recognized what it was in her voice that was so evocative for me.

'You know,' I said, 'you sound very much like my grandmother. She spoke the dialect of Madaripur all her life – as a child, I used to try to copy her . . .'

And even as I was speaking I could feel the intonations of that dialect seeping back into my own speech. That my memory had preserved those sounds through all those years, was so astonishing to me – and so disorienting – that I had to glance over my shoulder, at the lane beyond the window, to remind myself of where I was. I could scarcely believe that it was in Venice, after half a century, that I was speaking this tongue, the dialect of a place that I had never seen, and which I had only ever spoken with my grandparents.

'Have you ever been to Madaripur?' Lubna said.

'No. But when I was little my grandmother used to talk about Madaripur all the time. She grew up in a house near the Arialkhan river.'

Lubna's face lit up: 'Is that true? Really?'

'Yes. She often spoke of it.'

Reaching down, she pulled open a drawer.

'I want to show you something.'

After rummaging around for a minute, she withdrew a large Manila envelope and took out an old photograph.

'*Dekhun* – look!' she said. 'That's my father's house, where I grew up. Our village was right next to the Arialkhan river!'

The colours of the photograph had faded into a monochrome shade of violet: the picture was of a large family group, standing in front of a single-storey brick house with a roof of corrugated iron.

'Ours was the first pukka house in the village,' Lubna said. 'We had just moved in when this picture was taken. My father owned a shop as well as land, and he put all of us through school. I was the oldest –' she tapped her finger on the face of a smiling teenager – 'and when this picture was taken I had just gotten engaged to be married.'

She tapped the picture again: 'See, that's my husband, Munir, over there – at that time he was living in Dhaka. His family were neighbours of ours in the village – they were farmers, very simple people, but Munir was a brilliant student and he got a scholarship to study in Dhaka.'

Her finger descended on another face: 'That's Munir's father, and those little boys are his brothers. They lived over there.' She pointed to a thatched hut in the background.

Until this point she had been speaking in the cheerfully nostalgic tone in which people usually reminisce about the past.

But now a shadow fell over her face and a note of bitterness entered her voice.

'*Shob gasé!*' she said. 'Everything's gone now; the house, the people – the water's taken it all.'

'What happened?'

'A few months after this picture was taken there came a cyclone, a really fearsome *tufaan*. The winds were so strong that they carried off the roof of our house. Then the water began to rise. It kept rising till it was halfway up the walls. We had no choice but to take shelter in a tree. Somehow my brothers managed to get all of us into the branches. But then we discovered that the tree was full of snakes; they had climbed up to get away from the water, just as we had. My brothers drove some of them off, with sticks, but one of them was bitten. He fell into the floodwaters and we never saw him again. One of my nieces was bitten too – she died later that night.'

She grimaced. 'Can you imagine what it was like? Being in that tree, with the wind howling and the flood raging below, not knowing whether you would be killed by the storm or a snake?'

The photograph was still in my hands; the scene became almost unbearably real as I looked at it: I could see the faces of her family; the water below and the snakes on the branches.

'It was Munir's father who saved us,' Lubna continued. 'He came in a boat and got us out. But after that we knew we couldn't live in that village any more. We sold our land and moved to Khulna. Munir and I got married later that year and he decided that instead of wasting three years chasing a degree in Dhaka he would go overseas. It was easier in those days – he went first to Russia and then came to Italy, through Bulgaria and Yugoslavia. After receiving his papers he sent for me – that was almost twenty years ago.'

'And what does your husband do now?'

Turning away from me, she put the picture back in the envelope. Then, lowering her voice, she said: 'He died last year.'

'Oh?' I said. 'I'm sorry to hear that. May I ask what happened?'

'He was in Sicily . . . it was very sudden. We're still not sure what happened.'

I murmured a word of sympathy, but she brushed it away.

'It's all right,' she said, pursing her lips. 'Munir's younger brother is here now, so I don't feel as alone as I used to. He is working in the same construction crew as Rafi. You probably saw him there.'

She looked me in the face again and said, with a tight-lipped smile: 'These boys are very young and they've been through a lot, back home and over here. I know that you had a bad experience today, but I hope you won't hold it against them.'

'Of course I won't,' I said, with a smile. 'Luckily no harm came of it – to the contrary. I got to meet you, which was the best thing that could have happened.'

She raised an eyebrow. 'Oh? Why?'

'I should explain,' I said, 'that the reason I am in Venice is to help a friend – an Italian friend – who is making a documentary on migrants. Perhaps you could help us find some people to interview?'

A veil seemed to descend on Lubna's face. 'I'll have to think about that,' she said, hesitantly. 'It's not easy to arrange these things you know. In the first place, it's hard for these boys even to find the time – most of them work all day long, doing several different jobs. They barely get any sleep. On top of that, some of them haven't yet had their *incontro* – that's the meeting with the committee that decides on their status. And I'm sad to say there have been problems in the past for those who spoke with journalists – anything they say to the media can be used against them. You understand? And there are other problems as well. Sometimes right-wing troublemakers see things on television and get all worked up – you know how things are nowadays. We've all had to become more careful. Before, I would always help media people. But now I have become more cautious. I only help journalists if I know them really well . . .'

Her voice trailed away and she fell into a silent reverie, steepling her fingertips and staring at her desk.

'On the other hand,' she said, as though she were conducting an argument with herself, 'we have nothing to hide, and it might be good if people knew more about our lives. Perhaps they would learn to see us as ordinary human beings, with the same needs and desires as anyone else.'

Her lips curled into a smile as she came to a decision. '*Thik achhé*,' she said. 'All right then, I'll talk to some people to see if they're willing to be interviewed. In the meantime maybe you could ask around as well? Perhaps you could even start with Rafi? After all, he does owe you for not making more of a fuss about what happened today.'

She scribbled a number on a piece of paper and handed it to me. 'Rafi gets off work at four. You can call him after that. But please be careful.'

'Of course,' I said. 'Don't worry. I don't want to get them into trouble any more than you do.'

'Good. And if there's anything else I can do please let me know.'

'I will,' I said. As I was getting up I added, in a rush: 'I can't tell you what a pleasure it was to speak to you – I haven't heard the Madaripur dialect since I was a boy!'

She smiled. 'You are going to enjoy yourself in Venice then – it's full of us Madaripuris.'

'No! Really?'

She tapped my elbow. 'Come, let me show you something.'

We walked to the far end of the lane, where it joined the Rio Terà San Leonardo, a busy street, thronged with tourists and vendors.

'Look there – and there – and there,' she said, pointing first to a waiter in a café, and then a man who was selling chestnuts and another who was wheeling an ice-cream cart. 'You see,' she said, with a note of pride in her voice, 'they are all Bengalis, and many of them are from Madaripur.'

I began to listen carefully now and soon I was hearing echoes of familiar words and sounds all around me. I wandered down the street, starting conversations in Bangla almost at random: the idea that it might be possible to do this in Venice was, for me, something so novel as to be astounding. For even though Bangla is spoken by a great number of people – more than twice as many as speak German or Italian, for instance – I was not accustomed to thinking of my mother tongue as a 'global language'. Crossing paths with Bangla speakers in faraway places had always been for me a matter of pleasurable surprise, precisely because such encounters were very rare. Generally speaking you took it for granted that Bangla was a language of intimacy, to be spoken only with people you were already acquainted with – and I could tell from the expressions that passed over the faces of the Bengalis I spoke to that it was the same for them. First they would look disbelieving, as though they could not believe that someone who looked like a tourist was addressing them in Bangla. Then slowly their faces would light up and we would soon begin to exchange that immemorial question: 'Desh koi – where's home?'

Of all the gifts that Bangla had given me, this was by far the most unexpected: that it would help me find a context for myself in this unlikeliest of cities – Banadig, Bundook, Venice.

Rafi

Cinta's apartment was a ten-minute walk from the Ghetto: they were both in the same *sestiere* – Cannaregio. Cinta loved this district: she had grown up in it as had many generations of her family before her. She claimed that her father's ancestors had made their home in Cannaregio since the fifteenth century, ever since they were first brought to the city as slaves, from the far eastern reaches of the Venetian Empire. She liked to boast that only in Cannaregio was it possible any more to think of Venice as a proper city, where ordinary people lived: this was the one district that still had a substantial number of residents as opposed to tourists and transients.

Cinta's apartment had been acquired by her mother, with her Kentucky money, a few years before Cinta was born. It was on the third floor of a palazzo that was modest in everything but its location: it had the distinction of overlooking the Grand Canal. The entrance lobby even had a recessed dock, with steps and mooring posts, so that the residents could get into their gondolas without leaving the building.

When I had last stayed in Cinta's apartment, twelve years before, the palazzo's ornate gateway, overlooking the Grand Canal, had still served as the building's principal entrance. But this was no longer the case: the lobby's marble floor was now underwater much of the time. When the tide began to rise the building's *portinaio*, Marco, would lay down a wooden gangway – a *passerella* – so that the residents could cross the lobby without getting their shoes wet – but at high tide, when the water was sometimes knee deep, even the passerella was often swamped. Of late the floods had become so frequent that the residents had more or less stopped using the front entrance: they now went in and out through a walled garden at the back, where there was a small door that had once only been used by tradespeople.

Cinta's apartment faced away from the Grand Canal and looked out instead on the palazzo's backyard where wisteria and climbing roses had run wild. Beyond lay a view of winding lanes and jumbled red-tiled roofs. On clear days the peaks and ridges of the snow-covered Dolomites could be seen in the distance. Although the Grand Canal was not visible from the apartment, vaporettos could be heard from the kitchen window, as they pulled in and out of the nearby water-bus stop of San Marcuola.

The apartment was unchanged since my last visit. It had made a powerful impression on me then and it did so once again; it was the only space I had ever been in that was literally, palpably alive. This was partly due to what lay underneath the palazzo, which was not earth or rock but rather the soft mud of the Venetian lagoon, a substance that tended to shift over time, subtly changing the alignments of the buildings above. This meant that the terrazzo floors of Cinta's apartment had ripples running through them while some of the door frames were so crooked that it was impossible to shut the doors. So alive was the apartment that it even possessed its own language: at all hours creaks, groans and sighs would emanate from its corners as if to express changes of mood.

The animation of the apartment's outward shell was perfectly matched by the life that Cinta had breathed into it, a spirit that was entirely her own. Chaises longues, draped in Turkish kilims and knitted rugs, stood positioned to take advantage of the breezes and views offered by the tall windows; stuffed chairs sat invitingly in niches and corners, with intricately inlaid tables beside them, waiting for a cup of tea or a glass of wine. And everywhere the eye could go there were books, crammed into towering bookshelves, piled on tables and roll-top desks, heaped in corners and stacked against the walls.

On one of those shelves I had spotted a copy of James's *Aspern Papers*, and had been quickly drawn into it. I had intended to finish it on returning from the Ghetto, but when I opened it now I found it hard to go on. It wasn't just that the novella was about another time; it depicted a Venice in which it was impossible to imagine evocations of Madaripur, or a reunion with someone from the Sundarbans. It struck me that the Venice I had encountered today harked back to a time before that of *The Aspern Papers* – it was closer in spirit to the city that the Gun Merchant would have seen in the seventeenth century, another era when unaccustomed forces were churning the earth. Except that now it was unimaginably more so; it was as if the very rotation of the planet had accelerated, moving all living things at unstoppable velocities, so that the outward appearance of a place might stay the same while its core was whisked away to some other time and location.

As I closed *The Aspern Papers* my eye was drawn instead to another book that was lying on the table. It looked like an old children's book and was evidently set somewhere in India: the cover showed a tiger stalking some men in turbans. The title was *I misteri della giungla nera* – *The Mystery of the Black Jungle* – and on looking at the flap copy I discovered, to my surprise, that the book was set in the Sundarbans.

I guessed that this was the book that Cinta had mentioned to me: this copy had probably belonged to her daughter. My guess was proved correct when I opened the book. The name 'Lucia' was written on the first page, in ink.

Closing the book I glanced at the shelves around me and quickly discovered where it belonged: there was an empty space on a shelf with a set of books with similar covers. I got up and was just about to reshelve the book when my phone rang.

It was Cinta. 'Ciao, *caro*! Are you nicely settled in?'

'Yes, Cinta, thanks. I'm very comfortable here.'

'Good. What are you doing now?'

'Actually,' I said, 'I was just looking at this book called *The Mystery of the Black Jungle* . . .'

'Oh yes!' cried Cinta. 'By Salgari! Lucia loved that book – she used to say she could see the Sundarbans in her dreams.'

'Speaking of the Sundarbans,' I said, 'I had a very strange run-in today, with someone from there.'

'*Sul serio?* What happened?'

I told her about the incident in the Ghetto, and my meeting with Rafi. To my surprise, she reacted not with a show of concern, but laughter.

'It wasn't a joke, Cinta!' I protested. 'I could have been badly hurt.'

'But you weren't, were you? Your Gun Merchant seems to be keeping an eye on you.'

'What do you mean?'

'Never mind, *caro*. Look after yourself and I'll see you soon.'

The call had just ended when my phone beeped to let me know that I had a message. It was from Gisa: 'Something has come up – I will call later. Hope all OK in Venice. Let me know if u find some interviews for me. Ciao!'

As I was slipping the phone back into my pocket my fingers brushed against a slip of paper. Taking it out I saw Rafi's number scribbled on it and decided to give him a call.

Rafi answered after a couple of rings, in Italian: '*Pronto?*'

I answered in Bangla: '*Ami bolchhi* – it's Dinanath Datta here.'

His voice hardened. 'How did you get my number?'

'Lubna gave it to me.'

He gave a snort of irritation. '*Ki chai?* What do you want? Why are you calling me?'

'I wanted to ask you something.'

This seemed to give him pause. When he spoke again his voice was more evasive, almost anxious. 'What do you want to ask?'

I was puzzled by the sudden change in his tone. 'I'll tell you when I see you,' I said. 'When do you think you'll have time?'

He thought this over for a bit. 'I have time right now,' he said. 'I'm meant to be working except that I don't have any customers. We could talk if you came over here.'

'Where are you?'

'I'm near San Marcuola, selling ice cream. Do you know the church across from the vaporetto stop? I'm on the other side of it – you'll see me if you head this way.'

'I'm very close to San Marcuola. I'll be there in a few minutes.'

Stepping into the backyard I discovered, to my surprise, that the sky had darkened and the weather had changed: a chill had descended on the city and a thick, clammy fog had rolled in from the Grand Canal.

Opening the back door I found I could not see the far side of the adjoining lane, even though it was only a few feet away. I knew that the church of San Marcuola was somewhere to my right so I stumbled along in that direction, staying close to the side of the lane.

On reaching the walls of the church, I stopped to look around; I saw no sign of Rafi though I knew he had to be nearby. Then I heard his voice: '*Eijé* – here I am.'

He was behind me, leaning against a wall, with a handcart positioned in front of him. His plastic windbreaker was zipped up and a scarf was knotted under his chin, covering his head and ears in the fashion of a Bengali 'muffler'. The scarf's edges extended outwards, like a bonnet, shadowing Rafi's face.

When I went over to the cart I understood why he had positioned it there: the spot was a kind of crossroads, with a number of lanes converging on it, including a narrow, curved *calle* that led to the Rio Terà San Leonardo. Had the weather been better the place would probably have been thronged with tourists. But because of the fog there were only a few stragglers drifting forlornly by, like clouds within the murk.

'Who's going to buy ice cream on an evening like this?' said Rafi glumly.

'No one,' I said. 'So why don't you stop for the day?'

He gave me a pitying look. 'That would only give the owner an excuse not to pay me.' As an afterthought, he added: 'He probably won't pay me anyway but I don't want to give him an excuse.'

He looked me in the eyes now, frowning. 'So what is it that you want to talk about?' he said, sounding a little tentative, as though he were testing the waters.

'It's nothing very complicated,' I said. 'I just want to know how you ended up in Venice.'

'Why is that of interest to you?'

Although his tone was abrupt to the point of rudeness, I had the sense that he was actually quite relieved; that he had been expecting some other, more difficult question.

I began to explain about Gisa's documentary but Rafi stopped me after a couple of sentences. 'No, I don't want to do this. Ask someone else.'

'All right,' I said. 'You don't have to do it. But can I ask why?'

He made a dismissive gesture. 'I'm sick of people coming around, asking these questions: "Who was your dalal? What was his name? Who were the men who helped you cross over borders?" Or they'll want to know: "Who goes to which mosque? What's being said there?" It's hard to tell whether they're police stooges trying to get you to report on jihadis or whether it's the other side trying to get you mixed up with the police. And they could even be the same, for all you know—'

Cutting himself short, Rafi gave a cry of alarm and brushed something off his shoulder. A moment later he lunged in my direction. Taking hold of my arm he gave it a vigorous shake.

'*Makorsha!*' he said. 'That was a spider – it jumped from me to you. Look, there it is.' He pointed to the ground and I caught a glimpse of a large, long-legged spider scuttling away into the shadows.

Rafi looked at me again and his eyes slowly began to widen. 'What's the matter?' I said. 'Why are you staring at me like that?'

He shook his head as though he were trying to rouse himself from a trance. 'It's nothing – it's just that they have some bad spiders over here. You should be careful.'

I was puzzled, not so much by his words as by the way he said them. 'What are you trying to tell me?'

'It's not important.'

'But tell me anyway.'

'It's just that I remembered something,' he said reluctantly, 'from the story – you know, that story about the Gun Merchant?'

'What did you remember? Tell me.'

He looked me up and down and then glared defiantly. 'Why should I? I've been answering your questions since the day I met you, at the dhaam – and what have *you* done for me? Nothing! Isn't it time that I got something from you? You act like a rich tourist – I'm sure you have plenty of money.'

'Do you want money then?' I took out my wallet. 'How much?'

He snatched the wallet out of my hand and looked inside. I had withdrawn three hundred euros the day before and had spent hardly any of it.

Rafi pulled out four fifty-euro notes and held them up. 'What if I took these?'

'That much?'

'Don't you think you owe me at least that?'

'Oh, all right,' I said. 'Take them. But you'll tell me the story then?'

'Yes.' Pocketing the banknotes he handed me my wallet. 'Do you remember – back at the dhaam, I showed you a panel that had some criss-cross lines on it?'

Pulling out his phone he called up some kind of touch-enabled app and drew four lines that intersected in the middle, like the crosses on a Union Jack. In the centre he placed a small dot.

'Do you remember seeing something like this?'

'Yes,' I said. 'I remember that panel. But what does it have to do with spiders?'

'How many legs does a spider have?'

'Eight?'

He thrust the screen of his phone at me and pointed to the diagram he had just drawn.

'And how many lines do you see, coming out of this dot at the centre?'

I stared at the lines. 'Eight?'

'So you see . . .'

'But what do spiders have to do with the Gun Merchant?'

'Some spiders are poisonous, aren't they, just like snakes?'

'Oh, I see what you're saying: they too could be Manasa Devi's creatures?'

He shrugged and turned away.

'Come on, Rafi,' I said. 'What are you trying to get at?'

He shot me a glance, from under his lowered brow. 'I just remembered a little bit of the story, as my grandfather used to tell it.'

'Yes? Go on.'

'It goes like this: when the Merchant reaches Gun Island he thinks he is safe at last because no snake will be able to reach him here. But one day he sees Manasa Devi's face, in a book, and he knows that this is a warning. The next day, seized by fear, he tells his friend Nakhuda Ilyas that he wants to spend this night in the most secure place on Gun Island, where no creature will be able to find him. The safest place on the island is a room where guns are kept, a room that is made of iron. So

Nakhuda Ilyas takes him there and locks him in, with all the guns, thinking that he will be safe there. But in the morning, when he goes to check, he finds the Gun Merchant desperately sick – he has been bitten by a poisonous spider! It is then that the Merchant realizes that he can no longer remain on Gun Island.'

My mouth fell open. 'But you never told me this part of the story. Not when we were there, at the shrine.'

Rafi nodded. 'I didn't tell you because it wasn't in my mind then. It's only now that it came back to me, when I saw that spider.'

'What else do you remember of the story?'

'Only that. Nothing else.'

'Are you sure?'

But Rafi was no longer listening to me. His eyes had flickered away from my face to the narrow, curving *calle* behind me. He gave a start and his head snapped up, as though he were coming to attention. Then, lowering his voice to a whisper, he said: 'You've got to go now.'

'Why?'

'Never mind, just go.'

'All right.'

As I was turning to go I looked over my shoulder. The fog had thinned by this time and I spotted a man walking towards us, down the *calle*. He was wearing a green baseball cap and I couldn't see his face. On an impulse I turned around and began to walk towards him.

A few tourists had appeared now, and when I passed the man in the cap there were a couple of people between me and him. But I could feel his gaze on me, scanning my face, and we briefly locked eyes. He was a tall, swarthy-looking European, with a heavy jaw that was shadowed with stubble.

On reaching the end of the lane I stole a backwards glance.

The man was leaning over the ice-cream cart, his face thrust menacingly close to Rafi's. As I was turning the corner I caught a glimpse of him stabbing the boy's chest with an extended forefinger.

My phone began to ring just as I was stepping into Cinta's apartment.

It was Gisa, calling from Rome.

'Listen, Dino, I am very, very, very sorry,' she said, the words tumbling out of her mouth in a breathless rush, as always.

'*Mi dispiace molto, molto, molto* . . . but I will not be able to join you in Venice for a few more days. I have had to postpone my arrival . . . something has happened and I must stay in Rome a little bit longer.'

She went on to explain that a big news story was breaking: a boatload of refugees had been spotted in the eastern Mediterranean. They were believed to be steering in the direction of Sicily. The boat had precipitated a crisis; the interior minister in the newly formed government in Rome, a right-wing hardliner who had campaigned on an anti-immigration platform, had declared that he would not allow refugees to land in Italy at any cost, and had claimed that this policy would serve as a successful deterrent. This was the first refugee boat to head towards Italy in a long time and the minister was determined to stop it – he had even threatened to deploy the navy if necessary.

'Where are these refugees from?'

'They're probably a *gruppo misto* with Eritreans, Egyptians, Ethiopians, Sudanese, and maybe some Bengalese as well. That's been the pattern with boats from Egypt.'

'Is that where this boat is from?'

'*Sì*. At this time there's nowhere else that it could have come from.'

Over the last year, said Gisa, the European Union had been able to shut down most of the usual migration routes – through Greece, Turkey, Morocco and even Libya. But the traffickers were nothing if not inventive and they always managed to find new launching points. Currently Egypt was their preferred point of departure – the Sinai Peninsula to be exact.

'The Sinai!' said Gisa, on a note of bitter irony. 'Where Moses received the Ten Commandments! I went there once, on a holiday, many years ago. I remember visiting the monastery of St Catherine, where we saw a *roveto* that was directly descended from the Burning Bush of the Bible. The Sinai was such a beautiful, tranquil place then. And now it is the most dangerous place on earth, at least for *gli immigrati*.'

'Why is it so dangerous?'

'I can only tell you what I have heard from the rifugiati that I've interviewed. They all say that the Sinai is a wild place, even wilder than Libya. No one controls it and the tribes who live there are at war with the government in Cairo. Their source of finance is smuggling – I suppose in the past they smuggled drugs and arms and things like that. But now it's much more profitable to smuggle people, and easier too, because they have connections with the tribes of the Sahara, who send them rifugiati from Eritrea, Ethiopia, Somalia, and South Sudan – all the places that people are fleeing from. When they reach the Sinai, the rifugiati are put into big depots known as "connection houses". After that, in order to come to Europe, they have to make further payments, for the crossing. *Capisci?*'

'Sure.'

'What I've heard from the rifugiati is that the connection houses of the Sinai are equipped with special operating rooms, completely modern, with all the latest equipment, including solar-powered refrigeration units. Those who can't pay the ransom are given drugs to make them senseless. Then they're taken to the operating theatres, where an organ is removed, usually a kidney. Then these organs are sold – often to Europeans.'

I gasped. 'That's horrifying!'

Gisa sighed. 'I know – it sounds too terrible to believe, like the worst horrors of the slave trade.'

'Exactly.'

'There is something demonic about it, isn't there?'

'Yes.'

'Except that here too, in Italy, there are those who would turn a blind eye to all of this. Across Europe the question of immigration is now the single most important issue in politics and this boat – the Blue Boat, as it is being called – could bring it all to a head. This could be *molto molto importante* for my documentary. So I must stay in Rome a bit longer, to see what happens. You understand, no?'

'Yes, of course.'

'*Grazie, grazie, Dino. A presto!*'

Strandings

I found it hard to sleep that night: my mind was over-filled with disturbing images – of masonry crashing down at my feet; of people trying to escape floods by climbing into snake-infested trees; of refugees in the Sinai being preyed upon by demons.

In the small hours I gave up trying, picked up my phone and tapped my email app to see if I had any messages. There was only one, and much to my surprise it was from Piya: she was in India and wanted me to call as soon as possible.

I checked the time: it was 4 a.m. in Italy – 7.30 a.m. in India. I dialled Piya's Indian mobile through an Internet telephony service, and she answered almost immediately, sounding startled.

'Deen? Thanks for calling. I didn't expect to hear from you for a while yet.'

'Really? Why?'

'Well you're in Venice, aren't you? It must be very early there.'

How did she know where I was?

I was so surprised that the phone dropped from my hands and disappeared under the bed-sheets. I was scrabbling around for it when I heard Piya's voice calling to me, muffled by the covers: 'Deen? Deen? Are you still there? Can you hear me?'

I fished out the phone and put it to my ear. 'Yes, here I am.'

'Good. For a minute I thought I'd lost you.'

'No, I'm still here. But tell me: how did you know that I was in Venice?'

'I saw a status update or something on your social media. You posted some pictures yesterday, didn't you?'

'That's right,' I said. 'But it wasn't really me – it was my phone that did it, which is why I didn't remember.'

A pause, and then: 'Are you okay, Deen? You sound a bit woozy – we can talk later if you like.'

'No, no,' I said quickly. 'I'm fine. Tell me why you wanted me to call.'

'It's just that I've been dealing with a bit of a crisis and I thought you might be able to help.'

'Sure, of course! Tell me what I can do.'

'Thanks. But I'll need to give you a bit of background first. How are you doing for time?'

'No problem there,' I said. 'I have plenty of time. Take as long as you want.'

Two weeks before, in Eugene, Oregon, Piya had received an email message from an unknown sender. The message was written in the style of a news report and it described a mass beaching of dozens of Irrawaddy dolphins at Garjontola Island in the Sundarbans.

The message had startled Piya. She had heard nothing about a recent beaching event in the Sundarbans: if there had been one she was sure her assistants would have let her know. Beachings of Irrawaddy dolphins were very rare and an event on this scale was unheard of. The entire population of Irrawaddy dolphins in the Indian Sundarbans probably did not exceed eighty or ninety individuals: if dozens of them had died then it would mean that the species would not survive in this habitat.

Piya took some time to search the Internet and drew a blank. Nor was there any mention of a beaching in any of the professional threads and chat groups that she belonged to.

This should have set her mind at rest but it didn't. The specificity of the details in the message worried her; the fact that there was a mention of a time, 'soon after daybreak', not to speak of a place. Garjontola was a small and little-known island; it was not the kind of detail that would crop up at random.

She read the message again and saw that she'd made an error with the dates: the mass beaching was still a week away. She realized now that this wasn't a report of something that had already happened.

It was a prediction.

That raised the possibility that the message had been sent by a crank or a troll. Ever since she'd started speaking out against the refinery upstream of the Sunderbans her social media feeds had spilled over with angry messages: 'Why u trying to stop poor people getting jobs bitch? Who paying u to stop development? Go back where you came from foreign whore.'

But this message didn't look as though it had been sent by a troll: for one thing, it had appeared in the mailbox she used for private correspondence, not on her publicly available university account or any of her social media feeds. Piya could not rule out the possibility that it had been sent by a whistle-blower in the refinery, someone who had advance knowledge of an upcoming dump of effluents. If so, she might be able to prove her hunch about animal die-offs in the Sundarbans being linked to the dumping of toxic effluents. And that in turn might help to shut down the refinery.

As it happened, Piya was due to attend a conference in Berlin soon. Checking her schedule she discovered that by juggling a few flights, and leaving earlier than she had planned, she would be able to make it to the Sundarbans in time for the predicted beachings. She logged on to a travel website and was able to book flights that would get her to Lusibari the day before the date mentioned in the message.

During a layover in Frankfurt, Piya had a moment of in-spiration. She remembered a journalist who had been asking to be taken along for a field trip in the Sundarbans. Piya sent her a carefully worded message, inviting her to come along; she made it sound like a routine field trip and made no mention of a possible beaching. The journalist jumped at the chance and wrote back to say that she would bring along a photographer.

Piya arrived in Lusibari to find that everything had been set up according to her instructions. The journalist and photographer were already there and her assistants had loaded their equipment into one of Horen's steamers. The steamer set off as soon as Piya had boarded and reached Garjontola at sunset. Anchoring near the shore they began to collect water samples, to be sent to Hyderabad for testing with the latest solid phase adsorption toxin tracking technology.

Sunrise next morning was at six.

Piya made sure that she was up in time but she didn't wake the others. Armed with her binoculars and GPS monitor she went on deck to keep watch.

A half-hour went by, and then another, with no dolphins in sight. Soon her assistants began to stir and come on deck; everyone was surprised to find Piya already up and on watch. What was the matter? Was she expecting something?

She deflected the questions with smiles and shrugs. She had got up early because of jet lag, she told them, and rather than lying awake in her bunk she had decided to collect some more water samples.

As sunrise gave way to morning, Piya felt increasingly conflicted. On the one hand it was a huge relief that nothing terrible had happened. Yet, here she was, waiting, binoculars in hand, having travelled halfway around the world on tickets that she had bought with her own money.

Breakfast was served and cleared away and there was still no sign of any dolphins. Fortunately Piya had prepared a briefing for the journalists, on the long-term impacts of the refinery; it took her the better part of an hour to get through all her maps, charts and slides. Then her assistants took turns describing the mass mortality events that they had recently witnessed: shoals of dead fish; the decline of crab populations, and so on.

Piya wrapped up her talk at 8 a.m. Then, thinking that she might as well kill a little bit more time, just in case, she asked

Horen to speak to the journalists: he was the oldest person present, and a good storyteller to boot, so she guessed that he would be able to give them the kind of material they needed (the science communication department in her university had long been urging the faculty to focus on 'human interest' stories).

Horen was still talking when a dolphin was spotted in the distance. Piya immediately snatched up a record sheet and noted the time: it was 8.35 a.m. She made a mental note that this was a good two and a half hours after the time predicted by the whistle-blower.

Soon more dolphins appeared, dozens of them. They were swimming not in their usual meandering fashion but almost in straight lines, heading directly for Garjontola.

Up to this point Piya's voice had held steady over the phone. But now she broke down and began to sob.

'I don't know what to tell you, Deen: it was the most devastating thing I've ever seen. So many of them, throwing themselves up on the shore. I've heard of other cetaceans doing this but never *Orcaella*.'

Soon after the beachings started Piya and the others went ashore in a dinghy. She and her assistants managed to put half or more of the animals back in the water, but around twenty were beyond saving.

The writer and photographer were not idle either; they took notes and shot a ton of footage. Knowing that they had a scoop, they insisted on racing back to Kolkata. Their paper ran the story the next day, placing it prominently on the front page.

The article, and especially the pictures, had already had a huge impact.

'I just heard from an environmental lawyer,' said Piya. 'She's putting together a coalition of groups to file a case in the Supreme Court in New Delhi. She thinks that on the basis of this story there's a good chance that we can get a court order to shut down the refinery. She's planning to show clips of the dead dolphins lying on the beach. Some of the judges are vegetarians; they get really upset when they see stuff like that – maybe even enough to rule against corporate interests.'

She swallowed a sob.

'She – the lawyer – kept saying how *lucky* we were to be there just at that time . . .'

'Did you tell her about that anonymous email?'

'No! I haven't told anyone, except you. I don't want it to get out that there's a whistle-blower in the refinery.'

'Are you sure that it was a whistle-blower who sent you that message?'

'Yes of course.'

'But how did this whistle-blower get your private email address? Do you have any idea?'

There was a moment's silence and then she said: 'Actually that's what I was just getting to – it's why I needed to talk to you.'

Everything had happened so fast that Piya had neglected to let Moyna know that she was coming to Lusibari. But Moyna got to hear anyway and she had barged in on Piya, at the trust's guest-house.

'Why didn't you tell me you were coming to Lusibari?' Moyna said accusingly. And then, much to Piya's surprise, she proceeded to dissolve into tears – something that was very rare for Moyna.

'Don't you know how lonely I am here, without Tipu?'

Suddenly guilt-stricken, Piya put everything aside and sat down to spend time with Moyna. They talked about her health, about the hospital, and about Tipu. When Piya asked whether Tipu was still being good about keeping in touch with her, from Bangalore, Moyna shook her head. No, she said, Tipu hadn't called in a while; the last time she'd heard from him was two weeks ago, when he'd sent a picture of himself in Bangalore, with his colleagues.

Pulling out her cellphone Moyna handed it to Piya: 'Look, here's what he sent.'

The picture was a group photo, taken in front of an office building. Three rows of young men and women were looking solemnly into the camera.

'Which one is Tipu?' said Piya.

Moyna pointed him out: he was in the back row, wearing a suit and tie, like the other men.

'Doesn't he look ever so grown-up?' said Moyna proudly.

Piya agreed – but there was something about the picture that didn't seem quite right. She forwarded the photograph to herself and pulled it up on her computer. When it appeared on the screen she knew that the image had been doctored. A tiny picture of Tipu's face had been photoshopped on the image.

Moyna was thunderstruck when Piya told her this; she had never heard of photoshopping.

'It's not difficult to do, Moyna. For someone with Tipu's skills it's very easy.'

The two of them then went through Moyna's phone and social media logs to see if they might reveal anything of Tipu's where-abouts.

Piya saw that for the most part Tipu had been careful to communicate with Moyna through social media accounts. But every now and then he'd also made phone calls and sent text messages, from numbers that were preceded by international dialling codes.

Piya showed some of these codes to Moyna: + 880, + 92, + 98 and + 90.

'Moyna, didn't you notice that these calls and messages were coming from foreign numbers?'

'I did,' Moyna protested. 'I even asked Tipu about that. He said he was using some kind of dialling service that was routed through foreign servers. It's cheaper that way he said.'

'And you believed him?'

'What else could I do?' said Moyna, sounding uncharacteristically helpless. 'Tipu knows so much about these things. And I know so little.'

'Have you tried calling any of these numbers?'

'No,' said Moyna. 'Tipu doesn't like me to call him in Bangalore. He says that he has to work odd hours and his office has strict rules against receiving private calls. If I want to speak to him I send him an email and he usually calls back within an hour or two – but not these last two weeks. I've sent message after message and I still haven't heard from him.'

Piya was now both mystified and alarmed. She asked Moyna to show her the other pictures that Tipu had sent. They were all group photos taken inside offices, or in parks, or in what seemed to be a hostel. After looking at a few images Piya knew that they were all doctored. Tipu must have found them on the Net, on someone else's social media feed.

It was clear now that Tipu had put a lot of thought into deceiving his mother. Instead of taking a job in Bangalore, he appeared to have made his way to Bangladesh. On the evidence of the dialling codes that he had used, it seemed that from Bangladesh he had travelled to Pakistan, Iran and Turkey. But to what end? And how had he got the money for these travels? Piya could not believe that his sources of income, from the work that he did on the Net, would enable him to finance the journey.

Tipu's last message to Moyna did not show a country code. But Piya noticed that it had been sent on the same day, and almost the same time, as the anonymous message about the beachings. That was when she began to think that Tipu might have had something to do with that anonymous email.

At Piya's insistence they had gone to Moyna's house and entered Tipu's room. Glancing around it Piya noticed a locked closet. 'Have you looked inside that?' she asked Moyna.

'No,' Moyna replied, 'but I know what's in there. Tipu keeps all his electronics in that almirah, including all the things you've given him over the years.'

'Let's make sure they're all there,' said Piya. 'Do you have the key?'

'No.'

Fetching a hammer, Piya knocked off the lock. When the almirah's doors swung open they saw that it had been cleaned out: the shelves were empty except for a few discarded odds and ends. The gifts from Piya – the old computers, monitors, keyboards, gaming consoles and all the rest – were gone. Piya guessed that they had been sold to raise money for Tipu's journey.

On the bottom shelf there was an old plastic bag, stuffed with paper. The bag looked as though it had been hastily filled and forgotten. Piya ran her eyes over a few sheets and saw that they were random printouts, from the Internet.

Putting the bag aside, Piya said to Moyna: 'Does Tipu have a passport?'

'No,' said Moyna, 'not as far as I know. He never bothered to renew the one you got him before he went to America.'

It was clear to Piya now that Tipu had set off on a clandestine journey, with forged papers, and had somehow ended up in Turkey. The journey had evidently taken many months, through which time he had been careful to stay in touch with Moyna. At no stage had he fallen completely quiet as he had in these last two weeks. Piya could not help feeling that there was something ominous about this long silence: Tipu was probably in some kind of trouble.

Through a friend Piya contacted an NGO that dealt with refugees and migrants. She talked to someone who told her that Tipu's was not an unusual story; over the last couple of years there had been a huge increase in reports of teenage boys and young men leaving home without informing their families. She also confirmed that the overland route from Pakistan through Iran to Turkey was a major conduit for migrants. But as for helping to find Tipu, the woman said there was very little any NGO could do; they were all overwhelmed and under-staffed. Piya's best hope lay in finding people who could tap into migrant networks, to see if something could be learnt through informal channels.

The image of Tipu, stranded in Turkey, made Piya frantic: it was as though she were witnessing another stranding. She made many more calls over the following hours but to no avail. Only when she was at her wits' end did she think of delving into the plastic bag that she had found in Tipu's almirah.

Going through the stack of papers, she made a startling discovery.

'The bag was full of printouts, as I had thought,' she said, 'but they weren't random. You'll never believe it, Deen, but a lot of the material was about Venice, of all places! I think Tipu had been doing research on the Net, taking printouts of all kinds of stuff – history, geography, even fauna. (Can you imagine that? What fauna could there be in Venice?) I'd never have imagined that Tipu would be interested in stuff like that. There were even detailed maps of neighbourhoods, which he'd drawn on with a pencil. It's like he'd developed an obsession with Venice. And it wasn't just a passing thing, either. I checked the dates – you know how printouts from the Net usually have a date at the top? – and I saw that he'd been at it for two years.'

'Two years?' I said. 'So then he must have started gathering this material soon after he was bitten by that snake?'

'I guess so. And he'd also been doing research on the overland routes from Iran to Turkey and Europe. He'd even filled out some forms for passports, not just for himself but also for Rafi. That could only mean that they had decided to travel together, so I called Horen and asked if he knew where Rafi was. He told me that Rafi had left Lusibari a year ago and gone abroad – he had sold everything he owned, including his boat, and then he had disappeared. There had been no news of him until recently, Horen said, but a month ago Rafi had sent a friend a picture of himself from somewhere in Europe. So then I asked Horen: "Do you know where exactly the picture was sent from?" Horen said no, but he would ask the guy to forward the picture. I said, "Please do," and within an hour I had the picture on my phone – it was of Rafi, standing on a bridge with a canal behind him.'

Piya paused to catch her breath. 'I'm more or less certain, Deen, that the picture was taken in Venice. That was when I sent you that text, asking you to call: I was hoping you'd be able to look out for Rafi while you're over there. I mean, of course, I know there's only a very remote chance . . .'

The word 'chance' hit me with such force that I lost track of what Piya was saying. Shutting my eyes I silently embraced the word, clinging to it as though it were my last connection with reality.

Yes, of course, it was all chance, these unlikely encounters, these improbable intersections between the past and present; that almost fatal accident that had brought me face to face with Rafi in the Ghetto: all of this was pure coincidence, of course it was. To lose sight of that was to risk becoming untethered from reality; chance was the very foundation of reality, of normalcy. There was absolutely no reason to imagine, as I had done, that such an encounter, in such a place, was outside the range of the probable. Because no such thing existed; nothing was outside the range of the probable – wasn't that why I had insured myself against the possibility of living till the age of one hundred and three? Because that too might happen no matter how fractional the chances?

But even as this was going through my mind a tremor of doubt crept through me. How could one know? Was there some kind of abacus somewhere that allowed one to determine whether an experience fell within the realm of chance? No, of course not, because any number of inexplicable things could happen without disproving the possibility of their being connected by chance. In this, chance was like God – nothing that happened, no event or eventuality, could either prove or disprove its immanence. And at the same time, like God, chance provided reassurance, safety, cleanliness, purity. Wasn't that why chance was so often said to be 'pure'? – because it flowed over the world like a fresh mountain stream cleansing everything that it touched. To cease to believe in it was to cross over into the territory of fate and destiny, devils and demons, spells and miracles – or, more prosaically, into the conspiratorial universe of the paranoiac, where hidden forces decide everything.

I could not permit myself to go that way. I had to have faith – that was the thing that had been missing in my life of late, faith. I had to cling to my faith in chance, at all costs. It was almost as though my fidelity were being tested, through trials and ordeals, like the Buddha by the demoness Mara; like St Anthony in the desert; like Yudhishthira on his final ascent.

All of this was spooling through my mind when I became aware of Piya's voice. She was saying, probably not for the first time: 'Hello? Are you still there, Deen? Hello?'

'Yes, I'm here, Piya,' I said.

I took a deep breath and tried to compose myself.

'This may surprise you, Piya,' I said, 'but I saw Rafi just yesterday.'

'You're kidding! You saw him? Really?'

'Yes, I know! What are the chances?'

'Hmm. I guess Venice isn't a large city, area-wise, and the population's only a few hundred thousand, so it's not all that unlikely.'

'I suppose not. Anyway, I had a talk with Rafi and even asked him about Tipu. He said he had no idea where Tipu was and seemed annoyed that I'd even asked. I assumed they'd broken up so I dropped the subject.'

'Could you speak to him again, please?' I could hear gratitude brimming in her voice. 'I'd be really glad if you could! I know it's a very long shot, but . . .'

It struck me then that far from being a long shot, it was almost a certainty that Rafi had some inkling of Tipu's whereabouts; this was probably the very question that he had been half expecting and half fearing that I would ask.

'Of course I'll speak to Rafi again,' I said. 'I'll do whatever I can. And please don't worry too much. Tipu is a very smart kid, and he knows what he's doing.'

'But he's still a kid,' said Piya. 'So I can't help worrying. I guess I blame myself for all that's gone wrong for him. After all, his father was working for me when he died.'

'It's really not your fault, you shouldn't blame yourself.'

She sighed. 'When it comes to Tipu, I've never been able to do anything right. Anyway, let me know how it goes with Rafi. I'll be in Berlin tomorrow and I'd be glad to come to Venice – it's a short flight.'

'All right,' I said. 'But first let's see what Rafi has to say. I have his number so I'll call him straight away. I'll get back to you as soon as I can. Later today, if possible.'

'Good. Let's stay in touch.'

Friends

The dread that I had managed to hold off while talking to Piya seized me with a vengeance when the call ended. I sat in bed as if paralysed, staring at the wall ahead. What was happening to me? To us? There seemed to be a pattern in my encounters with Tipu and Rafi. Yet that pattern was not of our own designing; it was as if something or someone had taken possession of us for reasons beyond our understanding.

And then I recalled the resolution I had made while I was on the phone with Piya: that I would keep faith with myself. I reminded myself that it was possible that this was all an outcome of the randomness that is always immanent in the world – pure chance in other words. Wasn't it said that monkeys pounding on a typewriter would eventually reproduce a play by Shakespeare? Surely the odds against that were far greater than whatever it was that was happening to me? In any event that was what I had to believe if I were to preserve my sanity.

I forced myself to say aloud 'This is all chance and coincidence, nothing else' – and the words had the effect of a prayer, breaking the spell that had descended on me. As my mind cleared it became more and more obvious that Rafi was the key; the first thing I needed to do was to talk to him.

I looked at my watch. It was seven in the morning, not too late to catch him before he started his day job, at the construction site. I called his number but only to find that his phone had already been switched off. Hoping that he would check his messages, I sent him a text asking him to call when he had a break.

Over the next few hours I called and texted Rafi several more times, but with no result. Lunchtime too came and went with neither a message nor a call. Feeling increasingly desperate I decided to go over to Lubna's office to ask if she knew when Rafi would be getting off work.

The door of her office was ajar and Lubna was seated inside, staring raptly at her computer monitor. Her eyes left the screen briefly as she looked up to greet me and then veered away again.

'*Dekhechhen?*' She pointed at the monitor. 'Have you been following the news?'

She turned the monitor a little so that I could see the screen from my seat. I found myself watching a news clip of a small blue boat, chugging slowly across an azure sea. The top deck was crowded with dark-skinned people in ragged clothes. Many were looking up at the camera and waving forlornly.

Following the boat, at a wary distance, was a string of coast-guard vessels, all flying different flags.

The clip faded away and was replaced by a shot taken some-where else, of a squadron of sleek grey warships. On the foredeck of the largest vessel, a platoon of sailors could be seen, standing at attention and saluting the Italian flag.

'I suppose you heard?' said Lubna. 'The navy has been ordered to stop that refugee boat from approaching Italy. And every other country in the Mediterranean has sent coastguard vessels to make sure that they can't land anywhere else either.'

'So the minister carried out his threat, did he?'

'Yes. He did.'

She nodded at the screen, which was now showing live footage of a press conference.

A youngish, forceful-looking man with heavy-framed glasses and slicked-back hair was pounding on a desk and shouting into a microphone: '*Queste persone non metteranno mai piede in Italia!*'

206

'*Bujhte parchhen?*' said Lubna. 'Do you understand what he's saying?'

'Not all of it.'

'He said: "These people will never set foot in Italia."'

'*Salvo che succeda un miracolo.*'

'"Not unless there's a miracle."'

Lubna shuddered. 'I can't bear to listen to that man.' She turned the show off and looked at me with a raised eyebrow. 'So? Did you hear about Rafi? What happened last night?'

'Has something happened to him?' I said. 'I've been trying to reach him but his phone seems to be turned off.'

'Rafi was beaten up last night,' said Lubna grimly. 'I think he lost his phone. He's in hospital.'

I stared at her, aghast.

'Yes, it was a shock to me too,' said Lubna. 'I got a call late at night. The man who told me about it thought it was a gang attack, like those we hear about in Roma and Napoli, where right-wing thugs carry out planned attacks on migrants. It was a frightening thought because nothing like that has happened in this region yet. This would have been the first time.'

'So it wasn't that?'

'No, apparently not. This morning one of Rafi's house-mates came by. He told me a very different story.'

'I see.' I didn't know whether to press her or not. 'Is it something you can talk about?'

Lubna's eyes strayed to her watch. 'I don't mind talking about it but unfortunately I don't have the time right now. I have a meeting to go to. It's better you talk to Rafi's house-mate directly – his name's Bilal, and I've already spoken to him about your documentary. He said he was willing to talk to you. Come, I'll introduce you to him straight away – he works nearby.'

Not far from Lubna's office was a small marketplace, with a row of cloth-covered stalls running down the centre of the street. The stalls were stacked with colourful vegetables, fruit, herbs and other produce. Prominently on display were *fondi di carciofi* – artichoke bottoms – little white roundels swimming in basins of water.

These, and many other kinds of vegetables, were artfully arranged to create an impression of quaint and picturesque authenticity. Yet, the men behind the counters were almost all Bengali.

We found Bilal sitting at the side of the street: he was older than Rafi, maybe in his early twenties, tall, broad-shouldered and striking-looking, with flashing eyes, a sharp nose and a coppery complexion. Dressed in pale blue jeans and a striped Juventus T-shirt, he was seated in a plastic chair that looked too small for him. On one side of his chair was a bucket filled with small artichokes; on the other was a bin for the peel and parings. A basin of water lay between his feet and he had a knife in his hands, which he was wielding expertly to strip down the artichokes until all that remained of them was the ivory disc at the bottom.

After making a quick introduction Lubna hurried off to her meeting. Then Bilal signalled to me to pull up a nearby chair; his hands flew as he talked, producing a steady stream of *fondi di carciofi* for the basin between his feet.

The night before, said Bilal, Rafi had received a last-minute call, asking him to fill in for someone who washed dishes in a restaurant. He agreed and by the time he got off work it was quite late. To go back to his shared room in Mestre at that time of the night would have meant that he would have got hardly any sleep since he had to be back in Venice early in the morning, for his construction job. So he had decided instead to spend the night in an abandoned warehouse at the edge of Cannaregio – Bilal had discovered the place last year and had shown it to Rafi and a few other friends.

That part of Cannaregio was often deserted, especially at night. Rafi was passing through a dark *calle* when two men slipped out of the shadows and attacked him.

Afterwards, a passer-by had found Rafi lying senseless on the *fondamenta* and had called the Ospedale Civile, which had sent a water-ambulance to bring him to the hospital. He was still there and none of his friends had been able to speak to him yet.

'Was it just a robbery then?' I asked.

Bilal nodded: 'Yes, they took all his money. He was carrying quite a lot.'

Bilal took a quick look around, glancing from side to side. Then dropping his voice, he said: 'You see, Rafi had taken out a big loan recently and had missed a couple of payments. I don't think they meant to beat him up so badly. I suppose he fought back and the matter must have gotten out of hand.'

'Why had Rafi taken this loan?' I said. 'And from whom?'

Bilal's voice dropped to a whisper. 'The loan was from a *scafista* – a trafficker. Rafi had taken it out for a friend of his. They had left Bangladesh together and had got separated at the Turkish border – this often happens over there, because you have to run like crazy, over steep slopes. The soldiers on the Turkish side shoot if they see anyone trying to cross. Rafi got lucky and managed to get across, but his friend got hurt and had to go back into Iran. He managed to get over the border later but was stuck in Turkey for a long time. Anyway, a few weeks ago this boy called Rafi and said that he had spoken to a local dalal who had offered him a way out, through some other country. He would be able to get on a boat if Rafi could arrange for a payment to be made in Italy. So Rafi began to ask around and someone put him in touch with an Italian scafista who was willing to accept payment in instalments. Rafi was able to make the first payment, but he missed the second and the third. So . . .'

'Did Rafi ever mention his friend's name?'

'No.' Bilal threw me a glance and shrugged. 'Some of us had warned Rafi not to get involved with the scafisti; they're dangerous. But what could he do? He was desperate. And I don't blame him. When you set off on this journey with a friend and one of you makes it and the other doesn't, you feel terrible.

It's hard to live with that feeling. You'll do anything you can to help.'

The depth of emotion in his voice startled me. '*Tomaro hoye-chhilo naki?*' I asked. 'Did it happen to you too?'

He nodded, eyes downcast, his gaze fixed on his knife. 'Yes. I too left Bangladesh with a friend. His name was Kabir and he was from the same village, in Faridpur district. We had known each other since we were little. We played together, went through school together, and always stood by each other.

'A few years ago there was a dispute in my family, over land. One of my uncles is mixed up in politics and his sons are the local musclemen for the ruling party. For a long time they had been using their political clout to try to grab a part of what was rightfully my father's property. Every time there was a flood – which was happening more and more – they would try to move the boundaries. If we protested they would threaten us.

'One day there was a fight. My uncle and cousins attacked my father and me, so Kabir came to our defence and knocked my uncle down. After that it was like a riot. Kabir and I managed to get away, but from then on, we had to be constantly on the run. My uncle and his sons would hunt us down, wherever we went. They had henchmen everywhere, because of their party connections. They even got the police to charge us with a made-up case.

'After a year of hiding we realized that we would be killed if we stayed on in Bangladesh. A relative put us in touch with a dalal who said he would get us to the Emirates in exchange for 350,000 taka. It was a lot of money but somehow we managed to raise it and the dalal gave us each a piece of paper, saying that this was an "airport visa". He sent us to Chittagong where we boarded a plane that took us to Sharjah. Only when we got there did we realize that we would not be able to leave the airport.'

Bilal laughed, in self-mockery. 'What did we know? We were just eighteen-year-olds, simple village boys who had never even been in a plane before.

'Anyway, we had to remain in that airport, day after day, growing more and more desperate all the time. We had only fifty US dollars with us and we paid ten dollars for a prepaid card with thirty minutes of talktime. We called our dalal and he told us that we had only two choices. One was to go back to Bangladesh. The other was to go to Libya through Sudan. He said there was a war in Libya but it wasn't all that bad – many Bengalis had chosen to go there.

'What could we do? To turn back now was impossible, so we decided to take the second option. We said to ourselves: "After all, how bad can it be? It isn't as if things weren't bad for us back home."

'The next day we boarded a plane that took us to Khartoum. There were many other Bengalis at the airport, all waiting to go to Libya. After a day we flew to Tripoli. The airport was a shambles, with craters in the roof and shattered windows. Men with guns were walking in and out as they pleased. Some of these men surrounded us and took us outside to a minivan with darkened windows. Only then did we realize that we had been kidnapped.

'For the next year and a half we were beaten, tortured, and sold by one gang to another. They made us work from morning to night, paying us almost nothing and giving us only bread to eat. We were like slaves; what we went through was something that should not happen to any human being.

'But somehow through all of this Kabir and I managed to stay together and we even saved a little money. As the months went by we also became more worldly-wise. We learnt that there were Bengali dalals in Tripoli who could arrange for you to take boats to Europe. One day, with some careful planning, we were able to slip away from the gang that was then holding us. We made our way to Tripoli and paid a dalal who sent us to a town called Zuwara where they put us in a "connection house". This was just a concrete warehouse with a tin roof; some two hundred other people were already there – Nigerians, Sudanese, Eritreans, Iraqis, Afghans, and also some other Bengalis.

'A couple of months dragged by and then one night we were woken at 2 a.m. and told that it was time for our "connection" and we needed to get to the seafront quickly. We were herded to the beach and stripped of every belonging other than the garments on our backs.

'It was about 4 a.m. when the boat appeared – it was just a small, battered fishing vessel. To get to it we had to wade through chest-deep water. After hauling us in the scafisti told us where we had to sit: those who had paid extra were on the upper deck and those who hadn't were sent down into the hull below. Since Kabir and I had not been able to make the extra payment we had to go below deck, and were seated near the engine, which was belching clouds of black smoke.

'Once the boat began to move, water started to seep into the hull. We tried desperately to bail it out but it only got worse. By noon the next day the rear part of the boat was almost submerged, and we were hardly moving. We thought we would die, but then, like a miracle, a helicopter appeared above us – we could hear it, even down below. On the deck above, people became very excited and began to jump up and down, yelling and screaming. It was then that our boat began to go down.

'A frenzied scramble broke out, with all of us trying to claw our way out of the hull. Kabir and I managed to get out just before the boat sank. We had grown up swimming in rivers and ponds so neither of us was afraid of the water. We tore off our jeans and shirts and started to swim, trying to stay close to each other. We thought for sure a rescue ship would come soon and we would be safe. But a long time went by with no sign of either the ship or the helicopter. The sea was not rough that day but there was a steady swell. To fight the waves was tiring and after a time it became hard for us to stay close. We slowly drifted apart, losing sight of each other.

'By the time the rescue ship finally came I was exhausted and barely able to stay afloat. I managed to catch hold of one of the lifebelts they were throwing out; I clung to it while the speedboat was rescuing others. I looked around for Kabir and didn't see him, but I wasn't worried. I thought that he had probably been rescued already. When at last the lifeboat came for me I got in and looked around to see if Kabir was there. He wasn't.

'I was one of the last to board the rescue ship. Looking at all the people on deck, I felt sure that Kabir was among them. They were handing out those shiny silver blankets and I wrapped one around my body and went up and down the ship like a madman, hoping to find Kabir. Every time I saw a Bengali, in the distance, my heart would lift, in hope – and then I would see that it wasn't Kabir. In the end I collapsed, out of exhaustion, but when I woke up I started looking again. It went on like that until we got to port, and even afterwards, when we were taken to the camp. I could not bring myself to accept that Kabir hadn't made it. To this day I keep thinking he will turn up somewhere.'

There was a break now in the rhythmic motion of Bilal's hands; holding his knife at an angle, he raised his wrist and drew it across his eyes. Then he scooped up a handful of white artichoke bottoms and held them out towards me.

'Do you see these?' he said. 'For every euro I make from doing this work, I keep forty cents for my own needs. Of the rest I send thirty to my own family and thirty to Kabir's. He was an only child and his parents have no one to support them. For as long as they live I will send them money. I have to, don't I? It's only because Kabir was my friend that he's not here today. And the strange thing, you know, is that never once, through all that we suffered, did he blame me.'

Bilal wiped his eyes again, with the hand that was holding the knife.

'If I had got a call like Rafi did, from his friend, do you think I would not do everything possible to raise the money that was needed? I would do exactly what Rafi did, even if I knew I wouldn't be able to pay and would get beaten up for it.'

He looked me in the eyes and gestured at the left sleeve of his T-shirt. 'If I had to cut off an arm I would gladly do it.'

I was walking away from Bilal when I felt, in that indescribable, animal way that we sometimes feel the gaze of others, that I was being watched. I looked to my left and there he was, the pale, heavy-jawed man I had seen the day before, sticking his forefinger into Rafi's chest. He was leaning casually against a wall and picking his teeth; under the bill of his green baseball cap his eyes seemed to glow with an intensity that was almost demonic.

Our eyes met only for an instant, but I knew, with absolute certainty, that this was the scafista that Rafi had been dealing with.

By this time I had almost reached the turn for Cinta's building, but I ignored it and walked straight on, in the direction of the Rialto Bridge. At that moment it was suddenly of pressing importance not to reveal where I was staying.

I wandered aimlessly for an hour, allowing myself to be swept along by waves of tourists. On the way back I took a vaporetto and even though I was much calmer now, I couldn't get rid of that prickling sensation at the back of my neck. Almost involuntarily I kept looking around, checking the faces around me.

The sun was setting when the vaporetto got to San Marcuola. I joined a moving throng of tourists and slipped quickly through the back gate of Cinta's building. A sense of relief came over me as I closed the gate, yet when I entered Cinta's apartment and looked into the mirror that faced the doorway I half expected to see those eyes looking over my shoulder.

Walking through the apartment I caught a faint smell of wisteria blossom, wafting delicately through the air. It seemed to be coming from the room at the far end of a long corridor: that was where I had set up my computer.

The room was small – it had probably once been a maid's room – but it had a table, a chair, and a window that looked out over the flower-filled courtyard at the rear of the palazzo: the window frame was wreathed by the wisteria vines that covered the back wall.

Stepping into the room, I saw that the window was open. Had I left it like that? I couldn't remember. Nor did I stop to think about it for in front me lay a spectacular sight: the snow-covered peaks of the Dolomites, tinted with the rosy glow of the setting sun.

I was reaching for my phone, to capture the view, when my eyes fell on my laptop. I saw, to my shock, that there was a spider perched on the cover. It was about two inches across, brownish in colour, with jointed legs that rose high above its body.

Suddenly an image of criss-crossed lines floated past my eyes and I recalled Rafi's words: 'Some spiders are poisonous, aren't they, just like snakes?'

I took a couple of steps backwards and found myself pressed up against a wall. The spider, in the meantime, had stayed where it was, with its eyes apparently fixed on me. Since my phone was still in my hands I raised it, reflexively, and managed to snap a picture. The flash startled the creature and it leapt out of the window and disappeared.

Hurrying across the room, I pulled the window shut. But my heart was racing now and I had to lean against the window frame to collect myself. I knew I was having some kind of panic attack and forced myself to draw several deep breaths.

This had the right effect and my panic gradually subsided. As my heartbeat slowed I began to get annoyed with myself. What was the matter with me, jumping at shadows like this? Spiders were everywhere; they were just a part of the texture of the world, like flies and ants. If I allowed myself to read some kind of meaning into this it wouldn't be long before I lost my sanity.

I sat down at the desk, opened my laptop, and wrote a message to Piya, explaining that Rafi was in hospital but I had spoken to a friend of his who had told me a story that basically corroborated what we had already surmised: that Tipu and Rafi had left Bangladesh together and travelled overland through India, Pakistan and Iran, to the Turkish border where they'd been separated. As for the rest, I said, I would tell her over the phone once she arrived in Berlin; she should call me as soon as possible.

I was just about to hit the send button when my phone came to life and asked if I wanted to share the picture I had just clicked, of the spider. I transferred the picture to my laptop, attached it to my message, and added a postscript: 'My latest encounter with the animal kingdom.'

Upon rereading I decided that this sounded a little sententious, so I added a string of random emojis.

Dreams

At ten o' clock the next morning I went back to Lubna's office. I had half expected it to be closed, but the door was ajar. I stepped in to find a young man sitting in Lubna's chair, a diminutive Bengali with raven-black hair and a large pair of eyeglasses.

He rose to his feet and looked me up and down with an expression of puzzlement. 'Are you looking for Mrs Lubna Alam?' he said in English. He appeared to be in his mid twenties and was dressed in a neatly pressed shirt, trousers and jacket. Behind his lapels the tops of two pens could be seen, protruding from the breast pocket of his shirt.

I replied in Bangla. '*Hā, uni achhen?* Is she here?'

His eyes lit up suddenly, as though he had solved a riddle. 'I know who you are,' he cried. 'You're that Kolkata Bengali! The one who was almost brained by Rafi?'

'That's right,' I said. 'I'm Dinanath Datta.'

'And my name is Fozlul Hoque Chowdhury,' he said, shaking my hand vigorously. 'But everyone calls me Palash. Please sit down.'

I noticed that his Bangla accent was different from that of the other Bengalis I'd spoken to; he sounded like a street-smart, city-bred college student.

'I'm looking after the office today,' he said. 'Lubna-khala had to go to a meeting with a group of activists. They're busy trying to raise money to hire a boat.'

'A boat?' I said. 'Why do they need to hire a boat?'

217

'Oh, haven't you heard . . . ?'

Palash explained that human rights activists across Italy had decided to take up the cause of the boatload of refugees that had been so much in the news of late. They had decided to send out boats of their own, to confront the right-wing activists who had pledged to turn back the refugees.

'If a fleet of civilian vessels shows up to support the refugees,' said Palash, 'then maybe it'll speak to the world's conscience. Across the planet everyone's eyes are on the Blue Boat now: it has become a symbol of everything that's going wrong with the world – inequality, climate change, capitalism, corruption, the arms trade, the oil industry. There's a lot of hope that this will be a historic moment. Maybe now, while there's still time to make changes, people will wake up and see what's going on.'

'That must be exciting for you.'

'Yes, it is,' said Palash. 'I'm excited about going out there. This boat's journey could be a turning point.'

He flashed me a grin. 'Maybe you should come with us.'

'Me?' I was so taken aback that it took me a while to answer. 'But I'm no activist.'

'Lubna-khala said that you were working on a documentary. Wouldn't this be good footage for you?'

It struck me that he might have a point. 'That's an interesting suggestion,' I said. 'I'll pass it on to my friend, the director.'

'Good. It'll be a big help to us if you could share the costs. I'll tell Lubna-khala when she gets back.'

'And do you know when that will be?'

'Not for a while, I think.'

My disappointment must have been evident on my face for he added quickly: 'But maybe I could be of help? Why don't you tell me what you need from her?'

'Actually I wanted to ask her about Rafi,' I said. 'I was wondering whether it might be possible for me to talk to him today.'

Palash shook his head. 'I don't think it would be a good idea for you to go to the hospital today. There's a rumour that the *polizia* are going to question Rafi again.'

'What about?'

'The attack. I suppose they've figured out that it's more complicated than it appears.'

'How so?'

'In the first place because Rafi was carrying a lot of money – for a boy like him anyway. He had over 400 euros with him actually; he had put it together by begging and borrowing because he needed to pay back a scafista who had been threatening him. Apparently last night Rafi promised the scafista that he would pay him back today.'

I recalled the glimpse I had caught of the man in the green baseball cap, poking a finger into Rafi's chest.

'Who is this scafista? Do you know him?'

Palash nodded. 'He's a tall, thuggish-looking man, often wears a cap.'

'I think I saw him talking to Rafi on the night of the attack.'

'Quite possible,' said Palash. 'He often hangs around Cannaregio; he's a sort of labour recruiter, except that he's probably connected to the Mob. Those people are always trying to trap migrants into going down south, to work on farms where they're basically treated as slaves.'

'But I thought you said he was a scafista?'

'There's not a big difference,' said Palash. 'It's all tied together. The Mob has close ties with crime syndicates in Nigeria, Libya and Egypt. They often smuggle people into this country and put them to work on their farms and construction sites. These scafisti are always on the lookout for boys like Rafi – once they fall into their clutches it's not easy for them to get out.'

'But Rafi was going to pay this scafista back, wasn't he?'

'Yes,' said Palash. 'And the scafista must have tipped off the thugs who attacked Rafi and stole his money.'

'So it was a set-up?'

'That's right,' said Palash. 'These scafisti don't actually want to be paid back. It's to their advantage to keep people in debt. That way they can force them to do whatever they want – it's like bonded labour back home. The scafisti will stop at nothing, even . . .'

He looked into my eyes. 'Do you know the story of Lubna-khala's husband?'

'Not really. She told me that he died last year, in Sicily.'

Palash nodded. 'It was very sad; Munir-bhai was an amazing man, an activist who worked tirelessly for migrants and their causes. He was actually on a city council – the first Bengali to hold such a position. His death was a tragedy for everyone – especially since he was so young, just forty-two.'

'What happened?'

'He got on the wrong side of the Mob. For them, migrants and rifugiati – not to mention the whole Italian "reception system" – is a lucrative business, a big cash cow. Munir-bhai was a thorn in their side: he made a fuss about the money they were skimming from the funds earmarked for refugees. Then it came to his ears that a group of Bengalis was being held captive on a farm in Sicily and he decided to go down there to enquire. We tried to stop him but he wouldn't listen. He insisted on going and after a few days we heard that Munir-bhai had died, in a car crash.'

I sat back, stunned. 'That's terrible!' I said. '*Bibhotsho!* And terrible for Rafi too, that he got mixed up with such people.'

Palash nodded. 'Yes, we warned him, but he was desperate I suppose. He wanted to help his friend at all costs.'

I was going to ask Palash another question but my phone began to ring. Glancing at the screen I saw that the caller was Piya.

'I have to take this,' I said to Palash. 'But I hope we can talk again later.'

'Sure. Any time.'

Stepping outside I put the phone to my ear. 'Hello? Piya?'

'Hi, Deen. I'm calling from my hotel in Berlin. I just saw your message. So it looks like I was right then? Rafi and Tipu travelled to Turkey?'

'Yes,' I said. 'That's how it looks. They seem to have got separated at the border. Rafi made his way to Europe while Tipu got stuck in Turkey.'

'But I don't think he's there now,' said Piya, 'I think he's managed to get to Egypt.'

'What makes you think that?'

'I'll tell you. You remember that message – you know, the one about the beachings? I'd sent it to a friend of mine who's a whiz at digital forensics. He was able to trace it back.'

'And . . . ?'

'Apparently, it was sent from an Internet café in Alexandria, Egypt. So that's where Tipu must have been when he sent it.'

'Egypt?' For just an instant I toyed with the idea of telling Piya a little of what I had learnt about human trafficking in that country. But then I decided that there was no point in adding to her anxieties.

'Isn't it a bit odd,' I said, 'that he'd be thinking about dolphin beachings in Egypt?'

'My guess,' said Piya, 'is that the whistle-blower managed to reach him there through social media or something.'

'You're still sure, are you, that the tip-off came from a whistle-blower?'

'Well what else could it be, Deen?' she said impatiently. 'I hope you're not going to tell me he had a vision, or that the dolphins spoke to him in his sleep or something like that: that stuff is really not helpful.'

Then suddenly her tone changed: 'There is an odd thing though.'

'Yes?'

'You remember how I told you that the beachings started not at sunrise, as the warning had predicted, but two and half hours later, around 8.30 a.m.?'

'I remember that, yes.'

'I was thinking about it and it struck me that 8.30 a.m. Indian time would have been around sunrise for Tipu – that is, if he was still in Egypt the week after he sent the message.'

'That's interesting . . .'

Piya cut me off abruptly. 'If you're going to say Tipu saw it in a dream or something, please don't. What's important now is to figure out why Tipu was in Egypt in the first place.'

'My guess,' I said, 'is that Tipu was planning to get on a boat, to cross the Mediterranean. It's just a guess, but I think Rafi would know.'

'Yes, that's why I wish you could talk to him.'

'Listen, Piya,' I said. 'I'll do my best but I don't know when it'll be possible, what with him being in hospital and all.'

'Doesn't the hospital allow visitors?'

'I'm not sure. I'll ask.'

'Anyway, do keep me posted, Deen. I could come over at a moment's notice.'

'Well, *I* would certainly be happy to see you!' I said.

Then, sensing that I had startled her, I added: 'But don't do anything yet. I'll have another go at talking to Rafi and then I'll get back to you.'

'Okay, I'll wait to hear from you.'

I was about to say goodbye when she broke in suddenly: 'Hey, Deen! Could you just hang on for a minute? Something's just turned up, on my screen.'

'Sure.'

I heard her clicking on her computer and after a minute she gave a little gasp. 'Deen, remember that picture you sent me? Of the spider?'

'Yes. What about it?'

'I forwarded it to Larry, a friend of mine who studies spiders.'

'Why on earth did you do that?' I said, feeling suddenly panicky. 'It was a . . . a joke.'

'I don't know why I did it,' said Piya. 'I just did. And the email that arrived right now was from Larry. He was excited to get the picture – apparently the res was high enough that he could blow it up and make an identification. He says I should warn you as soon as possible.'

'Warn me? About what?'

'The spider in that picture is a brown recluse, *Loxosceles reclusa*. Its bite can be very painful; its venom is more potent, by weight, than that of a rattlesnake; it breaks down the skin and eats into the flesh. Larry wants to know: is it the only such spider you've come across or have you seen others?'

'I did see another spider,' I said. 'Or actually, it was Rafi who saw it. It landed on his shoulder and then jumped on me. I don't know if it was the same kind of spider though. Are they meant to be common around here?'

'Larry says this is the first time he's heard of one turning up so far north. But he's not surprised either. He says the brown recluse has been increasing its range very quickly because it's getting so much hotter in Europe. And there's a related species, the Mediterranean recluse, that's already widespread across Italy. Those're quite dangerous as well. A couple of years ago, in southern Italy, a woman died after being bitten by a Mediterranean recluse. She ignored the bite at first, thinking it wasn't serious, and within a day she was so sick she couldn't be saved. The antivenin had to be flown in from Brazil. She died before it arrived.'

'You're joking.'

'Not at all. I'll send you a link to the story: I'm looking at it right now. Apparently what happened was that there was a Mediterranean recluse infestation in the house next to hers and some got into her cellar. I just hope there's nothing like that where you are.'

'An infestation of poisonous spiders?' The very thought made my flesh crawl. 'In Venice? Surely not?'

'Well just be careful, okay?'

I could feel another panic attack creeping up on me now and to hold it off I started walking. The right thing to do, of course, would have been to check Cinta's apartment for spiders straight away. But I couldn't face it at that moment so I headed in the other direction.

I had not gone far when I sensed that someone had fallen in step beside me, someone much taller than myself. Glancing sidewise I caught a momentary glimpse of a green baseball cap and a pale, stubble-covered jawline.

With a jerk of my head I wrenched my gaze away and kept on walking, looking fixedly ahead.

'Hello, mister. How are you?'

His English was fluent but heavily accented. I noticed now that there was a tattoo coiled around his forearm, of a python.

'I'm fine,' I said, trying to keep my voice steady.

'Enjoying Venice?'

'Yes. I am.'

'But you are not tourist I think.'

'Why do you say that?'

'I see you all the time talking to Bengali *ragazzi*. Is there something you are looking for?'

'No,' I said. 'I too am a Bengali, like them. I find their stories interesting. That's all.'

'You like stories, eh?'

'Yes I do.'

'Be careful. Sometimes stories can be dangerous.'

I still couldn't bring myself to look at him. 'What do you mean?'

'Maybe you've heard, mister? There is a story called *Morte a Venezia*?'

He made a sound that was something between a laugh and a growl. 'Enjoy Venice, mister. Have a good time but remember to stay safe.'

His voice faded slowly, and I kept on walking, without looking around.

Strangely I no longer felt panicky now; instead a kind of numbness had begun to set in, a feeling of not knowing what I was doing or where I was. I wasn't even sure whether I had really spoken to that man or whether I had imagined it.

At a certain point I looked up and saw that I was in the Ghetto, walking past a small bookstore. I had almost left it behind when something caught my eye and brought me hurrying back.

Taped to the store's window was a flyer for an exhibition. My pulse quickened as I stared at it; I could hardly believe that I hadn't known about this exhibition.

The show was about one of the rarest and most valuable books on earth: the Aldine Press edition of the *Hypnerotomachia Poliphili*, a fifteenth-century allegorical text. The Aldine Press edition is widely thought to be the most beautiful book ever printed: it was produced in Venice in 1499 (which makes it technically an incunabulum, or 'early book') and the printer was none other than the great Aldo Manutius, who spent much of his life in the city and died there in 1515.

The very sight of the name was a tonic to me. Sometimes referred to as the 'Michelangelo of print', Aldo Manutius was, after Gutenberg, probably the most influential bookmaker of all time, a man whose legacy permeates our lives to this day. He designed the prototypes of some of the most widely used fonts of our day, including Bembo, and Garamond (my personal favourite); it was Manutius who invented italics, introduced the semicolon and gave the comma its distinctive hooked shape. As if this were not enough, he also created the ancestor of the modern paperback, because of which he is credited with forever changing our relationship with the written word: it was only after Aldo Manutius that people began to read not for instruction, or edification, or for purposes of piety, but purely for pleasure.

Looking more closely at the flyer I saw that the exhibition was at the Querini Stampalia Library. This name too had many resonances for me: when I had last come to Venice it was for a conference at this very library.

This sealed the matter and I set off at once.

As I made my way down the narrow, winding streets I remembered other details from my earlier visit to Venice. I recalled especially Cinta's presentation at the Querini Stampalia. She had described Venice as the 'publishing capital of the early Enlightenment'; for the first two centuries after the invention of the printing press, she had said, no less than half of all the printed books in existence had been published here; Venice had been the world centre of the book trade; it was here that the first printed Quran, in Arabic script, had appeared, in 1538; here too were published the earliest printed books in Armenian, Greek, and a variety of Slavic languages and scripts, including the Glagolitic (how I had marvelled at the ease with which that word skipped off her tongue!).

It had been amazing also to follow Cinta around the city, stopping at the places where bookshops had once stood, listening to her as she explained that 'books' in those days were merely printed broadsheets; buyers purchased the uncut sheets and then chose the binding in consultation with booksellers.

Now, as I walked towards the library, it struck me that many of those old shops and printing presses would still have been in operation when the Gun Merchant was in Venice: walking through these streets he would have seen, all around him, a universe of books.

And even as these impressions were passing through my mind, I had the strange feeling that they were no longer thoughts but memories, so vivid as to be dreams.

On my last visit to Venice I had spent many hours wandering around the Querini Stampalia Library. A labyrinth of gilded reading rooms and sleekly modern courtyards and galleries, it offered distractions at every turn. But today I had no thought for anything but the *Hypnerotomachia* exhibition.

On walking into the gallery I was surprised to find myself alone. Evidently rare books were not of interest to many tourists.

The incunabulum was in a large vitrine at the centre of the gallery. Arranged along the walls were many other vitrines and several screens. Some of the screens displayed translations of the text in different languages; others provided information on its historical background and the controversies over its authorship (which was generally attributed to a Franciscan monk by the name of Francesco Colonna).

I stopped in front of a screen that featured an English translation published in 1592, under the title *The Strife of Love in a Dreame*. Scrolling through the pages I began to remember bits of the story: it was told in the voice of a man who sets off to search for an always-absent beloved and finds himself lost in a forest where he is surrounded by savage animals – wolves, bears and hissing serpents. He wanders on and on until he falls into an exhausted sleep and dreams a dream in which he is dreaming a dream at once terrifying and erotic, filled with fantastical creatures, sculptures and monuments, some of which are engraved with cryptic messages in Latin, Greek, Hebrew and Arabic. In this dreamt-of dream voices and messages emanate from beings of all sorts – animals, trees, flowers, spirits . . .

As this started to come back to me I had an uncanny feeling that I too had lost myself in this dream; it wasn't so much that I was dreaming, but that I was being dreamed by creatures whose very existence was fantastical to me – spiders, cobras, sea snakes – and yet they and I had somehow become a part of each other's dreams.

It was as if in a dream that I went at last to look at the incunabulum, which was lying open in a velvet book cradle. Displayed around it were beautiful facsimile reproductions of some of the illustrations that graced the pages – the volume's fame rested in large part on these magnificent woodcuts (thought by some to have been executed by Mantegna).

As I circled around the vitrine, looking at those mysterious, cryptic illustrations, I began to feel that I knew some of them, that I had seen their like somewhere not long ago. Suddenly I remembered the images on the walls of the Merchant's shrine and then at once the conviction began to grow in me that the Merchant had seen these very pages, these illustrations, that this was the book in which he had seen the face of Manasa Devi. Then I came to an image of writhing snakes and all doubt disappeared. I was sure of it, sure that I, like the Gun Merchant, had entered the dreamtime of the book; that he was somewhere near me.

So much was I within this dream that I did something I would never have done had I been in my right mind. I began to struggle with the vitrine, trying to open its cover.

An alarm must have gone off although I wasn't aware of it. When I looked up again it was to find myself surrounded by uniformed guards, librarians . . . they were staring at me just as intently as I had been staring at the book.

The next I knew I was being hustled off, quite roughly, possibly to a police station or even a jail. The shock of it helped me regain my wits: I cast a quick glance over my shoulder and caught sight of a bespectacled woman. She had the look of a librarian – there comes a time when one learns to recognize them – and I cried out: 'Wait! I can explain . . . I'm a friend of Professoressa Giacinta Schiavon . . . I'm her guest.'

It was fortunate for me that Cinta was well known to the staff of the Querini Stampalia. Her name worked like a magical mantra: the librarian had a quick talk with a policeman, who had appeared out of nowhere, and then a phone call was made. An animated conversation ensued after which the phone was handed to me.

Cinta was at the other end and I tried, as best I could, to explain to her that it was all a mistake; I hadn't meant it; I would pay if the vitrine had been damaged . . . and so on.

'*Calmati, Dino*,' said Cinta. 'It's all right. I have told them about you. There is nothing to worry about. You're probably just disoriented from travelling. You should go back to the apartment and rest now.'

'Thank you, Cinta,' I said.

I was about to hand the phone back when I remembered Piya's call.

'Cinta, there's something else you should know. You may have an infestation in your apartment.'

'An infestation?' she said, sounding puzzled. 'Of what?'

'Spiders. I've been seeing them around and a friend told me that they could be poisonous.'

There was a sharp intake of breath at the other end. '*Orribile!* I will ask Marco to check at once. Anyway, you must not worry – I will come home myself tomorrow.'

'I am so glad to hear that, Cinta.'

'*A presto, caro.* Ciao ciao ciao!'

Marco, the *portinaio*, materialized in front of me just as I was about to slip away upstairs. He was a burly man with a bushy moustache and a big belly. I had made his acquaintance on the day of my arrival – it was he who had handled my paperwork and given me the keys to Cinta's apartment. I had run into him several times since and on some of those occasions I had tried to speak to him in Italian. But he wasn't having any of it – I was a tourist as far as he was concerned and was therefore fit only to be spoken to in English.

Now, I could tell, from his expression, that he had been waiting for me and was none too pleased that I had come back late.

'Ah, mister,' he said, holding up a hand. 'Wait, one minute!'

'Yes? What is it?'

'Is true, no,' said Marco, 'you see something in Professoressa Schiavon's *appartamento*? Insect? Spider?'

'Yes,' I said, 'I saw a venomous spider there yesterday. A friend told me that there might be an infestation.'

'I look everywhere – there was nothing, *niente, nulla*. I come with you now. You show me where you see spider.'

We went up to the apartment together and he picked out a

key from the jangling bunch that was attached to his belt. Unlocking the door he ushered me in: '*Prego.*'

I stepped in and he followed, closing the door with a thud. An instant later we heard a sound, of something falling, in the living room. I went to the door and looked in: there was a book lying open on the floor.

'These old *palazzi Veneziani*,' sighed Marco. 'Any time you shut a door, something jumps off a shelf.'

'This one must have jumped a long way,' I said.

The book had fallen beside a chair in the centre of the room. Picking it up, I saw that it had a brightly coloured tiger on the cover: it was Salgari's book about the Sundarbans. I was almost certain that I had reshelved it after taking it out.

Or had I?

Meanwhile Marco was growing impatient. '*Forza!*' he said. 'Show me where you see spider.'

I replaced the book and turned to Marco: 'Come, I'll take you there.'

I led him to the maid's room and switched on the light. I was stepping forward to show Marco the spot where I had seen the spider when something fell against the windowpane with a thud.

I jumped backwards, in fright, and Marco began to laugh.

'Nothing to worry, just a bird.'

I focused my eyes on the window and saw that there was a small brownish bird perched on the sill. It looked at me for a moment before flying away.

'It happens sometimes,' said Marco. 'They fly north and they get tired. When they see a light they fly to it. It is their season of . . . how do you call it?'

'Migration?'

'*Sì. Migrazione.*'

'Anyway,' I said, pointing to the table. 'It was here that I saw the spider. It was on my laptop.'

'*Sarà!*' Marco rolled his eyes in exasperation. 'I look in this room already. Nothing. *Nulla!* I live here twenty years never see spider. You come two, three days and you see. *Ma come?*'

'I don't know but I did see it. Here, look.' I showed him the picture on my cellphone.

He was unimpressed. 'Many spider in your country, no? Maybe you see there?'

'No. It was right here.'

He threw up his hands and turned to go. 'You see again you call me, okay?'

'Okay.'

On his way out Marco gave me a pat on the back, as if in reassurance, which left me feeling both foolish and guilty for having alarmed Cinta unnecessarily. After I had closed the door I pulled out my phone and sent her a text: 'Marco has checked the apartment. There's nothing here. Don't worry. All is well.'

She answered within minutes. '*Grazie, caro!* Sleep well. See you tomorrow.'

I went to the kitchen and was about to pour myself a glass of water when something began to knock on a windowpane. I spun around and saw another brown bird, perched on the sill: it was pecking at the glass. When I stepped towards the window the bird flew off, wings flashing. I stood at the window looking outside, at the flower-filled garden at the back and the dimly lit lane beyond the wall. I saw nothing of note but suddenly I had an odd feeling at the back of my neck. I turned around, to find nothing there – but somewhere in the apartment there was a creak and a groan, the sound of centuries-old wood slowly settling into the soft mud of the lagoon.

There was nothing untoward anywhere in sight, yet everything around me seemed to be alive, even the air, which was brushing against my face as though there were a draught blowing through. Yet the windows were all closed.

Trying to calm myself I put a call through to Gisa and told her about the boat that Lubna was hoping to hire.

'Maybe it will be interesting for you to go on this boat, Gisa? What do you think?'

She thought for a bit. 'Maybe you are right, Dino. It could be *molto interessante*. I will discuss it with my team and call you back.'

When I got off the phone I realized that I was very tired. I decided to go to bed but sleep eluded me and I lay awake a long time, listening to the apartment's nightly litany of creaks and groans, which seemed louder and more insistent than ever before.

At some point I drifted off, but only to wake up, some hours later. My heart was pounding and I was beset by a sense of urgency, as though something were imminent. Even the air seemed heavier, as in the hours before the breaking of a thunderstorm.

I went to the kitchen again, to get some water, and on the way back to the bedroom, when I shut the door behind me, I heard a sound in the living room – a sound of something falling, as if out of startled hands.

I ignored it and went back to bed.

Warnings

Early next morning I was sitting at the kitchen table, with a cup of tea, when I heard the clicking of a key in the apartment's front door. Then Cinta's voice rang out: 'Dino? Are you there?'

'Yes. I'm in the kitchen.'

'*Aspetta!*'

She veered off to the living room to draw the curtains. When she came out again she had a book in her hands. She waved it at me and laughed.

'I see you're reading Salgari . . . ?'

Then she caught sight of me, sitting at the kitchen table, and came to a sudden stop. '*Caro mio!* What's happened? You look terrible.'

Coming into the kitchen, she put a hand on my shoulder. 'That expression on your face – it's like you're trying to frighten away a ghost!'

'You caught me unawares,' I said. 'I didn't expect you to arrive so early.'

'I left as soon as I could,' she said. 'I could tell from your voice yesterday that something was wrong, that you were not yourself. And now I see that I was right: you're shaking.'

'Am I?'

'Yes. What is the matter, Dino?'

'I don't know, Cinta. But you're right – I'm not my usual self.'

She seated herself across from me, on the other side of the table. 'Tell me, Dino, what is wrong? *Dimmi!*'

'I don't know that I can explain it, Cinta. It's just that lots of things have been happening that I can't account for. It's a strange feeling, as though I'm not in control of what I'm doing. It's as if I were fading away, losing my will, my freedom.'

'What has made you feel this way? Tell me.'

'It's a lot of little things, Cinta, happening in quick succession. And I feel silly even saying this, but that whole business with the spider was really unsettling – the way it appeared in front of me and was just standing there, as though it were looking at me, as if there were some sort of connection between us . . . and then finding out that it was extremely venomous. I mean, I'm sure I'm making too much of it. I know it has nothing to do with me, that there's a perfectly natural, scientific explanation.'

'Really?' said Cinta frowning. 'And what is this natural, scientific explanation?'

'Oh you're as familiar with the explanation as I am, Cinta,' I said impatiently. 'You know – temperatures are rising around the world because of global warming. This means that the habitats of various kinds of animals are also changing. The brown recluse spider is extending its range into places where it wasn't found before – like this part of Italy.'

'Yes, I understand that,' said Cinta. 'But why is the world warming? Is that natural too?'

'Yes, in a sense it is,' I said. 'It's happening because there's more and more carbon dioxide in the atmosphere, and other greenhouse gases too.'

'And where do these gases come from?' said Cinta. 'Do they not come from cars and planes and factories that make –' she looked around the kitchen, pointing with her forefinger – 'whistling kettles and electric toasters and espresso machines? Is all this natural too – that we should need these things that nobody needed a hundred years ago?'

'Oh come on, Cinta,' I retorted. 'You know as well as I do that there's a long history behind all of this.'

She seized eagerly upon this. '*Eccolo!* There you are! So you cannot say that this spider's presence here is "natural" or "scientific".

It is here because of *our* history; because of things human beings have done. It is linked to you already – you have a prior connection with that spider, whether you like it or not.'

'So what are you saying then?' I shot back sarcastically. 'That the spider was brought here by some sort of magic or witchcraft? That it's carrying a message? Or trying to take possession of me?'

Cinta smoothed back her long white hair.

'Didn't you just say, Dino, that you feel yourself fading away, that you're losing your will?'

'So I did.'

'Do you know what that is a symptom of?'

'Maybe depression?'

'You can call it that if you like. But there are other ways of looking at it as well. When I was writing my book about the Inquisition in Venice I read hundreds of case files that described those symptoms. The cases were adjudicated by Inquisitors, and many of them were about magical practices and spirit possession. That may lead you to think that these cases were about ghostly apparitions or things flying about in the sky – but that was not it at all. Almost always the cases were about the loss of "will" and "freedom" – *volontà e libertà*. A victim thinks that she is being prevailed on to do things she would not normally do, of her own will. Or someone feels that a spell has been put on them or that they have been given a potion that has made them fall in love with someone they would not otherwise have cared for. A wife might believe that someone has put a spell on her husband to steal him from her. A son may imagine that someone has bewitched his father so that he is wasting his wealth. A girl is convinced that she has been robbed of her will to the point that she cannot get out of bed or even move her limbs. They are all beset by a feeling that inexplicable forces are acting upon them in such a way that they are no longer in control of what happens to them. Most cases of possession are exactly like that.'

She looked into my eyes and smiled. 'And are these not your own symptoms?'

I stared at her in disbelief. 'Cinta, are you really trying to tell me that I'm possessed? That my soul has been stolen?'

She smiled. 'No, Dino, no. That is not at all what I am saying. You and I don't live in a world where it is possible to be possessed in the old sense. These things happened to our ancestors because their will, and their sense of their presence in the world, were essential to their very survival. To get by they had to depend on the soil, the weather, animals, neighbours, family and so on, none of which would yield what they needed just for the asking, in the manner of, say, a cash machine, or a ticket agent at the *stazione*. Everything they depended on for their livelihood could fight back and resist, no matter whether it was a spouse or a horse, let alone the wind and the weather. Merely to survive they needed to assert their presence or they would have been overwhelmed, they would have become shadows of themselves. That is why possession – the loss of presence – was a matter of such anxiety for them. You and I face no such threat. We live in a world of impersonal systems; we don't have to impose our presence on a cash machine in order to get our money; we don't have to exert our will on our cellphones in order to make them work. In our circumstances no one needs to assert their presence in order to get by from day to day. And since it is not needed, that sense of presence slowly fades, or is lost or forgotten – it's easier to let the systems take over.'

It took me a couple of minutes to work out the implications of what she was saying. 'But if that's true, Cinta,' I said, 'then what you're implying is that people today – people like us – are *already* possessed?'

She smiled in her enigmatic way. 'All I can say, Dino, is that when I look at this world – our world – with the diagnostic tools of an Inquisitor, it becomes impossible to avoid a simple conclusion.'

'Which is . . . ?'

'That the world of today presents all the symptoms of demonic possession.'

I gasped. 'What? You can't be serious, Cinta! In what sense does it present the symptoms of demonic possession?'

'Just look around you, *caro*.' There was a touch of weariness in her voice now. 'Everybody knows what must be done if the world is to continue to be a liveable place, if our homes are not to be invaded by the sea, or by creatures like that spider. Everybody knows ... and yet we are powerless, even the most powerful among us. We go about our daily business through habit, as though we were in the grip of forces that have over-whelmed our will; we see shocking and monstrous things happening all around us and we avert our eyes; we surrender ourselves willingly to whatever it is that has us in its power.'

She smiled and reached out to pat my hand. 'That is why whatever is happening to you is not "possession". Rather I would say that it is a *risveglio*, a kind of awakening. It may be dangerous of course, but that is because you are waking up to things that you had never imagined or sensed before. You are lucky, Dino – some unknown force has given you a great gift.'

She got up and went to look out of a window. 'I envy you, *caro*, but I am grateful too – you have brought the Gun Merchant into my life as well. I think that imposes an obligation on us, don't you?'

'What kind of obligation?'

'To retrace his footsteps; to try to see Venice as it was when he was here.'

'And how do we do that?'

'I think we should go for a long walk, to look at some of the things that the Gun Merchant would have seen when he was in Venice. How do you feel about that?'

I jumped eagerly to my feet. 'I think that's a wonderful idea! When shall we go?'

She smiled. 'In a while, *caro*. Let me settle in first. Maybe after lunch?'

That afternoon, as so often before, Cinta stepped out in an outfit that was at once eccentric and mysteriously elegant: she had

237

matched a flowing black dress and a fuchsia-coloured Indian dupatta with a pair of blue sneakers and a tan fedora that had a feather sticking out of the hatband.

It was a clear day and the city was thronged with visitors. The noise of the crowd filled the streets with a sound that would once have been an indistinct hubbub to me but within which I was now aware of a constant murmuring of Bangla. It was as though I were in a forest and the whispering voices of a certain stream, or a kind of tree, were reaching out towards me, not to draw me into the spirit of the place, but rather into its living flesh.

To Cinta, on the other hand, the forest whispered of absences: 'My aunt lived there . . .' she would say, lifting a finger to point, 'and over there was the best hat maker in the city'; or, while passing yet another souvenir shop, 'My friends and I would go to that shop, after school, for a *sfogliatina*.'

From time to time she would spot an acquaintance and they would greet each other with the melancholy ardour of the last members of a vanishing tribe: 'There are so few of us Venetians left now that we all know each other. I can hardly describe the joy it gives me to speak our dialect.'

'I know exactly what you mean, Cinta.'

At one corner she stopped to show me an alley. 'Over there is the house where Marco Polo is said to have been born. I'm sure someone would have pointed it out to the Gun Merchant – the Polos were, after all, the most famous of merchant-travellers, even then.'

After a short while we found ourselves on the Rialto Bridge. Cinta stabbed a forefinger in the direction of a magnificent palace with a crimson facade, pierced by rows of tall, pointed windows.

'This is the Palazzo Bembo,' she said. 'It belonged to the family of the great poet Pietro Bembo.'

'After whom Manutius named the Bembo font?'

'Exactly! Long after Pietro Bembo's lifetime, a great traveller was born into the same family, Ambrosio Bembo – he was younger than the Gun Merchant but a contemporary none-theless. In 1671, at the age of nineteen, young Ambrosio set off on a long journey; he travelled all the way to India and back.'

Cocking her head she began to scratch her cheek.

'It is not too far-fetched, I think, to imagine that Ambrosio Bembo may have met the Gun Merchant. After all, he is sure to have made enquiries about the route, amongst people in the know. Someone or the other would have told him about Captain Ilyas, who in turn may have mentioned that a native of India was present right here, in Venice. *È abbastanza plausibile, no?*'

In the meantime, a young Bengali had appeared in front of us, carrying a bucket that was filled with ice and bottled water. Succumbing to his entreaties Cinta bought a couple of bottles, one for me and one for her. Then she whispered to me, in an aside. 'Ask this *ragazzo* where he's from and how he came here. In Bangla.'

'*Desh koi?*' I said to the boy.

The boy was astonished, as I knew he would be, at being addressed in Bangla by a random customer.

The look on his face delighted Cinta. 'What does he say? *Dimmi! Dimmi!*'

The *ragazzo* listened as I translated his words. 'He's from Madaripur, in Bangladesh, my own ancestral district. He left when he was eighteen and went to work in Libya. After two years he crossed the sea in a rubber raft and ended up in Sicily.'

'He came in a *gommone*?' gasped Cinta. 'But didn't he fear for his life? Ask him – wasn't he afraid to take such risks?'

I put the question to him and then translated his answer. 'He says he never thought about it like that. He was in a group and they crossed over together, giving hope and courage to each other.'

Here the young man broke in, with a grin, challenging me. 'And you?' he said. 'How did you come here?'

'In a plane.'

'And is there no risk in that?' he said, grinning. 'Did you study the risks before you got on the plane?'

'No.'

'Nor did I,' he said. 'Sometimes things seem normal just because others are doing it. And anyway, when you're young you don't think so much about risk.'

Picking up his bucket he went racing after another customer.

I explained what he had said to Cinta and she nodded as though I had confirmed something that had long been on her mind.

'Sometimes I ask myself,' she said, 'what would happen if those great Venetian travellers – the Polos, Niccolò de' Conti, Ambrosio Bembo – were to come back to the Venice of today? Who would they have more in common with? Us twenty-first-century Italians, who rely on immigrants to do all our dirty work? The tourists, who come in luxury liners and aeroplanes? Or these *ragazzi migranti*, who take their lives in their hands to cross the seas, just like all those great Venetian travellers of the past?'

We went over the Rialto Bridge and then Cinta turned right, into a piazza that adjoined an arcade. Under the shade of the arches lay a row of old shopfronts, most of them now boarded up.

'This,' said Cinta, 'was the market where your Merchant would have come to dispose of his cowrie shells. Here he would have bargained with wholesalers who needed shells to provision ships bound for the Atlantic. In West Africa the currency of cowries was essential for the fastest-growing commerce of the time – chattel slavery, intended for the New World. It was at this time that the trade in African slaves was becoming a pillar of the colonial economies of Europe.'

She walked on, leading me across a crowded street and into a narrow, quiet lane. 'You must remember, Dino,' said Cinta, 'that at the time when your Merchant came here, in the 1660s, Venice was a shrunken, haunted city. Its best days as a commercial power were over – they had ended with the discovery of the new sea routes, to the Americas and to the Indian Ocean. And this was, after all, the calamitous time of the Little Ice Age, when everything was in disorder, in the heavens and on earth. For Venice the crisis peaked in 1630. On the far side of the Alps a terrible war was raging, the Thirty Years War – just as a new thirty years' war is raging now, across the Mediterranean. And then amidst all of this, the weather too turned against humanity; the skies opened up, deluging the plains of northern Italy – no one had ever seen rain like this before, rain that swept away crops and destroyed harvests. The price of food shot up and hunger stalked the land – and where there is hunger, disease always follows.

'In 1629 German soldiers brought the plague to Milan and within weeks tens of thousands were dead. The epidemic leapt from city to city – from Mantova to Padova and then Venice, where it is said to have been brought in by a diplomat.

'The disease was not new to Venice; there had been other outbreaks of the plague before and much had been learnt from them: many tracts had been published on governing *la peste* and permanent boards of health had been set up as far back as the fifteenth century. You could even say that modern sanitary protocols, for dealing with epidemics, were invented in Venice. So when the great plague of 1630 broke out the city fathers were not slow to act.'

She stabbed my arm with her forefinger, as if to prevent me from jumping to a mistaken conclusion.

'Do not imagine, Dino, that these councillors were credulous men. Most of them had been educated at the University of Padova, which was a great centre of rationalism – that is where Galileo had once taught, and his doctrine, of the orderliness of nature, was like scripture to the men who presided over Venice. They were like the EU bureaucrats of today – competent, well-educated administrators, not given to flights of fancy: their faith in the power of human reason was limitless.

'They got swiftly to work, enacting measure after measure. Quarantines and curfews were put into place; all who were suspected of infection were transported to a quarantined island, while the few who recovered were sent to yet another island. All public places were closed and people were forbidden to leave their houses; only soldiers could move about freely. The streets were so empty that plants began to sprout between the paving stones. Specially appointed marshals, whose faces were covered with beaked masks, would go from house to house, fumigating and checking for signs of the disease.

'But the plague was relentless. People died in the thousands – workmen and fishwives, noblewomen and priests, not even the most exalted *probiviri* were spared. In a few months a quarter of the city's population perished. The barques that carried away the dead could not cope with the numbers; the canals were choked with corpses; in the Arsenale – where today they hold exhibitions of art – bodies lay stacked in piles, men could not be found to pour lye on them.

'But in the midst of this horror there was one tiny corner of the city, an alleyway called the Corte Nova, that was almost unaffected. A young girl who lived there had made a painting of the Blessed Virgin and hung it at the entrance of the *corte*, saying that the plague would not be able to get past the Madonna – and strangely, miraculously, it transpired that the people who lived in that alley were spared the horrors of the plague.

'The Blessed Virgin has always been greatly venerated by Venetians; now the whole city threw itself on her mercy. Even the city fathers, those competent men of reason, recognized their utter helplessness and passed a resolution pledging to build a great church dedicated to the Madonna. And when it happened, soon after, that the plague began to recede, it was said that a miracle had been wrought by Santa Maria della Salute – the Madonna of Good Health.'

She came to a halt and pointed ahead, to a great grey dome that had come suddenly into view ahead of us, towering over the Grand Canal. 'And there it is: Santa Maria della Salute. Today the church is one of the great icons of the city.'

'Yes, I remember the Turner paintings.'

'There have been many others as well – La Salute has probably been painted and photographed as much as any place on earth. Yet it could also be said that it is a monument to a catastrophe, a memorial to the terrible afflictions of the Little Ice Age.'

We paused to admire the soaring, octagonal church as the reflected ripples of the Grand Canal played upon its bright white surface.

'Your Merchant would not have seen La Salute in this form,' said Cinta. 'It took almost fifty years to build. Just to lay the foundations, in the mud, took many years. In the 1660s, if that was indeed when your Merchant was here, he would have seen only the octagonal rotunda that supports the dome. But he would have observed the great church rising and he would have known why it was being built. How could he not? The Venice of his time was a place where the terrible plague of 1630 was still a vivid memory.'

As she was speaking a vaporetto sped by, on the Grand Canal, and the ripples on the church's surface changed into a turbulent, shimmering vortex of reflected light. I saw then that the church was not merely beautiful; it was imbued also with dread and foreboding; it was a cry of warning from a moment of desperation so extreme that it had turned itself into stone.

I followed Cinta up the monumental steps, into the church, and we walked around the circular aisle to the high altar, at the centre of which was a glowing, gilded icon of a dark-skinned Madonna and Child.

'She is the Black Madonna of La Salute,' said Cinta. 'The Panaghia Mesopanditissa, Madonna the Mediator: it is she who stands between us and the incarnate Earth, with all its blessings and furies.'

She turned to smile at me. 'As you can see, the icon is Byzantine in style. *Infatti* it was brought here from Heraklion in Crete – a city that is famously associated with A-sa-sa-ra-me.'

She arched an eyebrow at me: 'Do you know who that is?'

'No.'

'She is the Minoan goddess of snakes.'

Turning away, Cinta knelt to say a prayer and light a candle while I wandered off by myself and went to look up at the great dome. As I was staring into that cavernous hollow, the church's bells began to peal. In the past I had always taken that sound to be an expression of joy and celebration; I remembered now that bells were also rung in warning, when great danger is in the offing. It was as if a voice were crying out from the past to remind the world that the limits of human reason and ability become apparent not in the long, slow duration of everyday time, but in the swift and terrible onslaught of fleeting instants of catastrophe.

Then I felt Cinta's touch on my elbow.

'We are very lucky today,' she whispered, leading me into the circular nave. 'The centre of the church is usually roped off, except on 21 November when thousands gather to celebrate the *festa* of the Madonna della Salute. Only then are we allowed to approach the navel of the church, which is, for me, also the omphalos of my world.'

She pointed to the floor where lay a circular rose mosaic of flowers entwined around a few words of Latin. She whispered in my ear: 'Remember these words, *caro*, think of them whenever you despair of the future: *Unde origo inde salus* – "From the origin salvation comes".'

High Water

As we were stepping out of La Salute, Cinta said: 'Now that we are in this part of the city, there is something else I would like to show you, something contemporary. You must not miss it.'

We turned right, crossed a small square, and came to a narrow pathway, flanking a low, freshly painted building.

'This is the old customs house,' said Cinta. 'It was built at about the same time as La Salute. When I was a child it was a dilapidated old place. But some years ago it was restored by a Japanese architect, and now, like every other building in the city, it is an art gallery. You should take a look: I'm told they have an interesting show on right now, of modern art.'

The path we were on ended abruptly at a triangular headland.

'This is the Punta della Dogana,' said Cinta. 'Customs House Point. As you can see, the two main thoroughfares of Venice meet here, the Grand Canal and the Giudecca Canal.'

Directly ahead of us lay a striking vista of St Mark's Square and the lagoon beyond.

'Let's go in,' said Cinta. 'The show will be closing soon.'

We stepped inside to find ourselves in the midst of a dramatically lit exhibition space. On display were some rather dull installations, which most of the viewers had chosen to ignore in favour of a work that was positioned at the far end of the gallery.

We had to wait a while before we were able to make our way through the crowd that had collected around the exhibit. When at last we got there we found ourselves looking into a long, brightly lit tank of water: it was like a large aquarium and submerged in it were several long, tentacle-like forms, coiled around each other. They were covered with tiny metallic scales of brilliant, parrot-like colours. Viewers were encouraged to interact with the piece by touching it and stirring the water. With every touch the tentacles would undulate and uncoil and change shape – and the lighting was so ingenious that the writhing forms seemed almost to come to life.

Cinta and I were both quite taken with the piece. She looked it up in the catalogue and gave a little laugh. 'Why,' she said, 'it's an old friend!'

'The artist?'

'No! The creature – *il mostro*.' She showed me the title: '*Il mostro di Punta della Dogana – The Monster of Customs House Point*.'

The write-up in the catalogue explained that the piece had been inspired by an old Venetian legend about a monster that had its lair beneath the embankment of the Punta della Dogana.

'Weren't we there a couple of minutes ago?'

'Yes.' Cinta laughed, tugging at my elbow. 'Come – let's go back and see if we can spot the creature.'

She led me out of the gallery and went straight ahead, to the point where the two big canals met. The tide was coming in and the water was only a couple of inches below our shoes.

'Over the centuries,' said Cinta, 'there have been many reported sightings of *il mostro*, in different parts of the Venetian lagoon. Some say that a giant squid – perhaps a whole *famiglia* – had moved into these waters. The last sighting was in the 1930s, and the two fishermen who reported it claimed to have seen the creature near the Punta della Dogana. That was how the story grew that *il mostro* lived here.'

Cinta dipped the tip of her shoe into the water that was lapping against the embankment.

'But tell me, Dino,' she said, with one of her playful smiles, 'does this look to you like a place where a *mostro* would live? At the busiest point in the city's network of canals? With so much traffic going by?'

She pointed to the vaporettos that were roaring past us.

'No! that's a tale only tourists would believe. This cannot have been the place where it lived.'

I glanced at her face and saw that her eyes were sparkling mischievously.

'No, Dino,' she said, leaning closer. 'When I was little I knew for a fact that *il mostro* lived on the other side of the city. My uncle had seen it, you see.'

She tapped my arm and started walking briskly. 'Come, Dino,' she said. 'I'll tell you the story while I take you to the place.' She gave me a wink. 'And when we get there I'll show you some real monsters too.'

I could tell from the febrile brightness of her eyes that she was in one of her moods and that I had no choice but to follow.

Cinta's grandfather, on her father's side, had been a fisherman. Although neither of his sons had followed him into the trade they had both liked to fish, especially Cinta's uncle Ruggiero, who would often go out to the Fondamente Nove to try his luck.

The Fondamente Nove is the kilometre-long embankment that runs along the city's north-eastern edge. Being a good distance from the main streets and piazzas, it remains to this day one of the least frequented parts of the city. Back in the 1920s it was a dark, lonely place with splintering piers. This made it peculiarly well suited for catching squid and cuttlefish: a lantern would be hung over the water and the creatures would come floating up to the light, needing only to be scooped up with a net.

One night Cinta's uncle Ruggiero, then a teenager, went to the pier with an expensive new gas lantern that the family had recently acquired: he smuggled it out of the house without his father's permission, thinking that the bright light would fetch him a good catch.

He was right: squid and cuttlefish came up in swarms when he hung up the gas lamp; his bucket filled up in record time. But as he was bending down for one last scoop his net was suddenly snatched out of his hands. He waited for it to float up – it had a wooden handle – but it didn't reappear. It was as if some large and powerful creature had caught hold of it and carried it away.

But how could that be?

Ruggiero hung the lantern on a hook, lay flat on the pier and stared into the water, thinking that the net had snagged on something – but instead of the net he saw two little shining discs, deep in the water; they seemed to reflect the light back at him, like the eyes of a cat. The discs began to grow larger as he watched, as though they were rising towards the surface.

That was enough for Ruggiero to take to his heels – abandoning the lantern, he sprinted down the pier. He hadn't got very far when he heard a splash and a sizzling sound. Glancing over his shoulder he saw that the lantern had been pulled off its hook and dragged into the water: it glowed faintly for a moment before sinking below the surface.

'I heard the story many, many years later of course,' said Cinta. 'I was just a child and it caught my fancy. For a long time I was desperate to see the creature. My friends and I would go there sometimes, to that exact spot, with torches and lamps.'

'And . . . ?'

'We never saw anything. By that time electricity was everywhere. People said the lights had driven the creature away.'

The story was told with many interruptions because we were passing through streets that were so narrow and crowded that Cinta and I could not long remain in step. And of course every once in a while Cinta would bump into an acquaintance which would lead to a chat, introductions and so on, which delayed us still more.

Our progress was so slow that the sun had already set when the Fondamente Nove came into view, in the distance. We were now in a neighbourhood of tunnel-like lanes and crooked little houses, many of which seemed to be abandoned or uninhabited. It was clear at a glance that this had once been a working-class area.

Veering suddenly to the right, Cinta stopped in front of a small two-storey house that was leaning sideways at a giddy angle. 'This was where my father's family lived,' she said. Raising a finger, she pointed to a tilted window. 'My *nonna* would sit there every evening, watching people go by. My *zio* Ruggiero lived here all his life. His son, my cousin Altiero, grew up here but he moved away after his marriage – Gisa is his daughter.'

She looked up at the dimming sky. 'It was at this time of the day that *zio* Ruggiero would go to fish.'

Turning around she led me out of the lane and down the street, to the Fondamente Nove. It was almost dark now and lights were winking on the surrounding islands; the silhouettes of innumerable spires and towers could be seen outlined against the twilit sky.

But the embankment, and the buildings that lined it, were all dark. 'Do people live in this neighbourhood?' I asked.

'I doubt it,' said Cinta. 'I think most of the buildings are abandoned . . .'

She was interrupted by the wailing of a siren, in the distance.

'Ah!' said Cinta, cocking her head. 'It's a warning, for the *acqua alta*, the high water. There will be a flood tonight.'

The water was now only a couple of inches below the level of the pavement. I glanced along the embankment, in both directions. There was no one in sight, so far as I could tell, but it was hard to be sure, in that crepuscular light.

'Shouldn't we head back now, Cinta?' I said.

She laughed. '*Beh!* We're already here and there's still time.' She started to walk briskly along the embankment. 'Come along. Who knows? Maybe *il mostro* will rise with the flood.'

She stepped on to a narrow wooden pier that extended some ten metres into the water. On either side of it, rising high above the pier's wooden planks, were tall timber pilings made of pairs of logs that were fastened together with rope.

Cinta walked to the end of the pier, holding on to the rails that flanked it. On reaching the end she turned back to beckon. 'Come, *caro*, come – don't be afraid, we are there. This is where my *zio* Ruggiero saw the *mostro*.' She patted a pair of pilings. 'This is where he hung the lantern.'

Pulling out her cellphone she turned on its flashlight and shone the beam into the water. 'Come here, Dino,' she said. 'Where's your phone? Turn on your light.'

Stepping to her side, I shone my cellphone's light into the watery darkness, which was now just below the surface of the pier. The two beams formed rippling circles on the murky, greenish brown water.

'Alas, the *mostro* of the lagoon does not want to be seen,' said Cinta with a chuckle. 'So I will show you a different kind of monster, much more dangerous.'

Turning slightly, she shone the flashlight beam on the piling beside her. 'Here – look!'

I saw that her beam had landed on a section of the piling where a concave indentation had been carved neatly into the wood.

'Look closely,' said Cinta, 'and you'll see the monsters.'

Turning my own flashlight beam on the piling I saw that the surface of the indentation was pitted with holes, like the inside of a book that has been attacked by termites. Then suddenly I realized that there was something alive inside the piling, not just one but many; they were wriggling, moving.

Pulling out a hairpin Cinta dug into the indentation, picking at the rotten wood. Suddenly one of the creatures plopped out and fell on the pier, near our feet. I managed to move my flashlight beam quickly enough to get a look at it. It was about two inches long, the colour of congealed coconut oil. Its tapering body widened into a funnel-like mouth that was ringed with tiny filaments.

It was so hideous that it was difficult to believe that it was real.

In a moment it slithered away and fell into the water.

'What is it?' I said to Cinta.

'A shipworm. A friend of mine who works in the *municipio* brought me here a month ago to show me these creatures and the damage they are doing: it was he who made that cut in the wood. More and more of these are invading Venice, with the warming of the lagoon's water. They eat up the wood from the inside, in huge quantities. It has become a big problem because Venice is built on wooden pilings. They are literally eating the foundations of the city.'

We turned our cellphones on the pilings again and focused the beams on the worms, wriggling inside the wood. Cinta knocked on a log with her knuckles. 'From the outside it looks *saldo*, doesn't it, really solid? But inside it is probably hollow.'

She was still speaking when the rail we were leaning on slipped sideways, catching us both off guard. As we snatched at the rail our cellphones flew out of our hands and vanished into the water.

I heard a creaking sound and shouted to Cinta, 'Quick! Move to the other side!'

No sooner had we moved than a section of the rails toppled over and fell into the water, tearing chunks of wood out of the pilings and exposing its hollowed-out interior. We watched in horror as a mass of squirming shipworms came pouring out of the broken logs. They fell on to the pier and came swarming towards us.

I grabbed Cinta's arm: 'Run! Run!'

But the worms were all over the pier now. We had taken only

a few steps when Cinta stepped on them and slipped. I tried to catch her as she tumbled forwards but was unable to arrest her fall. She let out a scream as we both fell on to the planks.

And then the worms were swarming over us – our legs, arms, faces, heads. It was as though the earth itself had sent out tentacles to touch us, to feel the texture of our skin and see whether we were real.

We were thrashing about, clawing at the worms, when a wave swept over the pier, washing most of the worms away. When the water receded I heard Cinta moaning softly.

'What is it, Cinta?'

'It's my leg and my ankle; they hurt *molto, molto*.'

'Do you think you can stand up?'

She made an effort to push herself up and then collapsed with a grunt of pain. 'No. *Non posso*.'

I put my arm around her and glanced at the water. It was rising fast now; I knew we didn't have much time – soon we would be marooned.

'Wait here, Cinta, just for a minute.'

Struggling to my feet, I looked at the shore to see if it might be possible to get Cinta to the end of the pier and back to the Fondamente Nove. But the embankment was itself under water now and a section of the pier was leaning heavily to one side: even if I were able to get over it myself I knew there was no way I could get Cinta across. Even to try would be to risk having her fall in the water – and in her present state, she would be helpless.

The lights of the city were glowing in the distance and things seemed to be carrying on much as usual, despite the flood. I could even hear a band, playing somewhere far away. But our immediate surroundings were in complete darkness; there was not a single light to be seen nearby.

A tide of disbelief washed over me as I stood in the ankle-deep water, looking at the illuminated spires in the distance. How was it possible that in this most civilized of cities we should be so utterly alone and helpless, so completely at the mercy of the earth?

Cinta was mumbling now; I caught the word 'Madonna' and knew she was praying.

It had been so long since I prayed that I did not know who to pray to. When I knelt beside her and shut my eyes the image that appeared before me was that of an open palm sheltered by a cobra's hood.

'Look!'

It was Cinta, tugging at my elbow. '*Guarda!* Over there – *laggiù.* Look!'

Following her finger I spotted a dim glow, like that of a candle. It seemed to be coming from one of the abandoned buildings on the Fondamente Nove.

'I think there's someone in there,' said Cinta. 'Maybe a *senza-tetto* or a squatter. They may be able to help. Why don't you try shouting?'

I cupped my hands around my mouth: '*Aiuto, per favore, aiuto!*'

There was a moment's silence and then a voice rang out: '*Dove sei? Che succede?*'

Although the words were Italian the voice was not; in fact it sounded somehow familiar.

'*Bilal naki?*' I shouted in Bangla. 'Is it you, Bilal?'

'*Hā!* Yes.' He sounded startled.

'It's me, Dinanath Datta. I talked to you the other day. I'm stuck on a pier and my friend is badly hurt. Can you call an ambulance or something?'

'Of course!'

I saw that the water had risen to Cinta's waist now.

'*Taratari* – please hurry, Bilal.'

A couple of minutes went by before I heard Bilal's voice again. 'An *ambulanza* will be here in a few minutes. Do you want me to come over there to help?'

'No,' I shouted back. 'There's nothing more you can do. It's lucky for us that you were here. *Grazie! Grazie mille.*'

'*Prego*,' he said. 'I'm glad I could help. But one thing please: don't tell anyone about where I was. This is our secret place.'

'I won't say a word,' I said. 'Don't worry!'

I seated myself beside Cinta and tried to warm her hands between mine. The water was almost up to our chests when we heard a siren, wailing in the distance. It grew louder and louder until suddenly a white and orange launch appeared beside us.

Crossings

The reason for the prompt arrival of the ambulance was that the hospital – the Ospedale Civile – was very close by, at the other end of the Fondamente Nove. The journey there took only a couple of minutes.

The hospital was well prepared for the *acqua alta*: the ambulance pulled into a covered dock where an emergency nurse and technicians were waiting with a stretcher. I followed them down a plastic-enclosed tunnel into an immaculately clean modern building. Cinta was whisked through a door marked *Pronto Soccorso Traumatologico* while I waited at the reception desk in my dripping clothes. After a while a kindly nurse took pity on me and handed me a set of green overalls and a pair of hospital slippers. When I had changed she gave me a plastic bag for my wet clothes and then led me through a warren of corridors, cloisters and staircases into what seemed to be an old monastery. Ushering me into an immense, empty loggia, she left me to wait for news of Cinta.

I went to a tall, stone-framed window and gazed down at the strange spectacle of the flooded city. Wooden *passerelle* had appeared everywhere, tended by gumboot-wearing migrants; and at every corner there seemed to be a group of Bengalis, selling boots, galoshes and plastic shoe protectors.

So absorbed was I that I didn't notice that someone had come up behind me. I jumped when he began to speak, in Bangla: '*Bané bhalo rojgar hoi.* We earn well on days like this. For us it's like home – we're used to floods.'

'Rafi!'

He was wearing a blue hospital gown and slippers. One of his arms was in plaster and he had a black eye and lacerations on his face.

'I saw you walking past my ward,' he said. 'What's brought you here?'

I told him the story, briefly, and he said: 'So Bilal was at that old warehouse on the embankment, was he?'

'Yes. It was incredibly lucky for us that he was there, at just that time.'

Rafi nodded. 'I know that place well. On flood days we sometimes spend the night there. I've been on those jetties. I've heard them.'

'Heard what?'

'The worms. It's just like the Sundarbans. There, if you put your ear to the embankments you can hear the crabs burrowing inside. My grandfather showed me how to listen to them. Sometimes, if you listen carefully, you can tell if an embankment is going to collapse. It's the same over here.'

Rafi's evocation of the Sundarbans made me recall my first encounter with him, when I was inside that shrine and he was staring at me wide-eyed through the entrance. I remembered how he had retreated as I advanced on him – and a shiver went through me at the thought that the cobra had been following me all the while, with its hood upraised. I remembered also the tenderness with which Rafi had cared for Tipu on the way back to the hospital in Lusibari.

'There's something I need to ask you, Rafi,' I said, looking him squarely in the eyes. 'And this time I want you to tell me the truth. I need to know. Did you and Tipu leave Lusibari together?'

He swallowed. 'Yes.'

'And is it true that Tipu had many more seizures?'

'Yes,' said Rafi. 'But they weren't like what happened that day in the steamer. When the fits started up again they were different.

Sometimes he would be quiet, sometimes he would start shaking; sometimes he would seem to be sleepwalking; sometimes he would be talking and arguing, with his eyes closed.'

'Were you always with him when they happened?'

'No. The first couple of times it happened at his home. His mother got very worried and wanted him to see a doctor and take medications, which Tipu didn't want to do. So after that, whenever he felt a seizure coming on, he would call me and we would go somewhere in my boat. He liked to be on the water; he said it reminded him of his boat trips with his father, when he was little.'

'Did he talk to you about what he saw during these seizures?'

'A bit,' said Rafi, 'not much. He said most of the time he himself couldn't understand what was going on. He would hear voices, or sense a presence, or see a place – even places that he had never been to. Sometimes he would hear his father's voice – that always made Tipu happy. But there were times when he was terrified – and he could never explain what it was that he was afraid of. He said he could see a kind of darkness closing in around him. And the more it happened the more restless he became. He kept saying he needed to get away from Lusibari. I'd been thinking of moving too so we decided to leave together. Had I been on my own I would probably have gone to some city in India – but Tipu wasn't interested in moving to Kolkata or Delhi. It was he who persuaded me that we should try to get to Europe – he said it would be easier for us to be together here. He began to make arrangements and we started to collect money. He insisted that it be done in secret; he was sure that his mother and his aunt Piya would try to stop him if they found out that he was planning to leave the country. He thought they might even put him in a mental hospital. So he made up a story about a job in Bangalore.'

'But the two of you went to Bangladesh instead?'

'Yes. Tipu already knew some dalals in Bangladesh and he made arrangements with them over the phone. One night we crossed the Raimangal River and went over to Dhaka. The money that we had put together – most of it was Tipu's – was just about enough to pay for the cheapest kind of journey, overland, with a little left over, to see us through on the way. We spent two weeks in Dhaka and then the dalal put us on a minibus, along with a group of other men. I was carrying only a backpack, and so was Tipu. We had some clothes, a bit of food, and around 250 US dollars each, that's all.

'There were around twenty-four men on the bus, but they weren't all paying passengers, like us. Some worked for the dalal; it was their job to get us across the border. They were tough, hard men, and you couldn't argue with them; you had to do exactly what they said. They weren't all bad, some of them were friendly and helpful. But Tipu didn't like them, he used to call them "jackals" – he said that's what men like that are called in America, except that he used some other word.'

'"Coyote"?'

'Yes, that's it. From then on, all the way to the Turkish border, we always had some jackals with us – they would change after each leg, but they were always there, keeping an eye on us. Much of the time we didn't even know their names.

'That first minibus brought us from Dhaka to the Indian border, at Benapol in West Bengal. Our dalal had already paid the necessary bribes so all we had to do was walk through the immigration checkpoint. There was another minibus waiting for us on the other side, with a fresh set of jackals.

'We got into the bus and a few hours later we were in Kolkata. We were taken to a connection house and locked inside. We stayed there for three days, twenty of us hidden in two rooms with one bathroom between us. You couldn't step out, even for a breath of air. If you complained, or asked too many questions, you'd be slapped or beaten; sometimes the jackals would hit you with pistol butts.

'On the third night, very late, we were woken abruptly and told to be ready to leave in fifteen minutes. Outside the house was an old truck, with brightly painted sides: its cargo area was fully enclosed with wooden panels, so that people couldn't look in. One by one, we were packed into this space, like cows or goats – there was just about enough room for each of us to sit.

'The truck was slow, with a bad suspension. Every time the driver changed gears clouds of exhaust would blow in, choking us. During the day it was like an oven. There were no windows to look out of. We just had to sit there, bumping against each other as the truck rattled on. From time to time, after many hours, the truck would stop and let us out to relieve ourselves. Sometimes people would get car-sick and throw up inside; the smell was so bad that others would throw up too.

'Most of the time we had no idea where we were. Sometimes, if we asked, they would say "near Agra", "near Indore" – but often they wouldn't answer. Then one night the truck stopped at a connection house in a place that looked like a desert. They told us that we were close to the Pakistan border but if we wanted to go any further we would need to arrange for an extra payment of fifty US dollars each.

'This came as a huge shock to us, because we thought we had already paid in full. We didn't know what to do. We had not planned on using our dollars so early in the journey; we had thought that we would need the money later.

'Tipu flew into a temper and began to argue with the jackals. I tried to shut him up but it was impossible; he was beside himself with rage, shouting and cursing. One of the jackals slapped him, and when that didn't stop him two of them dragged him into another room. We heard some hard blows followed by cries from Tipu. Then suddenly his voice changed and became very strange, like the howl of an animal. I'd heard him do this before so I knew he was having one of his fits. This went on for a minute or two and then the two jackals came rushing out, looking shaken. They told me to go inside and get Tipu.

'I found him lying on a bed, with his pants down. There was a stick on the floor – Tipu told me later that they were going to shove that stick into him but his seizure had come on before they could go through with it. Tipu can be frightening sometimes when he gets into one of his fits, and I think that's what saved him that day. Anyway, we paid up quietly and the jackals didn't stop us from going on with the others.

'When we next got out of the truck it was very dark. We were told to start walking, although we couldn't see where we were going. At some point we crossed into Pakistan without knowing it, and after a while we spotted someone who was signalling with a torch. Now we were handed over again, to another set of jackals. They made us walk until we came to a road where a truck was waiting.

'Then the whole thing began again: long stretches on the road with occasional halts at safe houses, in places whose names we never learnt. And as before, one night our vehicle came to a stop and we were told that we had now come to the Iranian border and would need to make further payments.

'This time it was not a surprise and no one argued, not even Tipu. He had become quieter after that incident at the India border. One day while we were crossing Iran, he told me that he could feel that there was trouble ahead, for us. Then he turned to me and said: "Rafi, if something happens to me and we get separated you must go on, no matter what."'

Rafi's voice had been level all this while but now it began to shake and he raised a hand to wipe the corner of his eye.

'*To ami oké bollam*,' he continued, 'I said to Tipu: "I would never leave you and go." And he said: "No, you must. If we're parted you must go on by yourself and you must have faith that we'll find each other again." It was almost as if Tipu knew what was going to happen.

'In Iran our jackals were Afghans and Kurds: they had dealt with so many Bengalis that they could even speak a little Bangla. After many days of driving we reached a range of mountains, in western Iran. It was very cold now and we caught glimpses of snow. Most of us had no warm clothes or even shoes – Tipu and I had left Bangladesh wearing rubber slippers. We had to pay the jackals whatever they asked to obtain anoraks and sneakers – we had no choice.

'We came to a small Kurdish village in the mountains and the jackals took us to a house that was already full of dozens of other men, mainly Hazaras, from Afghanistan, Pakistan and Iran. We were told that we would have to wait until a guide came to show us the way across the border, into Turkey.

'After a few days some Kurdish men came and loaded us into a truck that was covered with tarpaulin. We were told that when the truck stopped we would have to run as fast we could. They warned us that if we were spotted by Turkish border guards they would open fire. If that happened we had to keep running, they said, in the hope that the soldiers wouldn't see us in the dark. If we managed to make it over then we would be met by guides, on the other side.

'Our truck came to a halt near a steep slope. When the tailgate was lowered we jumped down and began to run, just as we had been told, falling and slipping on the loose rocks. Tipu and I were terrified of being separated; we did our best to stay close to each other.

'Suddenly we heard the sound of gunshots. There were spotlights and red flashes behind us. We were going downhill now and we began to run for our lives, faster and faster, tumbling and falling. The shots hit some of the men ahead of us; we saw them lying on the track, screaming in pain, but there was nothing we could do. We kept on moving, jumping over the bodies as if they were fallen animals. There were maybe thirty or forty of us, running blindly, in a panic: it was like a stampede.

'I don't know how, but I ended up taking shelter in a hiding place with a dozen Hazaras. I'd thought Tipu was beside me but when I looked around he wasn't there. I began to shout his name but the others stopped me, saying that I would give away our location.

'I told myself that Tipu was probably lying low somewhere

and that I would find him in the morning. But next day he was not among those who came out of hiding to join us: there was no sign of him anywhere.

'You can imagine my state then. I had no idea where Tipu was and nor did I know what to do next. It was Tipu who had studied the routes and knew where to go. All I could do was follow the others.

'We went down the mountain and were met by some Kurds who led us to a town and showed us where we could get a bus to Istanbul. After a few hours on the bus my phone rang: it was Tipu, calling through a social media app. He told me that he had taken a fall while we were scrambling downhill and had hurt his foot badly. During the night he had slowly crawled back the way we had come and had managed to reach the Iran border. The next day a group of Bengalis had helped to get him to the Kurdish village where we had stayed before. The people there had remembered him and had helped him get his foot treated. He told me that he was planning to stay there till his foot healed; after that he would make another attempt to get across the border.

'But in the meantime, Tipu had gone online to make arrangements for me. He told me that I should get off the bus at a town near Istanbul and join a group of refugees who were planning to walk to Europe. Following his advice I joined the refugees – there were a few Bengalis among them, but the others were from Iraq, Syria, Afghanistan, Somalia, Pakistan and some other countries too. I followed them over the border into Bulgaria, and then on through Serbia, into Hungary and Austria.

'All through this Tipu stayed in touch with me; it was he who said that I should try to make my way to Venice. I had often heard him talk about this place so I agreed – where else was I going to go anyway? At that time I knew nothing about Italy and Europe.

'In Austria I took a train that brought me to Italy where I was entered into a *Centro di accoglienza* near Trieste. After a few days I was moved to a camp outside the city – and it was while

I was there that Tipu made his next attempt to cross into Turkey. This time he succeeded, and I thought he would try to join me as soon as possible. But somewhere along the way something happened to change his mind. He had a dream in which a woman, an Ethiopian, had appeared before him, – she was like a *forishta*, an angel, he said. After that he could talk of nothing else – he became desperate to find her. I tried to tell him that he was crazy to think that he'd be able to find a *forishta* he'd seen in a dream – but then one day, about three weeks ago, he called to say that he'd been able to contact the woman he had dreamt of, and that she had asked him to come to a town somewhere in Egypt. He had already spoken to a dalal in Turkey who had agreed to make all the arrangements. Now it was just a question of finding the money.

'By this time I had left the camp and come to Venice, so I was earning a bit. I had offered to send Tipu money many times before but he had always said no, he would ask when he really needed it. Now I could tell that he was desperate, and I couldn't turn him down. I didn't have enough to make the payment – it was quite a large sum – so I contacted a scafista who agreed to let me pay in instalments: it was the scafista who transferred the money to Tipu's dalal.

'Tipu flew to Egypt as soon as the payment was made, which was about sixteen days ago. He called me once, from an Internet café somewhere in Egypt. He said he didn't have a phone any more and anyway it wouldn't be of any use to him because it would be taken away when he was moved to the connection house where he was going. He told me not to worry, he had met up with the people he had been looking for and it wouldn't be long before we saw each other again.

That was the last time I heard from him.'

It took some time for the story to sink in.

'What I don't understand, Rafi,' I said, 'is why you didn't contact Tipu's mother, or Piya? They could have sent him money.'

Rafi shook his head. 'Tipu didn't want me to do that. He was adamant about this – he said under no circumstances was I to ask for help from his mother or Piya. He made me promise not to tell them anything – or you either.'

'Then why are you telling me now?'

'I'll show you.'

Thrusting a hand into his hospital gown, Rafi pulled out a piece of paper that he had folded into a small square.

'This was one thing they didn't bother to take when they beat me up,' he said wryly, unfolding the sheet.

It was a picture that he had torn out of a newspaper, a photograph of a blue fishing boat, crowded with refugees.

Tapping the picture with a fingertip, Rafi said: 'Do you see this face over there? That's Tipu. You may not be able to tell because the picture's faded a bit. But, it's him, I'm sure of it. Tipu is on that Blue Boat.'

We were still talking when I realized, suddenly, that a couple of hours had passed with no news of Cinta.

Rafi helped me find my way to the reception area where I learnt that Cinta's injuries – a twisted ankle and a fracture in her tibial shaft – had been attended to and she was now under sedation, sleeping peacefully in a private room (arranged by the *direttore* of the hospital, who happened to be a friend of hers).

There was no need, said the nurse, for me to remain in the hospital any longer. I wouldn't be able to see Cinta anyway; it would be best if I came back the next day.

With that settled my first thought now was of finding a phone.

'Is there any way we can call Lubna?' I said to Rafi.

He nodded. 'There's a public phone in the waiting area. We can try her from there.'

'Won't we need a phonecard?'

'I have one,' said Rafi. 'A nurse lent it to me.'

He led me to the phone and dialled a number. 'Here,' he said passing me the handset. 'It's ringing.'

Lubna answered after a couple of rings and I wasted no time in getting to the point. 'Lubna? *Shunun* – listen, are you and your colleagues still planning to set out to meet that refugee boat?'

'Yes,' said Lubna. 'We've hired a rescue ship – it's at Marghera, not far from here. Palash and I will be going there tomorrow to join the others. Why do you ask?'

'Because I'd like to come with you.'

'Really?' She sounded more than a little surprised. '*Keno bolun to?* May I ask why?'

'It's a long story,' I said. 'Let me just say that I think I may know someone who's on that boat. He's a Bengali – Rafi's friend actually.'

'Oh? Will Rafi want to come too?'

I glanced at Rafi, who was standing right next to me, listening intently.

'Rafi is in no condition to travel,' I said. 'But I have some other friends who might want to come. Would that be okay?'

'*Shomoshya nai*,' said Lubna. 'It's no problem, so long as you can all contribute to the expenses. The boat's quite big and there's plenty of space. How many of you will there be?'

'I'm not sure,' I said. 'I have to speak to them first. I'll get back to you in a couple of hours.'

'Sure. Let me know.'

I rang off to find Rafi glowering at me.

'Why can't I come with you?'

'Because you're injured and in hospital, Rafi – just look at yourself! You're in no state to travel.'

He began to argue but I cut him short. 'Rafi! *Bas!* Enough! There's no point in dragging this out. You can't come and that's that.'

The circumstances being what they were I decided to permit myself the extravagance of a water taxi. Within half an hour I was back in Cinta's apartment, seated in front of my computer.

Once online, everything was surprisingly easy: Gisa was eager to join the expedition and as for Piya, nothing could have held her back after she had heard Rafi's story and learnt that Tipu was on the Blue Boat.

That Gisa's presence would be a great asset was soon evident. It was she who took charge of the practical details, arranging for sleeping bags and provisions, and booking a minibus to take us from the airport to Marghera to meet the ship that Lubna and her fellow activists had hired, the *Lucania*. She even managed to find a flight that would get her and her crew to Venice at about the same time as Piya, the next day. So it was arranged that Lubna, Palash and I would meet them at the airport, at midday, and that we would all go on to Marghera together.

Winds

I woke next morning to find that the weather had taken an odd turn. While the *acqua alta* had receded, the sky had turned dark. Banks of cloud, of many shades of colour, ranging from silvery to almost black, were scudding and whirling across the heavens, swept along by fierce and changeable gusts of wind. Every now and again the apartment's windows would rattle and draughts would whistle through, but only to die down a minute or two later, amidst a chorus of indignant creaks and groans from the ageing timbers.

I ate a quick breakfast, packed a bag, and set off at once for the Ospedale Civile, thinking that I would drop in on Cinta before proceeding to the airport.

By the time I left the building it was around 9 a.m. In the surrounding streets migrants were out in force, taking down the passerelle they had set up for the *aqua alta* and sweeping away the silt that had been deposited by the flood.

Sudden bursts of wind made it hard to keep from slipping on the wet paving stones; I had to stop every few minutes to huddle against a shopfront until the gusts died down. During one of these stops I heard a man call out, in Bangla – '*Kono din dekhi naai* – never seen anything like this . . .' – and a moment later a flowerpot came crashing down from a balcony above, shattering into pieces on the flagstones, no more than a yard from where we were standing.

Under ordinary circumstances it would have taken me fifteen to twenty minutes to walk from Cinta's building to the Ospedale

Civile. But today, after half an hour, I was only two-thirds of the way there. I was crossing a small campo when I heard a pounding noise around me. A moment later something cold struck me on my back, and then on my shoulders and head. I clapped a hand to my neck and found myself clutching a hailstone.

Running to the side of the square, I took shelter under the awning of a café. There were some other people there and we watched in astonishment as the hailstones came hammering down, shattering windows and cracking shopfronts. Then someone shouted, '*Guarda! Attenti!*', and I looked up to find that the awning above had filled up with hail and was sagging dangerously downwards. I managed to move away just as the awning tore open, sending down an avalanche of hailstones.

And then, just as suddenly as it had begun, the hailstorm passed and the sun appeared. Soon steam began to rise from the melting hail; it was through this shimmering, mirage-like fog that I finally made my way to the hospital.

A nurse showed me to Cinta's room and I stepped in to find her sitting in a wheelchair, with her left leg and ankle in plaster.

I had assumed that Cinta would be alone, but no sooner had we exchanged *baci* than she pointed over my shoulder. 'Look, Dino, your friend is here too.'

I turned around to see Rafi sitting in a chair, smiling sheepishly.

'This morning,' said Cinta, 'the nurse told me that a *ragazzo Bengalese* had come by to ask after me. So I told her to send him here and we have been talking ever since. Rafi's Italian is better than you might think.'

She paused to run her hands through her flowing white hair.

'I gather, Dino, that you've been very busy. Rafi says that you are about to go off on a little sailing expedition.'

'I would hardly call it that.'

'I'm disappointed, Dino – why didn't you think of including Rafi? Or me?'

'That's obvious, Cinta,' I cried. 'You're in hospital, with your

268

leg in a cast. How could you possibly come? And why would you even want to?'

Cinta wagged a finger at me. 'I think you know very well why Rafi would want to go, Dino. After all, his *benamato* is on that refugee boat. And as for me, I have a different reason.'

'Oh? What's that?'

'I have received a sign.'

'What sign? From where?'

Cinta made one of her dramatic gestures. 'It is from the story of the Gun Merchant – you will no doubt be interested to know that Rafi and I have solved the last rebus in the legend.'

'Which rebus?'

'The one near the end, after the Merchant leaves Venice and is taken captive by pirates. You remember, no, that they are taking him to be sold as a slave, on an island? But on the way there is a *miracolo* and he is set free by the creatures of the sky and sea?'

'Yes, I remember.'

'And do you remember the name of the place the slavers were taking him?'

'Certainly,' I said. 'It was "The Island of Chains".'

'Say that in Bangla.'

'Shikol-dwip.'

'There you are! That's the solution – *shikol*.'

'What do you mean?' I said in puzzlement. 'How is that the solution?'

'Because,' said Cinta, 'the Arabic name for Sicily is "Siqillia" – the resemblance to *shikol* is not incidental I think. The word must have metamorphosed as the legend was passed down from mouth to mouth. At any rate, I am sure that Sicily was where the Merchant was going when the *miracolo* happened. And as you know, Sicily is exactly where that refugee boat is headed.'

I stared at her incredulously. 'Let me get this straight,' I said. 'You want to come with us because you think that a scene from that story will repeat itself?'

Cinta laughed.

'Well, maybe something will happen and maybe not. Whatever it is, I am not going to miss it, you can be sure of that! Especially now that I know you're going.'

'But Cinta!' I protested. 'It's not I who's hired the boat. It's not in my hands.'

'I am well aware of that, *caro*. With Rafi's help I have already spoken to one Signora Lubna Alam. She said she would be glad to have us join your expedition.'

Cinta shot me one of her mischievous smiles. 'Of course, the fact that I made a sizeable donation may have had something to do with it.'

'Well, Cinta,' I said resignedly, 'it seems that you've thought of everything.'

She nodded. 'So I have, *caro*. It is all arranged. Rafi and I are both coming with you!'

I glared at Rafi: 'Was this all your doing?'

'Not really.' He shook his head but I could tell that he was quite pleased with himself – and I have to admit that I was not unimpressed by the dexterity with which he had outmanoeuvred me. But that didn't stop me from making one last half-hearted attempt to dissuade Cinta.

'Look outside, Cinta – have you seen what the weather is like today? I was caught in a hailstorm on the way here. This isn't a day to be out of doors in a wheelchair. And how are we going to get you to the airport anyway?'

Cinta patted my hand again. '*Non ti preoccupi, caro*,' she said. 'You worry too much. You shouldn't – it's all been taken care of. My friend, the hospital's *direttore*, has reserved a special, wheelchair-enabled water taxi to take me to the airport. And the *pulmino* that Gisa has hired to take us to Marghera also has all the right equipment too. *Sta' tranquillo* – we will travel in great comfort, all of us, but especially me.'

Because of the strange weather, and the whipping winds that were tearing across the lagoon, the journey from the hospital to the airport took much longer than expected. The driver of our water taxi told us that he was under orders to be very cautious; already that morning there had been several accidents, on the water and on the roads.

Luckily no flights had been cancelled and by the time we arrived at the airport some of the others – Lubna, Palash and Piya – had already settled into the minibus. But Gisa and her four-man crew were still busy, loading their equipment into the luggage hold, along with piles of sleeping bags, cartons of bottled water and provisions of all sorts.

It was evident at a glance that Gisa had taken charge. I realized now that she was, in her own way, a formidable figure, with her streaked blonde hair, her thick, pink glasses and her quick tongue. Quickly and efficiently she saw to it that Cinta's wheelchair was properly strapped in and that Rafi had some sleeping bags piled on the seat beside him on which to rest his plastered arm.

I found myself growing nervous as I waited to get on the bus: I hadn't seen Piya in a very long time and I had no idea what to expect. But when at last I climbed in, it was to find that she had kept the seat beside her for me. My heart leapt – but my hopes were quickly dampened when she greeted me with a perfunctory 'Hi!'

'Hi!'

I noticed now that she was wearing the same expression of anxiety that I had seen on her face at the hospital in Lusibari. 'Have you been waiting long?'

'Almost half an hour,' she said. 'I hope we're not going to miss the boat. Are we?'

'No way,' I said. 'It's just one o'clock now and the ship doesn't leave till three. I gather that the drive from here to Marghera takes only twenty minutes, on the autostrada.'

But as if on cue, the driver announced, a moment later, that the high winds of that morning had caused an accident on the autostrada so we would be taking an alternative route. There was no cause for worry, he said; we would still be in Marghera with time to spare – the drive wouldn't take more than an hour.

Within minutes of leaving the airport we were hit by whirling squalls. At times the rain was so heavy that our pace slowed to a crawl. From our windows we could barely see the edge of the road. Even when the rain abated there was a strange menace in the sky, with eddies of inky cloud standing out against fields of deep grey.

Then abruptly the rain stopped altogether while at the same time the cloud cover thickened.

We were on a winding country road now with lush, green fields on either side. Piya was sitting by the window, looking outside. Suddenly she grabbed my arm and cried out: 'Look! Look at the sky over there!'

Glancing up I caught sight of a patch of dark cloud, heaving and shuddering, almost as though it were trying to give birth. Then all at once it split apart, like a bursting eggshell, and a thin, grey extrusion emerged from it and began to descend towards the earth, twisting like a whiplash as it grew.

'Oh my God!' cried Piya. 'It's a tornado!'

The fear in her voice startled me, for Piya had never struck me as someone who would be quick to take fright. But then she did something even more unexpected: taking hold of my lapels she buried her face in my chest. Almost unconsciously I put an arm around her and hugged her closer.

Every eye in the minibus was now gazing out of the window, looking leftwards, where the twisting, serpentine form was spinning and dancing above a green cornfield. For a minute its mouth hung above the ground, almost touching down but only to pull back at the last minute. This happened three or four times until suddenly it bit into the ground.

Instantly a fountain of matter shot up above the field, accompanied by a thundering sound, like that of a speeding train: branches, fence posts, stalks, grass, dirt and soil began to spin in the air, rising into the sky as the tornado swept towards us.

I was dimly aware that the minibus had come to a standstill and that there were many voices screaming around me; I was conscious also that Piya's nails were digging into my back and her teeth were biting the fabric of my jacket. I too was terrified now; I couldn't bear to look out any more so I buried my face in Piya's neck. The only thought in my mind was: 'If we're going to die, let it be quick.'

The noise outside rose to a deafening pitch and the bus began to shake and quiver, windows rattling. Then suddenly there was an explosive, tearing noise and a moment later the ground shook, as if under the impact of some immense weight.

Looking up I saw that the tornado had narrowly missed us, crossing the road twenty yards ahead, and knocking over a tree on its way.

Then the noise faded away to be replaced by an eerie, seething silence. We could sense that the tornado had lost contact with the earth and shot back into the sky. But the air was now so filled with dust and leaves and soil that it was as though night had descended. It wasn't until the driver switched on the head-lights that we saw that the road ahead of us was blocked by the fallen tree: its branches were heaving and shaking as if in the last throes of death.

And then, by the light of the headlamps, I caught sight of something moving on the far side of the tree trunk: a dimly visible figure had materialized out of the dust cloud like some unearthly apparition. A moment later the figure leapt over the trunk and began to walk towards us.

We saw now that it was a man, dressed in a flowing yellow robe; wrapped around his head was something that looked like an ochre-coloured turban; his face was brown, with a trimmed, greying beard.

There was no hesitation in his movements as he approached the driver's window and tapped his knuckles on the glass; he seemed to know exactly what he was doing. It was the driver who jumped in shock, fumbling as he lowered the window.

The man asked no questions but simply pointed down the road. '*C'è una altra strada*,' he said. 'There's another road – it'll be on your right after two kilometres. If you stay on it it'll get you to Marghera.'

Without another word the stranger turned on his heel and walked away.

'*Grazie!*' the driver called out after him. '*Grazie mille!*' There was no answer.

On the seat beside mine I heard Rafi murmuring under his breath, 'It's him – Bonduki Sadagar. It's him.'

My nerves were now so fraught that I couldn't keep my voice down. 'Nonsense, Rafi!' I snapped. 'He was just a migrant in a jellaba, a North African.'

We glared at each other and then suddenly the driver chimed in: '*Ci sono tanti marocchini qui* – there are many Moroccans around here; they work on the farms.'

A wave of relief swept over me.

'You see,' I said to Rafi. 'Didn't I tell you?'

But almost at once Cinta, who had been watching us quietly, reached over from her wheelchair and patted Rafi's hand. '*Ti credo, Rafi*,' she said. 'I believe you. I think someone is looking after us.'

The *Lucania*

With her bright green hull and white superstructure, the *Lucania* was a sturdy workhorse of a ship. Built in Germany in the 1970s, the vessel had been in the coastguard fleet for thirty years before being sold to a Gibraltar-based charter company; in recent years she had twice been hired to serve as a rescue boat for refugees.

At Marghera, surrounded by giant cruise ships, the *Lucania* seemed tiny. But this was deceptive for the ageing coastguarder was by no means small: from stem to stern she measured over 250 feet and her hull and superstructure could accommodate several hundred people. Since our numbers were much smaller, there was plenty of space to go around.

Thanks to Gisa's persuasive abilities Cinta was allotted a comfortable cabin on the main deck. The rest of us were accommodated below, in large, echoing, neon-lit compartments that were empty of furnishings.

We were still stowing our luggage when the blast of a klaxon brought us up on deck, in time to watch the cranes and gantries of Marghera falling behind. As the port receded the landscape beyond came gradually into view, a flat estuarine plain lying prone beneath a lowering sky.

Suddenly someone shouted – '*Guardate! Guardate!*'– and we all turned to look northwards where, miles away, a long serpentine form could be seen, dropping down from the heavens. It seemed to bounce a few times as it hit the ground and then it vanished into the sky, like a top being pulled back on a string.

Barely had it disappeared than there was another shout. We spun eastwards this time, where another twister had appeared; it touched down on the Venetian lagoon, sucking up a whirling spout of water that hung above the surface as though it were a spinning column of crystal. It too was gone in a few seconds, but now the captain sounded an alarm and issued orders to clear decks.

Our group crowded into Cinta's cabin, which commanded a panoramic view, with windows on three sides. Cinta insisted that her wheelchair be positioned by the port window and she beckoned to me and Rafi to join her there.

'You see, that island over there?' she said, pointing to a speck of land as it slipped past us. 'That's San Giorgio in Alga; there's been a monastery there for a thousand years. The Gun Merchant would have sailed past it just as we are now. And that island over there? That's San Clemente and when the Merchant was here it would have looked much the same as it does today. And over there is the Lazzaretto Vecchio, where those who were stricken by the plague were sent. Thousands of skeletons have been found there, in mass graves; it hasn't changed in centuries; what you are seeing is what the Gun Merchant would have seen . . .'

And all the while the dark, swirling heavens continued to heave and churn, occasionally extruding twisters that sometimes made contact with land or water and sometimes not. The sight was like nothing I had ever seen before; it seemed to belong not on the earth of human experience but in the pages of some unworldly fantasy, like the *Hypnerotomachia Polyphili*.

Soon we learnt that the strange weather was not just a local phenomenon: all of Italy had been affected in different ways. Some northern cities had been deluged with rain and hail; many parts of the country had been struck by gale-force winds; in the mountains of the Sud Tirol entire forests had been flattened; elsewhere too trees had been knocked down, damaging houses and blocking roads.

A member of Gisa's crew rigged up a monitor in Cinta's room which enabled us to watch some live footage – of devastated forests; of people sheltering from hailstorms; and of cars floating through city streets. Then came some extraordinary scenes of Rome where many towering stone pine trees had been uprooted and knocked over.

As the images were flashing past, Gisa gasped. 'That's Trastevere – where I live!' Pulling out her cellphone she ran out of the cabin.

She was gone for so long that Cinta grew worried and turned to me: 'Can you go and see where Gisa is? I hope her family is all right.'

The *Lucania* was in open waters now and strangely, considering what was happening elsewhere, we had run into some good weather. The clouds had parted allowing the setting sun to light the sky with a rosy glow.

With the easing of the weather many of our fellow passengers had returned to the main-deck. This meant that I had to scan dozens of faces as I circled the deck, searching for Gisa. When I finally spotted her she was half hidden behind one of the *Lucania*'s lifeboats. She looked as though she were in shock, staring glassily at her phone.

'Gisa?' I said. 'What's wrong?'

She gave me a dazed look, blinking rapidly behind her thick glasses. 'Oh it's nothing, *niente* . . . I'm just relieved, that's all.'

She explained that she had had a great deal of trouble getting through to her partner, Imma, who hadn't picked up for fifteen or twenty minutes. But in the meantime, Gisa had managed to get through to a downstairs neighbour and had learnt that the winds had toppled a tree on their street and it had hit their building. This had made her completely frantic; she was almost beside herself with worry when Imma finally called back. She told Gisa that that tree had indeed crashed into their apartment, breaking many windows. Their adopted daughter was in her room when it happened, and her window had shattered, scattering glass everywhere. She wasn't hurt, none of them were, but they were in shock. They'd left their apartment and moved in with some friends; they were planning to spend the night there.

Gisa brushed her hands over her eyes and struggled to summon a smile.

'Can you believe it? In Rome – of all places! – my family have become refugees.'

Later in the evening one of the cameramen broke out some wine while Lubna and Palash served up plates of panini. That was when I noticed that Piya wasn't in Cinta's cabin, with the rest of us.

I wasn't entirely surprised because Piya had been strangely silent since we came on board; I'd had the impression that she was embarrassed about how she had responded to the tornado.

I took a turn around the deck and spotted Piya standing at the bows of the ship, staring ahead at the moonlit sea. My approach startled her, and I froze in my tracks.

'Sorry,' I said. 'Am I intruding?'

'No, no!'

She reached out to put a hand on my sleeve. 'Actually, I'm glad you're here. I wanted to apologize for my meltdown back there, in the minibus. You must have taken me for an idiot.'

'Not in the least,' I said. 'I was scared too.'

I could see that she was struggling with herself, and when she spoke again it was with an obvious effort.

'It's not that I scare easily,' she said. 'It's just that I had a terrible experience once, in a storm. It was a cyclone, not a tornado . . . I'd thought I'd gotten over it but I guess I haven't. Maybe I never will.'

'Is that the storm in which Tipu's father was killed?'

She nodded. 'Yes. I'd have died too that day if it weren't for him. His name was Fokir – he protected me, gave his life for me. And I'm sure Tipu knows that, which is one of the reasons why our relationship is so complicated. Tipu was very, very close

278

to his father and I suppose, in his heart, he blames me for his loss.'

'Well, Piya,' I said, 'you've done a lot for Tipu and Moyna; as much as you could possibly do.'

'I've tried,' said Piya, 'but in some ways I think I've only ever made things worse for them. Nothing I do seems to help. Like taking Tipu to the US for example – I should have known that it would end badly; I'm just not the motherly type. But he so much wanted to go; I couldn't say no.'

It was disconcerting to see Piya, always so self-contained, looking confused and helpless. Nor was it easy to think of something consoling to say: she was too honest a person to be comforted by empty words. Finally I said: 'Moyna understands, you know. She's grateful for all you've done. She's told me so.'

Piya nodded. 'She's sort of forgiven me, I think. But the truth is that if something were to happen to Tipu she'd have nothing left. And it would all be on me then, wouldn't it, all the guilt?'

'You're getting ahead of yourself, Piya,' I said. 'We're here to bring Tipu back, aren't we? Don't start imagining the worst before it's happened.'

'You're right.' She gave me a tight-lipped smile. 'Thanks.'

'You don't need to thank me, Piya.'

Her hand fell on my sleeve again. 'No, really, I mean it,' she said. 'Thank you. I don't know what I'd have done without you these last few weeks. I thought I'd lose my mind when we found out about Tipu's disappearance. You were the only person I could depend on.'

Her words were so unexpected that I was struck, literally, speechless.

It had been explained to us when we boarded that the usual practice, on migrant rescue boats, was to provide separate sleeping quarters for men and women (an exception being made for families travelling together). The same procedure was followed on the *Lucania*, with the compartments on the starboard side being reserved for women and those on the port side for men.

When it came time to turn in I wandered around for a bit, looking for a quiet place to lay down my sleeping bag. It didn't take long to find a small cubicle-like space that was being used as a storehouse for supplies left over from previous rescue missions: donated clothes and blankets lay jumbled together with some forlorn-looking toys.

Pushing the clothes and toys into a heap, I managed to make a small nest for myself and slipped quickly into my sleeping bag. The metal deck was none too comfortable, and there was nothing to be done about the glare of a distant nightlight. Yet somehow I did manage to fall asleep and was soon lost in a dream in which I was looking down on the earth through the eye of a tornado, with everything in motion around me. Through the whirling haze I caught sight of the man who had appeared in front of us after the tornado, dressed in robes and a turban.

His gaze was so piercing that I woke abruptly, only to find myself staring into three pairs of eyes: two stuffed animals and a large doll were sitting atop a pile of clothes, looking down on me.

I sat up with a jolt wondering whether it was I who had put the toys there. Or had someone come in while I was sleeping and rearranged the supplies? But surely the tread of feet, on the metal floor, would have woken me up?

I was now too unsettled to shut my eyes again. Instead I pulled on my jacket and climbed up the ladder to the main-deck.

The night air was cool and bracing. Taking a couple of deep breaths I turned towards the bows – and to my surprise I spotted Cinta's head and shoulders silhouetted against the moonlit sky. She was sitting in her wheelchair, talking to Gisa.

They seemed to be deep in conversation so I decided not to disturb them. But just as I was about to turn back Gisa caught sight of me. Raising a hand she gestured to me to join them at the ship's bows.

'I suppose you haven't been able to sleep either?' said Cinta. 'That's right.'

The silvery moonlight was lying brightly on Cinta and I saw that she had a faraway look in her eyes.

'Gisa was just telling me about something that happened today,' said Cinta, 'when she was trying to call Imma in Rome . . .'

At some point, during the twenty anxiety-ridden minutes when Gisa was unable to get through to her partner, she had heard a voice, a girl's voice, saying: '*Sta' tranquilla, Ella* – don't be upset; they're all right, your children. Nothing has happened to them . . .'

Gisa had looked to the right and to the left and over her shoulder: there was nobody there.

'The strange thing,' said Gisa, 'is that there was only one person who ever called me Ella. It was Cinta's daughter, Lucia. Ella was her little *nomignolo* for me.'

Cinta smiled and tossed her head, letting her hair float freely in the wind.

'Lucia is here,' she said with calm certainty. 'I can feel her presence.'

Sightings

To everyone's surprise the weather was exceptionally fine the next day.

I was already on deck when I spotted Piya coming up, her face shaded by a big canvas hat; she looked briskly professional, with her field glasses strung around her neck and a backpack dangling from a shoulder.

'Don't tell me!' I said incredulously. 'Are you really planning to do some dolphin watching?'

'I might as well,' she said with a shrug. 'Or else I'll go crazy worrying about Tipu.'

'But do you think you'll actually see any dolphins?' I asked.

'I don't see why not,' she replied. 'Cetaceans are quite abundant in the Mediterranean and many of them will be migrating in this season.'

Placing her backpack at her feet she positioned herself at the bows and was soon sweeping the horizon with her glasses.

But in the event, it wasn't Piya but Rafi who was responsible for the first sighting. '*Oijé*,' he cried excitedly, 'look over there Piya-didi. I think I see something.'

A frown appeared on Piya's forehead as she focused her glasses on the spot he had pointed to. After a couple of minutes she said, almost grudgingly: 'Wow, Rafi! *Tomar chokh khub bhalo to!* You have good eyes!'

'What do you see?' I asked.

'There's definitely a school of cetaceans ahead. I'm not sure of the species though – it's too far to tell. I can't believe Rafi spotted them without glasses.'

She handed me the binoculars: 'Wanna have a look?'

I pushed up my eyeglasses and squinted into the lens, but to no avail: it was all a blur to me.

'You'll see them soon enough,' said Piya. 'They seem to be travelling in the same direction as us. We should be abreast of them in a bit.'

She trained her glasses on the waters ahead and in a short while even I was able to make out an occasional ridge of white surf, where dark, curving humps were rising to the surface.

'They're long-finned pilot whales, I think,' said Piya excitedly. 'Maybe five or six of them. We see them around the Sundarbans sometimes, especially along the coast. They rarely go upriver any more, although in the nineteenth century they used to be seen as far inland as Calcutta.'

She turned to Rafi: 'Have you ever seen this kind of whale before? With the big balloon-like swelling at the front of the head?'

He nodded. 'Once or twice.'

Piya reached into her backpack, pulled out another pair of field glasses and held them out to Rafi. 'Do you think you'd be able to use these, with one hand?'

'Yes.'

'Would you like to go on watch with me then?'

Answering with a nod, Rafi put the glasses eagerly to his eyes. Within minutes he had made another sighting. 'There! There!'

Piya turned in the direction he had pointed to and focused her glasses. 'Hey!' she cried after a minute. 'I think we might have ourselves a pod of Risso's dolphins!'

She reached out and gave Rafi a thump on his back. 'Good job!'

In a while Cinta too came out to join us. She watched Piya for a bit and then tugged at my sleeve, gesturing to me to lower my ear to her lips.

'*È in gamba questa ragazza*,' she whispered. 'She's smart this girl.'

'So she is,' I said.

Cinta searched my face with her eyes. 'You like her, don't you?'

I nodded.

'And are you doing anything about it?' said Cinta.

I laughed nervously. 'Oh, I don't know that she's at all interested in me.'

'Don't be a *babbeo, caro*,' said Cinta. 'This *ragazza* is not the kind to bare her heart. But I can sense that she's going to open a door for you, maybe just a crack. When she does you must step through. *Capisci?*'

'Oh Cinta, I don't know that anything like that is going to happen.'

'But you're hoping that it will,' said Cinta. 'Aren't you?'

'I suppose . . .'

'See!' said Cinta, smiling. 'Your Merchant has already made your life better, hasn't he?'

'How?'

'It was because of him that you met her – *non è vero?*'

Now that the weather had cleared people began to mingle: Lubna and Palash went off to circulate amongst their activist friends while Gisa sought out the other journalists on board.

At lunchtime, when we were gathering in Cinta's cabin again, Gisa came running in, with a fresh story about the Blue Boat: she had heard it from a friend who was a foreign correspondent; he had called her from Egypt.

Through an analysis of satellite images it had been established that the Blue Boat had started its journey somewhere near the town of El-Arish, in the Sinai. The area was notoriously lawless but a couple of intrepid correspondents had managed to make their way there. Some local people had led them to a wrecked building some thirty kilometres from the town: this, they said, was once the site of a notorious connection house, where large numbers of refugees had been kept captive by traffickers. The place was known to have been a hub for the trade in human organs.

The connection house was cunningly designed: the refugees' dungeon-like cells were below ground and difficult to detect. Above ground there was only an unremarkable-looking house; that was where the traffickers had their quarters. Looking at the structure, no one would have taken it for a connection house.

Some three weeks before, said the locals, a new group of migrants had been brought there, in a darkened minivan: this was an unusually motley lot, consisting of Ethiopians, Eritreans, Somalis, Arabs and Bengalis. Among them was a woman, a tall Ethiopian.

A couple of nights after their arrival, a boy who worked in the connection house, as a servant, had come running to a nearby village. He had a strange story to tell. The connection house had been hit by a sudden storm, he said, soon after nightfall. A tornado had struck the house with such force that the building had collapsed, killing some of the traffickers and rendering the others helpless. It had also torn off a part of the floor, so that the refugees were able to climb out of their underground cells and overpower the traffickers.

Then, after seizing the traffickers' cellphones and extracting the hard disks from their laptop, the refugees had forced their former captors to lead them to one of their boats – this was none other than the so-called Blue Boat. All of this, said the boy, was done under the instructions of the Ethiopian woman; she had led the refugees on to the boat and once they had boarded – more than a hundred of them – the boat had sailed away into the night.

Looking into the story, the journalists had confirmed, from meteorological data, that a tornado had indeed hit that stretch of coast at around that time. They had learnt also that such freak storms were becoming increasingly common in that area; this was thought to be an effect of changing weather patterns.

'Who knows what really happened,' said Gisa. 'But one way

or another, it seems that these rifugiati may have in their possession a huge amount of data on human trafficking. Everybody knows that the traffickers have connections everywhere – not just in the criminal underworld but in the highest places, among the police, and even inside European governments. All these networks could be exposed. It's being said that this is the reason why so many governments don't want to accept the Blue Boat. This group of refugees may know too much.'

Lubna had some news too.

'There are all kinds of rumours going around,' she said. 'People are saying the *Lucania* may be boarded by commandos, or attacked by drones.'

'Seriously?'

She nodded sombrely. 'Yes. And it seems that we are going to be hugely outnumbered by right-wingers: apparently they've chartered a whole fleet of boats. It's not surprising, I suppose, since right-wing parties have so much money now. They may even block us or ram us.'

'You really think they would try that?'

'Who knows? They're capable of anything. It depends on how the navy handles the situation. Let's hope that Admiral Vigonovo keeps his head.'

The name made Cinta's ears perk up. 'What was that?' she said. 'Who did you say was the admiral?'

'His name is Alessandro di Vigonovo,' said Lubna. 'Do you know the name?'

'*Certo!*' Cinta slapped the arms of her wheelchair in delight. 'Of course I know him! I've known Sandro since he was a little boy. The di Vigonovos are an old Venetian family. Sandro's uncle was the *parroco* of the church of Santa Maria dei Miracoli, in Cannaregio, and Sandro was an altar-boy there for many years. Everybody thought he would be taking the orders but then he met a girl and fell in love, so he decided to join the navy instead. He is a good man; an honest man . . .'

She was cut off by a cry from Piya, who was looking out of a window: 'I don't believe it! Fin whales dead ahead!'

There was a concerted rush to the deck rails, just as a huge whale leapt slowly out of the sea and crashed back again. It displaced so much water that the *Lucania* was rocked by a wave a couple of minutes later.

'*Uau!*' cried Gisa. 'And they all seem to be travelling in the same direction as us! It is strange, no?'

'Not really,' said Piya. 'It makes sense that they'd be heading towards Sicily, like us. They need to pass through the Strait of Sicily to get to the western Mediterranean. In some seasons it's one of the busiest marine mammal corridors in the world.'

An hour later Piya gave another shout: 'Sperm whales at three o'clock!'

We ran out in time to see a jet of spray shooting up into the air.

'This is amazing,' I said. 'How many species have you seen today?'

'Four already,' said Piya. 'And there are only eight species of cetaceans in the Mediterranean.'

'Is it normal,' I asked, 'to see so many of them at the same time?'

'It depends on what you mean by normal,' said Piya. 'It changes from season to season.'

Both Lubna and Palash were much in demand among the media people on the *Lucania*, who interviewed them at length about matters related to migration. But Palash, unlike Lubna, was careful to conceal his identity: he always insisted on speaking anonymously and when a TV journalist asked him to appear on camera he flatly refused and pushed Lubna forward instead.

At one point a journalist challenged him: 'Why are you being so secretive?'

Palash brushed off the question by saying, 'It's just that I don't like being in the limelight.'

But later he came over to offer me an explanation. 'You must think I'm a shady character or something.'

'No,' I said. 'Not at all.'

There was an awkward silence and then Palash led me over to the deck rails, where we leaned into the wind.

'It's just that my family,' said Palash, 'don't know about my life here.'

'Really? Why's that?'

'I came to Italy as a student you see, which sets me apart from most Bengali migrants. Back in Bangladesh, my circumstances were completely different from theirs. Most of them are from villages and small towns, while my father is a banker, in Dhaka. My older brother is a civil servant, quite high up. I studied at Dhaka University and even have a degree in management. For some years I worked as a manager in a multinational corporation. I used to go to work in a car every day, wearing a suit and tie.'

He gestured at his clothes. 'I suppose that was where I got into the habit of wearing a coat and trousers. But somehow all that was not enough for me. From an early age I'd wanted to leave Bangladesh. I had a close group of friends and we decided, when we were still quite young, that we wanted to go to Finland.'

'Finland?' I said in surprise. 'Why Finland?'

Palash smiled self-deprecatingly.

'I know it sounds strange – to want to move to Finland! – but in Dhaka there are many young people who have that dream. My friends and I thought of Finland as everything that Dhaka was not: quiet, clean, cool, uncrowded – and, of course our first cellphones were Nokias, made in Finland, so we always had a soft spot for that country. Anyway, whatever the reason, we all wanted to go to Finland, it was our fantasy, our dream. One boy in our group actually succeeded in getting a scholarship to study at a Finnish university. This made the rest of us even more determined, especially after our friend started sending us pictures of the place where he was living – we could not imagine anything more beautiful! I applied for the same scholarship, a couple of times, but didn't get it. So I decided then that I would pay my own way, at a university somewhere in Europe, and transfer to Finland later.

'By this time I was already working and making good money so I started saving up. I knew that I could not expect any help from my family; they were completely against my going abroad – they wanted me to stay on in Bangladesh. So without telling them I started sending out applications to European universities. The University of Padova accepted me so I decided that I would go there. Between my savings, and loans from friends, I was able to obtain a student visa and a plane ticket.

'But things didn't turn out as I had hoped. I took classes in Italian and learnt to speak it quite well – but I still couldn't keep up with the coursework. After a year of trying, I gave up on my studies and put in an application for a work permit. When it was turned down I appealed, and kept on appealing, again and again. In this way four years have gone by and I am still in a kind of limbo – not just in terms of my status in Italy but also in regard to the other Bengalis who are here.'

'Why is that?'

'Because everything about me is different, you see,' said Palash. 'My Bangla accent, my manners, my background. The others can tell when they hear me speak; then they find out that I did not come here in the same way that they did; that I have not had to deal with the same kind of suffering or hardship. They assume that I won't be able to do the kinds of work that they do, so they don't share information with me – for example about such and such a shop owner needing a delivery boy or about a hotel that is looking for someone to clean the toilets. I would be happy to do that kind of work over here, although back at home I would have scorned even to work as a clerk, in an office. But here I would be happy to deliver pizzas or wash plates. I myself can hardly believe that there was a time when I worked as a manager, dressed in a suit and tie.'

'Why don't you go back home then,' I said, 'and take another job? Surely your family would help you find one?'

He smiled ruefully but I noticed that his eyes had begun to glisten.

'It's impossible for me to go back now. My family still does not know that I dropped out of university and am now scraping by on the streets. My parents would not be able to imagine that a son of theirs was doing that kind of work. They think I'm still a student going to lectures and writing papers, at my university. If I tell them the truth now I would have to admit that I had been lying all along; that they were right to tell me not to go abroad; that I had made a terrible mistake and would have done better to listen to their advice. I would have to acknowledge that in chasing a dream I destroyed my life.'

'Was your dream a kind of curse then?' I said.

'I suppose so,' said Palash wearily. 'But everyone has a dream, don't they, and what is a dream but a fantasy? Think of all the people who come to see Venice: what's brought them there but a fantasy? They think they've travelled to the heart of Italy, to a place where they'll experience Italian history and eat authentic Italian food. Do they know that all of this is made possible by people like me? That it is we who are cooking their food and washing their plates and making their beds? Do they understand that no Italian does that kind of work any more? That it's we who are fuelling this fantasy even as it consumes us? And why not? Every human being has a right to a fantasy, don't they? It is one of the most important human rights – it is what makes us different from animals. Haven't you seen how every time you look at your phone, or a TV screen, there is always an ad telling you that you should do whatever you want; that you should chase your dream; that "impossible is nothing" – "Just do it!" What else do these messages mean but that you should try to live your dream? You ask any Italian and they will tell you that they have a fantasy, maybe they want to go to South America and see the Andes, or maybe they want to go to India and see the palaces and jungles. And if you're white, it's easy: you can go wherever you want and do anything you want – but we can't. When I look back now and ask myself why I was so determined to go to Finland, I always come back to this: I wanted to go there because the world told me I couldn't; because it was denied to me. When you deny people something, it becomes all the more desirable.'

As he was speaking, a strange sense of recognition began to dawn on me: it was as though I were seeing myself in Palash. I remembered the restlessness of my own youth and how it had been fed by another, very powerful medium of dreams – novels, which I had read voraciously, especially savouring those that were about faraway places. I thought of my teenage years and all the time I had spent hunting for cheap paperbacks in the alleys and back lanes of Calcutta (Aldo Manutius might well have had me in mind when he pioneered the publication of inexpensive books; I was addicted to them in much the same way that people of Palash's generation were to their phones).

Back in those days there were very few bookshops in Calcutta and their wares were far beyond my reach: instead I had frequented libraries and second-hand bookshops. Reading was my means, I thought, of escaping the narrowness of the world I lived in. But was it possible that my world had seemed narrow precisely because I was a voracious reader? After all, how can any reality match the worlds that exist only in books? Either way, the fact was that novels had done for me exactly what critics had anticipated when 'romances' first began to circulate widely, in the eighteenth century: they had created dreams and desires that were unsettling in the exact sense that they were the instruments of my uprooting.

If mere words could have this effect, then what of the pictures and videos that scroll continuously past our eyes on laptops and cellphones? If it is true that a picture is worth a thousand words then what is the power of the billions of images that now permeate every corner of the globe? What is the potency of the dreams and desires they generate? Of the restlessness they breed?

Towards sunset some twenty dolphins appeared suddenly, and began to frolic in the *Lucania*'s bow wave, right under our noses. Piya identified them as yet another species, striped dolphins, and even she was impressed now. 'This must be some kind of record,' she said. 'We've sighted more than half the cetacean species of the Mediterranean, in one day. It's incredible.'

'Or maybe miraculous?' said Cinta slyly.

Piya frowned. 'Not even close! It's just a little bit unusual. But I've been in places where you can see a dozen different cetacean species in an hour.'

The sight of the frolicking dolphins created a buzz of excitement on the ship and people began to cheer and clap. The mood seemed to communicate itself to the animals, who responded with an extraordinary display of acrobatics, leaping, somersaulting, and even looking us in the eye as they flipped over in mid-air.

'They're great old hams, these striped dolphins,' said Piya with more than a touch of disapproval. 'They know exactly how to play an audience.'

'Really?' I said. 'But wouldn't that imply that they can understand human feelings?'

'It means nothing of the kind,' said Piya sharply. 'It's just something they do.'

The show certainly had a transformative effect on the *Lucania*: the atmosphere on board suddenly lightened, changing from a mood of misgiving and apprehension to one of festive camaraderie. Soon bottles of wine and grappa began to circulate and cauldrons of steaming pasta appeared in the galley – apparently a Catholic charity had brought along large stocks of food. In a while the sound of guitars and accordions began to echo across the decks, sometimes accompanied by snatches of song.

It was a very clear night, with bright moonlight. Even after nightfall the dolphins continued to keep pace with the *Lucania*, leaping high every now and then, as if to keep an eye on us.

At some point Piya fetched me a heaped plate of pasta and some wine. We raised our glasses (disposable and organic) in a silent toast and covered our knees with a metallic blanket. Our shoulders rubbed gently against each other as we devoured our pasta.

After her last mouthful, Piya lowered her fork and turned to me. 'Tell me, Deen,' she said, 'do you think you could ever live somewhere other than New York?'

I was about to say no, when I remembered what Cinta had said about a door being opened, just a crack . . .

'Why do you ask?' I said guardedly.

'Because it struck me that you might like Eugene, Oregon,' she said. 'It's got great weather and a good library. You should check it out sometime.'

'I don't know about that,' I said. 'Where would I stay?'

'I guess,' she said tentatively. 'You could stay with me; I have a guest-room.'

My heart was now beating so hard that I was afraid she would hear it. I knew that saying too much might turn her off forever, so I forced myself to sound casual. 'Sure,' I said. 'I'd like that.'

'And you know what? If you like Eugene, and feel like hanging around with me a bit longer, it would be easy to arrange something more comfortable. The apartment next to mine just fell vacant.'

It was a struggle not to betray the joy that was building inside me. Trying to keep my voice steady I said: 'It's certainly something to think about. I guess I could let out my apartment in Brooklyn – the rent would bring in enough to live on.'

'You should look into it.'

'I will.'

I fell silent, overtaken by an overwhelming feeling of gratitude – towards the Gun Merchant, to his story, to Manasa Devi, and even to that king cobra: it was as if they had broken a spell of bewitchment and set me free.

My eyes wandered to the moonlit sea and I was reminded of a phrase that recurs often in the Merchant legends of Bengal: *sasagara basumati* – 'the ocean'd earth'. At that moment I felt that I was surrounded by all that was best about our world – the wide open sea, the horizon, the bright moonlight, leaping dolphins, and also the outpouring of hope, goodness, love, charity and generosity that I could feel surging around me.

The Storm

The camaraderie and optimism of those hours faded quickly the next day when a motley flotilla of vessels came into view ahead of us. They were all charter boats, hired by activist groups of many stripes: their varying opinions were evident from the flags and banners that were on display on each vessel.

Return to Sender!

No room here; go home

No human is illegal

We are Indigenous, the only Owners of this Continent

Climate migration = invasion

Refugees are not your enemies

Immigrants are all God's children

Enough is ENOUGH

Send them back with birth control

As we closed on the vessels ahead it became clear that right-wing, anti-immigrant groups had indeed mustered by far the larger force, with many more boats and supporters than we had. On the evidence of the flags that were fluttering above their decks it seemed that some of their supporters had come a long way to support their cause – from Germany, Hungary, Russia, Singapore and Australia.

As the ships drew closer, the mood on the *Lucania* grew increasingly sombre. When word went around that a meeting was being convened on the rear-deck, Cinta insisted on attending, in her wheelchair. I pushed the chair to the stern and stood behind it while the other passengers seated themselves around us, cross-legged.

My experience of meetings of this kind dated back to my college days in Calcutta, when 'leaders' would stand behind microphones loudly haranguing their audiences. But here there were no leaders and no microphones either. Those who had something to say held up their hands and took turns speaking. The default language was English even though only a sprinkling of those present were native speakers.

The first to speak was a woman in a big, shabby-looking caftan. Expressing herself in halting English, she said that the question we most urgently needed to discuss was what our tactics would be in the event that another vessel tried to block our way or even ram us. This agenda was accepted by a show of hands and then speaker after speaker rose to express their views on the subject. For the most part the feeling was that we needed to be patient and non-violent. A few of the more fiery young activists took the view that if projectiles were thrown at us then we should retaliate in kind – but this proposition was voted down and it was decided that in case another vessel approached us in a threatening manner we would join hands and face the other ship resolutely, but without resorting to violence of any kind.

The meeting was not yet over when a ship was seen to be approaching ours, from the rear. We hurried to the deck rails and once again Cinta insisted on joining us, despite my protests.

An angry howl rose from the other ship as it drew level with us. The people on deck were near enough that we could see their faces clearly. They were mainly young men, many with their faces painted in the colours of their football clubs. Many appeared to be drunk.

When they began to shout slogans – '*Close borders now! L'Italia agli Italiani!*' – we joined hands and shouted back: '*No to xenophobia! No to hate!*' – but these simple slogans seemed completely mismatched to the phenomenon that we were confronted with, about which there was something truly apocalyptic, not least because the anger that was on display was so clearly fuelled by fear.

I glanced at Rafi thinking that this vision of rage might have unsettled him. But instead his face was glowing and his eyes were glittering brightly.

'Remember what happened when the Merchant was trying to escape from Venice?' he said.

'You mean when his ship was attacked by pirates?'

'Yes. It could have happened right here, couldn't it?'

Piya alone remained oblivious to the clamorous confrontation that was unfolding around us. Her gaze remained fixed on the water and her hands were as steady as ever on her binoculars.

'Can you still see the dolphins and whales?' I asked.

She nodded. 'They're a long way off – they veered away from us when we caught up with those other ships. But many of them are still in sight.'

'Are there as many as there were yesterday?'

'Sure! In fact I'd say there were more – this is clearly a major migration event.'

'Really? That's lucky for us.'

'Not so lucky for them. I wonder what they're going to do when they run into those warships up ahead.'

Long before the Italian warships came into view we knew that something very unusual was going on in the waters around them.

A few TV journalists had already reached the area and were broadcasting live from there.

That morning a big screen had been hung up in the *Lucania*'s stern, so we were able to watch the footage. We found ourselves looking at a stretch of water that had come to life in an astonishing, almost unbelievable, fashion: the sea was calm, sparkling in the sunlight, and everywhere in the frame plumes of spray were rising and falling as schools of whales and dolphins surfaced to breathe; every now and again a dolphin would leap out of the water and somersault through the air. There must have been hundreds of them, concentrated within a couple of square kilometres.

'Have you ever seen anything like this? I said to Piya.

She shook her head. 'I've seen cetaceans gathering in large numbers, but never so many different species. What's even stranger is that they seem to be circling in one place.'

'Any theories?'

'My guess,' she said hesitantly, 'is that those navy ships are blocking their migration route.'

'But surely they could go around the ships?'

'I guess.'

'Then why aren't they doing that?'

Her jaw twitched. 'I can't answer that,' she said, with a touch of annoyance. 'There's a lot that we still don't know about cetaceans and their behaviour.'

It was late afternoon when we sighted the warships. There were four of them, arrayed in a line, looking watchfully eastwards: it was as though they were waiting to ambush an enemy armada.

The activists on the *Lucania* had assumed that they would be able to intervene directly in the fate of the Blue Boat when it finally showed up. But unbeknownst to them the navy had already taken measures to thwart those hopes.

The warships were still a long way off when a flotilla of grey speedboats came swarming out to meet us. Shouting out orders through megaphones, they formed a cordon around the vessels to make sure that the charter boats maintained a safe distance from each other, and from the warships.

On the *Lucania* there was a general feeling of disappointment when it came to be realized that we were to be mere spectators. But we were lucky in at least one respect: the *Lucania's* position was such that we had a good view of the waters ahead of the warships.

There was, as yet, still no sign of the Blue Boat – it was not expected to arrive for a couple of hours. But what was happening in the stretch of water that faced us was riveting enough: a forest had risen there – of dorsal fins and spouting fountains of spray.

Piya was beside herself with excitement: 'Sperm whales . . . pilot whales . . . fin whales . . . bottlenoses – they're all there! The only Mediterranean species I haven't seen yet is Cuvier's beaked whale!'

Sunset was nearing when a thin trail of smoke was spotted rising above the horizon. An eternity seemed to pass before the long-awaited vessel came sputtering into view. Following the Blue Boat, at a distance of about a kilometre, was an array of coast-guard ships, all flying different flags: every one of those vessels dwarfed the forlorn little fishing boat with its clinkered hull and flaking coat of blue paint.

The refugees on the deck of the Blue Boat now began to wave at us. An answering cheer of welcome went up from the *Lucania*, but it was quickly drowned out by the angry roars that rose from the vessels around us.

'*Go back where you came from . . . ! Not needed here . . . ! Europe for Europeans!*'

The fishing boat's pace slackened as it limped towards the warships. Then its engine died and it began to drift, amidst the whales and dolphins, encircled by columns of spray.

'Let's hope the boat doesn't get hit by a surfacing whale,' said Piya. 'A sperm, or even a fin whale could easily overturn it.'

Raising her glasses to her eyes she began to scan the deck of the Blue Boat, going over it minutely.

'Are you able to see their faces, Piya?'

'Yeah, sort of.'

'Have you spotted Tipu?'

'No. Not yet.'

But just a few minutes later Rafi cried: 'There he is! I see him! Right there, by the smokestack.'

He began to jump up and down, yelling wildly. Piya threw her arms around him and they hugged each other, laughing and crying.

A German TV journalist happened to be nearby. Intrigued by the celebration he came up to Gisa to ask: 'Do those two over there actually know someone on that boat?'

'That's right,' said Gisa. 'That woman there is the foster-parent of a boy who's on that boat. And that fellow with the cast on his arm? He's the partner of the same boy. In fact they started their journey together, in Bangladesh. It's an amazing story.'

'Wow! Do you think they'd be willing to do an interview?'

'I don't see why not,' said Gisa. 'Why don't you ask them?'

A few minutes later Piya came over to ask. 'Do you think Rafi and I should do this interview?'

'Absolutely, Piya!' I said, and Gisa added: 'You should tell them everything – about you and Tipu, and also about his relationship with Rafi. You must do everything you can to put a human face on those refugees. You'll be doing them a great favour.'

Piya looked still unconvinced so I added: 'It'll be a great human interest story.'

'Human interest, huh?' said Piya. 'I guess the sci-comm guys in my university would be happy about that.'

She smiled and handed me her field glasses. 'Look after these for me, will you?'

I didn't have much luck in focusing the glasses on the refugees: the faces on the deck were so blurred by fountains of spray that

I could hardly tell them apart. But in the crimson light of the setting sun the softened outlines of the boat, and the roiling waters around it, took on an unreal, and strangely pictorial, appearance. I was reminded dimly of images I had seen somewhere.

Sitting beside me, Cinta too was reminded of an image. 'Dino,' she said, 'have you ever seen the Turner painting of a slave ship, with a tempest approaching?'

'Why yes!' I said. 'I was just thinking of that. And also of some pictures I once saw, of coolie boats.'

It struck me now that the resemblances were not incidental: in some ways the plight of these refugees was indeed similar to that of the indentured workers who had been transported from the Indian subcontinent to distant corners of the globe in order to work in plantations. Coolies too had been mainly young, and overwhelmingly male; then too, dalals and other middlemen (*duffadars* and *mahajans* – recruiters and contractors) had been essential cogs in the machinery of transportation; and then too debt and moneylending had been vital to the oiling of the machine. Then as now, trafficking in human beings had been an immensely lucrative form of commerce.

There were similarities also in the circumstances under which they had travelled; like refugees, coolies too had been policed and preyed upon by 'coyotes' and overseers; they too had been crammed into confined spaces and had had to subsist on meagre rations. Beatings and whippings; seeing their own die before their eyes – all of this would have been familiar to the passengers of a coolie ship.

Yet there was a vital difference – the system of indentured labour, like chattel slavery before it, had always been managed and controlled by European imperial powers. The coolies often had no idea of where they were going or of the conditions that awaited them there; nor did they know much about the laws and regulations that governed their destiny.

The coolies' colonial masters, on the other hand, knew

everything about *them*. They recorded in obsessive detail where the coolies had come from and which castes and tribes they belonged to. Even their bodies were studied with close attention, special notice being taken of scars and other marks of identification. It was the colonial state that decided where they would go and when; on their arrival it was the state, again, that allotted them to owners of plantations.

But all of that was now completely reversed.

Rafi, Tipu and their fellow migrants had launched their own journeys, just as I had, long before them; as with me, their travels had been enabled by their own networks, and they, like me, were completely conversant with the laws and regulations of the countries they were heading to. Instead, it was the countries of the West that now knew very little about the people who were flocking towards them.

Nor had I, or any of the young migrants I had met, been transported across continents in order to become cogs in some giant plantation-like machine that existed in order to serve the desires of others. Slaves and coolies had worked to produce goods like sugar cane, tobacco, coffee, cotton, tea, rubber, all of which were intended for the colonizers' home countries. It was the desires and appetites of the metropolis that moved people between continents in order to churn out ever-growing floods of saleable merchandise. In this dispensation slaves and coolies were producers, not consumers; they could never aspire to the desires of their masters.

But now, just as much as anyone else, young men like Rafi, Tipu and Bilal wanted those very things – smartphones, computers, cars. And how could they not? Since childhood the most attractive images that they had beheld were not of the rivers and fields that surrounded them but of things like these, flashing across the screens of their phones.

I saw now why the angry young men on the boats around us were so afraid of that derelict refugee boat: that tiny vessel represented the upending of a centuries-old project that had been essential to the shaping of Europe. Beginning with the early days of chattel slavery, the European imperial powers had launched upon the greatest and most cruel experiment in planetary remaking that history has ever known: in the service of commerce they had transported people between continents on an almost unimaginable scale, ultimately changing the demographic profile of the entire planet. But even as they were repopulating other continents they had always tried to preserve the whiteness of their own metropolitan territories in Europe.

This entire project had now been upended. The systems and technologies that had made those massive demographic interventions possible – ranging from armaments to the control of information – had now achieved escape velocity: they were no longer under anyone's control.

This was why those angry young men were so afraid of that little blue fishing boat: through the prism of this vessel they could glimpse the unravelling of a centuries-old project that had conferred vast privilege on them in relation to the rest of the world. In their hearts they knew that their privileges could no longer be assured by the people and institutions they had once trusted to provide for them.

The world had changed too much, too fast; the systems that were in control now did not obey any human master; they followed their own imperatives, inscrutable as demons.

Suddenly Lubna came rushing over, her face flushed, her eyes shining in exhilaration.

'*Apni janten?*' she asked me. 'Did you know all this? About Rafi and his friend and everything?

'I suppose so. Why?'

'Their story seems to have struck a chord around the world!' cried Lubna. 'The interview isn't even over yet and we've been getting calls non-stop. Donations and offers of help have been pouring in! Groups that have never shown any interest in our issues have been sending us messages. It's incredible – we've never seen anything like this . . .'

Something in the distance distracted her now and her gaze drifted over my shoulder, to the horizon. The expression on her face changed suddenly and she stepped up to the deck rails, shading her eyes.

'What's that over there?'

I spun around to see a darkening smudge spreading across the southern horizon.

'Maybe it's a cloud,' I said.

'No, that can't be it,' said Cinta. 'There's something different about the way it's moving – it seems to be coming towards us.'

The smudge was growing quickly, spilling over the horizon like a stain, expanding rapidly in our direction. I could only gape uncomprehendingly.

'What on earth could it be?'

Then suddenly Piya was beside me. Snatching her field glasses out of my hands she focused them on the horizon.

'Birds,' she said. 'They're birds – hundreds of thousands of them. No. Millions. They must be migrating northwards – they're going to pass right over us.'

Rafi too had appeared beside us now. Gazing at the sky he said: 'It's just as it says in the story – the creatures of the sky and sea rising up . . .'

An awestruck silence descended on us as the dark mass came arrowing through the sky: it was as if some limb of the earth had risen into the heavens and were reaching out to touch us. Everything seemed to stand still, even the air; I felt that I had somehow ceased to breathe.

'Time itself is in ecstasy,' said Cinta softly. 'I had never thought I would witness this joy with my own eyes, pouring over the horizon.'

And then there they were, millions of birds, circling above us, while below, in the waters around the Blue Boat, schools of dolphins somersaulted and whales slapped their tails on the waves.

'*Uno stormo*,' said Cinta, gazing upwards, using the Italian word for a flock of birds in flight – and it seemed to me that this was indeed the right word, the only word, for the phenomenon that we were witnessing: a storm of living beings, *bhutas*.

Now, turning his glasses on the Blue Boat, Rafi cried, 'Look! Look over there!'

His finger was pointing to the prow of the fishing boat, where a robed figure could be seen standing erect between the bows.

'It's a woman!' cried Piya.

'She must be the Ethiopian,' said Rafi, 'the one who called Tipu to Egypt.'

The woman lifted her arms now, raising them until they were level with her shoulders, palms facing upwards. And almost instantly a funnel-like extrusion appeared in the storm that was spinning above us. It began to extend downwards, forming a whirling halo above her head.

She stood absolutely still for what was perhaps only a moment, with a halo of birds spinning above her, while down in the water a chakra of dolphins and whales whirled around the boat. And then an even stranger thing happened: the colour of the water around the refugee boat began to change. In a few moments it was filled with a glow, of an unearthly green colour, bright enough that we could see the outlines of the dolphins and whales that were undulating through the water.

'Bioluminescence!' cried Piya. 'I don't believe it!'

For a few moments more we were transfixed by this miraculous spectacle: the storm of birds circling above, like a whirling funnel, and the graceful shadows of the leviathans in the glowing green water below. Then all of a sudden a siren went off on the admiral's flagship and a few seconds later a helicopter took off from its foredeck.

And now it was as if a storm had passed: the birds flew on, the water ceased to glow and the spouts died down. By the time the helicopter reached the Blue Boat the water was calm and the sky was clear.

Hovering above the boat the helicopter made an announcement, in English, over a powerful megaphone: 'We are from the Italian Navy and we are here to organize your rescue. You will shortly be taken to a navy vessel. Our first concern is for your security. Please do not panic and please follow our orders. You have nothing to fear; you are safe now.'

Even as the words were ringing across the water, two naval cutters were seen in the distance, approaching the refugees.

On the *Lucania* there was an amazed, disbelieving silence. Then a great cheer of relief rose from our throats – but barely had it been heard before it was drowned out by angry roars from some of the other charter boats: '*Treason . . . ! Send them home . . . ! The admiral is a traitor . . . ! Try him . . . !*'

I felt my hand being squeezed and looked down to see Cinta smiling up at me. 'What did I tell you, Dino? Sandro di Vigonovo is a good man, a man of honour, a true Venetian. I am sure it was he who ordered the rescue.'

Beside us Rafi and Piya were spinning around and around, in an embrace, with tears of relief running down their faces. Then Piya broke away and flung her arms around me. 'I can't believe it,' she said, planting a kiss on my cheek. 'Tipu's safe at last!'

By the time the cutters reached the Blue Boat darkness had fallen so the evacuation was carried out under the glare of bright spotlights. When the refugees had all been moved, demolition experts climbed into the little blue fishing vessel. A little later a series of small explosions went off and the Blue Boat began to capsize, very slowly. On the decks of the cutters, the refugees lined up to watch their vessel go down; many of them raised their hands to wave it goodbye.

Then Gisa's voice echoed across the *Lucania*'s deck: '*Venite! Venite qui!* Come, come, the admiral's addressing a press conference. Come and watch.'

Rushing to the stern-side screen, we saw a sombre-looking man in uniform facing a roomful of journalists. A chyron was unspooling across the bottom of the screen, translating what was being said.

'Admiral, did you order the rescue of the migrants on your own authority?'

'Yes I did,' said Admiral Vigonovo. 'The responsibility is mine alone.'

An uproar broke out. A couple of minutes passed before the next question could be asked.

'But Admiral, you were under direct orders to prevent these refugees from landing in Italy, or even from boarding an Italian vessel. Are you not aware that you have acted in contravention of your orders?'

'I do not accept that I have contravened my orders.'

'But you are aware surely that the Minister's orders were to prevent the refugees from setting foot in Italy, at all costs?'

'I beg your pardon,' said the admiral, 'but I would like to set the record straight. What the Minister has said, in public, was that only in the event of a miracle would these refugees be allowed into Italy.'

There was a pause.

'And I believe that what we witnessed today was indeed a miracle.'

In the hubbub that followed I heard Piya's voice whispering in my right ear: 'He's wrong you know – there's a scientific explanation for everything that happened there. It was just a series of migratory patterns intersecting in an unusual way.'

'Even the bioluminescence?'

'Sure. That kind of bioluminescence is caused by dinoflagellates, and some species of dynos are known to migrate.'

'Have you heard of anything like this happening before?'

'No,' whispered Piya. 'But animal migrations are being hugely impacted by climate change so nothing is surprising now. I'm sure we'll see more of these intersecting events in the future.'

'But don't you think it's strange, Piya, all of this happening at the same moment?'

'I don't know,' said Piya, shaking her head. 'I really don't know. All I can say is that I'm grateful that it happened the way it did.'

I noticed now that Palash had also come to sit beside me, on my left, and that he was weeping silently into his hands.

'*Ki hoyechhe Palash?*' I said. 'What's the matter, why are you crying?'

'It *is* a *miracolo*,' came the answer. 'It *is*! Everything we had hoped for is coming true. There is an awakening happening around the world – this could be the moment when everything changes . . .'

In the meantime, a journalist was shouting on the screen. 'The Minister has just released a statement saying that you've broken the law, Admiral, and you will be brought to justice. What do you have to say to that?'

'I have nothing to fear from the law,' said the admiral, standing ramrod straight. 'I have acted in accordance with the law of the sea, the law of humanity and the law of God. If I am tried, those are the laws that I will answer to.'

Now all order broke down and the journalists began to hurl questions at random.

'Admiral, what gives you the right to prioritize your religious beliefs over your orders . . . ?'

'Admiral, is it true that in your stateroom there hangs an icon of the Black Madonna of La Salute . . . ?'

These last words made me think of Cinta. Looking around me now I saw that she wasn't with us and it struck me that a couple of hours had passed since I had last seen her.

Stepping away from the stern I took a turn around the *Lucania*'s deck and was unable to find any sign of Cinta. A twinge of unease went through me and I hurried to her cabin. There was no answer when I knocked so I tried the handle and to my surprise the door swung open. The cabin was dark but there was a nightlight glowing in one corner. I saw that Cinta was lying on her bunk, with her eyes closed, her head encircled by a halo of white hair.

I thought she was asleep and was about to step out when she opened her eyes and smiled. 'Come here, Dino.'

I went up to her and she reached for my hand. 'How are you, *caro*?'

'I'm fine, Cinta,' I said. 'But what about you? Why are you here, all by yourself? Why aren't you celebrating with us?'

'But I *am* celebrating,' she said, smiling peacefully. 'I am celebrating with Lucia, my daughter. She is here with me.'

'What . . . ?'

She gave my hand a gentle squeeze. 'Don't try to look for her, Dino – you will not see her. But she is here, believe me.'

'That's crazy, Cinta. Why should she be here?'

'She has come to take me away. It is time at last.'

'What the hell do you mean, Cinta?' I could hear my voice rising to a wail. 'You're not going anywhere, Cinta. You need a doctor, that's all! You're not well.'

'No, Dino,' she said calmly. 'You are wrong. I am very well. In fact I have never been better. And for that I want to thank you. You have given me a great gift – as I always knew you would.'

'What gift? What are you talking about?'

'Well, Dino – as you know, I sometimes have these . . . intuitions. And I had one the very first time we talked, outside that library, in the midst of that Midwestern snow. I knew that one day you would give me a great gift, a boon . . . and I just wanted to thank you.'

I had become quite frantic now and could not bear to listen to her. 'Cinta, you need a doctor. I have to go find one.'

I stumbled out of the cabin and rushed around the deck, calling for a doctor. But with everything that was going on, people were so distracted that it took a good fifteen minutes before I found one, and then too it was only with Gisa's help.

When we reached the cabin a sense of dread seized me and I hung back when the doctor and Gisa went in. I could not bring myself to follow them so I closed the door and stood by it, waiting, with my eyes shut, and suddenly memories, from all the years that I had spent in Cinta's orbit, began to flash through my mind, starting with that bitterly cold Midwestern day when we had talked in the faux grotto outside the library, and ending with the words she had said to me in the cabin, a few minutes before: 'I knew that one day you would give me a great gift'.

Now at last I had an inkling of why she had chosen to bestow her friendship on me: it was as if she had had an intuition that someday we would bring each other *here*, to this juncture in time and space – and that not till then would she find release from the grief of her separation from her daughter. In that instant of clarity I heard again that familiar voice in my ear, repeating those words from La Salute – *Unde Origo Inde Salus* – 'From the beginning salvation comes', and I understood what she had been trying to tell me that day: that the possibility of our deliverance lies not in the future but in the past, in a mystery beyond memory.

Then I felt something like the touch of a hand, brushing gently against my cheek. My eyes flew open and I began to say – 'Cinta?' – when I realised that it was just a draught, created by the opening of the cabin door.

It was Gisa who had opened the door and she was standing in front of me now, wiping her eyes.

'We came too late,' she said. 'Cinta's gone.'

Acknowledgements

With many thanks to Shaul Bassi, Haznahena Dalia, Elisabeth Crouzet-Pavan, Roberto Beneduce, Shail Jha, Aaron Lobo, Kanishk Tharoor, Antonio Fraschilla, Sara Scarafia, Norman Gobetti and the Civitella Ranieri Foundation.